OVERMORROW

THE OVERMORROW RITES

BOOK ONE

LANCELOT SCHAUBERT

Schaubert, Lancelot

OVERMORROW / Lancelot Schaubert

ISBN: 978-1-949547-14-6

FICTION / Fantasy / Dragons & Mythical Creatures

FICTION / **Science Fiction, Fantasy & Scary Stories > Fantasy & Magic / Mystery & Detective**

FICTION / **Teen & Young Adult / Science Fiction & Fantasy / Fantasy / Paranormal & Urban / Mermaids**

FICTION / **Children's Books / Science Fiction & Fantasy / Fantasy & Magic / Visionary & Metaphysical**

FICTION / **Science Fiction, Fantasy & Scary Stories / Fantasy & Magic / Paranormal, Occult & Supernatural**

FICTION / Science Fiction / Space Exploration

Printed in the United States of America

Lemniscate Of Bernoulli Props - Right Hand Loop Of Lemniscate —for image between chapters.

This book is dedicated to my niblings — the children of my siblings and in-laws — L., C., S., M., É., C., C.2.0, E., E., C., C., as well as those who never had a name — may you be, be born, be washed in gilded light, become the real you.
See the author's note at the end for a letter to you.
(And acknowledgments for everyone else).

CONTENTS

1

THE MAW IN THE DEEP, DARK STAIRWELL

Ellie's mother showed the worst of her memory loss where most stories, days, and many lifetimes end: during a bedtime story. The bedtime story was going very, very poorly.

Charlie, Ellie's oldest brother, had long fallen asleep in his own room. He'd probably read himself to sleep with a memory puzzle mystery. In Ellie's room, her two younger siblings — Annie and Levi — had drifted off in their own bunks after her mom's first round of stories. It was dark. Only the sequins, stickers, and costumes caught twinkles of refracted light to match the stars outside. That twinkling dark left Ellie and her mother to share a long by the glow of Ellie's yellow lamplight.

Ellie's wide eyes had a special case of heterochromia iridium. Two different colors, one in each eye. One eye was as green as wet grass, one eye was as turquoise as the Turkish ocean. She had inherited that exact trait and those exact colors from her mother's eyes. Her hair matched too, more on that in a moment. But when mom's eyes met Ellie's across her yellow lamplight glow, it was green meets turquoise, turquoise meets green. "Mom?"

"Sorry honey, what was it?"

First, Ellie feared her mother had blanked out like she kept doing lately. Then she hoped her mother's mind was off in her own little world. "You were telling the story about the pilgrim baby, momma. Did he have a black suit and one of those gold buckled hats?"

"Oh Ellie, he wasn't a *puritan*. Not that kind of pilgrim. They didn't even have those kinds of image breakers where this baby came from. No protestants. No, not that kind of pilgrim."

"What kind? You stopped telling me his story."

"History not… not… his story? Odd. Oh. Yes, right, the baby could travel."

"By himself?" Ellie asked.

Mom cocked her head at Ellie's phrasing, but nodded.

"Babies can only crawl, Mom. If they've learned how, I mean."

"Not like that, Ellie. This baby could jump from world to world."

"Jump?" Ellie asked.

"Not with its legs."

"Then how?"

"Something about a crib. Or maybe the baby's house? Could he househop? Cribcrawl? Roomroam? I don't remember how it goes, the right word for it. Something about thinking about his home? I'm sorry." Mom looked ashamed. Then lost. "I don't remember."

Ellie's breathing quickened, then caught up high. "You don't remember the story or his power?"

"Both."

Ellie sighed, frustrated. Mom's memory kept getting worse. "The baby was a globetrotter?"

"Sure," Mom said.

"A baby Harlem Globetrotter. Could the baby shoot hoops?"

"No," Mom said and she shifted her angle on her propped arm. "Not like that. It could travel. It had seen many worlds for a baby."

"What happened to him on his travels?"

"Some worlds don't like to be discovered. Some worlds hide.

And the baby had found them out. So people from the hidden world came to snatch it away."

"Did the baby fight them?"

"In its own way," she said, then swallowed. "It was a baby emissary. So it had ways of hiding even from them, ways of getting the truth out."

"Like us?"

Mom nodded, her eyes drifted towards the window, towards the stars.

"Mom, where are we emissaries *from*? Emissaries always come *from* somewhere. They said in government class and social studies that ambassadors are from other countries. Are we from another country?"

Her mom turned her eyes first to Ellie's wall and all of their travel photos, then to the drawings Ellie had made outside of school. After that she slowly turned, almost horrified. She froze that way for a moment, then searched, deeply, into Ellie's eyes. "Of… a kind."

"Why did you tell Dad that we were hiding under protection? Are we in witness protection?"

Mom laughed a dark laugh. "Who told you about witness protection?"

"Movies. Podcasts."

Mom said nothing, but there was a naked honesty in her eyes and she searched her daughter further, pursing lips as if desperate to tell.

"Mom?"

"Yeah?"

"Are you okay?" Ellie asked.

Her mother locked color-complementary eyes with her once more. Then she looked up at Annie in the other bunk. Down and over at Levi. Was she making sure they were still asleep? Then she turned back to Ellie. "No."

Ellie's breath caught high in her chest. "How can I help you, Mom? I can help. Are we gonna be okay?"

"You will be more okay than I will be."

"What about the others?"

Her mother shrugged, almost despairing with the shadows in those beautiful bicolored eyes.

Seeing her mother in that state crimped Ellie's heart, seized it, as if some great bedrock had cracked beneath her and the world itself were hanging onto her arteries for dear life. "Does Charlie know?"

"No."

Mom did this sometimes, sharing things with Ellie that no one else in the family knew. Ellie wondered if it was because they looked so similar and she *was* the eldest daughter. She looked over to the corner of the room where her diorama of Central Park that she'd built with Charlie. They'd promised each other to visit the park together, but Charlie didn't know about the problem.

"Dad?" she asked.

"He knows," Mom said. "He's a good man."

"What's wrong?" Ellie asked.

"Big things keep going blank in my head. Like your sister today."

"What's her name?" Ellie asked for the second time that day without thinking.

Biting her lip, Mom winced.

Ellie sat up in bed. "And my brother?"

Mom shook her head, almost desperate.

"Mom, what can we do? How can I help?"

"I wish I could travel like that baby did. Travel again."

"Again? Again? What do you mean again? Like the way we went to Paris?"

Her mother looked out the window one more time, searching the skies. Searching. She turned back to Ellie and said, "Just sleep and dream of babies going on adventures, Mrs. Wright."

"Mom?"

"Yes?"

"I'm *not* married."

"Right, Ellie, right. Of course you're not married." She kissed her daughter's forehead. Nibbled a piece of her hair oddly. "Dream and sleep of babies."

Ellie desperately searched for a mathematical truth or a fact of rote memorization that might hide deep within her mother's mind. Something, anything she could use to shake her free, wake her up. Why not two plus two or one minus one? But she, having just learned about exponential power in math, impulsively asked instead, "What's zero to the power of zero?"

Mrs. Wright waited a long, long time and then answered, "One."

That basic forgetfulness crushed Ellie: of course the answer was zero. How could her mother answer so wrongly?

"Goodnight," Mom said and kissed her forehead and both eyelids, the way she did every night.

Ellie tried to lay down and sleep, but her mind reeled from that answer: *One.* Had her mother forgotten the number zero too? Looking down, she realized she'd been picking at the cuticles on her nails, tearing at her own flesh. She didn't want to tear herself in half, but she sometimes her journey left her with no other choice, having the mind she had. So she tore at her nails.

Minutes later, judging by the clear rustling, her mother had gone to bed quickly. Across the hall, Ellie's mother snored. In response to that snoring, that apathy, Ellie sat bolt upright in her squishy bed, wrapped in the softest pink blanket. Her quicksilver hair whipped around her. She would have been an aloof, dark-haired girl were it not for the hair that matched her mother's.

She *was* an aloof girl, it's only that rather than *being* dark, her hair caught the true essence of shadows when the light hit it. Her hair *caught* darkness. If you've ever looked into a dish of mercury, you know true liquid mirrors reflect the shadows of a room as much as the light. Her hair did that.

It was odd hair.

As she stared at the picture of her mother she'd washi-taped to her wall, she touched it with her left hand's callused fingertips, the only rough thing on her, and wished for healing. Or for mom to wake up.

Ellie was afraid for her mother's fading memory. The whole month, Mom kept saying she *should* be remembering something. Something important. Something nefarious about their post in Missouri. What had Mom forgotten?

Why couldn't she even remember a basic bedtime story? Or, frankly, just finish the dadgomn thing by making up an ending?

But mom's memory loss didn't explain all of Ellie's fear. The night before, Ellie'd had a terrible dream, one she'd woken from screaming. Her screams had woken the whole house. Now she feared drifting off again and seeing *him*. Death, the Grim Reaper, maybe it was Father Time eating his children? She'd dreamed a psychopomp had ferried her across some great threshold of grief while she watched — *let* — her brother die. Something was wrong. She panted like a winded dog when it leaves off chasing a fox because it worries a bear has caught its scent. She looked over at the beds of her siblings, angry that they hadn't woken to help fend off whatever was coming.

Why did the base of her neck crawl as if something *had* caught her scent? And the scent of her siblings?

Had something truly done so?

It would have been far, far better for her had it been a bear that had caught her scent.

Outside her room, firecrackers. A young girl cried. Loud romance. Flying planes. A churning of earth. Inside her room, those sounds increased Ellie's fear for her mother's memory and for her own sanity. But mostly, the sounds grew her terror that something mighty and big approached. She clutched her pink fluffy comforter to her chattering teeth, hoping to silence them for her sister's sleep. As frustrated as she was that neither was awake to help calm her fears, she also felt a kind of sadness for the moment that they would *have* to wake up. Let her siblings sleep as long as they could.

Instead her anger moved back towards her mother.

Because none of these loud night sounds awakened Mrs. Wright.

As she looked out into the yard, a horse continued watching the windows of Mrs. Wright and of Ellie. A horse?

That young boy two streets down set off some more firecrackers. At that sharp sound like distant gatling guns, the horse below returned no whinny or flinch. A young girl cried again from a third-floor window. Teenagers made brazen loud romance on a nearby flat balcony. A low-flying plane passed over their heads.

None of this dampened the horse's resolve, who steadily munched on the early blackberries and raspberries growing wild along the oak-brown neighborhood fencerow. While munching, the horse used the night light glow from all of those gold-fairy-crowned sable wrought-iron streetlights to stare down at a perfectly flattened and normal grey stone in the Wrights's front yard.

A stone Ellie had often played upon, had often read her fantasy novels while perched upon.

That great grey stone gave way to reveal a tunnel made of identical stone. The entire rock deflated like poorly baked apple cake, sinking into a funnel. The funnel collapsed into stairs. The stairs decayed into a tunnel made of that very rock. A shortcut through rockiness to… who knew where?

The horse remained stoic and turned his attention from the magically manifest rock tunnel back towards Ellie's window instead.

Out of the newly formed stone stairwell climbed a white wolf larger than the horse.

The horse, though it raised one eyebrow, did not bolt. Nor freeze. Nor rear up and try to put its hooves through the eye socket of the wolf. It *lifted* its *brow* and *winked*, swallowing its berries. Then the horse transformed into the man in a clean white robe, yet the hooves still poked out the bottom.

The wolf sniffed but remained a wolf. "Did you see anyone?"

"Not yet, but I hear tell it's coming. Ellie did not get her normal, boring day."

Upon hearing her own name echo in through the cracked window, Ellie's breath caught short.

"We seldom do," the wolf said. "But one in nine, we still try to get them all to stop."

"We shouldn't interrupt her," the horseman said.

"Which?" the wolf asked.

"Yes," the horseman said. "Her. Let her have a little more normal, a little more boring."

"They're coming."

"Yes, I know," the horseman said. "And quickly."

"Then we must move. She must move. *They* must move. Their time has not yet come."

The horseman hoofed at the dirt, and let his bushy brows look over the robe towards the dark horizon and light pollution of the small city. "Shame to wake what wants to bore. Boring things delve the deepest."

The wolf grunted and hummed. More creatures and people clambered out of the hole with the stairwell and headed towards the house. The man with hooves raised his other eyebrow up at the window where Ellie shivered, watching him.

Ellie, who had already risen in the night from the loudness of her mother's fitful sleep, felt her heart hammer harder. She clutched her comforter tighter to her teeth, very happy her siblings were still not awake. Rather than clutch it to her as a shield, she found herself perched on all fours on her bed, up on the balls of her feet and fingertips, ready to pounce. How had the sounds not woken them yet? How had Charlie, Levi, and Annie stayed asleep during that series of loud noises, silver wisps, and golden flashes in the night?

Framed by the eldritch light of their bedroom's open doorway stood not their parents, but a man. Dear God, a man. *A strange man in her room.* Blood went to her fists, her feet. She showed her teeth. She looked for something to swing as a scream caught in her throat. A man.

No, two.

Two men. An exceedingly tall old man and a hunched young man with a golden yoke over his shoulders. And then that HUGE white wolf with a blue leather saddle. On the saddle now rode a young black girl whose hair was woven into dreamcatchers. Real, white twine dreamcatchers serving as fancy hair clips or hair pins. The wolf's nostrils flared sideways and flipped... backwards? Inside out? He sniffed out the door, down the hall. The wolf seemed somehow concerned with the scents behind them all, not those before them.

Not the scents of the children.

Had her mother forgotten to tell Ellie that this kind of event was a possibility? Forgotten enough to warn Ellie that this could happen to her at some point in her short life? None of her story-time pictures had warned her. None of her studies, none of her shows, none of the things that her parents had taught her: none of their poetry, none of their prose. (She'd not only never seen such a quartet in her life, in all of Carthage, Missouri, Ellie knew no one *who knew of anyone* in living memory who'd ever encountered such a quartet like the four now standing, menacingly in her doorway). Her worried mind searched and searched for some answer or morsel of wisdom or lived experience. Absolutely, positively nothing came to mind. Ellie *really* wanted to wake up now. But a worse idea came to mind:

Maybe she *had* woken from whatever Mom had forgotten into the actual living memory?

Was she waking up in the dreamworld and had "reality" been the lie?

Ellie tensed the balls of her feet and felt it all. The realness of wolf, its whiteness of fur. She bet it felt fluffy under that girl's fingertips. Dusty odor, roadside tar wafted off the tall one along with something bitter. Sulfuric. What was it about Mr. and Mrs. Wright, their job, and their understudies? What was it about that failed bedtime story? Why were they all in witness protection?

Dad had remembered more than mom, it seemed. He had mentioned many odd things before. In fact, odd things made up the bulk of what Dad remembered most. But Dad also protected Mom by sharing less and less about their history together and was a bit of a bad bluffer. Ellie thought she'd caught her Dad not only changing details, but fabricating stories whole cloth. Quite the storyweaver, Dad. Ellie had learned to value the bits that he repeated over the carefully fabricated tall tales.

Yet it was one thing for Ellie to hear her father recall stories, to learn from them strange words like *eldritch* and *prestidigitation* and *wombrover* and *storyweaver*. There were many such words: she'd been keeping a journal of them during childhood throughout her life..

It was another thing entirely for Mom to suddenly recall one of those words when she seemed desperate to forget for whatever reason. Or tried so hard to remember that she had forgotten despite her sincerest efforts.

Now Ellie had found herself ramrodded inside the kind of story Dad told.

After the initial mental shock of the quartet wore off, their cloaks stuck out first. Not made of velvet or wool or some elven fabric like in the stories. Nor even made of shadow or shaed like in Peter Pan or Kvothe the Bloodless. *Their* cloaks, Ellie somehow *knew* deep in her guts, were woven of the fabric of nested universes like the little dolls the Ukrainian emissary had brought them. How could she know the cloaks did that? It felt like a memory, the cloaks. Those painted symbols… no. Not painted. Embroidered?

Maybe embroidered cloaks?

If it was embroidering it was so, so tight. But the cloaks transfixed her. They moved with imagined (and therefore real) sunbursts. They streaked with comet tails and an ever so faint music. The pictures *danced* even while the quartet stood still in her doorway. The very orbs on each composed a kind of symphony. Each one different. Each one personal.

It dazzled her. The spirals of the galaxies hypnotized her. Made her want to know these worlds of hints and whispers. A tremor took over, shifting her fear to pulsing thrill, hiding a kind of nostalga beneath. She had no word for the feeling.

She only knew she somehow wasn't scared anymore. Her whole skin had gone slick with sweat as if a fever had broken.

The child riding the wolf had a cosmicloak. How did Ellie know the name? Megacosm cloaks. Starling wear. It came unbidden to her mind, the name. She wished it hadn't. The child's cloak, to Ellie, appeared quickly sketched with a white sharpie on a black piece of construction paper, tied around her neck with a bread tie. It seemed as substantial — or perhaps even more substantial — than most of the other cloaks.

The first man stretched out before her in every direction: taller and lankier than even Mrs. Wright or Charlie. He had the sort of good-bad-ugly ancient cowboy look you might find in any archival western film. Perhaps he could fight a bear while naked and maybe — just maybe — win. A film camera wouldn't quite catch the whole of him unless fitted with a certain lens. He carried a crowfoot in his palm and had a tattoo of a weeping upside-down tower under his left eye.

The man to his left from where Ellie stood was younger, shorter, and wore a great golden ox yoke around his neck. She wondered if it weighed a thousand pounds. How did he stand at all beneath the weight of that gilded neck anchor?

Annie stirred beside Ellie. Woke up bolt upright, rubbed her eyes. She did not scream or clench her fists. Her sister, rather, said, "Huh."

Ellie shook her head, and then, pulse pounding in her neck, looked again. Now there were five or six others crowding in the hall, passing. One of them was a barefoot man in tweed and a cape with a universe like a cathedral on it. An expensive brimmed hat topped that one's head, who stopped and looked in her room. Another one of them was the horse-hoofed man from outside her window.

Unlike the horse's proud manner, the wolf obviously didn't resist the girl riding on his back. What was the difference?

The wolf was immense enough to be ridden, large enough to

eat a lion king. How did he keep from breaking up the drywall and tearing down the studs? What a horrid ride. Pecos Bill had ridden a tornado. Had the worst tornado in history taken on wolf form, it was this wolf. The subtle cream markings on his paws looked like her father's paratrooper jumping boots.

To all of this, Ellie's normally receptive mind reeled. She grew dizzy and collapsed, the speech knocked clean out of her. Something crashed elsewhere in the deeps of the house, but she barely registered it in her blinded, passed out state.

When Ellie woke moments later, the wolf seemed unconcerned with the flashing and banging about in the other end of the house behind the crowd. He sat down his back haunches so that the young girl had to adjust her posture to stay in the saddle. Then he bent his head inside a special leather satchel tied to the wolf saddle, rooting around.

Ellie looked at them all, once more, one by one. Her mouth was dry and fetid. Her eyes were dry and crusty. She fought to wake further, go *back* to boredom. Ellie said to no one in particular, "My sister Annie sometimes has day terrors."

The wolf said, "Hypnopompic and hypnogogic hallucinations."

"What's that mean for her?" Ellie asked. "For me?"

The wolf said, "She's afraid of dreaming while waking up and afraid of walking while falling asleep."

The cowboy before her sighed and cleared his head of cowboy hat.

The man in tweed shuffled and squeezed himself between them to get further into the room.

The wolf grinned before them all, what big teeth. He turned to face the lanky man full-on. "I find it best to remain curious and playful in the teeth of fear." He could have been snarling or smiling. Was he hunting or laughing? "Would you like some dandelion wine? I picked it up before making my way." He pointed with his snout to a little bottle hanging off the side of the saddle.

"Some what?" the cowboy asked.

"Dandelion wine. Made in Bellhammer, Illinois at the Tonti cidery."

"Did you really?" asked the man in tweed and the cloak.

The wolf smacked his lips. "The Bellhammer folk really know how to make a weed tasty."

"Grandpa Remmy made dandelion wine," the man in tweed said.

The cowboy snorted. "I bet they think weed's tasty."

"You know what I meant, Black Jack."

Levi snored on and Ellie turned towards him. Her gaze was followed by the rest of the waking eyes in the room.

After that awkward moment of eight grownup strangers's eyes mirrored the course of her own throughout the room, the cowboy glanced at the girls, mostly at Annie, then watched the wolf master, scoffing. His foot shuffling sounded to Ellie like the susurration of several winds over many waters. The wolf had noticed other ways, sniffing, twitching ears. He merely nodded at Ellie and glanced at the others. The cowboy went on. "Pleasant banter's well and good, but the tabooed name of the One We Ought Forget still comes."

Ellie noted the word forgetting. What did that mean? She'd been so worried about her mother's memory — about her own memory regarding her mother, about her own memory if she'd become a mother — that she'd never stopped to consider the source of her mother's forgetfulness. Was it possible something *outside* her mother's body had forced her to forget?

"Call him Oblivion. He is and does that."

The lines deepened in the furrows — the elevens — of the brow and nose corners of the old cowboy. "Yes, and I don't want to forget. Anything."

"Stick with me and you won't," the man in tweed said.

Ellie also did not want to forget.

The wolf said, "You don't forget just by mentioning Forgetfulness, silly goose." A wolf saying goose was an odd thing for Ellie to behold: it hissed, just like a goose, but one with what big teeth. "And you don't prevent forgetting simply by *forgetting* Forgetfulness, silly goose." The tongue hit his lupine teeth in that anserine hiss. "In fact, to remember to say Forget — even to remember to forget something — is itself an act of Memory. Oblivion. Call him thus."

Ellie didn't follow, but *did* get a rush in her chest at the word Memory and the sight of the wolf. Her arms went numb to the shoulder.

"Fine," the cowboy said and heaved in air, enough that Ellie felt it rushing past her. He ignored the girl for a moment. "Oblivion," he projected loudly into the room, matching its resonant frequency so that the whole room shook and rang with the name. Almost a summons. "But I'm at risk of forgetting things, doctor, you aren't. You can't forget anyone, anything, any phenomenon. Oblivion doesn't apply to you: your powers outweigh his. It's you — your memory — he'd have us and my master forget. If that happens, Sickness, War, Strife, Grief, Fear, Hunger, Poverty, the Abyss will wash over a world that has forgotten who they are and what they're made of, why they exist, whence they came, and whither they—"

"Hush, child," the wolf said to the giant, ancient cowboy.

Ellie focused hard on their conversation, though she understood little of it. It was all so new, she wanted to make sure she could explain later to her sleeping siblings and help her mother's mind heal and remember. Especially if her mother's forgetting sickness could catch like a cold. In that case she needed to work all the harder to remember what they'd said, this haggling of wolf and cowboy.

The source of her thrill and fear and frustration had moved past this small, strange crowd towards something beyond and behind. Something outside, bigger, both less and more present in the room, but woven with Ellie's personal journey. Almost story-woven into a lemniscate knot.

The wolf smiled. "Why call me Memory? No one can remember it all but the Alone."

The man in tweed cleared his throat. "Oblivion isn't better at remembering. He's caught in the promise of memory, not the reality. Competent evil's still just evil. Your only competence is The Good."

The wolf flushed. Ellie didn't get the feeling the wolf was ashamed: he'd flushed the way she did after riding dressage. Horrified there in the dark, she felt like a hunk of lead had sunk into her bed. She gasped, worried about being eaten by some big bad wolf.

They — to a beast — stared at her.

She held in the gasp. It stretched the corners of her lungs painfully.

"Can we hurry it along?" the man in tweed and brimmed hat said, checking a cold iron pocket watch (the hooved man hissed at this). The man in tweed checked behind them, deep into the hall.

The wolf tsked. "Curiosity and play in the teeth of fear." It simpered its muzzle and then put his snout back in his pouch and pulled out a diamond-encrusted something. Ellie met eyes with Levi, who was now awake and shaking. Levi looked back and forth from the thing the wolf had pulled out.

"What?" she whispered to Levi.

Levi said in a shaky little voice, "It's like dad's lasers when he squares off a room while framing a house."

With that in his teeth, the white wolf pointed it at the wall and bit. A soft click. A rainbow of lasers formed a grid of light. That grid took in the back wall where sat the main bunkbed that held Levi and Annie. He bit again and it scanned the other wall and Ellie's bunk. Ellie thought this, too, would make it hard to fall to sleep. Or to wake up, were she dreaming.

Was she dreaming?

"Doctor…" said the man with the golden yoke.

Crashes came closer.

"Doctor…" said the girl on the wolf's back.

More banging, higher up. It was on their staircase's landing.

"Doctor!" shouted the man in tweed.

The white wolf gritted its teeth, ignoring all three of them. A third click. Ellie winced at the sound. The rainbow of lasers moved out once more to scan the third wall, another brilliant grid.

Monstrous banging and breaking and smashing crashed up the stairwell towards her room. The others were banging around in the room next door. Banging around in *Charlie's room*.

Was something hurting Charlie?

Ellie's heart beat a cold climb up and then on into her collarbone. She looked at the young girl with dreamcatchers in her hair. Mouthed, *Please*.

After breaking eye contact with Ellie, the last question came again from that young girl on the wolf's back: a low, low whisper. "Doctor…?"

A fourth click of the scanner. It took in the room. The booming and banging up the stairs increased. Ellie's chest went all warm and started pounding as if to kill her clean. She grabbed whatever pole or handful of sheets she could. Crap, she thought. Crap, crap, crap *I want to go back to bed now, I don't want to be awake anymore now.* The room began to spin, surrounded in a green and red and yellow and blue and violet and orange and indigo grid. The last image behind them was massive feathers, scales, and fur passing in a blur. The growl in the stairwell.

"No, no, no, no," Ellie shouted at the stairs.

That *thing* whipped and turned, opening its maw at Ellie from the deep of the dark stairwell.

Every fiber in her body froze.

2

LIGHT WELLS

The room pulled away from the maw of whatever it was that chased them. They clung to their bunkbeds. Felt the cold steel of the red rails under their palms. The sheets with pixelated adventure prints had given her rug burns in that spinning. Her pulse bounced her wrist against the bed rails. The panic in her now-floored heart prompted Ellie to look around frantically towards her siblings. "Where's Charlie?" she asked as the room spun.

Amid the spinning, one clear form emerged: a white wolf bowing, saying slow and somber to her, "Charlie is taken."

Ellie moved nothing. Said nothing. Felt nothing. The room spun on.

Annie screamed loud enough to physically hurt Ellie's inner ears. "Mama!"

"She comes," the wolf said.

The room settled. It hissed. Something like a latch clicked, and the door had been replaced, now a bi-fold door, bluish and hard plastic and filled with kevlar, something that opened inwards. The wolf cracked it open with his nose.

Ellie felt the wind leave her lips. *Whooooo*. She picked up

Annie and they bolted with Levi through the door. "Where where wh—"

"Your parents?" the man in tweed asked.

She stared through the bi-fold door *across a fuselage of an airplane.* Another bi-fold door across the aisle opened, revealing a fat pirate captain, a cat shaped like a grown woman standing up on her hind legs, and a very large creature made entirely out of onyx. Or at least what Ellie assumed was a creature (she could only see it from the waist down). The barefoot man in tweed walked up to them. The rooms vanished behind both of them as did the people in cloaks. Airplane bathrooms replaced them one and all. They were somehow flying to New York City from Carthage, Missouri.

"Where's Charlie?" Ellie asked again. "Where are our parents?"

At that, Annie once more started to sob.

Levi, for once in his life, had nothing to say.

The wolf turned towards the man in tweed.

That man said to them, "I'm your fairy godfather. I'll have to do for now."

"My what? A fairy?"

The wolf shook its head and rolled its eyes.

"Not exactly," the man said, "Sorry. I've always wanted to say that. But I am your godfather." He opened a folder full of paperwork showing guardianship, signed by Ellie's mom and dad.

"Where are *our parents?*" Ellie asked once more.

The man in tweed sighed and looked to the wolf, who nodded at the papers.

"What of my Uncle Corey?"

The man in tweed snapped his attention to Ellie and said, "What do you know about Corey?"

She bowed her head softly and whispered, "He's a drunk. And a creep."

The man sighed in relief. "Is there someone else who can take you? And legally?"

And Ellie, cold, went still as a damp, rainless, mossy hunk of lead. The difference between her and a rolling stone? She was *alive*, however still. A living lead. She had woken something within, but normally she wanted to wake from a nightmare to see her same old boring life. Or maybe stay inside the sweetness of the dream when life was far too hard. This time, she'd neither woken up to a sweet life from a nightmare nor gone to a sweet dream from a hard life. This time, she'd woken from her boring old sweet life into her personal, custom-made, living nightmare.

Ellie and her siblings flew from Carthage, Missouri, to New York with the barefoot man in tweed and his bride. After the strangest boarding process she had ever experienced, Ellie realized she knew both of them. The man in tweed had been long friends with her parents in Joplin. Why was he caught up in all of this? The flight had Ellie gripping the handles of the seat, white knuckled.

She wasn't afraid of flying. Only little kids feared flying. She was afraid, rather, of this second plane transforming *back* into their house in Missouri. Though the monster likely wasn't there anymore, she feared he might return. Or worse: she feared finding herself *still* inside her house 35,000 feet in the air. What a crash that would make.

Because of this crippling fear the whole flight long, she refused to go to the bathroom. Because of having refused to go to the bathroom, she refused to get off the plane when everyone else debarked. The Author, her barefoot godfather in the tweed and cosmicloak, grew tired of waiting and deplaned with the other children. However the maker, her godmother, waited and waited and waited. Finally she asked Ellie what happened.

The poor twelve-year-old girl, who hadn't had this happen in years, finally whispered in a soft whine, "I peed my pants." She cried a little. "And… and the seat."

The flight attendants — both women — understood. The Maker asked Ellie, "Did you pack a carry on?"

"How could I possibly have packed?"

"Use mine."

Ellie might have had to use the Maker's carry on luggage even had her mother made it with them. Had she been on the plane, Ellie believed that her mother wouldn't have remembered a carry on anyways. Remembering those memory lapses made her worry all the more for her mother. More wetness spread along her pant legs. As bad as she felt for herself, she felt worse thinking about Mom and all women as this other woman helped her: were their situations reversed, Ellie had imagined cleanly how horrible it would be a mother trying to help a blushing daughter and not even remember *remembering* to bring pants.

Where was Mom now? And could she remember enough to be safe and sound? Could Mom even protect herself? Speak up for herself?

But the Maker was already passing a second pair of pants over the seat of the row in front of her.

However when the flight attendants again suggested Ellie use the restroom, she *wailed* against that. The flight attendants couldn't figure out why. But they walked out in a platoon formation, arm in arm, to shield Ellie as they would for a foreign dignitary. They escorted her all the way to the family restroom right outside the flight gate, where Ellie met eyes with a set identical to Mom's in the mirror: water drop in ocean, bit of moss in jungle.

A quick change between scenes.

Ellie came out of the family restroom and faced their escort. "Where is my mother?"

The Author said, "Not here. There are too many eyes and ears to talk right now."

"She was taken like Charlie, wasn't—"

"*Not here.* Soon. We will talk soon."

A walk into the great expanse of whiteness. White marble and glass in a huge multi-story atrium decorated by drips of black ichor like oil: half sculpture, half painting, all mobile. Then out into a city that would have screamed GOOD MORNING at you had its first inclination not been to keep its silence prior to nine a.m.

But for its taxi horns.

"Now?" Ellie asked, but received no answer.

They would have taken the black car, but the Author enjoyed

escorting folks. So he helped them take the first M60 Select Bus Service. In Astoria where (at the time at least) most of the comedians lived, he helped them transfer to the train. They took the N all the way through Manhattan, back over the Manhattan Bridge. From that vantage they saw the sun setting to backlight the Brooklyn Bridge, Lady Liberty, and the financial district, ferries all aglow below. It looked as if the stars had leapfrogged over the sun's path and had dived into the dark abyssal deluge of the East River to light the way home.

After every transfer on their commute, Ellie asked to talk about what had happened, but on the last train she finally let the rocking lull her to sleep.

They disembarked from the subway at the double express station — DNR stop. Folks on the platform seemed excited to take photos there: some famous girl named Sylvia had entered through that entrance the night before.

A few blocks walk up the second highest hill in Brooklyn...

Four flights of stairs, no elevator, with tight curves for... well if they had had time to pack suitcases...

They arrived in the apartment of a thirty-year-old Author and his bride, herself a Maker. Ellie felt water in the tips of her eyes: these two had no children of their own, though they wanted children very much. They did have an adorable and grouchy English Cocker Spaniel, Blue Rhone in coloring, named Echo.

Ellie offered to walk the dog down the stairs and to the street to give herself time to breathe, to explore the block. They had a 24-hour diner, a laundromat two blocks away where they carried their 150 pounds of laundry over five feet of snow in the winter, and a park that overlooked the whole of New York City. The dog Echo was quiet on the walk except when arguing with Kiko, the downstairs Chihuahua, and Rio, the other neighbor's macaw. Once, on the way back up, Ellie thought she heard both dogs. But Echo was silent on the leash beneath her. She worried that she was losing her mind the way mom had, wherever mom was.

Then both barks sounded again: the downstairs parrot mocked *both* dogs. She did the math. That made three dogs. No, four, two dogs and then two. Sounded like five animals in two floors.

As annoying as they were, they seemed familiar. Memorable because forgettable in the good way. And therefore safe. So did the library ten blocks down, the pool four away, the diner's donuts. The Author seemed safe to Ellie — though he was thirty, he looked fifteen most of the time.

He had hair she called "hobbit hair" and Annie named "Jesus hair." Levi whispered to Ellie in the landing that the Author had eyebrows like a wizard. Grey and wispy, bits of stray steel wool. He'd hollered at his bride when, near the bathroom, she threatened his wild eyebrows with clippers, "Don't take my wisdom!"

Annie looked the man up and down, curls to parachute boots, said, "You look funny. Did you grow out your hair?" Ellie laughed at this. The middle child, Levi, ran laps around the Author.

The Author asked about the various marathons the boy had run — the Frisco, the Mother Road, the Camino de Santiago, and so forth. Levi's stories about his races involved lots of leaves, pumpkins, and apparently he always ate lots of spaghetti the night before. "FOR FUEL!" Levi said, lapping and lapping. "CARB LOAD!"

"Now?" Ellie asked. Would he ever tell her?

The Author eyed her. He had eyes like blue springs of living freshwater congealing into great grey hunks of lead. Those disturbed Ellie. But not so much as the lines on his brow, lines only the very, very old have. Lines that didn't fit the rest of him or even most seventy-year-olds. Lines that seemed to have come from many, many lifetimes of many, many characters. Lifetimes looping over and again in his mind because of revisions and editing and too many real-world losses.

Ellie sighed: he'd never tell. But she *was* in New York. She'd eaten Omani food and Cherokee food from the reservation, so stomach growling, she relented when they ordered a New Yorker meal. She brought the breakfast up those black iron stairs. The Author giggled and added a bunch of tandoori chicken spice to his eggs.

The Author eyed her as he ate in silence. Then, nodding to no one, he holed himself up into his tiny bedroom. Their bed touched three walls. One wall had a turned-off radiator, a window. Beside the radiator and the mattress, a bookshelf slid between the bed and wall. It towered, leaning towards them both while they slept. Ellie supposed there were worse ways to die than "book avalanche." From that leaning tower and other shelves hidden throughout their tiny apartment, he plucked strange books about other worlds, about the nature of thinking, about remembering to remember.

After a time flipping through their pages, he returned to the main room (kitchen, living room, dining room, hall) and turned to Ellie. "Ask."

"Mom. Dad. Where did they go?"

"They agreed if something ever happened that we would take you and the other team would take them."

"Team? Why is their godparent plan a *team*?"

He eyed her and didn't answer.

"Why would you divide us?" Ellie asked.

The Author looked deep into her eyes and seemed to be looking right, left, right, left, unsure which of Ellie's eyes to focus upon. Or perhaps searching for some hint of something lost. "It is the safest way for you. They planned this."

"Why didn't Mom tell us? Why didn't Dad let us know?"

The Author shook his head. "They had their reasons."

"But everything is changing so fast," Ellie said. "First the girl on the wolf, Charlie being taken, now *they're* gone?"

"They're not gone. Think of it like a mandatory vacation for you guys. They went underground."

"She said we were in *witness protection*."

He said, "Then little has changed other than the location."

"And that we're divided," Ellie said.

"So now we're which cup is the ball in with the enemy."

Ellie clicked her tongue loudly. "How long are you going to watch us?"

"We're your godparents."

Annie piped up and said, "They didn't *die*. Right? They didn't die, did they?"

"No, Annie. We would know. But they had to go… away."

"Where?" Levi asked.

"Wherever the other team took them. That is all I know right now in the flow of the Narrative we're living. I could guess, but I do not know yet. I am not supposed to know. We were all worried this might happen, but they had insisted on giving you a normal, boring life in Missouri."

Ellie sighed and groaned in the sigh. "They knew the world was like this?"

The Author locked eyes with her. "They knew so much more than they let on."

"Even with Mom's memory loss?"

"With what?" The Author stood up tall. "What was that?"

"She kept forgetting things."

There was silence for a long while. "We will see what we can do. For now, let's eat, get warm, settle in a little. Have you ever been to New York?"

"No."

"Well let's make it as fun as we can for you."

When Ellie saw their tiny hundred-square-foot living room, she saw strange books in the author's little nook, little reading hole. She asked after these. He responded to her with the strangest of eyes. One that seemed to extend inward as if his eye were actually the eyepiece to some spyglass or telescope that went *inside* him, rather than out. The look shook her to her core. She swallowed and asked, "Do you ever write stories?"

He laughed. "How about you all go to sleep and we'll tell you when you wake up? We did, after all, wake you in the middle of the night."

By the end of the sentence, Levi was yawning. They made a pallet in the back room from unzipped sleeping bags they spread out and flattened into comfy little poofs — there were only three rooms that weren't the bathroom in the apartment. When they woke, they woke to the sound of more food and immediately sat down to eat again, strangely still hungry.

Ellie said, "I know you're an Author, but stories?"

"Yes."

"What about?"

"I often Author stories about what it's *actually* like to remember stories. Like this one, eh?"

"This one like the dog?" Ellie asked.

"No. *This one.*"

She didn't understand him. But she liked that he was obsessed with memory. That felt like a reprieve from her mother's forgetfulness. Had her mother run off and forgotten her?

This strange Author remembered himself, his family, other worlds, thoughts, languages from bygone days. He talked about locations in the memory, imagination, and dreams. He told her a loci was *a place in your mind*. And he could read memories.

Ellie called them "books."

But he did not. He called his books *memories* and said he could *read* those too. Memory, for the Author, was magic. That's because it is. Books are portable imaginations, embalmed master spirits, minds caught in little pulp prisons. Ghosts bound by buckram and ink. Stephen King calls books "uniquely portable magic." Another called books "dreams you hold in your hand."

To cast a long form spell: write a book.

Ellie realized, in talking to the Author, that buying books for her friends would end up much cheaper than buying each one a universe. Some universes have infinite libraries in them. The books in those libraries each hold whole worlds inside them, whole universes. Some of those universes in those books have infinite libraries in them...

And so on.

Ellie thought through more of this than most girls of twelve. The cosmicloaks of the guests who'd saved her, each depicted a unique universe. She thought of hearing about Charlie, "He is taken." Her chest ached, her skin vibrated remembering the monster of the feather and the blood and bone and scale.

Timidity filled her, cautious silence to protect her. She backed away from the Author, the Maker, even her siblings. Her quicksilver hair reflected more shadows than light. She proffered no hand to shake. Said nothing. She'd been hiding her shell-shock since Carthage. It's one thing to have a cold bucket of water poured on your head in the midst of a *good* dream to wake in the boring world.

But what about when in the wake of that chill splash you rise from boredom into a nightmare?

Ellie didn't know what to do anymore, what to believe. She hadn't wanted some weird reality, she'd wanted... basically? Another boredom, just a more interesting one. She needed a place of peace and curled her toes on the large ceramic tiles the Author's landlord had used in the remodel. New York was no countryside.

It was noisy. Or could be.

Would noise distract her for a while?

She needed at least distraction. Or normal again. Even a weird, noisy normal. Being a part of the real world, New York was normal enough. Being a major global city, it was also weird enough that it *felt* like it satisfied both of her needs of boredom and waking — all the people and four hundred languages spoken in the city. What was one girl who felt caught in a nightmare amid such motley cultures?

And yet... she also *wanted* the nightmare. Or at least to figure out what the nightmare meant, to mete out why it had happened. Where the monster had gone. Where he'd taken *Charlie*. It wasn't the nightmare she wanted, it still terrified her. Made her rage. Wish for a time before it had existed. No, she wanted the brother the nightmare had stolen.

So boredom *was* enticing. Or at least a relaxing trip in New York? If she could relax. Could she do both? Did she have to choose?

Yes, the Author's apartment was smaller than their kitchen back home. Ellie, having cornered herself and backed away from the others, felt like her eyeballs would strain from going so wide at something so small. She paced (in that happy-anxious way) around the house, thumbing the Maker's thimbles, basking in the Author's books.

She breathed. Smelled. Forced herself to feel the room.

What did she see?

It all felt so homey in a city not her home. She said, "Well at least we got away from all of the arguing people. I'm sure we'll find all kinds of curious things here in New York. And this Author and his wife will let us go anywhere and do anything."

They all turned towards Ellie in the hall, watching her fiddle the thimbles.

The Author laughed.

"What?" Ellie asked, shy.

"Away from arguing people?" he asked. "This is New York City, the birthplace of American argument."

Levi ignored them both with a grease mesh shield in hand, wielding it like a sieve for rain, and said, "I think the Author wants to run with me to different places."

Annie stirred again. "He probably will watch us the whole time and tie us down with kiddie leashes."

The Author raised his eyebrows. "What... are... kiddie leashes?"

Ellie said, "I remember this one: kiddie leashes are dog leashes that over-protective and generally whiny parents use to treat children like dogs."

"They work?" The Author asked curiously, looking down to Ellie with a wry grin.

"As well as dog harnesses work."

Annie said, "I want to pull a godparent around the way sled dogs pull sleds."

"See?" Ellie asked.

The Author said, "Ah. No I don't think I will tie you down with kiddie leashes, dear Annie. While we're at it, I won't tie down my dog."

Annie said, "Are you calling me a dog?"

"To be fair," the Author said, "there are several similarities between wee toddlers and dogs. They both eat things off the ground, you have to keep both away from glass vases. Both poop and pee on everything and everyone. And drool. New parents drastically underestimate the sheer volume of drool a newborn can—"

"I'm not a baby," Annie said.

"Sure," the Author said, "But also: dogs and toddlers will proudly bring you a dead rat. There's something deliciously monstrous about that, but not so monstrous as to return the favor of monstrosity. No leash."

Even if they did need kiddy leashes, Ellie thought Annie didn't want to be tied down. Annie, like many immature adults who talk about how other adults need to be mature, concerned herself with being a grown up and not doing anything a kid might do. Young things ought to want to grow. Annie would grow out of that, but Ellie wondered what happened if Annie became the kind of adult who *still* feared looking childish. The kind of adult who couldn't indulge a young adult fantasy novel.

She shivered at the thought.

Ellie watched as Annie, while whispering *just in case, just in case*, started collecting anything that could be conceived as a kiddie leash – Echo's dog leash, an apron string, a tin box of twine. Once she had collected all of the potential leashes in the Author's apartment, Annie stuffed them all in the miniature galvanized steel trashcan where they kept the dog food. She slammed the lid shut and shouted, "There!"

Ellie wondered if *she* was tied down. Tied to boredom. Tied to mystery. She didn't want to choose: she wanted to be "free" in her dilly-dallying. She wished she had — and could see — her guardian angel for that moment. Had she, she would have named it Daliel: the dilly dallier of God.

The Author, he chortled at Annie's collection.

"Will you let us wander?" Ellie asked, bouncing her leg in a jitter.

He said, "Of course I will. Kids get metro cards in the sixth grade here, it's just that one of you needs to stick with Annie, cause—"

"Hey!" Annie shouted. "No kiddie leash! I'm big!"

Ellie made up her mind. Boredom wasn't enough. And it wasn't enough either to wake from boredom into a dream state that had nothing to do with when and where you were. She'd had a nightmare happen to her and she would have to brave it right there, right then, in normal New York. So she started again to look, in earnest. A sudden ferreting amid the normal. A game to play with the others inside this normal-ish city, because this city is all the evidence she had right now. All she had to work with.

The Author asked, "What are you looking for?"

"A way to get back together with Mom and Dad," she said.

"And Charlie?" he asked.

"And Charlie."

The Author grabbed her shoulders. "Ellie. That will happen soon enough. Not any sooner than you and I would like, but that is exactly what we want to happen, okay?"

"Alright."

"So what can I help you with? What are you looking for?"

She turned on him. "Mysteries," she whispered louder than whispers.

"Mysteries?"

"You know," Ellie said. "An unsolved question that needs answering."

Levi sat up ramrod straight and said, "Like a dead body."

Annie said, "Or a stolen cookie with only crumbs left."

Ellie stamped like a little soldier, fists on her hips, and grinning wide and well. "Or proof on paper that somebody lied. Or forgot." She didn't say which somebody, which lie, which dead body… or kidnapping. Which act of forgetting.

"Are you detectives, then?" the Author asked them.

"Yes," Ellie said.

"And what mystery do you want to solve?" the Author asked them, only half-jokingly.

Annie mumbled something.

"What was that?" The Author asked.

Annie whispered, soft as an uncorrupted church mouse.

"I still didn't hear."

Ellie had no idea what her sister said, but blurted out, "What happened to our eldest brother?" She grabbed hold of the radiator pole: it reminded her of the bed pole on kidnapping night. "Charlie," Ellie said.

"They said he was taken," Levi said.

"Died," Ellie said.

"So you're not the eldest, Ellie?" The Author asked.

A hollowness came into that poor child's eyes, a weight unbearable. She was *supposed* to have been the middle child, not brought up from the bench in the final quarter to take over Charlie's varsity spot on the family roster. She was *supposed* to have been the overlooked one, not suffering the piercing gaze of Charlie-level attention. She didn't like feeling like the eldest suddenly, today, without Charlie in the room. Ellie shook her head softly, slowly, the tiniest oscillating fan: no, not eldest. "Charlie died," Ellie said.

"You sure?" The Author asked.

"Taken," Annie whispered.

"It feels like he died," Ellie said, "taken or no. It's only been a few hours." She frowned, she felt it in her cheeks. Her eyes skidded back and forth and looked the room around. She shrugged.

"Where was this? That he died?" the Author asked.

All three children stopped moving, stopped looking at him, and focused all of their undivided attention on the door frame in the room as if they expected a small crowd in black cloaks to silhouette its frame. At last among them, Ellie breathed and said, "Missouri. It was in Missouri."

"Are you sure?" The Author asked again. Hadn't he been there? Why was he asking?

She went still as hunks of lead in a river. "About Missouri or *when* Charlie died or *that* he died?"

"Any? All?"

Ellie breathed in the shallowest amount of air to the tight corners of her collarbone. "I don't know." There was no new mystery. All that remained was the grief of the old one and the hopeful pain of the normal, boring world. And not even the normal or boring that she wanted.

No dream, no mystery, no nightmare, no boring — nothing but New York City.

At least it had *New* in the name. And *City*.

Heavy-bellied clouds blocked out the sunlight over the apartment complex's white painted alley.

"What's that?" Ellie asked.

"Light well," the Author said. "Light wells in old cities like New York showed up before lightbulbs and electric switches: they help reflect light from the sun down into the shadowy depths of apartments that face a three-walled alley. Gets the light down to the darker apartments, with windows on the lower levels. Helps with air flow too."

In the moment of Ellie's doubt, it began to rain. She'd failed to find a new mystery and felt as heavy-bellied and dark inside. She needed a *place* to find one. Times Square? The Gowanus canal was supposed to have bodies in it, if *Law and Order* had told it true. Had New York changed since 1970?

The Author seemed to be watching the rain, squinting. "We'll see if this normal rain lets up enough that we can make a beeline to the subway station."

"Normal rain?" Ellie asked, so tired her eyelids drooped.

The Author cleared his throat and looked at The Maker. Then he shrugged and said nothing.

She thought as she dozed off again that bees seldom flew in a line.

OVERMORROW

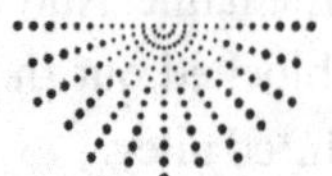

Ellie insisted on calling it not a nap or quiet time, but her "book time." After a quick doze during book time, she often preferred to read herself a book about trolls and magic waters. During book time, her quicksilver hair acted as a tent protecting her from others, keeping her aloof. She read by flashlight beneath her hair's silver shadowed canopy.

Once the others stirred, the Author took them downstairs. They passed the neighbors's doors on their way down and the dogs and parrot went at it again.

They passed an apartment with an open door where family members of that girl named Sylvia lived. The press stood outside asking the mother questions. Sylvia was not home according to her mother Maria. Maria was standing in the door, answering questions between shouting at her boys to "¡Suelten Conception!" Conception, their sister.

"You okay, Maria?" The Author asked.

"She'll come back," Maria said. "She'll come back."

"Of course," the Author said. Getting children down four flights of stairs takes…

a…

long…

time...

to...

...do. But they finally got outside.

The Author and the three kids all got meatball sandwiches from Murat, the Turkish chef and restaurant consultant downstairs. Turkish meatballs — Kofte — are nothing like Italian meatballs. More like steak. Levi called them "little juicy burgers."

"I want to go to Central Park," Ellie said at the restaurant's little combined tables.

"Why?" Levi asked.

"A promise," Ellie said. After seeing the clouds, she'd thought of Charlie and The Taking of Charlie. The thought of Charlie reminded her of the man with hooves outside their home in Carthage, which called to mind trees and other horses. Charlie had always dreamed of visiting Central Park. They had made a diorama of the whole park together when it was just the two of them — not for class, just for fun. They'd *promised* one another that they would go together, not with anyone else: hot dogs, pigeons, and a calm boating day. And now Charlie was gone. Part of her thought maybe, just maybe, he'd be hiding there and keep the promise. It was a frail, childish part of her, but it was optimistic. Optimistic, not hopeful. Hope is a different thing and never so frail.

"Okay," the Author said. "Why?"

"For the rocks and maybe for clues to our mystery." She did not mention that Charlie had always wanted to go to Central Park. That was her real reason. A wistful gloom filled her slight cheeks.

"Aren't there pirate ships?" Levi asked and shuffled his feet the way a small little sandpiper might when deciding which way to turn.

"Something like that," the Author said. "Rentable row boats."

"I don't want pirate ships," Ellie said. She savored the charred black meatballs, sweet white baba ganoush, and savory red lentil soup. The colors stirred her and she thought of the colors of the park. "Central Park is magical enough." Or would have been. For

Charlie. "Central Park should have *a* mystery somewhere." Any mystery to distract her. Or maybe she would find a new mystery connected to the one she, deep down, didn't want distracted from. "Or maybe, if we're lucky, *The* Mystery."

The restaurant owner offered them Turkish delight.

The children, having read many stories, turned him down.

The Author, having read many more, accepted.

"But it's *Turkish delight*," Ellie said.

"The point," the Author said, "is the desire. I desire the thing behind the Turkish delight and therefore will only have this little piece, no more. Plus unless my eyes deceive me, no witch poisoned this candy. Rather, my friend Murat made it for me."

Murat said, "Made with love."

"You want to find a mystery at Central Park?" The Author asked and swallowed. "Be careful what you desire." The Author wiped his hands off on a black cloth napkin. "But we'll go." They paid and went out the glass door, tiny silver bell ringing like a lost memory of The Polar Express rendered in Turkish.

Two bus mechanics stood outside smoking, wearing the traditional blues of the MTA, its gold embroidered patch sewn to their jackets and hats and everything else. One wore fuzzy black earmuffs. "I swear," that one said, "it attacked us last night — looked like a moonwolf had a baby with a spacewyrm."

"Listen to you," the other one said. "Drunk again."

"It's true! It's true!"

"Saying you seen you a dragon."

"Not a dragon. A wolf dragon. I seen him with my own two eyes the once."

"Listen to you," the other one said again.

Ellie stared. Her eyes, they bugged at horrors of a wyrmwolf.

"Come on," the Author said.

They continued towards the subway.

THE TRAIN CONDUCTOR ANNOUNCED THAT THERE WERE DELAYS due to a police investigation and track maintenance. Ellie raised her eyes at that. The Author nodded at her, affirming her concern, but seemed unworried for their sakes.

She blushed and shuffled her feet, while seated on one of the D train's orange seats. She didn't want to mention the awkwardness she felt. They detrained, took an elevator up, hit the streets of Columbus Circle. A pang of loss for her grandma's people came to mind, looking up at that Italian merchant prince, that early capitalist who once said, "With fifty men we could subjugate them all and make them do whatever we want."

She spat towards his direction as she passed.

Then the Author took the three children through the Merchant's Gate. It was carved in great capital letters right into the stone.

"Merchant's Gate?" Ellie asked.

"The park builders made a park for the poor — for all people — so every gate has a kind of people or vocation in mind. A specific category of New Yorker. This one is the Merchant's Gate." They crossed the gate's limestone threshold to the one place they'd really wanted to see: Central Park.

Ellie, who felt a cool rush every time she passed one of the chert boulders in the Southwest Missouri and Northwest Arkansas rivers, wondered if the rocks at the park would cry out any secrets to the mystery they'd hunted. Similar black rocks poked up all around Central Park like the bones of old giants through the mossy green flesh of earth. She didn't mention that directly, neither the crags of Arkansas nor the giant association. She asked, rather, "Will we boulder? Will we get hot dogs, pigeons, and a calm boating day?"

The Author laughed. "We can touch rocks, yes."

She didn't take her eyes off of her swinging toes. "I meant climb."

His head jerked and cocked, a left side roll and pitch as if to prepare to nod his head *yes*. His eyes squinted instead. "No?"

With her next step crossing the street by the white Cinderella horses and carriages, she kicked a stone that had come loose from the cobbled planters. It hurt. She wasn't ever going to experience the *real* Central Park the way she wanted. The toe flared, something like a melon ripe to bursting, leaking fire all up her foot and ankle. She was going to be stuck in this boring, normal stubbed-toe world with nothing but a memory of a nightmare to haunt her waking hours and no solution to the main Mystery and no other mystery to keep her occupied. It galled her. It made her flinch at her own steps.

Now Central Park, depending on how you look at it and where you're looking, is laid out like the space between all the great worlds making up The Vale. It's the great outdoor cathedral in our corner of the universe. If you come into Central Park through The Mall as Ellie did with her siblings and the Author, you'll encounter many of the great Authors of history cast in bronze. A triad of great women Authors gathered around a table.

Benches and trees flanked her way. Those benches had filled up with sundry artists and sugar-coated nut vendors. Guys gathered large crowds of tourists who watched them dance for real money. Others painted for real money. Still others sang for real money and were filmed by filmmakers making real money. People blew bubbles for real money, others sculpted for real money, still others *posed as fake statues for real money*. Ellie had no idea so many arts could make money, nor that so many people could make money off their arts. "Huh," she said.

"What?" asked the Author.

"An artist is a real job. With real money. It's a thing I could do."

"Yes!"

Oddly, many of the lampposts had their lamp heads cut off. Far more than every weird raven lady covered in birds, far more than endangered American Elms tarnished in profane graffiti tags, these decapitated lampposts drove chills down the cuticles of her cute nails. Perhaps they'd lose their way back in the dark without the light? She missed the wrought iron lamps of her old street in Carthage, the black ones crowned like gilded fairies. The ones that had revealed that strange man with the hooves. Who would decapitate light itself? She thought of the Author's light well and searched for the other lampposts. Those spare few glowed gold.

The street crossed over that great walkway. Ellie led them across, pitter patter pat.

A horse-drawn carriage full of fat tourists cut her off even though she had the right of way according to the bright foggy glow of the white walk sign. The carriage also looked like it contained one fat tortoise.

Ellie blinked.

The tortoise had vanished, tourists remained. Tourist. Tortoise. Surely she had confused herself, hearing the word in her head. But upon closing her eyes, no, she'd realized seen a shell. She'd seen the leathery lichen-colored reptilian flesh. A tortoise that seemed to be waxing and waxing like a green moon that wouldn't wane. Odd. That felt like a mystery.

Or maybe she was falling back into the dreamworld. She tried to shake it off, to lead her siblings and the Author again.

A battery of long distance cyclists cut them off again.

Once m—

Moms with strollers.

Ellie looked over to where her mom normally would have stood, imagined her standing there. Felt as if she saw her outlined there. Felt a rush in her belly. She'd remember her mom even if her mom had forgotten her. She screamed — her bicolor eyes squeezed tight — and sprinted across the way. *"Arrrrrgh!"* Fast footsteps of the others clattered close behind her. Her face smashed something cold, and she fell back on her butt. Cobblestone on ischium. Anger vented out her in a guttural growl as she rubbed her sore nose on a nearby grass patch. She felt livid that rather than climbing stones, the stones had climbed her.

Her nose started to bleed from the smashing. Why couldn't she see Central Park without her stupid watering eyes preventing even *that*? Why should it be so hard? This wasn't how their diorama of Central Park had looked at *all*.

Northeastern and British rich white kids had dressed up like bands of Appalachian white trash kids. They'd taken to the bandstand. The bandstand and music enchanted Ellie, the blackened glamour. She couldn't help but walk up to them and ask, as a child, if she could try the guitar. Almost all of them hesitated or refused, but the lead man boldly thrusted his out his ax.

Using her callused fingertips for the first time in a while, she strummed out a tune and started to sing her mother's favorite song. It made her sad. Then anxious. But she kept on until she was done. And then she felt tired and ashamed that she couldn't share that with her mom right now, only these strangers. She handed back the six string.

They walked down a great set of steps into a tunnel where you could shelter from the sun or the rain, a gorgeous little covered tunnel with a ceiling made of hand-painted clay tiles. This type of hand painted clay tiles were used on the floor in late medieval England.

The painted ceiling tiles disoriented her. At first, she had a hard time focusing on Central Park. Then the disorientation itself seemed to root her: yes, it *was* strange. Strange here.

Dark birth before breathing and light and sound: they emerged from out of the tunnel into an open air atrium surrounded by red bricks, trees. The angel of Bethesda faced them, cast in bronze on a high pedestal flourished like the cap of a Corinthian column. The angel seemed to stir the waters in her fountain to ward off cholera and other colds. Had that old statue moved? Truly stirred? The boat pond stretched out beyond. The boats on water stirred her soul with dreams of sailing off to newer worlds. "Rowboats," she said. "This *is* Central Park."

"Well yes," the Author said.

"Gondola." Levi pointed to the boat shaped like a brown ripe banana that a dude with a polearm punted forwards.

She shrugged. If she couldn't have her rowboats, she couldn't have her ideal of going to The Park with Charlie, whatever Levi thought about the coolness of gondolas.

They all looked at one another meaningfully.

Levi sprinted towards the gondola.

She sighed.

They all got there at various speeds. The Author and Annie meandered past the watercolorists and the twelve chairs for Chinese massages. They dodged around the skateboarders. Ellie stopped for a moment to admire the guy with the big five-gallon paint bucket full of dish soap and water who dipped a massive twisted rope tied to two poles into the mixture. No mystery there, but rather magic.

He pulled it out and whipped it around, and a bubble the size of Annie came out of it. It floated towards the statue of the angel of Bethesda. An imposition and inquisition of bubbleness. It ducked down and floated towards Annie then, who went wide armed, wide eyed towards it.

Ellie's pulse quickened. She shouted, "NO!"

Everyone in a wide radius around the fountain turned to look at Ellie, then Annie. The bubble swallowed Annie whole.

Then burst.

They gasped.

It, being a *silly old bubble*, did nothing. Annie giggled.

"What?" The Author asked.

Ellie blushed at her own overreaction, then sulked after the Author. Together they moved the siblings past the man who could make squirrels and sparrows do tricks for him. Over there the black wire fences gave the grass a break from the thousands and thousands of people standing on it every day. They got in line for the boat house.

Levi tapped his foot as if they'd waited there for centuries. Enough to vibrate Ellie's feet.

Ellie gently extended her hands at him and then folded them, leaning in. She sighed at them as her grandma had once sighed at Ellie in her hand-carved rocker. What a rocker: two arms doubled as seats for the other two children, so that all three could sit on her lap as she read to them. At least while she still had good eyes and good books. When grandma grew blinder, it grew harder to rock that way.

Luckily, Ellie had started reading her own books during book time.

She read the sign. For the price of a large pepperoni pizza, they could reserve a boat (and life vests) for four. They could then row around the lake below the statue of the angel of Bethesda. Ellie begged. Pleaded.

It didn't take much persuading. The Author ponied up and they three joined him in his boat.

Ellie took on a Brooklyn accent. "Get outta here! Fuggetaboutit!"

"Forget about what?" That Author asked her.

Ellie looked to The Author and away. "Did my parents trust you people?"

"More than anyone else they could have left you with."

"How long will they be gone?" Ellie asked.

The Author didn't answer.

"How long?"

The Author stayed silent.

"My *mom*?"

Another beat.

"They're just going to leave us like all the kids in the storybooks? Where parents leave or die and never come back?"

"Not at all," he said. "They're sending you and you're sending them. It's a mutual sending, a mutual seeking. You said you wanted a mystery? Well they do too: they want to solve the same one you want to, but they have their own path. They *will* be back. I promise. We will find a way to get them back. And they trust us with their own lives and yours." The Author handed off the oars to Ellie, who rowed for a couple of minutes. Then she passed them to Levi, who rowed for a couple more, then Annie, and back to the Author, who sang sea shanties.

Levi joined in, pumping his skinny little runner's arms in a pendulum. "Yo, ho, a pirate's life for me."

"Blow the man down."

"What shall we do with the drunken sailor?"

And when Levi came to the line about shaving his belly with a rusty razor, Annie asked, "Is that a song about Uncle Corey?"

Ellie shivered thinking about the old buffoon, Uncle Corey. The one the Author had agreed back during The Taking of Charlie couldn't care for them. Uncle Corey looked at her the way a sick king full of secrets might look. She opened a granola bar and started munching, mumbling indiscernibly under her breath, "It's about tetanus." She didn't want to be thinking about tetanus in Central Park. "The song."

The Author chuckled.

Levi continued with verses only the Author had heard before. *Keep him there and make 'im bail 'er. Put him in the bilge and make him drink it. Stick on his back a mustard plaster.*

They rowed past one of these great flowstones leaning from the grassy knolls and dipping into water. It looked like a discarded door of stone to the fae. Like Stonehenge had sprouted an American tooth.

They passed the keystone of one of the great elven bridges. Turtles hid on the other side of it (not to be confused with magical tortoise tourists). Normal red-eared sliders splashed into the water. Levi said, "Hello, brother turtles."

Various wedding photographers parked their rears up along the roughhewn gazebos on the shoreline. All other boats had started heading into shore.

The Author looked up at the sky. She followed his gaze. Her siblings followed hers. Blimps with OMT painted on the side. Rain in the distance flowed down in spiral formation, almost as if in an invisible funnel, a series of trees that stopped flowing in the breeze just outside the circle of trees that surrounded the pond, a coven of witches standing around a pot that was flashing lights, and several other oddities.

But the weirdest thing they caught – it was Levi who pointed it out – was a series of rainbow refractions high up in the otherwise cloudless sky.

The Author stood up in the boat, staring at them. "Overmorrow."

"What?"

"Row faster."

Ellie's breath caught in her throat. She didn't want Central Park ruined by rain, not the trip Charlie had wanted to take. So she tried to row as fast as her little bones would move and grunted while she was trying so that the others heard her grunt. "Because we'll get wet?"

"Because," the Author said, "you could get a chill that could kill you if you don't get wet *enough*." The Author looked at the sky and added, "That's not near large enough an Overmorrow thunderhead."

"What do you mean?"

"I mean," The Author said, "Normally in a thunderhead like that, we'd just sit out here in the rain."

The kids looked at each other with wide, giddy eyes. What kind of adult let all three of them get soaking wet in a rainstorm? It was almost too wonderful to imagine.

"But that one's so small you won't get wet enough. It causes problems. We have to find shelter *now*." The Author asked to switch her seats and he started to row faster and faster and then, at once, it started to pour rain.

Despair rose in her chest. She threw up the umbrella in her hand, and it too splashed in the lake. "Noooooooo."

The Author laughed. "Why despair? You're Undernaeht. There's a range. Undernaeht sleepers. Sleepwalkers and Daydreamers. Overmorrow folk. There are some others in-between."

"I'm what?"

"Non-magical. Or rather you're ignorant of the magic latent inside you. The rain will teach you the world of Overmorrow, we just need enough of it. Otherwise you'll be a daydreamer or worse, a sleepwalker. Sleepwalkers often die." His laughter prompted still more terror from deep within her. For the first time in many years, she wanted her mama. She shrank from the Author.

Maybe he knew more and could teach as they rowed fast in

the gathering dark? "Exactly what is Overmorrow?"

"Overmorrow is both a timeplace and a rite at the same time." The Author clicked his wedding ring onto his thumb ring. A steel anchor in a charcoal abyss ringing concave titanium ouroboros. "Overmorrow the place requires Overmorrow the rite to first notice and then enter. Or rather, it's more like Overmorrow, the rite, is light. It's not something you see. It's a means for seeing reality, the act of seeing it, and the reality itself. The waters of Overmorrow open your eyes to what's always been all around you, especially the deeper into the universe you go. The waters are one of seven rites that someone has been destroying or mucking up somehow. It's not the first time this has happened, sometimes someone tries to mess with the local manifestation of one of the rites, but this seems… almost stolen."

"How?"

"It depends," The Author said. "All kinds of ways this could happen."

"Who?" Ellie asked. "Who messed with this rain to make it so small we'll get hypothermia and die."

Annie laughed. Levi gasped.

"I have thoughts," The Author said, "but shelter first. It's dangerous."

"Seven?" Ellie asked. "Seven … rights like civil rights? I thought there were more civil rights than that?"

"Rites like ceremonies or special acts of reverence."

"A rite of passage?" she asked.

"Yes."

"Puberty," Levi asked. "You're talking about—"

"No," the Author laughed. "Heaven, I forget what it's like to be on the other side. No, it's more involved mentally and in terms of symbol and magic rather than… hormones. Overmorrow is the first rite."

"After you've made the rite of passage, can you cross back?" Levi asked.

"Of course not. It's permanent."

"More permanent than puberty?"

"Is even puberty still permanent these days? Yes, more permanent. You can't unsee what you see, now that you've partly been forced and partly have chosen to see it. Choose whatever you'd like, your choice doesn't change reality."

"Other six?" Ellie asked.

The Author answered: "Overmorrow, Yestereve, Yondertryst, Almshouse, Averrue, Bellwether, and Wayfare. All the rites both expose and preserve Overmorrow the place, allowing people to encounter the really real. Don't worry about the others, we have a thunderhead coming."

Ellie tickled her own lips by humming to herself, a honeyed buzz to keep her grounded and keep from growing nervous. "Preserve how?"

"They change the person, the better to see true with," the Author said, "The person changed by the rites changes society. Society sees truer and then it makes better people who can better see and therefore change first themselves and then illumine others. Like I said, it's not something you see so much as a means by which to see. Like glasses or a telescope or a prism or a mirror or a window that looks out of a house towards an Alaskan mountain. It's a rite of passage into a magical world. It's water that washes the scales from your eyes so that you can see the magic."

"What if I don't believe in magic?"

He stopped rowing to stare at her. "After everything that's happened to you three?"

She shrugged. He had a point. "It was worth asking."

He rolled his eyes and went back to his rowing, struggling to outrace the rain storm.

"What's the word mean? Overmorrow?"

"In English it means the day after tomorrow. It means something a bit different in Narrative."

"What's that have to do with some magic rite of passage?"

The Author let them coast for a second and his eyes rapidly looked between Ellie's and she knew, deep down, what he saw: green, turquoise, green, turquoise, green. He said, "Because you might have an idea for how tomorrow goes, but the day after tomorrow? That's a foreign place entirely, whatever your calendar says. Crossing through tomorrow into the day after that is as good as crossing a threshold into another world entirely. Think in terms of the future. It's like living the future in the past, now, with all times and places present to you. Like waves where different potential pasts and different potential futures all crash upon the island of RIGHT NOW. Overmorrow will wake you up to worlds and clockwork timelines happening alongside yours you've never dreamed about. Dangerous thing that." He scanned her eyes. "Dangerous."

He stopped talking to grunt and focus on speed.

The rain came down without a cloud in the sky, without a drop of murkiness like little liquid prisms A colorful, bright, wet rain. A golden rainbowfall. It splashed on the children's faces cold, bitter, shocking, and refreshing in what had seemed hot weather in the retrospect of moments ago, but the cold of it started to set into their bones. Deep in there. She felt it might vibrate her bones from within until they broke. So the Author rowed faster and faster, the sweat on his brow mixing with the Overmorrow rain. Grey and gold.

Ellie watched him work, wondered at his straining. Wondering at his worry. Of all the things to worry about in New York, he was worried about a rainbow rain? Over... what was it? Oh good grief, was her mother's memory sickness catching? She squinted hard until it came: worried over someone stealing it so that three children didn't get wet *enough*. How ridiculous.

They made it after several minutes in the pouring rain, made it to the closest bridge and took shelter underneath its grated surface. Two turtles splashed from the shallows into the swallowers and two coons ran off with used yogurt cups.

Between the grate above and their two cheap collapsible umbrellas, they kept off most of the coldness of that bright and wonderful rain. Levi called up to the various people running over the bridge. Ellie put her hand over his mouth.

A strange sound. One person clip-clopped over the bridge. Hooves?

Levi pulled her hand from his mouth. "Watch out, for we are a family of bridge trolls!"

The person crossing the bridge above their heads hooted out an, "Oh no!" And clip-clopped off, the sort of creature one expected — *in somno* — to find in the center of the West Village Labyrinth.

Was there any way to save her trip to Central Park?

Something else stirred in Ellie. A vague... curiosity? She stopped everything she was doing, thinking, feeling and turned so that her full face looked up to the bridge above her where the rain trickled down. "Were those hooves?" She remembered Nyssa the horse man.

The Author nodded. "Overmorrow."

"Overmorrow is hooves?"

"Overmorrow *reveals* hooves that were always already there, present in the pasts and futures you never knew."

Ellie, flushed, as if Overmorrow explained everything. She huffed under her breath. It *didn't*. At least not yet to her. She looked up through the grate above her. Various people taking shelter still wore three-piece suits and summer dresses, polos and baseball caps.

But all of them — or nearly all of them — were *also* fantastic creatures like fauns and centaurs and gnomes and satyrs. So, so many fantastic creatures. How had she never noticed them all over New York City?

Ellie, flushing deeper, shot back down into the boat. Without looking at anyone, eyes squeezed shut, then opened wide to do nothing other than stare at a stray shaving of grey metal. She said, "Levi, please tell me what you see up there."

4

THE SEER'S RAIN

Levi climbed up in front of Ellie, feet on the crossbar seat of the row boat. The Author wrapped his arms around Levi's knees so Levi could climb higher in the rain and the wet beneath the dripping grated bridge floor. He looked over the edge. "I see a juggling bear, a dragon with police lights on its belly, and six tree ents sipping three cherry limeades. They're sharing them with large bendy straws. Are you sure we're still in Central Park?"

"Good question," Ellie said.

Annie leaned past Ellie over the board of the rowboat, rocking the lot of them, precariously peering into the waters. "Mermaids down here are catching lead coins people threw in the lake. They're calling the coins plumbum?" Annie asked. And then leaning back over the edge to more stable seating and locking eyes with Ellie, she said, "Or is that how underwater breathing sounds? Plumbum?"

"Plumbum," the Author said. "A leaden currency based on symbolism."

Annie said, "They might be picking gems? Gold? Vials of the water of life? Hard to tell through the glare on the waves. The mermaids take all shapes."

"How big?" Ellie asked, thinking of wee mermaids she'd seen in a graphic novel at the Joplin Public Library.

"Mostly our size," Annie said. Then she doubled checked the size of her own belly and stretched out both legs and arms before her. Finished, she looked up at her elder sister. Nodded.

"Overmorrow," the Author said again, brushing bare feet on the floor of the boat, watching where toes hit dew. They moved water that had rained in and pooled. Somehow this guy was terrified of the water hitting *them* in too small of a quantity, of its chill. And yet he went barefoot out in it himself. Why?

"Overmorrow?" Ellie asked again.

"The seer's rain, as I said."

Ellie had dared to fan her pale lanky hands out from underneath the bridge into the wind and the rain of their beautiful frigid disaster. It had ruined her and Charlie's dream of Central Park by threatening hypothermia: she was so, so cold. It had shaken her bones. Oscillating those hands of hers out from underneath the bridge, dipping in and out of the waters, she asked, "You're saying this is all real? We're still in New York, no some weird parallel dimension or something like the way we travelled to inside of the airplane?"

The Author didn't speak.

When Charlie had been captured in Missouri, she'd thought, deep down, that she had imagined many of these things to cover the loss of her brother. She'd wondered whether her mind hadn't blocked the memory of a tragic car wreck or a house fire with wild, fantastic imaginings. She'd read all kinds of stories about this. Sometimes people slept when bad things happened, sometimes people forgot, sometimes people went crazy, sometimes — when there was nothing else for it — they died, whether by their own hands, some cancerous growth, or terribly foolish carelessness.

Was her imagination inventing tales to defend her mind from the real pain and horror of what had happened? Was *that* what had happened to Mom prior to Charlie's kidnapping? She understood a little: after less traumatic, but still serious events, Ellie had tried sleeping long hours. Sometimes fifteen hours per day. But now after Charlie, her body wouldn't let her sleep like that. Not yet, anyways. Before all of this had happened, her mother had moved past sleeping in forever and had tried forgetting. Now Ellie wondered if Mom had graduated to crazy.

It was perfectly reasonable to wonder if her own mind had made up stories to protect her.

Or...

Was it backwards to think her mother's imagination was hurting her own? What if the pain we inflict on one another comes from a *lack* of imagination? Had Ellie imagined more, would it have hurt any less?

Perhaps, she thought further, we dole out pain onto each other to suppress what imagination could do if turned loose? To suppress the help that imagination offers?

What if those who guard thresholds to other worlds became corrupted into those who invade other worlds to destroy thresholds? What if she wasn't crazy? What if someone had *wanted* her to stop imagining?

What if the rain had ignored their desire? Their destruction? What if the rain had knocked the truth loose in her mind and now the truest, most beautiful bits rattled around in her imagination so that she saw it with her waking eyes?

She shot up in the boat. This threw her off balance and forced the rest of them to counterbalance. The boat shook in a rocking barrel roll. If they flipped right now, Annie was sure to drown.

"Wait, wait," she tried again, still shaking the boat with wobbly knees, more aggressively, desperate with the rest of them to get it still. "You're saying this is all real?" She had planned on hot dogs, pigeons, and a calm boating day. Not some rainwashed gateway to a magical world. Certainly she had not planned on watching Pandora's magic rain stick lance some nightmare zit to watch bitumen, bile, pus, and infection spew forth from all kinds of sea monsters in the boat pond like the monsters she now saw leaping through the waters in the distance. She closed her eyes. Maybe it was only her imagination.

She opened her eyes again to the rain and magic creatures.

Nothing much changed except the pain in her eyes where more tears begged to come. "This is... real?"

The Author said calmly, "All things are real, child, but some are more real than others. Santa Claus is, in many ways, more real than the ideas of the historians and philosophers who disbelieve in him. Socrates's thought is real, whether Socrates lived in history or not, whether or not his plays by Plato feel like poetry. Otherwise why call it Socratic method? And Gandhi is a real historical person whether he captures our imagination and reason or not.

"There is one, though, who stands where Santa, Gandhi, and Socrates all play poker. Overmorrow shows the Socrates in Santa, the Claus in Gandhi, the Gandhi in Socrates. The other way as well. Overmorrow waters help you see the wondrous things hidden here in New York. And Elsewhere. One touched by Overmorrow has the seer's sight, if they choose, but—" The Author stopped to search the skies. The waters. The lampfires of the lanterns yet to be decapitated by whomever had cut the heads off the lampposts.

Ellie watched him watching. Following his eyes, she searched for whatever it was he had in mind in his search. And searched his eyes as well.

"But what?" Levi asked the Author. Then Levi started searching the skies too.

For what?

A crack behind her to the right.

Annie had strained her neck searching too.

"Someone is restricting the waters to a manufactured drought," the Author said, soft and low, eyes squinting. "The Overmorrow Cumulonimbus seems... hemmed. Hemmed in. It's only falling over the pond, and that just barely. Why?"

It was still raining stilted polychromatic drops, and the Author pointed to the sky. Ellie followed his fingers. Sure enough, if you looked closely, only the lake and bits of the shoreline were being kissed by waters, as if the cloud above had been a cookie and the lake below a cookie cutter. It was a Their-Lake-Shaped cloud. Just outside of the lake, hot clear sky spread out with no rain for miles. Certainly not Overmorrow rains.

"Who would steal such a beautiful thing?" Annie asked. "It's a mystery in a mystery. Maybe rain thieves kidnapped Charlie, too!"

Ellie felt a shiver in her spine but scoffed at her sister anyways. Not only was this the trip to Central Park that *Charlie* always wanted, not only was it ruined, not only was Charlie not here to enjoy it, but it turned out *she* hadn't been seeing things, imagining, or dreaming the night Charlie had disappeared and they were separated from their parents.

It had happened.

For real.

Charlie might even still be *alive* out there somewhere. Not murdered. Not eaten. Perhaps Ellie really *had* seen that monster, that white wolf, the crazy people in cosmicloaks, the transforming horse. If that was the case, she'd had to give up on the vacation Charlie had always wanted in order to search for Charlie himself.

And that was a stage of grief she didn't know she was ready for: that quick of an acceptance that he really, truly, was being held hostage somewhere.

It would certainly be easier to tick off Charlie's bucket list for him. But if Charlie still existed? And what if he could have been here in New York to do it himself? What if — deep down — Ellie hadn't wanted to check off his list for him? Visit Central Park to check their diorama without him? Or to please their parents who had always seemed to want her to fill in Charlie's shoes (whether they said so or not)? Or to lead their younger two siblings who now seemed unsure of everything other than still, as they had their whole childhood, wanting a leader like Charlie?

What if after all of it, she — without any help from the rest of the family — merely missed her eldest brother and wanted to be rowing out here on this pond alone in a boat with no one else but him? Wasn't there a kind of romance to a brother and a sister's relationship that had nothing to do with romance novels? That had everything to do with high Medieval romance? Courtesy? Kindness? A kind of ideal friendship that, when it worked well, complimented the world the way the dance of Mars and Venus complimented Earth?

Ellie missed Charlie. Yes, she wanted to be in the boat alone with her big brother and no one else, exploring. Tough. Together. And happy with someone who *got it*.

She decided there. She decided then. She'd do everything she could to figure out who had stopped this magic rain. Seer's rain. She'd have to figure out how they stopped it, why they stopped it, and how it affected all of these beautiful magical creatures. She'd have to figure out who was cutting the heads off of lampposts. Because Charlie would have done it if he were in the boat with her. And more importantly, Charlie would have encouraged *her* to do it alone simply because *she* wanted to do it.

Maybe whoever took away the capacity to remember the magical world was taking away the world's capacity to remember anything at all? Or at least her mother's? Perhaps whoever had just stolen Charlie had already locked him away in a safe the way gun owners do? "There's those actors back there with the cauldron," Ellie said. She squinted at them and their cauldron and wondered if she'd soon hear *When shall we three meet again? In thunder, in lightning, or in rain? When the hurlyburly's done. When the battle's lost and won.*

"The witches?" Levi asked.

She looked from him to the witches. Back and forth. Then to the Author.

The Author said, "Huh," and rowed the kids through the torrential downpour as Levi shouted back towards the bridge:

"We are a family of bridge trolls and we will eat you whole."

5

WARLOCKS

At the sound of the children's warning, more minotaurs and fauns ran squealing from where bridge met hillock on either edge. Hard keratin on riveted cold-pressed aluminum grates gave way to squishy dull thuds on mud, fanning out from either side.

The kids laughed as Overmorrow droplets touched their warm bodies. Skin made steam, little holy ghosts. Ellie glanced at the Author who rowed as fast as he could towards the west side of the lake. The Author's hobbit hair whipped wind. When wet, it took on a *ranger from the north* feel, lengthening, straightening, darkening.

Across to the other side, the witches (and one warlock) had taken shelter underneath a gazebo made of twisted driftwood, wicked vines that long had ceased their climbing. Perhaps a great eagle's nest had crashed to earth's salt and some old giant had upturned it for shelter? The witches huddled under it now. Had the witches stopped the rain? But how? Their cauldron sat along the rim of shoreline, fizzing and sputtering against Overmorrow droplets. Silver sparks and green flashes. Do *all* witches and warlocks make potions in cauldrons?

She didn't have a cauldron for making Overmorrow bigger or smaller or making any other kind of magic. Yet! she reminded herself. She didn't have one *yet*.

All a-shiver, Levi climbed out of the boat across her lap, sopping wet — *"Levi!"* — up to the driftwood arms of the Gazebo to get a better look.

Annie, Ellie realized, had already exited the boat in a clean leap from the back to a rock outcrop, had already run over to the cauldron, had already started poking at the bubbling, hot mixture with a stick.

Why?

Ellie, seeing all of this, felt drawn toward the witches however much she preferred hanging back, staying quiet. Journaling what she observed. Shoot, her quicksilver hair *almost* matched that of the witches, though affected a deadened grey. Did it know who had taken Charlie?

If they had done this to the waters, it seemed likely, knowing what little she knew about how the waters woke up the mind and helped you remember.

And what about her mother?

It all seemed connected to Ellie, she just didn't know *how* quite yet.

The Author watched this unfold from over the bulwark of his neck's silver afghan. The Maker had made him the thick scarf out of a silky cotton blend, had woven mirror thread in it, as if weaving the very fabric of the universe's story, or the story's universe. When his scarf wall caught the light *just so*, it glistened as chainmail glistens, but moved and vibrated with hardy songs where the metal chainmail rings ought to have gone.

The stress of it all welled up in Ellie's chest in a hot, sinewy knot. She ran to the warlock, a warlock she later learned went by the name Democritus Theocritus, and demanded, "Did you do this?"

"Do what?" The warlock asked and whipped around searching for the accusing phenomenon. Then, finding nothing of note on his plane, he looked up at the clouds. He pointed out and up at the rain and snorted. "Call Overmorrow? No one can summon the seer's rain. It is. It waits. It works any time someone without the seer's sight touches it."

"What about The Board?" The witch with the roughest hair offered almost absentmindedly.

He scoffed before Ellie and ultimately ignored the witch. "You should know this, child, if you can see us as we are."

The witch with the smoothest of skin and the roughest of garb — appearing half homeless, like a cheerleader-turned-prostitute down on her luck — shuffled belly-up fingertips at Ellie. "You're new here, aren't you child?"

Ellie, thinking of the cost if they couldn't figure this out quickly, ignored the witch and pointed beyond the gazebo to where the rain cut off before a wall of air. Or a wall of something. Beyond where it seemed restricted, it splashed in a funnel shape as if the rain were targeting some house. "That," she said.

The rain stopped falling altogether. At once. Everywhere. As if Ellie knew the name of the rain and, pointing out its restrictions, had made it shy.

"Did you do that?" The eldest witch asked and held aloft a large staff whose arboreal claws clenched forth a murky blue crystal. "Why would you *stop* this coming of the Overmorrow rain?"

Ellie lowered her hand. "No." While looking at the ground, she asked, "Did you restrict it to the lake?"

They all looked back around at each other. None of them answered Ellie. They seemed far more intent on understanding one another's role, watching to see if one another winced, flinched, feigned, or frowned.

She watched them all. She couldn't keep eyes on them all at the same time, but she searched them all.

None of their faces expressed anything.

Ellie dug into her satchel, grabbed hold of something cold, snap-flipped open a small notepad, bound at the top margin by ringlets. "What are your names?"

The older's husky voice hurtled phlegm. "Melvilla Melheure. The younger's Haley Wholewheat. The middle's Trog."

Trog grunted.

"What kind of creature could make this happen?" Ellie asked, scribbling.

"Witches," said the warlock Democritus Theocritus.

"Warlocks," said the witches.

"Rotten old stinky kids," said a random toad. "And princesses who kiss you without consent."

They all looked at the toad.

Even Levi.

"What?" The toad said. "I figure while we're taking shots, I could talk about non-consensual princess ki—"

"So you're confessing?" Ellie's head whipped between them all, especially the witches and warlocks, quicksilver locks flailing.

"No, no," the witches said.

"No!"

Ellie gave the toad a turn.

"Not in the least," said the toad. "I mean plenties of peoples could've done 'er. Boreas hisself gets fickle sometimes. Besides, that's what Averrue's for, ain't it?"

"Who?" Annie asked.

Ellie scribbled *Averrue* and *Boreas*. Maybe they didn't want her figuring out who did this, even if it wasn't witch, warlock, or toad?

"The North Wind, the wind of the Aurora to the north. Boreas brings the Overmorrow the way your postman brings mail."

"C-can't shoot the messenger," said Levi. He gave the weirdest shake as if someone had walked over his grave.

"Sure we can," the witch named Trog said. "We shoot who we wanna and you look shootable."

Levi gulped.

Democritus Theocritus the warlock sniffed. The sound seemed wolfish to Ellie. Wolfish… "Perhaps Boreas grew tired of bringing Overmorrow to a city that doesn't much care for wonder anymore?"

"Who else?" Levi jumped up on top of the gazebo. He'd

brought out his golden spyglass and peered across the lake. "I see a great amount of hustling near the fountain."

An explosion sounded. Everyone looked down the hillock to the cauldron.

Over the edge of the cauldron peeked a char-faced, frizzy-haired Annie. "Guess this stuff's sassy to sassafras."

So much dread filled the pit of Ellie's belly that she brushed her hand over the top of it. "Oh Annie. Are you okay?" She couldn't lose two siblings.

"You put *sassafras* in that pot?" the young witch nearly shrieked. "Are you crazy? Which mitten? The three fingered, left, or right?"

"The one that looked like a right-hand mitten," Annie said. "The one I normally use to make sassafras tea."

They all looked at each other and laughed and shook their heads, warlocks and witches and siblings as one.

"Stop laughing at me," Annie said.

They laughed louder.

Annie picked up a branch.

"Annie, wait," Ellie said.

But her sister threw two more sassafras leaves shaped like right hand mittens into the cauldron. A great column of fire and smoke and brimstone exploded skyward.

It roared up to the higher sphere, the clouds, to singe the skies. It dissipated. Sulphur gas lingered as embers floated down. After a long silence, one that made them almost *wait* as one, the Warlock said, "She's nuts."

The other kids said nothing. Levi shrugged.

The Warlock said, "She could have turned her whole face into black soot. She could have been the worst kind of burn victim. She could have ignited *the atmosphere*."

Ellie, terrified within, started to nod ever so tepidly, but chose instead to outwardly shrug. "Who else?"

The warlock said, "The Angler King just switched over the whole water of the New York archipelago. It all comes from his private water company. He used a diversion in the aqueduct that runs up to Tarrytown and Sleepy Hollow. This goes beyond goblet tampering. Remember what the governor pulled on the water sprites in Flint, Michigan?"

"No," Ellie said.

"Well there's no good way to get water without going through his for-profit water pipes. If you talk to one of the fae here about that, they'll almost immediately vomit. Whoever did it, did it with the guy whose name is … Can't Remember."

Something pinged in Ellie's memory. She turned to the young witch, then back to the warlock. "Who?"

"His name is Can't Remember. That's his name: Can't Remember."

Ellie tweaked her lips. "What's the name of the place where he lives?"

"He lives in Overlook."

Ellie said, "What's the name of his place of employment?"

"Omit."

Ellie said, "I just need to know who he is, the name of the place where he is, and what he looks like."

"Can't Remember. Overlook. Omit."

"I WILL NOT DO *WHO'S ON FIRST* WITH YOU," Ellie said. She'd watched Red Skelton, Abbot and Costello, and the other classics in her grandpa's VHS collection.

"What?"

"I. Will not. Do *Who's on First?* with you." Ellie took a deep breath, way down into her diaphragm. Deep enough that it felt like it might stretch loose the deepest parts of her. A bone clicked into place, or perhaps a pinball dropped into the keyhole: she got it all of a sudden. Sort of. The words — the names themselves — felt as if someone had yanked them clean out of the warlock's memory.

Her fingernails picked at her thumbnails, each hand independently. Was this why it was so hard to find the culprit behind the Overmorrow drought? Memory loss? Like how her mother had forgotten most of her own life prior to having her kids? Ellie's head tilted sideways the way a dog's might, sounding for the depth of the thing before her. A sonar waiting for submarine pings.

Annie walked up the steps of the stairwell slowly and looked at Ellie and the spell casters while Levi climbed down from the gazebo.

Ellie turned to the older witch, Melvilla. "His name, please?"

"Oblivion," she said. "It means 'can't remember,' but people don't like saying his name so they say it's Can't Remember. Or the Forgotten One or This One Causes Men to Forget, but that seems to me to mean the same thing as Oblivion. Well, of course, there's a good chunk of the free folk of the Vale who actually *can't* remember his name because he took that and a great many other memories from them. He makes many things forgettable, himself among them. Oblivion. Warlock Jack over here—"

"Democritus Theocritus," said Democritus Theocritus.

"—thinks Oblivion has something to do with it because restricting the rain makes it harder for new folks to remember Overmorrow, to remember fantastic creatures and charms work right alongside the people of New York. A terrible thing to forget. Oblivion would be up to it, no doubt, no doubt."

Another voice said, "But sir, sir, if I may, sir, the evidence seems to show, sir, that the Zobrine ice dwarf union would benefit from an Overmorrow restriction such as this, would it not?"

Ellie and her siblings whipped around 180° to see a short, bent little reporter accompanied by a stocky cameraman interrogating an even shorter series of dwarves dressed like Wall Street bankers: pinstripes and crisp blue collars and black phones and class rings with Greek letters. The kind who only use Greek for parties or the names of culty inner circles and mispronounce all of the letter names.

The reporter looked so shriveled by the weathering of the city — its smog and concrete and steel – that Ellie wondered if the next straight wind might blown him away. He wore eyeglasses thick enough a cruel child could use to burn black ants or blacker oil.

Perhaps because he donned the horrible burden of torture lenses, he barely made eye contact. Who knows? Ellie didn't, that's for sure. Maybe the lenses would sear him blind if he wasn't careful? Yet he stood his ground against those greedy creatures (not to be confused with the other kinds of dwarves), even when they bowled into him to rough him up. Perhaps he cared too much about standing his ground. Or the ground in general.

"Answer the questions I asked, if you would, please, sirs. Doesn't the air conditioning union of the Zobrine ice dwarves benefit from hotter temperatures and a weakening of the Overmorrow rains?"

The lead dwarf, sporting a tie-dyed pocket square, the only color on him, growled. "I suppose we *could* pocket some extra cash in the short term."

"There you have it," the reporter said into this weird Overmorrow version of a camera that involved many plants.

Ellie did a double take. Plants? Yes, the *plants* seemed to be recording the reporter's moving pictures, moving vines and tendrils to hold up cameras and lenses, so many black eyes.

"Overmorrow rains have been *artificially* restricted in their reach to the shoreline of the boating lake. The air conditioning union admits to benefitting — at least in the short term — from these developments. We'll be back tonight at six with the Angler King to see whether these developments have benefitted his drinking water monopoly. I'm Sy Cada with OMT News Noon, signing off." Sy looked over at the children, away from the news camera plant. He strode towards them.

The dwarves argued over who was to blame for the bad press.

Ellie smirked at this, wondered if any of them had a *coffee* monopoly, turned, and whispered to Levi, "See what you can ferret out of them, little brother."

Levi already had his spyglass up to his eye. His hand shook badly. Why was his hand shaking so badly? He said, "I'll tell you right now, big one has pimple problems."

She ground her teeth. "Not helpful. We need someone who's willing and able to help us. Go."

Sy came up to her, his tiny, shaking form moving slowly, and stretched out a weathered hand, the kind you'd normally expect to extend from little old sassy editor ladies who have worked for some old publishing house for eighty years. "Silas," he said. "Short for Silvanus. Call me Sy. Did you see what happened here today, young lady?"

His leafy cameraman and leafier camera hovered behind him, taking it all into their photosensitive polychromatic leaves. A literal photographic memory.

Ellie said, "Yes, of course."

"Oh fantastic. Would you be willing to let us interview you for the evening special?"

Ellie snapped back, "Would you be willing to let me interview you for my case?"

He hesitated, looked around. He had never, in all his time, received *that* question. He nodded exceedingly slowly.

They flipped their notebooks open as one, duelists armed.

He laughed at her, even though he was only a couple of inches taller than her. "Case? Are we detectives now, little Miss…?"

"Ellie."

"Ellie…?"

"Alia Aenor Saga Fay Wright. One of the Wright children. Or Fay children, if you take my mother's side of things." She pointed in a careless circle around them. "They're around."

"Your mother?" He seemed suddenly very excited.

"The other Fay children."

"Well, Ellie Wright—"

"Just Ellie. Or just Wright. I'll ask the qu—"

"Well, Ellie, are you… are you…?" He took a swig of water, a gulp, a swallow big enough it pained him as it tested the tensile strength of his throat's long balloon. "Sorry, so parched. I stutter without a camera lens to w-watch me. When did you become a detective?"

"When I was born. Solving mysteries is my calling. My turn! What did you see here today?"

"Overmorrow rain. Do you know what that is?"

"Yes." She didn't reveal she had only just now *learned* what it was. "Do—?"

"Then you know it's very important we keep this revolution of seer's sight reserved for visitors and the like, don't you? Do we not live in a world that suffers for lack of wonders? It's a wonder we even have rain anymore. They say it's miraculous, though it does wear off in time, as I'm sure you'll see."

"But isn't the point of Overmorrow to wash away scales from our eyes so we can see the fantastic all around?"

He grimaced. "Not necess—"

"I mean, when it hit me, the rain felt like an answer to the great riddle of everything. It felt like I had discovered every answer to every mystery, at once, even if I hadn't read every answer yet."

He scribbled a ton and looked as if he'd misplaced his camera, searching around for the plant. Frustrated, he turned back towards her. "Was this… was this your first rain to help you see past worrying about tomorrow?"

First Overmorrow? She nodded, small, stiff. Wait, he was now *two* questions up on her?

"My God." He looked around. Over both his shoulders. Off in the sky to the west, where he squinted, and then back to her again. "You have had qu… quite the shock, are you okay?" He had almost the opposite reaction that the Author had had. He seemed *deeply* concerned rain had touched her. "Is your mind stable? Do you feel vertigo?"

She didn't answer.

"See how the whole rim has been restricted? Why a time ago the great monsoon of Overmorrow washed the Americas entire, back when a squirrel crossed from Maine to Mississippi Delta, never touching ground, what for all the dense forest. Squirrel hunters would get hit with the Overmorrow no matter where they stood and saw they hunted not squirrel, but rather porream or limwog."

"A what?"

"Porream or a limwog."

Ellie waited, but he offered no definition. That had become a theme: feeling awash in the *newness* of it all without a dictionary or a compass.

"Of course, that's what the tales say. You'll find nothing on the microfilm or in the papers." His eyes unfocused. "When I was a child, I think… I think I remember the rains washing over the shores of the New York archipelago. But when I was a child, I saw like a child. Now I have become a man, those times have passed."

The dwarf with the tie-dyed pocket kerchief walked up to them with Levi in his arms. Her young brother was beautiful for a boy, but when Ellie asked, "Levi?" he was nonresponsive. He moved, but only from the deep abiding shivers in his bones. Levi absolutely wouldn't respond to poking, to prodding. The Author had been right. She had been *right* to worry about the shivers she'd noticed and that made her worry all the more in horrid ways. "Levi!"

The Author ran up to the dwarf. "He's got a sprinkler's chill," the Author said. "This is what I was afraid of. We need to get him to my house and warm, *right now*. If we pull him all the way, it'll stop. Otherwise, his sputtering will choke him off."

"What happened?" Ellie asked.

Sy, the reporter, said, "He got too cold without getting wet enough with Overmorrow waters. I should mentor you girls in this. If you—"

The Author cut him off with a slice of his hand. "He's not warming himself within. It's like he's braved a winter blizzard to get to a well-lit warm glow of a cave beyond, but stopped halfway inside. A little enlightenment without awakening is worse than living in the dark."

Sy grimaced.

The Author ignored him and continued, "It's a range. Sleep-walkers are almost always more dangerous than sleepers. Sleep-walkers stand half *in somno* and half out, a foot on either side of the realm of dreams, stuck mid-Swevenfall, one foot in Somnolory, the realm of dreams, and one part in actuality, the waking world. Sometimes it gets bad enough, they can have an affixation on their brain." The Author hoisted her little brother into a fireman's carry over his shoulder.

"Affixation?" Ellie asked desperately.

"A demon latches onto your pituitary gland and sucks you dry."

Ellie gasped.

"Starts with bed wetting and gets worse from there," he added, grunting under the weight of her brother.

Ellie asked, "Did we do something wrong? Is that why he needs more of the waters?"

The reporter tsked.

"No," The Author said. "No one did anything wrong. Other than… I suppose the restriction could have made it more likely? So whomever restricted it—"

"Why aren't we shaking? Me and Annie?"

The Author turned and looked at the girls. "I'm not sure. Maybe because you had your hands and head out under the bridge more than Levi? Or maybe something in his disposition to the rain? I'm not sure."

"His disposition?"

"How his mind is arranged towards it. His temperament."

"Does Levi need to choose the waters? Or change his behavior in order to be worthy of them?" Ellie was panting. "What do we do?"

"No child," the Author said. "Overmorrow is a gift. Nothing but a gift. But you need the whole gift, not a sample size. This isn't a wholesale grocery store's taste testing in little muffin papers. This is *Overmorrow* we're talking about."

Levi looked so frail, so small dangling over the Author like that, his limbs like bruised saplings, swaying. A whimper caught in Ellie's throat: so, so helpless. It didn't even feel like her own brother, the way the empathy swelled in her chest. Levi felt like her own *child*, watching him dangle that way. What to do? She wished Mom was here.

6

SHABBY MAN

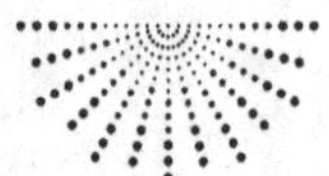

The Author unceremoniously and without turning said, "Good night Silas." He was off.

She chased The Author with her brother dangling at risk and no solution in sight. Ellie jogged with Annie behind them, remembering. Wondering if whoever restricted the rain had now both taken Charlie, and had also threatened her only remaining brother's life with some magical, haunting hypothermia? Or a demon affixed to his brain? "But I'm not done with my questions."

Without stopping, the Author said, "We have *got* to get him warm first, then home."

"Without staying, we won't find out who stopped the rain," Ellie said. "Who *hurt Levi!*"

"Without getting him home," the Author said, "your brother won't get enough Overmorrow and will die of underexposure. Do you want to solve an assault or a murder? We leave *right now* and I don't mean perhaps."

That stopped her short. She'd failed both brothers. Now what? "Levi..."

They walked cobblestone and past walkway lights when out of nowhere came a hard (yet normal) rain, somehow colder than

66

Overmorrow. Or perhaps it amplified the bitter cold within them? Great thunderclouds and fulminations poured down grey without the gold. Ellie barely walked forward in the mess, quick-silver hair dripping almost white, silent amid the pitter-patter-clap and sploshing.

They made it down the escalator to some grocery store, where they started to buy a collective gallon of hot chocolate (tea for the Author, who couldn't digest dairy) as well as more rugelach than their bellies could manage.

"I thought we had to make it home *right now*," Ellie said.

"We do," the Author said. "We have got to get him *first* warm, *then* home. We're an hour train ride from home. He will not make it without something in his belly to warm him."

She looked at Levi, worried, struck by the odd word. "What's rugelach?"

"Super sweet dessert." He pointed. One had melted chocolate, one raspberry jam in the middle. Both were wrapped alongside sweet piecrust and coated with rock sugar.

"Why have I never seen it before?"

"Polish Jews invented it, got everyone in New York addicted to the stuff." He pointed to his cup. "But it was Brits that got us addicted to the tea they bought or, in some cases, stole." There was a small napkin, a fifth one, with an extra serving of rugelach as well as a separate cup, this one half coffee, half cream, all sugar.

Ellie couldn't unstick the feeling. Chewing the dark chocolate pastries, she felt that she needed to give up searching for Charlie in order to save Levi. She clung her cold, sopping brother to her chest, trying to warm him.

But with one brother in her arms, she wished she had the other one too, the one whom she always felt closer to. She *couldn't* just give up on Charlie. Should she just give up discovering whether these folks were *capable* of finding Charlie? And. Then try to enjoy the rest of the trip, even with the Central Park portion spoiled? That or... explore more information about her own family. Considering Mom's mind, maybe Mom was somehow connected to all of this, even still. Or Uncle Corey, who still hadn't shown? She looked down at Levi, feeling him shake in her arms. She couldn't leave him. But his face reminded her of someone.

"Annie, can you flip open my notebook?"

Annie did so while mindlessly preoccupied in her chocolate treat.

Ellie had her flip past her notes. Give up or, once Levi was safe, sneak out and dive headlong back into the park, by herself. After dusk. In the rain. What to do? Abandon Charlie? Or the Overmorrow quest that might *lead* to Charlie? How would she begin to investigate absent people? Levi looked so peaceful in her arms, almost like a baby or a corpse. Investigate family? Or leave family to continue the investigation?

They'd hurt Levi too now, the monsters of this world. Yes, it was personal before, but she didn't know *for sure* that the person who restricted the rains had taken Charlie. But now? Now Levi was sick because of it. On death's door. "Shouldn't we call an ambulance?"

The Author didn't answer. He was dozing. What on earth? How could he doze at a time like this?

Ellie drew in breath to shout him awake and it caught in her chest.

A man approached.

Deliberately the man walked towards the two girls, their frail brother, and the sleeping Author. Vulnerable. Exposed. This man dressed shabbily, the stains of years of street living on him, barnacles of time grown over scraps of winter clothes that hid a once-handsome tuxedo with a blue bow tie.

She felt... haunted. The tuxedo appeared to have been dipped in the world's largest chocolate fondue fountain. Only instead of chocolate, the fountain poured molten time and molten time had ossified the very suit. She felt... as if the tuxedo should *mean* something to her.

Why?

A smell accompanied him, one you'd expect anyone to have if

they continued sweating through the same layer of clothing, year after year, without a washing machine or an easy-to-access shower. Acidic plus rancid umami. Cheap bourbon aged in rotten barrels. Distilled putrefaction. Was that sea salt caked on his lips? Now it was the breath of a scream caught in her chest as the main raised his unshaven jawline.

She felt familiarity of Levi's face in the man's face before her. If Charlie rotted away in some cell somewhere, unshaven, he too might look like at the man.

A flash of horror and delight and revulsion pulsed through Ellie's molars, painful as an impacted wisdom tooth. She recognized the unshorn, salt-caked face before her. Why was he experiencing homelessness? "Uncle Corey?" Her voice shook.

The man smiled thinly from beneath his tucked brow — the grimace a cancer patient gives a nurse for her administration of chemo and sat down in a chair too close for her personal space, and too close to Annie.

"I need more space," Ellie said.

He scooted back a touch, but not enough. He stared at her hair. "Like quicksilver," he said and then grabbed a fistful of the rugelach and shoved it in his face. Crumbs exploded over his beard.

"What is?"

"Fairy hair," Uncle Corey said, spitting crumbs. One hit her cheekbone, slimy and sticky and spiked with raw sugar. "Curly quicksilver with pointy ears sticking out. Lanky too."

On noticing her uncle, she again consulted her options:

Abandon Levi? She daren't.

Abandon Charlie? She couldn't.

Abandon the Overmorrow search? She wouldn't: not if it led to her elder brother Charlie or to whatever jerk was actively killing the brother on her lap. She looked at the Author. She should wake him. She opened her mouth and instead thought some more.

Leave her family and continue the search herself? She shouldn't, however tempted. She could, however, get information from family, right? They were no longer *all* absent. She snapped to attention. They *did* look similar, Levi and Uncle Corey. How hadn't she noticed before? Other than for lack of seeing her uncle very often?

Therefore:

"Uncle Corey," Ellie said, "what are you doing here in New York?" She nodded to Annie, who started scribbling messy notes.

"Protecting Overmorrow rains," he said, spraying sugary breadcrumbs by any consonant that brought his lips even vaguely together. He nodded at them — the kids, not the crumbs. "And her children."

She wished she was twiddling the fulcrum of her longpen rather than holding her brother's shaking body. She needed to put a stop to this, but... "You know about Overmorrow?"

"Of course." He belched. The burp smelled rotten: wet oak leaves. Decomposing corolla. Like what black squirrels bury acorns beneath for winter.

She wrinkled tear ducts.

"Who doesn't?" he asked with even more compost cloud.

Annie looked at her sister, at Levi, at the Author who slept calmly, serpentine brown locks now still, hands folded over tiny belly, eyes closed in contentment. "How long have you been here in New York?" Annie asked through squinty eyes.

"Since before you got on the boat," he said. "Since before you arrived at the Author's."

Sudden horror filled Ellie, a revulsion that made her wrinkle her full nose against now-invisible stenches. Against hypothetical ever-present, imagined future, or potential past disgusts. "You were watching us?" Could her nose itch or scrunch any higher and deeper?

"Always." He smiled. Orange chipped teeth, one rotting to the root.

The kids grew quiet, Levi even quieter than either of the other two, which felt doubly unsettling to the others, since he was already passed out and unresponsive. The cocoa wasn't working. Even in light of the creepiness the man had instilled into the both of them.

Levi started to convulse, stiff against Ellie. "AUTHOR!"

The Author snapped awake.

Uncle Corey, bored, pulled a flask out from his coat pocket and downed more liquid. Juniper berry aroma. He took the cap — a chain-bound thing with a human heart forged into the steel and the image of barbed wire — and squeaked it back on in a slow cranking motion. He looked at the table, left, right, left again, scanning every detail, and met eyes with the Author. "Did you fashion today after the seventh date in the calendar?"

The Author nodded vigorously, but snatched up Levi from Ellie's arms.

Corey drank, never taking his eyes off the Author. "I can't tell if that's cold blooded or heartfelt. Spleen filtered?"

"Both," the Author said. "All."

"What are you talking about?" Ellie asked. "We have to g—"

Corey wept. It was ugly and ridiculous. And smelly. He looked like a sick beggar king. Another fetidness accompanied him perceptible only in her mind's nose, not actual scent.

But why?

"Did you see Overmorrow shrink?" Annie asked.

Uncle Corey shifted awkwardly, then spat and stumbled away, crumbs falling out of his beard and trailing him.

How could Ellie get more info out of him?

Out of her own family?

How would she get Levi home?

Once most of the shivering faded from the bodies of the girls, the Author got them down the escalator, huddled wet and cold beneath the safety of a towel hidden in his backpack.

"Do you just carry around towels?" Ellie asked.

"A novel once taught me that towels can come in handy in an emergency."

"What all do you have hidden in that backpack?"

"Universes," he said mysteriously with weird hand-wavium. "We don't have *time* for the MTA or an ambulance, look at him."

The Author looked at Ellie's arms holding Levi, hoisted him back up on his own shoulder, and nodded. He pulled out a white ceramic compass, cranked it a few times, and placed it on the subway wall. It opened up a tunnel in the wall made of the same subway tile, stretching down a little stairwell and out.

To where?

Through what?

Ellie expected to feel shock at this, but didn't. She'd seen something very similar recently in the rock outside their house in Missouri when Charlie had been taken: of how many people clambered out of the rockness of their landscape rock. Because of that, it felt familiar, warm, cozy. It felt like coming home to a home she'd never known. Should she feel bad that she wasn't shocked about it happening again?

The girls descended behind them and they passed *through ceramic-ness* and watched the white tiles turn beige and then grayish purplish brown. It opened up a tinier hole in their floor with a ladder made out of ceramic. They climbed that and the Author hoisted Levi up through the hole.

Ellie emerged.

From the floor in the Author's kitchen. The shortcut sealed back, their frightful hourlong commute evaporated and avoided altogether.

Outside the tall windows with black aluminum trim it had started sprinkling again. Normal grey leaden rain again, no tiny rainbows and flecks of gold. It reminded Ellie of that deep abiding cold inside them that made them feel sleepy but not asleep, as if… as if sleepwalking. A burrowing cold. It snuck past numb skin and numb nerves and started tapping on her skeleton like a snow owl tapping on a frosted windowpane.

Ellie wondered if the cold would eat *her* heart from the inside out now. She'd gotten more of the icey water on her than Levi, but maybe it was also not enough? She moved so slow, as if it might freeze… her… very… the steel heart cap on Uncle Charlie's flask came to mind.

"Quickly, quickly," said the Author, but both Levi and Ellie collapsed this time, as one.

It fell to Annie, still young and small and ready for wonder. She took up the mantle, wide eyed and grabbing hold of Ellie's feet while The Author grabbed hold of her shoulders awkwardly with his other hand. He repositioned to better hoist Levi's frame over his shoulder as would an old fireman carrying little boys out of hell's besooted cauldron. As if to charge hell's own gates armed with nary a squirt gun and the last boy in the world on his shoulder.

Then, that Author fumbled with the handle on his own bathroom.

The latch wouldn't budge.

He raised his foot and kicked in his own door, getting them all into the three-foot-by-six-foot bathroom. All five. Once Ellie was inside, he stepped over everyone and went out to the oven to bolster the work of the radiators. They had no space heater, and the radiators had yet to kick on fully for winter, which made for chilly nights now and again during a cold snap. Somehow, he'd summoned their heat.

Next, the Author set Levi gently down on the stool and pulled out a tiny silver secondhand, the sort you might pluck from a priceless pocket watch. It looked like the conductor's baton of a mouse, the needle of a dwarven sewist, the very spear of Father Time's children. He conjured, moved lips, articulated words the kids would not know.

Here is what followed the incantation (not a summoning):

Strands of fire burst from thin air and attached to a stone sheet he had drawn from the marble tiles. With a whisper, he pulled up bits of water into a sheet — a literal sheet — of water. That he amalgamated through complicated needlework, wielding the quicksilver secondhand for a stylet, into a mesh that disappeared. This opened a hole in thin air with the stars of deep space behind.

Out of the hole of the womb of the worlds into their bathroom's thinning air emerged what seemed to be a tiny golden sieve.

7

THE GOLDEN SIEVE

Ellie's consciousness stirred at the great sucking sound coming from the caesura in their reality. Her eyelids refused to blink while looking at the sieve, and memorized it.

At the same time it distracted them from more important matters. The confluence of wonder (what could be, what unsettled, what *taught* wisdom) and frustration (what *is*, what comforted, what maintained boundaries) gave her weird wrinkle lines: her face read *wonder*; brow read *bitter*. "Can't we teach for Uncle Corey?" She felt so bad about Levi, which made her feel terrible again about wishing Charlie, which made her feel worse for ignoring Levi before her. And on and on. She just wanted whole and present brothers.

"Really, Ellie?" Annie asked.

Ellie shrugged. "What? Aren't you all upset? You saw him." She hesitated. "Or I did, at least."

Annie kind of shuffled her feet.

The Author, holding the golden sieve in midair above his hobbit locks, said, "Allow me a chance to repeat what you're saying back to you while I'm in the middle of saving your brother

Levi's life: you want to leave your brother Levi here in distress *right now* in order to chase after your drunk uncle whom your parents have been unable to fully remember?"

"So we can find out what happened here. To get vengeance for Levi. And from there, find out what happened to Charlie."

The Author sighed and tapped his bare feet. Then he grunted as he shifted Levi to the wall and the edge of the tub. It was a tiny bathroom and this was very awkward and tight, but it kept the boy from falling. "You're willing to abandon your second brother en route to finding — hopefully, with *no* guarantee — your first?"

She sat on the toilet seat cover, shifted her weight from one hip bone to the other, knees tucked up, arms folded across knees. On the one hand, she really wanted to find Charlie. She looked at Levi's pallor. On the other, the Author was right. Her youngest could die, right here, right now. "Yeah, sorry. How do we fix Levi?"

The Author fitted the sieve to the bathtub spigot. It was ridiculously big at first, but the sieve shrunk until it fit. The Author turned the faucet handle and the water flowed. Annie, at the Author's gesture, placed the makeshift rubber stopper on the drain.

"Ice, Kiddo," he said to his bride.

Ellie ran with the Maker downstairs to the bodega. A bodega is a convenience store without the gas. They used to sell wine, but now mostly sell Takis and seltzer and hummus and cheap umbrellas for days like today. Days when the city itself gets a second wind.

You can tell a lot about neighborhood changes by who owns the bodegas, delis, bakeries, and diners. Bodegas tend to have mischievous cats that look like furry pirates. Bobcats, in fact. All bodega cats are Midwest bobcats who migrated to the city and, now and again, shrunk. This bodega had one such pirate bobcat, missing an eye, peg leg where her front paw should have gone. Unlike her peers, she had a sword whip tail yet to be bobbed.

It hissed at Ellie every time Ellie reached for the bag of ice.

Reach.

Hiss.

Reach.

Hiss.

Reach-hiss-paw-claw-reach-OW! "This cat is going to be the death of my brother."

Ellie reached out, but the bobcat pirate cat scratched her. Eventually through the scratching storm, Ellie grabbed some cat food directly off the shelf, opened the can, and threw it away. As uncatlike as possible, the bodega bobcat chased after it. It worked, though it would cost her more than she planned on spending. What did she have left in American currency? She certainly had no plumbum or other currencies with her in NYC and only had what was left in her pockets.

The Maker, luckily, paid.

Both of them came back upstairs more slowly with three bags of ice and dumped them into the tub. Then halfway full of water, it steamed not from heat, but sublimation. The ice created a thick fog that filled the tiny bathroom. Ellie would barely be able to see, were it a normal fog, but the waters also illuminated dark places.

"Lights," the Author said. They dimmed.

The bathtub glowed up at Ellie's chin and chest as white fire glows. Or molten glass. As if he'd filled it up with gilded liquid rainbows. As if he'd drawn Overmorrow from the tap into the tub. It cast dancing shadows on the wall. Or rather it seemed to make their shadows dance from where they stood affixed to bodies. As if shadows forefelt what they'd forgotten.

Once the waters had grown to overwhelm a body, dead or alive, the Author turned to Levi, picked him up, unceremoniously put him in the bathtub, and slapped him. Hard.

Levi screamed.

"What are you doing?" Ellie said, tips of her canines *hurting* somehow.

"Giving him the rest."

Ellie said, "We're supposed to fix him, not—"

"Shush," the Author said. He smacked Levi again.

Great tears bowled Levi's ducts as his scream stilled.

"Stop hurting my brother."

There came a pounding from the apartment below: someone banging on their ceiling, the Author's floor, with the handle of a mop.

The Author shook his head to both interruptions. With wild eyes staring into Levi's two little grey eyes, he said, "Hear me, hear me quick, ye dead man, ye sleptling. Are ye awake, alert?"

"Yes," Levi whimpered, now very, *very* awake.

"Are you ready to remember, think, and imagine? Are you ready to renounce the machine?"

Levi had tears in his eyes and a look of betrayal on his cheeks, but he nodded slow to the one he felt, at least for now, had betrayed him someway, somehow. "Save me from the machine." One tear spilled over.

Ellie started crying sympathy tears for her brother, tears entangled, falling twine down her cheeks.

"Then repeat after me: I know by Is, I know by Thinkart, I know by Bliss."

Levi repeated. "I kn…know by… by Is." The tears slowed. "I… I know by Thinkart." He sat up straight in the tub, shoulders back and his teeth bared in a half smile, half growl though still shivering, he said, "I know by Bliss. Are you going to kill me?"

The Author said, "Might do."

"Oh God oh God oh God," Ellie said.

The Author ignored her.

She grabbed the Author's shoulder. "This will not fix—"

He shook her off. "Do you trust me?"

She shook her head. *No.* Her neck cracked at the shaking and she felt, in the pop, as if a great cinch of nervous rope in her spine had unsnagged and snagged again, the pain radiating up her face. Ask if this was too much, too hard.

"I do trust you." Levi pointed to the rest of them, his teeth chattering so loud Ellie feared his molars might crack. "But th-

th-they d-don't. Bring me back to them or them to me if you d-do kill me. How long will you hold me under?"

"Till I'm good and ready. Till *you're* good and ready. Brace yourself like a man: the waters will question you and you shall answer."

Levi gulped, but the child was no longer afraid. And no longer a child. "Okay."

The Author seized the little boy, yanked him up roughly — Ellie having seen, screamed — and he threw him into the arctic chill of a makeshift Overmorrow rain barrel. "I kill thee by Is, I kill thee by Thinkart, I kill thee by Bliss."

Ellie tried to pull the Author off of her younger brother. "Why does he have to *die* now? You're supposed to help!"

"He's dying one way or the other. If he chooses—"

She tried to grab at Levi past the Author. Twelve-year-old girl arms seldom match a thirty-year-old back.

Though the clawing did annoy the Author's elbows.

Levi went from relaxed, to struggling, to relaxed, to wide-eyed beneath the icy waters. Ellie hated to see it. She thought he might suck all that water into his lungs and have nothing but the fire of not-breathing left. Her own lungs hurt thinking about it.

"Please," Ellie said. Then she whispered, "Plea-hea-hease. He didn't choose this."

And the Author waited.

"He didn't choose *this*."

The Author had sad eyes, happy eyes. Eyes that looked like they were longing for a home they'd never known. He smiled softly.

"He did," she said.

And the Author unwhelmed the boy, still staring at her. After a long moment having surfaced, Levi gasped. And he no longer shivered. They'd fixed him. By killing him before it killed him. Why? How? To her, he looked as if he *had* chosen. How did that make any sense?

Why would someone choose to die? It wasn't like the Grim Reaper did anything but take and reap. Her brother had died.

She'd watched it, right there in front of her. Drowned at the hands of a man stronger than both children. He hadn't even fully understood the decision until afterwards. She certainly didn't.

She had gotten what she wanted, Levi alive. But only after—

"You're next," he said.

"On no," Ellie said. "Oh no no no."

8

SWEVENFALL

She had gone through the same set of questions, the same formalizing of the rite. The Author had pledged to kill her by Is, Thinkart, Bliss — whatever that meant. And then he too had said, "Brace yourself like a woman: the waters will question you and you shall answer."

She too had been thrown into the arctic chill of a makeshift Overmorrow rain barrel. And it had chilled her to her bones.

The waters, then, the waters now said, "Fear not, child."

And she relaxed.

"We must ask you."

There is another time to recount the struggle Ellie had with her questions, but it isn't here. Nevertheless, she went from struggling, to relaxed, to wide-eyed beneath the icy waters.

Ellie felt the pain of dying was badly named. For her, the pain of trying not to die when you had no choice in the matter hurt *far* more. It was bad enough when she watched her brother go through the waters in a more martyrous posture. But herself? It felt like some combination of being tickled by your best friend and strangled by your worst enemy. It felt like she'd lost a game she didn't even know she'd been playing. Somewhere in her lower chest.

81

It felt by losing, she'd gained everything back. And then some. That she'd won not only that game, but the set of all games. She actually felt… normal? More normal than she'd ever felt, in fact. She felt almost *too* normal. Was that a thing?

Then, once he was good and ready, the Author yanked her up again.

She gasped for air. Coughed.

Despite her protesting, Levi had stopped shaking and was very much alive. Almost painfully alive — it *hurt* Ellie to see him that vibrant — but in a good way. The way she might have hurt after a tumor or an infection was removed. Everything settled down slowly into its rightful place within her.

To her, he seemed horrified, as if someone had frisked him down for weapons he'd never owned. So what had she witnessed? His old self killed? His new self born? Would it take? He certainly didn't *seem* to be shivering anymore, almost as if he were warmed from within.

And if it did take for him, would it take for *her*?

Afterwards, they all, panting, settled down and ordered two large pizzas. They ate. They invited the neighbor girls from number fourteen to come over and eat. And compare experiences growing up between the city and the country. The youngest sister carried a toy hammer.

The neighbor girl Jasmine seemed shocked to Ellie, shocked that Ellie had a room the size of her whole house. Of how many *necessities* were simply taken care of by *space*. But it shocked Ellie that Jasmine could walk to school, pool, and bowling, and take the subway to any museum whenever she wanted by herself — an almost unfathomable level of personal liberty. On the other hand, how many necessities did Jasmine have taken care of simply by being around talented people? And how much freedom did Ellie have by being able to wander into the woods, alone?

Freedom and necessity, necessity and freedom…

As they talked, Ellie thought of her experience — her beautiful disaster submitting to the Reaper himself — at the hands of the Author. Jasmine's testimony moved Ellie, made her want to completely reevaluate her relationship with her family, with Uncle Charlie, with her parents, siblings, and the rest. Did it change who she was, deep down?

She couldn't really unsee what Overmorrow had revealed: a world of real dragons and witches and minotaur attorneys. What's the proper form of that? Minotaurs attorney? Attorneys minotaur? Minauttorney? When beans get involved do they shorten it to minestrone?

Now the waters had made her one of them, one of the mythic. Perhaps her family included magical folk now? Certainly it included Levi, who had also crossed over. Perhaps her search for Charlie should include the magic, as well? Perhaps she could pursue both at once?

No, she needed to follow the magical clues. Whatever got Charlie *was* magical.

Right?

Ellie called them to order after that, banging that neighbor's toy hammer like a gavel, though the squeaker in the hammer undermined her intended effect: SQUEAK SQUEAKER SQUEAKER.

Levi grabbed her squeaky hammer and threw it away. It bounced off the wall in a whispered, deflated *squawk*.

Ellie scoffed. "Now that they've made sure we won't fall into sleepwalking and are wide awake to Overmorrow, we need to lay evidence that magical people ruined the rains. Or stole them."

"Why?" asked Annie.

"It had to be a magical person, because non-magical people don't know about Overmorrow. They wouldn't miss it were it gone." Still, she wondered if it had something in common with Charlie's disappearance by now. But she didn't ask her siblings that. She still suspected Uncle Corey knew more than he was telling, but she wasn't exactly sure. Nor did she necessarily know how to find Uncle Corey to get what she needed to ultimately find and rescue Charlie. It felt as if Uncle Corey'd found *her*.

The Author brought in a pad of Post-it-notes the size of Annie, left them with Ellie. Then returned to the other room to communicate with someone named Steve by way of a compass made of crystal stone. Levi started scribbling on the top Post-it. Pizza sauce stained the notes.

"So," Ellie said. "We have witches, the Angler King CEO guy, boreas, the A/C union of the dwarves, possible unknown characters. Who else?"

Levi looked up at her from his note taking. "They're not going to want you to follow them."

Ellie stamped her foot. "We have to anyways."

Annie cooed, clipped a gilded braid of rope into her hair that she often stored in her bag. "We should probably investigate the dragon, the mermaid … everyone we saw when it hit."

"I doubt Overmorrow…" Ellie started. The pressure of all of her doubts burned within. She looked to the Author, the wince already on his face at her partial statement.

"Doubts…" he whispered to himself. "Doubts so plain to chase, so dreadful to withstand…"

She waited for him to explain.

He fiddled with a brass seal with his monogram on it and then sealed a letter in red wax. The smell of burning and sulfur hit the air. "Overmorrow is like this seal. It leaves its impression on hot wax and the wax is forever changed in its very form. You could know the brass seal existed without ever seeing the brass. The wax carries evidence of a reality beyond itself." He flicked some wax stuck to his finger. It clearly burned him.

Annie laughed at his wincing, finger flinging.

This all confused Ellie. She picked up a tea cookie and dipped it in her carob, barley, or chicory tea. *It* didn't taste like plastic. "How can someone mess with what's real? With Overmorrow?"

"They can't," the Author said.

"So…"

He started drawing a veil like a theater and a backstage treasure trove. He wasn't that good, but it was enough to get the gist. "Someone can make it harder to see and access reality. Muddy the waters and you can't see through the glass, even though the glass sits unchanged. Right now, we see through a glass darkly.

It's like someone hoarded the rites or the keys to realities back-stage somewhere. That's rendering them meaningless in society as if reality ought not be shared. Dragon and gold, vodyanoy and the souls of children."

Annie gasped.

Why?

"It's hoarding them and their meaning. Scattering good seed to desert winds." The Author thought for a moment. "No, I lied. Or, rather spoke too quickly. On reflection, there are some who can mess with the reality of the story you're living out right now. That's not the ultimate reality. They could mess with all you see and experience, but you'd still be you, you'd still have an imaginative will." He thought. "Hrmmm… Dr. Cirilla would say this better were he here… or Professor Pappas, Professor Wood, others… Professor Cirilla… well, he's certainly not as absent-minded as I… anyways, even still, the likelihood that any of this has anything to do with any of the ones you mentioned is very, very … " He smiled. "I just doubt that you'd know it if you saw it. Most of the beings you'll encounter in Overmorrow who have had anything to do with it are trying to keep more people asleep. Very few want to turn your story into a tax document." The Author pondered for a second. "Or an accidental life-after-death insurance claim." He smiled.

"Accidental life-after-death insurance?" Levi asked.

Ellie asked, "Wouldn't putting in a… claim… on the… policy… involve death?"

"Long stories," the Author said, "but yes. Accidental virgin birth insurance policies are similar. Very few of the beings in the megacosm want to turn your story into insurance riders, insurance adjustment reports."

The kids looked at each other. The girls, for once, had nothing to say.

"Why do they call him the Angler King?" Levi asked, clean out of the blue. It made Ellie turn her head hard enough her poor neck cracked again. "The guy who runs the air conditioner union?"

The Author turned his full attention to the boy, shoulders and sockets, buttons and brow.

"Not a guy," the Maker said with a slight smile. "Not the normal way."

"Ahh…." The Author said. "I think at this point, I should tuck you all into bed, then you can decide your path in the morning."

"But the Angler King?!" Levi asked.

"You'll see," the Author said, pawing at the afghan knitwear round his neck.

"What if you're just trying to keep us from finding clues that incriminate magical people!" Ellie shouted.

The Author laughed.

"Are you laughing at me?" Ellie asked. She felt herself blushing.

"At the idea, rather. I'm not trying to keep you from anything. Some seem to think that's half the problem: that I *don't* stop people from choosing."

"I didn't know."

On the corner of the tiny table sat a bonnet the Maker was knitting, pale and flecked with spots of purple and red and blue, for a baby named Sadie who would, one day, invite a boy to the Sadie Hawkins dance in a small Illinois high school.

"No clue chasing tonight," the Author said. "Soon."

Ellie groaned. These people and all their delays. The longer they waited, the further away Charlie floated, the colder the trail grew. Yes, Levi had been saved.

But what of catching his perpetrator? Who could also potentially have Charlie? Yet it seemed like it was always tomorrow, tomorrow, tomorrow for anything that wasn't entertainment — she felt surrounded by a bunch of antebellum southern belles.

What could she do? Leave. Sneak out. Sure, it couldn't possibly be safe in the East Village or Central Park for a twelve-year-old girl to be out all alone after midnight on the D train. But man, oh man, did she ever want to go. (Or potentially stay and never ask questions again. Bury her face in a book and use it to literally escape her prison). What if the delay was coming because the Author wanted a delay, because the Author wanted them to stay away from the crime scene? What if she interrogated the Author? Would she find out that he was behind it all? Wasn't the Author magical?

That could end the way stupid people who fall into bear pits end:

BAD.

Not badly, no.

BAD.

BAD BAD BAD.

Nah, she needed to sneak out of here and get to the magic folk. The other magic folk. But danger lay there, too. Sneaking away from the Author, whose wizardry she barely grasped. Especially after what she'd seen now? That conversation could go poorly. Very poorly. Wild and untamed. Which made her even more afraid to interrogate him than escape his clutches. Ignoring it all was an option.

But her dad always told her to do the hard thing, the thing you most feared. Typically that had more to do with homework, with handrails for an on-belay rock climb, than with magical madness.

Her heart hammered hard as returned to the pallet on the hardwood floor of the backroom. Her skin itched. Her brain vessels screamed against scalp.

Her leg jittered. Sphincters in her belly protested against undigested pizza, holding back a ship in the flood. It hurt. They — especially she — had a hard time falling asleep at first, what with the shouting of kidnappers down in the shady hotel's back alley, the fighting of giant raccoons over hardboiled eggs, the sanitation truck's beeping up backwards, the shriek of the D train taking the hard curve to 36th street, a boombox setting off a car alarm on 38th street, bus brakes in the Jackie Gleason Depot out back. An echo of what sounded like an honest to goodness wolf.

Dragon.

Both?

Good Lord don't let it be both, she thought.

ANNIE WENT TO THE RESTROOM. ELLIE KNEW ON THE EDGE OF THE tub sat the golden sieve. Annie came back out much later. Ellie didn't know why, but she went inside after her sister had left. Nothing was on the edge. Annie must have pocketed the sieve. Clean. Was it stealing? More like borrowing for safekeeping. Keeping safe wasn't — to her — the same thing at all. It felt like a gift to Ellie, perhaps she could give it to someone else?

But to whom? And when? And also why had Annie taken it? Especially without telling her or even flinching there on the floor where she slept on the red sleeping bag mat?

THE MAKER HAD LONG GONE TO BED AND SNORED, THOUGH SOFT and ladylike, from the other room. Yet when it became clear that, for all three, sleep would remain elusive, the Author made them more soothing tea and invited them back into the main room, which was also the kitchen and also the dining room, where he read them a story about a boy in a golden elevator.

As he read, Ellie went cold in her eyelids, borderline feverish. She got lost in the picture book: that great golden box snatched them into Neverness, a door that led beyond the Nothing. And she stirred her camomille tea, shifting on her chair, sit bone to sit bone. Finally, she could wait no longer.

Cue interrogation.

"You said you knew my brother was taken, but I don't know you as well as Mom and Dad do. What happened to Charlie?"

The Author dropped the book. "What do you mean?"

Ellie thumbed her lip. "When we talked, you didn't seem surprised about Charlie."

He stirred his drink with a glass stirrer normally used for chemistry or esoteric alchemy. It attached, at the end, to his quicksilver secondhand stylet. "How so?"

"The first thing you asked was if I was sure. At first, I thought you meant to as if I was sure about Carthage, Missouri. But the more I think about it, the more I know — deep down — that you asked me if I was sure about Charlie. About the way Charlie died."

The Author's face betrayed nothing.

"So… it feels like you know something." Ellie felt awkward enough to work her lips over with her teeth, to fold her hands above her crossed legs. "Now that I can see what the world's really like, I wonder if something happened to him, something worse than drowning."

Did she honestly believe that? She didn't know. Had she grown so tired of half truths and far fetched answers that she refused to talk — even on the inside — about the way Charlie had really left this earth? "The last few days, I seem to remember differently. I remember a wolf and a horse and a big old dread in the hallway. Like a shadow come to eat me. Did my parents not know? How much of you — of all of this — does my mother really remember? What if she's stumbling out in some alley or some random apartment in the world somewhere, forgetting everything, clueless deep down about who she really is? I can imagine a great deal."

The Author's face grew dark enough that Ellie wondered if it would snatch up the light of her flashlight, there in the story-telling dark. He pointed through the wall to where she knew the tub still sat with little droplets of golden water hanging about. "I would be surprised if any child of The Wrights could die of something simple as a drowning."

The golden droplet fell, splashed into a million tiny rainbows, the loudest echo of a splash. Many of the rainbows gave glimpses of other worlds: towers and tunnels filled with dwarves and giants, a world of water run by the Angler King, a world made of art, a *true* light well that drew *you* from yourself.

Levi and Annie were listening from a distance, still wrapped in their sleeping bags. Annie said, "If he didn't drown, what happened?"

"He was stolen," the Author said. "Some called it good, most called it terrible. Some called it most terrible."

"What do you mean?" Annie asked and fiddled with something large in her coat pocket. How had Ellie missed her sister donning her coat? "How could stealing my brother possibly be good?"

"It couldn't," the Author said. "I'm in the most terrible camp. But some good came, although that's complicated. Small goods always come of evil deeds. Even evil is rooted in someone's mistaken definition of 'greater good' to mean greater good for them. That's the only reason anyone does anything evil in the first place — they think that the small good they create in their own little world outweighs what The Good — the actual Greater Good — would put in its place."

"What good could come from stealing Charlie?" Levi asked.

Ellie nodded.

"People could remember. Very specific people."

"Charlie?"

"Use Charlie to remember."

"Remember Charlie?"

"So much more," the Author said. His blue-grey eyes went grayer, hazier. "For years, they suffered under Oblivion's rule, you see. He grew and grew in power, stealing up the loci of so many children, so many elderly, so many of the poor, so many magical folk."

"Loki?" Levi asked. "Thor's brother?"

"Loci like location. Locus. It's where we store things in our minds before they become part of The Archive. Stealing a loci is like stealing the deed to intellectual real estate."

Ellie said, "He made it sound earlier like a kind of memory magic. Like spells so long, they're the length of a fantasy series."

"What Archive?" Annie asked.

"ARC," the Author said.

"What's in it?" Levi asked.

"Everything. All of the ideas. The *logoi*."

But this made Ellie even more suspicious. She scoffed. Loudly. "What do you mean everything? No library can keep everything."

"It's the only one that can."

Levi said, "Does it contain all libraries?"

Annie asked, "What about every mac and cheese I ever ate?"

The Author said, "It has the record of them and what you thought about them. As well as the ones you didn't eat. And no, Levi, it couldn't hold everything. Where would you put it?"

They laughed.

"But it holds the record of every knowable thing, every imagined thing, every remembered thing, every dream. It has all the names. All the ideas. The things themselves exist elsewhere, of course, but what can be known about every thing? This it holds."

"What about unknowable things?" Ellie asked. "True mysteries?"

The Author scoffed.

"What?"

"The name of that would be God. Knowing all *unknowable* things is the job of no one and no librarian or library. But the collection of what's *knowable* has gone by many names over the ages. But if you're asking if the knowable ideas connect to all of the unknowable ideas, then who knows?"

The kids grew quiet.

"Who knows how deep The Archive really goes? It is creaturely sophia."

Levi made the *go on* motion with one finger and unrolled a fruit roll up. He handed it to Ellie, who opened it. He ripped off the wax paper, trashed that, and rolled the candy into a ball. He jammed it into his mouth in one great wad, baseball player.

The Author smiled and nodded. "Similar things have been talked about: The Library of Babel. Encyclopedia Galactica. The World Brain. The Akhashic Field. Collective Unconscious. Or, more classically, the Book of Life. But this is a little different: every knowable thing is in it, every bit of wisdom about everything. Every true thing and every true image and even every true thing that can be said about every lie."

"Our memories touch?" Annie asked.

"By a little door at the back of the gardens of our minds," the Author said.

"Mr. Rogers said you can grow ideas in the garden of your mind," Annie said. "What do you grow? I grow persimmons and clover."

The Author laughed, "Good fodder for whitetail deer."

"A white stag comes sometimes."

Ellie thought about that. She had no way of knowing if her sister was telling the truth, but Annie wasn't the lying type.

The Author said, "Yes, the secret garden door hides in the back of your mind's eye. It's really hard to see it, kind of like trying to see your own cornea or hear your own ear drums. It's like catching a mystical deemer out of the corner of your eye and noticing it isn't wearing soft leather boots, but hooves. Even still, if you know how to look, and you have the right tools, you can do it.

"Every door is different, sacred, special. Shaped to the shape of the mind of the maker it leads inside. And in your mind, there's that palace, that garden, that loci. It's unique to everyone: it's where you hide your memories, your dreams, your ideas when you don't want anyone else to know they're there.

"Oblivion was breaking into their memory's doors one at a time and stealing not the dreams and ideas, but those loci. He stole *the doors and the space*."

"You talk as if he stopped," Ellie said.

"Well," the Author said. "He's been ravenous. He's done this nonstop until your brother was captured. Now it's quiet in the archive and nothing to report. Prior to this one moment, many, many great and powerful magical creatures, storyweavers, and the like died or went vegetative as Oblivion and his lot stole their loci."

"Vegetative?" Levi asked.

The Author stood in the doorway. Everyone looked at the Author. "Or comas." His face had a pained expression, but he said no more other than, "We need to get you back to bed."

In the other room, the sound of the gentle swishing and clicking of the maker's needles resumed. That soft clicking needles soothed Ellie the way crickets or a distant starling murmuration's dawnsong chittering might. The child unbidden, unconsciously laid her head against the knee of her sister. They had peeked in earlier at the new needlework, the maker's own kind of storyweaving, a sort of binary write large in brioche stitching.

They all went to sleep.

When they woke, Levi broke the silence. "Really *all* libraries?"

"What? The Archive?"

Levi nodded.

"Yes."

"And The Archive's a library?" Levi asked. "Does it contain itself?"

The Author smirked. "Man named Russel asked that once in order to break math: the set of all possible sets that do not contain themselves. If it doesn't contain itself, then it's not the set of all possible sets. If it does contain itself, it breaks its own definition."

"What?"

"Except Russel didn't believe in pre-infinite choice."

"Wait, can you go back?

"Cosmic agency. Initiative dating back an eternity. Ur-cause for everything that could be — an intentionality at the finest motes of being and the highest heights of existence. His set isn't as much of a paradox as it seems. It's just a statement on whether or not you want to do math. So The Archive both does and does not contain itself. That antimony says something about wisdom."

Levi looked at Ellie.

Ellie shrugged.

He wrote out the formula disproving Russel on a used paper towel. "See?"

Levi looked down, then up at Ellie. She knew he didn't understand the symbols, the math. The quirks on his smirks implied he understood the *question*. He met eyes with Ellie, then turned to the Author. "Folks really went into coma when their memories were stolen?"

The Author whispered, "One by one, yes."

"But it's *just* memory," Annie said to them both, cuddled in her coat *in her bedroll*. "It's okay to forget some things, sometimes."

Ellie's face went slack, almost peaceful. Was it okay? She thought of her mom, of the fear of it, of the way her mother... well it was a sort of lying. The way her mother often lied about what she had and hadn't remembered. Ellie sat up straight with her shoulders back so that the sleeping bag slumped down around her hips. "Yeah, memory can't be that important, can it? I mean, it's not like Oblivion was torturing these people with horrors while they were wide awake forever and ever."

"Oh girls," the Author said. "Don't you see?"

They had blank stares.

Levi stood up and crossed his arms, adamant on getting it right.

Ellie picked at her left hand's thenar space.

He sighed. "Okay, listen. Ignore eternal torment for a minute. Imagine instead the final annihilation of your mind. Blinks out into nothing. Sure, it *seems* better than eternal torture. At first. But isn't it still an infinite price no one could possibly pay *and still* remain themselves on the other side of having paid it?

"Pressing the final delete button for *any* created mind and memory? Any imagination? Not imaginings, like my stories, but the minds that made them? *My* mind? Yours? My *capacity* to remember? My *capacity* to think and be myself, it speaks and spells, is known by every mind that knows me well? If you press that forgetting button, it is the last end. The last purpose. Carved into eternity. If it's lost forever and all the way, what's left, no matter how beautiful, still holds the bathtub ring of primal tragedy. If you forgot your mom forever, would that hurt a piece of you?"

"Forever," Annie said.

"Forever," Levi and Ellie agreed.

"Forever! It soils and spoils Happily Ever After. The loss of memory — the loss of the ability to remember anything — becomes the price of Happily Ever After. And so Happily Ever After gets founded on what's forgotten. Happiness becomes a deal with Oblivion. If any true mind forgets any of The Good, we can't regain the loss. What's your favorite memory of your mother, Ellie?"

"I remember how she pushed me to climb, how happy I was. I fell and broke my arm and she held me the whole time and took me to get a cast. And then when it was off, she made sure I could climb again."

"Would your feelings of your mom be the same without that memory?"

Ellie whistled low. "Okay. *That* I get. That I get because of Mom. If she forgets us, she's no longer Mom. If we forget the best parts of her, we're no longer her daughters."

The Author raised both of his eyebrows way, way higher than her comment deserved. Almost like he was acting or being melodramatic. But the longer Ellie watched him, the more she saw his sincerity.

"What?"

"What about your mom?" The Author asked.

"She's losing herself because she can't remember some of the oldest and best memories."

"Stuff you remember?" The Author asked.

It was quiet for a very long time as Ellie fought to remember something foggy, something grey and formless and void. But she finally said, "No. No, I think it came… before me?"

"What if an evil mind forgets itself?" Levi asked.

Ellie shook off the fog.

"Even then," the Author said. "Even then, it's evil."

"Whoa whoa," Levi said. "An evil mind forgetting is evil?"

"If evil doesn't substantially exist — if it simply cuts off some piece of the good from the rest of The Good — then evil itself cannot exist without The Good. It's really just a part of The Good deprived of the rest of The Good. The best thing you can do is to help it be less deprived. So yes, even in that case, if it's a true mind, evil or not, even the slightest hint of good forgotten means that all of The Good is not present in an author's alleged Happily Ever After."

"That's why Charlie died," Levi said.

Ellie nodded, added, "It's also why blinding people to Overmorrow is so bad."

Levi shivered the ghost of a shiver.

Ellie hugged him. Tightly. Then she retired back to leaning on her sister's knee.

"Can they ever remember again?" Annie asked. "Can the victims of Oblivion remember The Good?"

"They can," the Author said, "they will, in part, but also not yet. Now and not yet. We have begun to remember The Good now and yet we have not yet remembered The Good entire."

"I don't understand," Levi said. "But sounds good."

The Author smiled at the pun. "Good enough for now."

Ellie eyed the Author. She still did not trust him fully yet. She fiddled with the brass lion button on her pajamas. "Is Oblivion still working? Is he still out there?"

"That's the thing. Since Charlie the last… however many hours… it somehow stopped. All of it — the madness, the chaos, everything. Stopped for… well, as long as we've been together. Whatever Charlie did, it stopped Oblivion. If Charlie died, he died protecting all of us."

The kids grew quiet.

Ellie snarled and turned it into a clearing of her throat. "So, did Oblivion die?"

"Don't know. Until this Overmorrow restriction. There's nothing on the newswire, other than that. All quiet."

"The Archive knows," Annie said.

"Quick girl," he said with a smirk. "But The Archive is huge, and you have to know where to look."

"So…" Annie said. "Oblivion has disappeared somehow. People are out there on the street in the last day or so thanking Charlie. But what? What happened to Charlie?"

Ellie opened her mouth.

But Levi asked, "Is he still alive?"

"Stillborn into this world," The Author said.

Annie shivered. "He was *born*. He was a *baby*."

"I think so, that he's alive," the Author said. "In fact, I know so. I just don't know where. Not in my current state. I'm really sorry, gang, I wish I had better news to—"

"How do you know?" Ellie asked. "That he's alive, I mean."

The Author thought a moment. A longer moment. He looked out the window. It was not only a regular night sky above the light well. The dark clouds had cleared and the light pollution of the city blocked out starlight from the sky. A literal storm wall. He sighed at the shadowy coin in the firmament. "There are certain advantages to being an Author and certain disadvantages. I only now know the plots I already know. I know the whole of many, the ends of those I plan to write, at least, and those I see in full cloth that I've yet to touch. And those that I've finished, of course. But of the ends I'll write, details get fuzzy, you see. Or at least fuzzy to the me you're meeting now. I have no idea if the Maker and I will ever conceive a child, for instance, but eighty-year-old me knows. My own loci has not been spared The Archive: he plays with my mind too. I can't imagine what I've forgotten, much less what I'll remember later."

Ellie asked, "Is there someone who knows more than you?"

The Author stilled.

"Is there?"

The Author swallowed. "The Author of my story knows more, but he — like me — does not interfere with the desires and wills of his characters. When he shows up in my stories, he tends to surprise even me. Many of my characters don't."

The kids shrugged, almost in unison. This didn't get Ellie closer to a solution.

The Author sighed.

Ellie wondered why. At this point, she should trust him. But, she still had to ask and watch his eyes, "You didn't steal Charlie and hurt Levi the first time. Did you?"

The Author smiled a wan smile. "No, child. I have no desire to

steal your brother or anyone else. I don't think you realize how…
I know the names of things, the names of you children. I care.
How I wish you realized how much I care for you and them."

"Now I won't be able to fall asleep," Annie said.

"Why not?"

Her eyes drifted towards the wall, where shadows from the
smoldering light well danced.

"Wyrmwolves?" Ellie asked.

She said nothing.

"Let your mind wander to Overmorrow, child," the Author
said, "Swevenfall will find you."

"Swevenfall?"

"The hour of dreams. The ferry to Somnolory, the realm of
dreams. Dive deep *in somnio*. Sleep. You'll find your way."

He started singing a poem softly to them.

"*O Lady Flora, let me speak: a pleasant hour has passed away while,
dreaming on your damask cheek, the dewy sister-eyelids lay. As by the
lattice you reclined, I went thro' many wayward moods to see you
dreaming—and, behind, a summer crisp with shining woods. And I too
dream'd…*"

9

QUAFF TO QUELL

L evi woke early, alone and frustrated at the prior night's conversation. Frustrated at Ellie for interfering in his own way. If the Author hadn't stolen Overmorrow and Charlie, then Levi knew who had.

He could help Ellie find that perp. He'd helped her pick organic apples and a giant pumpkin at the orchard near Melrose, Kansas — *population 844* — a couple autumns back. He could find the guy. Run him down. Oh boy, to have the North Wind whipping at him while he caught him. Or he could just enjoy his trip.

Helping Ellie came with perks (1) Finding his brother, (2) the good feeling of being helpful, (3) chasing bad guys.

Then again, sometimes he just wanted to enjoy a thing. A painting, a meal, a run. A vacation. A run *while on vacation*. He didn't want to enjoy himself. It was his *self* that enjoyed... some*thing*.

So many people came to Central Park, but who circumnavigated it in an hour? At a jog, you could see *the entire park* in two hours. The whole thing. The Boat House, Reservoir, ball fields, mountains, The Ramble, Dairy House, Turtle Pond, bridges, Balto, carousel, Bethesda fountain, Chess and Checkers House, cop cot, music clock, Zoo, Met Museum, embassies (he'd forgotten they had embassies), that one Natural History Museum from Mrs. Basil E. Frankweiler (and *Night at the Museum*), and on and on.

Endless.

As endless as the peoples its many gates named.

Levi savored the press of foot on cinder, the pull of skin on shoe. Why worry? It already felt like Charlie'd been gone for years. Levi felt better now, compared to that fateful night. At least he hadn't freaked out the way Ellie had. She didn't know what it'd felt like to *him*, then or now. He felt alive while running. Alive at the hope of circumnavigating Central.

Why not enjoy his trip? He'd earned it, right? For now, anyways, his hunch could wait down in the deep muscle pain of his hip.

Levi liked to run early. Quick start, quicker stop his Papa Jimmy'd said. He hoped to run hard, long, and get back before breakfast with at least one task completed. Back with an appetite for a cabbie breakfast, an Irish breakfast, then a hobbit's second. Bunch of sausage and ham and bacon and beans and tomatoes. Also something called pudding. Banana pudding, hopefully. The hunger in him stirred, ready to rear its head higher.

He was young, sure, and his legs were not particularly long. Even still, Levi had run multiple 5k and 10k races with his father, most of them on asphalt. The Author himself had pushed Levi to do multiple laps around the coffee table in his parents's first apartment. The Author lived near them all back in Joplin. Ninety-nine laps around that coffee table at four years old. He was old hat at running now. The kind of running that would make one lose one's old hat: fast, against the wind.

Levi took off on a ten-mile run, ears deafened by breeze. He'd get back quickly after finishing his run and see if the girls and The Author had closed on a lead. The park opened like a fairy tunnel under gemel bays.

He hoofed up the East Side of Manhattan after jogging the Brooklyn Bridge. He ran past the STUNTAZ INC trucks faster than the sun itself could rise. When reflecting off the skyscrapers and East River waters, sunlight gives off almost as many colors as Overmorrow itself — as many as you can get without something magical happening.

A couple of times he hitched a quicker ride on the back of a loading truck or a bus. He wasn't set against running the whole nine miles to Central Park from the Author's, training for his marathon as he was, but getting there faster helped. So he hitched rides, mostly landing his butt on cold, damp, diamond plated steel.

Once he landed at the park and started running laps, he would have kept going. But he ended up north of the boat lake where he'd first encountered Overmorrow. He should have kept going. They had a Reservoir of freshwater around which runners ran in the baby blue and orange smoke evenings. Some people illegally fish. Some turtles semi-legally swam. At Turtle Pond, former pet owners dropped off decades worth of inconvenient red snappers. Betwixt the long years, mutant monsters grew and changed there beneath the surface.

And swam.

Someone long ago had named the Reservoir waters after a First Lady that'd been faithful to her cheating husband. A cuckol-dress. The reservoir was ringed in rigid fishing poles. The fishing poles of elderly Chinese men (cigarettes in mouth, shod sockless with high-gloss loafers). The fishing poles of young black girls (heads half-shorn or dreadlocks dyed neon pink and white). The fishing poles stood discarded, underused, lined up like river reeds stitched with gossamer webs.

Other folks draped their fishing lines from pole tips over the edge of the pond like wool knitting yarn, stitching waters to the concrete shores. Knits and purls and knits and purls of rods and lines on a quilt of waters. Levi squinted. The faintest edges of his vision give an old prismatic light to them, afterglow of dampness from the Overmorrow drowning.

It wasn't magic. Right? His equilibrium shifted.

Were those narwhals out in the Central Park Reservoir? Did tower-sized sucker fish clean the big deep below, some catfish left to mutate down in muddy depths? And most importantly: where could he purchase a decent bacon, egg, and cheese?

He was suddenly overwhelmed by a desire to start running again. Immediately. A fear welled up somewhere in his chest. He moved to flee.

"Hello, little story boy," a voice resounded from beyond the iron fence. "And what is your true name?"

Dangerous to give his true name so quickly. Even if what he'd give wasn't what would one day be written on his white stone. The true new name on the pebble known only to the giver and to the receiver. So as not to be rude, he couldn't help but say his calling name, "Levi."

When he turned, no one stood behind him. No one down his left side was staring at him. Nor down the right side of the shoreline, where waves lapped at angled limestone.

What about up in the sky?

Winged flying things ventured about. Winged fire ribbons, nothing like dragons or phoenixes. More like jellyfish of flame, yet high above. Nothing within speaking distance. The light of the dawn framed the great spray of the reservoir's fountain, bursting and disclosing itself to the world.

Waves blustered straight at him in the adverse wind. The waves had streaks in them reminding him of black silt erosion in sand.

Beneath all of that vista perched a mouth the size of an MTA bus. The maw gaped. Hooks dangled from it, bad Christmas tinsel. This was the proto fish, the überFische, The One That Got Away in every fisherman's fishing story ever told.

"Took you long enough," the overlarge largemouth bass said. "Not too quick on your feet, are you?"

"I run," Levi said. "So…"

"I didn't mean your literal feet."

Levi felt drawn to run again. "But—"

"You haven't said your name," the überFische said.

"Yes, I did. Levi."

"Priestly name. You come to Papa Fish for absolution of your sins, wee priest? My confessional is open for business, step right in." It opened wide its maw.

"Thank you, no," Levi said.

"No Averrue for you?"

"No what? Do I know you?"

"Do you know many kings, little priest?"

"Are you… wait … are you the *Angler King*?"

The fish laughed a basso laugh. It wasn't funny. Whatever the opposite of a fellowship laugh was, this was that. "I've eaten more fisherman than any fish I know. Angled out more kings. I am a kingfisher. Of a kind, at least. I suppose you could call me that. King of the angler buffet, if you catch my driftwood. The King over anglers who think themselves kings of fishes."

Levi felt vibrations on his head where horns go on goats. "A fisher of men?"

"If you follow me." The Angler King smiled. His teeth were barbs.

Levi swallowed against a throat that wanted to strangle itself. "Did you come here to eat me?"

"Not yet," the Angler King said, pock pock pocking his lips. "If I ate all boney little story boys, who'd be left to buy my freshwater? Who'd come back to tell how big and scary I am? How uncatchable? Who would feed the fishes?"

"You have fish food people use to feed the others?"

"I meant that others of my kin also like to feast on flesh."

Levi shook his head to get the image of *becoming* a fish feast out of his mind. He started stretching. He'd resume his run very very soon if he needed to escape, but for now he stretched to calm himself. The benefit of stretching on the ground is that the black iron worked more like a shark cage than when he was standing higher than it. Would a question help get him going in the face of such a tyrant? "Does your freshwater come from Overmorrow?"

The fish scoffed and gurgled. Choking on his own laugh. "God in heaven, no! Could you imagine quenching twenty million New York thirsts with intermittent magic rain? Let alone the problems it would cause if every soul knew Overmorrow? Harpoons-in-fins, how awful."

Wow. Actual *clues*. Ellie would be thrilled. Levi wished he had a pad of paper. Or a Sharpie for writing on his arm. "So you'd like for fewer folks to come awake in Overmorrow?"

The fish eyed him with his good eye. He eyed him with what was left of his bad one. Even moved a bulbous growth at the front of his head towards him. It reminded Levi of the bodega pirate cat, that growth. "Are you accusing me of something, story boy?" The bulbous growth roiled and pulsed like a third eye, an evil eye. "Are you saying something here?"

"You know that Overmorrow is restricted, right? That the waters are forgotten? Someone seems to have kept them from falling broadly."

"Of course. Everyone who's anyone has noticed that, silly goose." The fish honked to mock him. It was an odd, funny sound. It didn't have the intended effect, whatever that had been.

Levi had the feeling that the phrase "silly goose" had a darker, more insane bend in the mind of the Angler King. "Did you have a hand in that?"

The Angler King curled and uncurled its fins as if someone had not only set the strongest hook in his lip, but had hauled him up and out of water. "No."

"Do you know who did?"

The great fish hissed at him, more barbed teeth on its barbed lips. "No."

"Where are you getting your water?" Levi asked. "Upstate? The aqueduct?"

The fish started to sink back into the waves like so many blue blankets in the world's largest bed.

Levi smirked and leaned in. "Are the questions of a little story boy scaring you? Are—"

"DO NOT TAUNT ME, CHICKEN LIVER." The Angler King was somehow in Levi's face and not touching the water at all. A monster the size of a double stacked, double long city bus gaped at him. "DO YOU NOT SEE YOU ARE SPARE MORE THAN A

BUBBLE, A BURP? A SPLIDGET OF LIVE BAIT?" Its barbed teeth clicked and thwacked like so many reeds in a harsh sea breeze. "THE TINY COWBELLS WILL TING WITH CRIES, WITH LIGHTLESS DREAMS WHEN I DRINK YOU DOWN, WHEN I QUAFF TO QUELL YOU."

The whole of the greater fish did make the little story boy very, very afraid. But Levi swallowed and breathed. Breathed still again. "I do need to know, please. Where are you getting your water?"

"Upstate," he said at a normal volume, his fins returning to his side, pulsing normally. Levi noticed the other fishermen had long left. He wondered if they could see what he saw or if they simply felt the sudden urge to flee. "We're getting it from the sweet, sweet lady of the mist. She has been known to coat the world in ice and many roaring waters. Have you never seen Niagara in the winter?"

"I've never even seen Niagara Falls in summer."

The Angler King waited.

Levi, nervous, blinked and blinked and blinked and blinked. The sun stung his eyes.

"Her mist in winter looks of paraffin: the stairs seem dipped in molten glaciers seven thousand times only to be frozen once again. Wax coats. Now say, would you like a little bit of wine?"

"I can't have wine. I'm a *kid*."

"It's not alcohol. I would never give alcohol to a *child*. This is seawine."

Levi smiled. Swallowed, not nervous so much as choosing his words carefully before such a monster. "Wouldn't want to get an addiction."

"Addiction? To alcohol?"

"Yes."

"Plenty of people drink alcohol without an addiction. But this isn't alcohol. This isn't wine." The Angler King said. His mouth-barbs grinned. "This is different. It's *sea*wine. Wine?"

The questioning startled Levi out of his daze. "Oh, thank you, but I must get back onto my run. I'll be late for my sisters."

"Oh, come now. Would you break the rule of hospitality?"

Levi stopped up short after a couple of jogged steps. "I... I don't know what that is, but I'm sorry. However guilty I feel, I know I will feel worse if I don't—"

"Accept me? It's delicious! It's not Wayfare, granted, but I assure you that it'll connect you to plenty of folk here." He smocked. "Good folken. Some say better than the folken connected to Wayfare."

Levi looked at the goblet the great bass proffered, the way the glass floated towards him unbidden, unworried, unwiggling. The goblet had a gilded grey green crust made of barnacles (holes that looked like mud dauber nests), fossilized seaweed, coral, and the incrustation of centuries of sand.

Underneath at the base of the goblet, Levi caught a couple of glimpses of blackened ceramic and figures of the slightest bronzing: a man hiding in a cave with a bow, and men from some citadel coming to beg him to join them. The handles on both sides bowed out like great mouse ears, as if it were meant to be held two-handed by hands made clumsy with gauntlets.

He reeled back to his heels from the balls of his feet. "What is that?"

The great fish said. "It'll fill your belly more than anything. And it'll give you powers higher than anything you'll come across in Overmorrow. Plus, only a handful of people have had the honor of having drunk from *this* cup." He hissed and sucked. He bop-bop-bopped his fishy lips.

"Like a secret society?"

"Oh to be sure, sweet little story boy. A secret society of the secret cup."

Levi's eyes bugged out of his head. He snatched up the goblet. The barnacles felt rough on his fingertips. He drank.

The Angler King sniffed and hissed in only the way that a great catfish out of water might have sniffed and hissed. "You smell a middle child."

Levi searched around for another child. Several black squirrels nearby searched for dark acorns that wouldn't fall for a while.

"No, not them. *You* smell a middle child."

"I am of sorts," Levi said, then drank again, deeply.

"Of how many?"

"Four," he said, "but three right now." He took another plug from whatever was in the great grey goblet.

"Sissssssssters," the Angler King hissed. "You must bring me both daughters of men. I've fallen angels who would wish to sire wombroving giants." He smocked and smacked. "Wish Gabriel would fall and then I could get him wives, but I have mine. And I have mine. Yes, they would enjoy you in part or in whole. Mmmmmhmm."

"I don't think my sisters would like you very much."

He hissed and coiled his tail. Uncoiled. Coiled again. "Why the Pit not?"

Fishing lines tugged or untugged oblivious New Yorkers all around him. And some of the Overmorrow folk fishing, unnoticed, alongside them. One of the Overmorrow dryads pulled a great crappie out of the lake named after the faithful First Lady. The dryad pulled out a knife from his overalls and pulled back as if to stab a tiny fish.

The Angler King shouted, "NOT MY LITTLE COUSIN, YOU WRETCHCHCHCH—" He opened his mouth and swallowed the dryad — clothes and lunchbox and tackle and fresh catch and water dress — whole. After a quick swallow, he spat the little crappie back into the lake. "So what say ye, fisherboy?" he asked, his mouth now smelling of spring rains. No rain came from the heavens. "Bring your sisters to me. They are very very important to remember, and for all of us to remember things by."

"No, thanks. I think I'll just stay here and sip this seawine with you."

"No more seawine until you bring your sisters."

"But—"

The fish took it from him. "NO MORE! Sweet, sweet little story boy."

"He—" Levi said, interrupted by a burp. "—ey."

"Oh, there's more for you, but we wouldn't want you to get too taken by it, would we?" It smocked and smacked its lips. "Bring your sisters along. I have need of them for my plans with the Overmorrow rain."

"But I thought you said you hadn't stolen Overmorrow's rains, that you hadn't restricted it?"

"And so I haven't," the Angler King said. "But that doesn't mean I don't have *plans* for it and for you. Would you like another sip of this rich, pleasing, powerful draught that I've given you the secret honor of tasting?"

Levi paused. What about his run?

The fish held out the drink.

Levi sipped.

And was taken beneath the waves.

10

THE SCENT OF ORGAN MEAT

When little, Ellie had been in a visitation line for a great aunt. It had lasted for what seemed like forever. Well this felt like an uninvited, unexpected visitation line at a funeral. One that never ended. One that didn't have a backroom to escape to for a tiny break. A room of green where one could snag some bottled water, one of those flat round Saturn peaches, or a granola bar.

For the past month as they'd made their home with the Arthur and the Maker in New York City, she couldn't escape from the questions. The puzzle box she fiddled with wasn't helping. It sounded like it had an egg inside.

The pizza man asked if they were related to Charlie. So did the building's super: *are you Charlie's sister?* A lady on a video call with The Author stopped doing what she was doing mid-sentence. Hobbit hair whipped and swung, time's pendulum, to a stop. She peeked over his shoulder, then asked if the girls happened to have "Charlie blood."

The Author had the decency to scoff at the lady. He massaged a dark set of prayer beads.

These questions drove Ellie half mad. How far did the idea

that *everyone* knew Charlie reach? Did "knowing" Charlie mean they remembered him better than neighbors? Family friends?

What did any of them know? She wanted to be known. Known that deeply. Known that wide. If Charlie really did remember everyone and everything — from minotaurs who dragged e-trucks by the power cord to mohawked Sasquatches — then did that connect their memories through his missing loci?

The place in his mind connected to the place in hers through this Archive? Through this dreamscape?

Should she and Annie press forward? Forward towards those people (like the lady on the call) who had nothing to do with Charlie? Oblivious people?

Like Levi?

She didn't like to think about her other brother that way. It felt awful: shame on her.

Maybe oblivious was too strong of a word, considering?

Or should she try to find some people she didn't know existed yet? Folks that, had she known existed, might know something about Charlie?

Find people she knew who were ignorant of him? Or people of whom she was ignorant, but who knew him?

There wasn't an easy answer. As for the people who knew next to nothing, Ellie wanted to bring along Annie to try out the witches again. Melvilla Melheure, Haley Wholewheat, and Trog all had guilty names. "Or maybe," Ellie said, "it was the interruption and the changing of the concoction that made the storm subside?" She took a bite of her bagel and lox. Capers fell out and rolled all over the ground.

"Dang things," the Author said.

"Storms?" Ellie asked, whipping her quicksilver hair in mock maelstrom.

"Capers," The Author said. "They scatter everywhere. You never *really* hold them in."

Ellie smiled at the Author, but continued talking to her sister across the table. "Like, maybe they're conjuring a storm?"

Annie ate a Saturn peach. Ellie focused on her notepads and

scribbled over giant Post-it Notes she'd hung upon the back room wall. As if they'd *buried* walls in notes. The Post-it Notes accompanied books like *The Process of Investigation* and other memorabilia. the Author and the Maker brought the trinkets in the backroom with them to New York from Tunisia and Rome. Others, however, seemed to come from further, distant worlds.

Ellie looked over all of it, remembering their second conversation with the witches.

The notes, they worked like wallpaper missing aesthetics. A raw, untempered reason. Scattered data, stubborn syntax. Dots and outlines and footnotes every which way. Pink smaller Post-it Notes layered on top of the giants like icing. It was dissonant, yet it had a point. A riff. Jazz.

Which way to go?

If they went with the folks whom they knew didn't know about Charlie, would they find a thing? Probably not. She set down the little snow globe depicting molten lava on obsidian. It wasn't some known entity who had taken Charlie. Unconnected to the Overmorrow nonsense, someone strange had taken him. Why else would she feel so empty handed?

Something harsher. Something tied to Oblivion. But how could they find a soul they didn't know existed, yet who knew of Charlie? From the sound of it, half the world knew Charlie. They all knew his power, his cost, and seemed to know why Oblivion wanted him. The Wright kids didn't quite understand, but everyone else seemed to get it.

Charlie's wasn't fame, but renown. Word had traveled lightning fast among the Overmorrow folk. People didn't just know him. And they didn't know him for something bad, like infamy. They knew Charlie for a kind of heroic virtue the way that some folks know about martyrs quickly: here was the boy who had delayed the memory monster for a time. Living in the shadow of the man the world believed had beaten the memory monster. What kind of mind could kill a memory monster?

Assuming Oblivion was actually gone for good?

A deep one, deep enough to become famous. Renowned. But

how could they live in Charlie's shadow? Her, Levi, Annie? It's bad enough to feel the pressure to outperform, to be compared to her elder or younger siblings. To worry over favoritism. But this? His stalling the memory monster since Missouri was too much. She looked in the mirror: just a child. What could they even do? Her brother, as far as she knew, had just lost the genetic lottery. Charlie un-lucked out: his brain had something Oblivion wanted. He had been *stolen*, he alone.

Her thoughts felt so painful. So divided. Angry. Guilty. Sad. Especially for how worried she'd been, how worried she still was. How conflicted she felt.

Rather than decide whether to go toward the folks they didn't know or those they did, Ellie decided to suss out her own internal dilemma *with* the witches they didn't know.

It took some time for her and Annie to arrive at Central Park again, but they were already becoming old hat at navigating the subway.

The potion mastering of the witches over that cauldron by the shoreline had gone on for weeks. They had little interest in the Overmorrow rain. It interrupted their concocting.

The witches went back and forth with Ellie over which came first, the cauldron or the rain.

Annie said, "Witch came first? Get it?"

The witches groaned. They debated the use of the tails of subway rats. Also of street chestnut oils, pigeon feathers, and the bloody talons of the raptors thriving in the New York hawkeries.

The girls laughed at most of the nonsense ingredients (and some sense ingredients like the anteater nose). The witches explained the ingredients dealt more with classical taboos and less with the homeopathic bonds of pseudo-culinary ingredients. Ellie knew what none of this meant, but felt their passion in explaining it. She scribbled a note: perhaps it'd make a good soup. But in the back of her mind, she was remembering the way she was taken.

The witches steered the conversation to the A/C union. They finished the chocolate pastries from Slimak that Ellie had brought from the Author's neighborhood as a peace offering to grease their wheels.

Making their way home afterwards, Ellie and Annie quickly agreed on the innocence of the witches. Maybe the ladies had conjured a storm to ward off the Overmorrow rains? Ellie had scribbled on her notes: *Or maybe not.*

When they arrived in Brooklyn at the apartment, looking over it all, she realized that the witches knew them — knew Charlie — no better than any other. Less than average strangers. Perhaps they didn't know how dangerous the dearth of rains had grown. Still so few droplets, still so much chance of hypothermia. She wondered if, without the Author's intervention, others had died?

Who else could she find to interview?

Their uncle?

Back at the Author's apartment there was knock at the door. A firm and somewhat sloshy knock on steel.

Half afraid the arm would work between the crack and block the door from closing, Ellie gestured to her sister. Annie shrugged. The younger, braver went to the door as Ellie looked on. Munched on a Boston crème donut with chocolate frosting.

Annie went to the door and asked who it was. No answer. Annie dragged the step stool up, unfolded it, climbed its ionized black steel steps. She thumbed the swinging peephole cover widdershins on its pin-hinge, un-cloaking sight. "It's Levi!" she screeched and swung wide the door.

Ellie ran to her, back foot slipping on wet hardwood.

Levi stood before them both all soaking wet and covered. In what? In the freshwater moss and mire that forms water-to-soil gradients at the bottom of every country pond. A couple of slugs garnished his shoulders. Barnacles, which seldom moved from the underbelly of normal hardwood ship hulls, detached from Levi's belly and scuttled around on the black and white mosaic tile of the landing.

"Oh no, Levi, what's happened to you?" Ellie asked.

"Nothing, why?" He smiled. The briny, filthywet, organ-meat-scented dark water that squishes out of a boiled lobster when you crack its claws leaked out between his teeth. It fell on the floor, water the color of ground chicken livers. "Delayed my run. I mean, I hate I couldn't—"

"Gross!" Annie hollered.

Ellie gagged. "Are you serious?"

"Sure," Slime glugged over his tongue. "Couldn't finish. I am famished. Do you guys have everything to eat?"

Annie fiddled with a small ring on her pinky. The slightest star. "Anything to eat?"

"That too," he said. "Never really got to finish my run, but I'd love everything to eat. Or drink. Drink and eat, just not nothing, I think."

"What happened to you, Levi?" Annie said.

"What ya mean?"

"Oh, stop," Ellie said. "Just stop it. You're covered in seaweed. You're sloshing dark water everywhere. You look like Lancelot dragged you through his birth lake on the back of a grindylow chased by a fatberg."

"A fatberg?" Levi asked. He was genuinely curious.

The Author walked over to join them, "Giant iceberg-sized thing down in the NYC sewage system that grows from too many people pouring bacon grease and other unmentionables down the drain." He studied Levi. "It is a fair question, though. What happened to you?"

"I had a meeting," Levi said, dancing in place the way a bad date dances. "It was urgent."

"What meeting?" Ellie asked.

"Can I sit down?" He looked very, very wild. He was poking his head around the three of them, eying for the slightest bit of sun beyond. His skin seemed pale and... either chalky or wrinkled, Ellie couldn't tell which. "I really need food. Or drink. Drink would be wonderful."

The Author looked at him very, very warily. "Levi...?"

"Yes?"

The Author breathed three, slow, deep breaths into his belly and yawned out each. Yawn. Yawn. Yaaawwwwn. Thinking about yawning would make his readers yawn. He hoped it would work with Levi. When Levi didn't yawn, the Author asked, "Are you… alright?" He moved aside and gestured for the sisters to move aside.

"Peachy keen." Levi walked over the threshold into their apartment, a quick twenty steps to the kitchen. There he collapsed onto the little orange leather ottoman that had been hand stitched in Tunisia on one of the Author and Maker's trips. It was stuffed full of picnic blankets that still had bits of grass on them. Ellie knew this because they'd used one of them to sit on and watch a movie under the stars in Sunset Park and also because a single blade of grass poked out the edge of the zipper.

"You're getting the leather wet," the Author said.

The drips and occasional streams came out and down Levi's shirt sleeve — like a water hose, and drenched the delicate leather footstool. "I'm famished."

"I know what you need," the Author said.

The Author began making them a special soup. A secret chili filled with steak and ale, shrooms and chocolate, liquid smoke that puffed when poured. He fed it to Levi, who ate it, and then ate a second helping and a third.

The boy's mouth steamed, but the rest of him felt cool and slimy to Ellie's touch. Still Ellie wondered. "Are you alright?"

"Yes of course. Why?" Levi said. "I definitely don't think it's the Angler King who's taking Overmorrow, by the way. Whoever did it, it couldn't be a big old giant fish, that's for darn tooting."

Ellie laughed. "For darn tooting? Who are you?"

"What'd you do with our brother?" Annie added.

He started gnawing on his fork as dogs gnaw bones. Stainless steel. *Gnawing*. The sound of teeth on tines tore at Ellie's insides. "Still me," Levi mumbled unconvincingly over the metal in his molars.

The girls looked at each other.

The Author shook his head. Watching.

Ellie turned her attention back to her brother. "The Angler King did this to you, didn't he?"

The Author added, "He made you hungry for what couldn't fill you."

Levi cackled as might a darker elf. "Of course not. Why would he?"

"Why defend him?" Annie asked.

Levi blushed. Ellie knew he didn't have an answer. "More food," her brother said. "Please."

"This makes me *super* suspicious of him," Ellie said. "And of whatever he…" She jotted a note down in her notebook. She thought of what she'd decided then tried in quick succession: "I don't know him. What did he feed you? Did he know Charlie?"

"Wine."

Ellie said, "That's poison for boys."

The Author sat flush upright in his chair, suddenly very concerned. "Did he say anything about Wayfare?"

Levi giggled like an infant girl. "What a silly word. Why? What's Wayfare?"

"Something good, and the exact opposite of what he may have fed you." The Author looked up as if trying to see further down the boy's throat, then checked both pupils, pulse, and reflexes in the knees. When he did this Levi kicked over a whole tea tray, which crashed loud enough that it was all the more remarkable the Author didn't flinch. "Something less savory."

"It did too taste savory." Levi batted his eyelids and lashes fast enough to start a weed whacker. "I need more of what he gave me. It was really, really go—"

"What else did *you* find out this morning?" The Author asked the girls, trying to distract the boy.

"Well," Annie said. "The witches think it's harder for a human to stop the rains."

"Any rational animal is a human," the Author said, "If an animal comes up with ideas and embodies themselves and their ideas into bodies that make other makers, then it's any rational animal, not just the people witches like." He eyed the girls.

"What?"

"I was just thinking of your last name. Wrights. Means maker." The Author shook his head. "History gets nasty the moment we start saying someone isn't a rational animal who makes things to empower his kin."

Levi belched. Loudly. Wet. With salt spray. Bit of slug chemtrail.

Annie said, "I think the witches meant humans that look like us and don't have any magic in them. Harder for them to stop the rain."

"Everything that is in the world exists by magic," the Author said. "It exists, but shouldn't. Folks like us caught up early in the Overmorrow – who know they're in a story and therefore add to it — are called Storyweavers."

Annie huffed. "You know what I mean."

The slightest wince of recognition came over the Author's face.

"Wait," Levi said. "Do these magical storyweavers wear hoods with stars on them? Also, can you get me something to eatdrinkbemerry?"

The Author winked at Levi, but addressed Annie. "You mean earthbound."

"Earthlings," said Ellie.

"No no. Earthling is the sort of word aliens in a scifi film call us. As if we're another species. There are elements, plants, beasts, humans, angels (or gods or the long living souls or minds, whatever you want to call a bodiless thoughtformword, a tulpa, authors of authors, and so on). And then there's the Alone. Aliens are human too, even if they have weird bodies compared to ours. We're earthbound — Gaia bound — folk. Born of the Tor of Dewgloa's star. A Martian's still a rational animal who makes things to empower his kin. And that makes him one of us."

"Whatever," Ellie said.

"Not whatever," The Author said. "This stuff's important."

"To you," Ellie said. "Not to me. Not to Charlie."

The Author snorted and shook his head with a fae smirk.

"Anyway," Ellie said. "The witches think it's harder for an earthbound to make the Overmorrow disappearance happen cause of memory loss. They think Oblivion's behind it. They think that the memories of Overmorrow — the capacity to remember what it is, what happened to it — have been stolen. Or rather, the potential for wonder, for growing in those memories."

"Are they under his control?" Levi asked, in a reasonable tone, given his condition. "And why hasn't anyone helped me decide on whether I'm eating or drinking?"

Ellie turned to Levi and his *second* meal so fast her costume beads clacked. "Is The Angler King under Oblivion's control? Did he know Charlie?"

Levi scoffed. Huffed. Wrung his hands and said, "You got any more of them soups?"

"Stop delaying our investigation!" Ellie shouted. "We have to find those we don't know who *knew Charlie!*" Ellie gave up on the conversation. She focused on the table once again. She picked up a fountain pen and made a list on her little notepad:

1. Interview Angler King, Levi present.

2. Interview Boreas, witches suggested.

3. Interview private water CEO.

4. Interview A/C union.

5. Check cauldron for residue and test with someone who knows potions.

6. Where were parents? Still?

7. Ask journalist for more leads.

The Author, still cringing from the sound of Ellie's shouting, towered over her from across the table. "What about The Board?"

"You can read upside down?" she asked.

The Author ignored her. "And that one's dwarves: they'll find you soon enough if you *don't* ask them."

8. See if centralized board knows something of Oblivion's movements.

9. Separate warlocks from witches.

She hesitated, her eyes flicking to the man reading across the table and upside down, then wrote:

10. Buy Author some more toilet paper. He's out again.

"Bit passive aggressive, that," the Author said.

"I need to see the Angler King." She pinned the note to her inner lapel using safety pins. "Levi, take us to him."

Levi squirmed and squished in his now-mossy, sluggy, sludgy seat.

"Levi?"

Levi, still squirming and squishing said, "I suppose he'll give us all more wine."

"What kind?" The Author asked.

Levi stilled.

Ellie picked at the cream fleur de lis stitching on the seat her own chair.

"Oh, you won't be needing any more of that, but here, take this." The Author brandished a draught, a flask or a wineskin — full of glowing liquid.

"What's this?" Ellie poured a little out into her hand and tongued a drop. It looked like liquid rainbow. Cold, sweet, and savory at once.

"Overmorrow waters," the Author said. "To remember your Overmorrow rain."

"And drowning," Levi said.

"Your proper Overmorrow drowning, yes. Take the flask on your person into all the worlds. If you're finding yourself either not hot enough or not cold enough, indulge a bit." He sipped some from the flask himself. Then passed the flask to Ellie. One to Levi. Then a little plastic little one to Annie, capped in gold.

"How will we know?"

"You'll feel lukewarm. Far too comfortable. This should shock you back awake."

"Question," Ellie asked him. "Could a human—"

The Author cleared his throat. "You mean *an earthbound?*"

Ellie went pale and then nodded. Her fingers left the fleurs.

"Depends. Which earthbound?" the Author asked. "Some could steal the waters. The better question's why would any sensible earthbound with magical contacts *want* to do it?"

Ellie struggled to flatten her face. "Means and motive. Opportunity?"

"Who was there?" Annie asked.

"Good question," the Author said. "Very, very good question. Where are you off to?"

"The Angler King first," Ellie said, squeaking to a halt on the now-briny hardwood.

The Author sighed and hunted down their magic eraser mop. It wasn't magic, they just called it that.

Ellie said, "Before Levi's... squishy interruption, Annie and I meant to go find those who knew Charlie, but whom we did not know."

The Author cocked his head. "It makes... some sense."

Levi gagged and threw up water, as if getting CPR after being poorly drowned inside a mucky pond. "In fact, can we wait to head out? I have to do some research." He glanced at the Author's bookshelves.

"Sure," said Ellie. "We will get a bagel. Be right back."

The Author's stomach growled. His head turned down at the belly bulge his deformed spine had proffered him. Looking up he added, "If you need anything, utilize this." The Author handed Levi a little spinning gyroscope of paper pulp.

"What is this?" Levi asked.

"A spacetime gyrocompass."

"What?"

"A compass that shows where you're at in the Vale. And then when in the narrative. Also whether and how. Other necessary accidents as well."

Annie asked, "Accidents?"

Levi felt vertigo, learning of that kind of compass, especially right now. "Like a car wreck?"

"A property that isn't an essence. An accident."

"How will this help if I need something?"

"It's also a fancy walkie talkie."

Levi tried it out but got no answer. "Do you have any others?"

"Many. I'll have one on me, I'll give one to the girls." Then did as he said; theirs looked black.

"It's just made out of paper?" Levi asked.

"Yours is. They come in other elements and weaves."

"What if I wanted a compass of gold?"

The Author laughed. Ellie felt the laughter in her chest, as if his called to hers. He said, "A golden compass nobody gets. Who looks for direction *as such*? Who wants to meet *the way*? The whole point of obtaining a sign is having a thing to signify. Anyways, just think of us and talk." He tossed his to his bride, who whispered inside.

She might as well have whispered deep in Levi's mind. "Use it wisely."

The Author raised his glass and uttered, "Don't get et."

Levi's eyes bugged out.

The Author went out with the sisters for a promised ice cream run and the Maker went to work, so Levi was left all alone at the home with the dowager countess warspaniel.

"Think I decided to drink all the things that I see," he told the Spaniel. Asked her, "Do you have a coffee?"

11

B.I.T.U.M.E.N.T.A.V

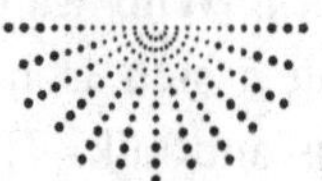

The warspaniel — called Echo after myths — shook her head. Commenced licking her paws, she cleaned herself more than a cat. Before the girls departed, Levi wanted to find out more about this Centralized Board. Did they know of Oblivion's movements? He searched the house for any cup he'd quaff to quell his thirst. Granted, he bore a bellyful of brackish wine. A mind full of slush had resulted. He hoped he'd find some more. Started looking at the covers of the books.

Ellie's voice resounded next to him.

At first he thought he'd dreamed it. Hadn't they just left through the front door? But then the compass in his pocket whirred. "Yes, Ell?" A slug gagged his throat. It shot out and onto leather-bounded books, leaving rainbow trails within its wake, ruining primeval pages. Levi frowned and picked a random tankard up. It wasn't seawine. He huffed, but held on tighter to the question mark handle.

Ellie's voice continued, "Levi, this is disappointing. I thought you'd be more helpful."

"I can help. I will help. I am helping." He swirled the draft in his cup around and around, augured for a future draft to pour from it.

"You can't even think with that stuff that you drank."

On the opposite wall, a shelf held the egg basket of coffee and espresso. His mother — even more, his father — had forbidden caffeine, which meant sodas and fine teas. Espresso? They would kill him if they found his hands on that. "Okay," he said to keep his sister talking, eyeing caffeinated beverages.

"Levi? I just want your help, you know? We need you."

"I will help. I promise, Sister." The tankard felt heavy in his hand.

"You're in no state to help right now," she said. "Why don't you sit this ice cream trip out?"

Levi eyed the shelf. How did one make coffee? "Pay for your ice cream, whatever you're out getting," he said to his sister. "When you get back here, how about waiting to decide until then if you think I ought to come or not?"

"Fair enough. Whatcha want?"

He smacked his lips. "I think I'm good."

The paper compass stilled.

He used his little arm muscles to drag out the footstool. He unfolded it, then climbed its fourfold steps with water still dripping out the bottoms of his pantlegs. Up on such great heights, he grabbed the stoutest caffeinated blend he found.

Then he grabbed the other blends and threw them to the oakwood flooring. Beans fell out, but ties kept bags cinched tight enough to stop the spillage. He farted. Seaweed filled his britches. Over that squishing moistness, using both his hands, he lugged the coffee grinder off the shelf. He knocked the woodblock *Peace on Earth* and clambered down.

He struggled on the floor to get the coffee grinder plugged because the outlet hid behind their maple table's folding leaf. But get it he did. He filled up the bowl to the brim with beans. He couldn't see them well, the world looked hazy, somewhat green. He replaced the plastic top and hammered on the black button.

It clicked like someone hitting the gas pedal on an electric car. Beneath his hand the blade spun and whirred and ground its chunks like rolling dice of teeth. He didn't know when to stop, and so he ground the coffee till it turned to finer, chocolate-colored powder.

He also didn't know enough to feel strongly one way or the other about this outcome.

Using the ladder, he came by a brazen old 1970's Ozark coffee mug and the glass beaker of the French press. He took his sweet, sweet time. If it cracked, the gig was up. He opened it carefully, filled up the bottom with ALL of the grounds. Then he poured in the previously boiled water for teas from a quicksilver thermos a telluric patriarch Broganer had once given the Author.

In both hands again, he muscled it up. Poured plenty. It spilled onto the tea bar's reddish runner. Put in the plunger. Not that plunger, the one for the French press. He waited, plunged it, poured.

He drank it down.

Too hot, but something deeply whispered, *Chug it*. He sloshed himself a second cup. Chugged it too. A third. The same.

It wasn't seawine, still it hit him hard.

The fog of seawine burned away. The world came alive, alight. "LET'S GO BILLY JOEL!" He shouted to the Cocker Spaniel, who wanted no war, but sighed and returned to sleep.

Carefully, Levi washed out his mug. Then he washed out the press and positioned it back. Put back the mug. Put back the bags. Then the grinder. The steps. He toweled up the spill. Then he went to the bookshelf and sped read through indices, looking for quotes about Centralized Boards that might show movements of Oblivion.

It took time to notice the filing system.

The Maker had sorted the books of the Author by color. The colors of the Author's books had favored some browns for his locks, some blue for his irises, green for what he'd wear as over-coat. Or was it brown for the earthen soil and the earthen stock of trees, blue for the ocean and sky, green for plant matter? Regardless, organizing a library by color was the opposite of function. Yet she enjoyed the look of it. The Author must as well, however unfunctional. He'd left it, after all. So Levi took time to find sources amid the chromatic rainbow panoply. That little choice of filing meant what little time Levi had left to search for his sources grew more precious than ever.

He scanned the red-spined books for what might mention Overmorrow. Or The Board or Charlie. Oblivion. He found a book on Wayfare —an Overmorrow rite. A magic spell they cast by eating a peculiar meal. Or maybe eating any meal in one specific way, he wasn't sure. It talked rather abstractly. The book smelled of matzoh, of real alcoholic wine.

Watercolors of Wayfare styles filled its pages, shapes of tables too. It went too deep for Levi. The forward said that Bellwether, Yestereve — both were somehow needed. That it could only happen after Overmorrow. But Levi hadn't gone through either (that he knew of anyways). The book also warned of falser fare that tried to take its place.

Halfway through that section squirmed a word. *Seawine*. He wanted to drink what all could be drunk.

Again.

He gulped. *Seawine*.

Slammed the book shut and he kept looking for big dirt on The Board. Not everything needs drunk. Not everything needed drinking, no. Searching, searching over dark wood shelves and their greying dust. A magical solution? No. Overmorrow solutions would only make him feel guilty, and he didn't want to have to face his conscience. He needed normal solutions.

One of the covers had tons of explosions on it. Pulling it down from the shelf, he discovered the opening sentence:

With enough pressure and heat, everything explodes.

Wow, how he grinned. From a book on the intimate habits of hydrazite monsters. He didn't explore much further. He could have drunk hydrazine, so thirsty was he.

But everything explodes? He liked the sound of that. He needed a firepower of that kind.

Don't think on drinking. Everything doesn't need drunk, no no. And don't think about the hydrazite monsters either: he had no need to learn about literally explosive mating rituals.

(He'd yet to read about the normal kind of mating rituals).

Another book described the shapes and sizes, functions, archives, names of things called "stylets." What might they be? They all looked long and slender. Other than that, what has a pillar to do with a pen? Where do spears and straws connect?

For drinking?

Oh, mentioning *drinking* was not helping.

Do not think about it.

He dug through covers on the genealogies and Hierarchy of Souls, books like *Travels with Marty through Time and Thresholds*. Marty was a pigeon on that author's leash: William Arthur Greenpeltz, a man confronting homelessness, took this pigeon through the Tors and stars of the Vale. Then, *Uncommon Applications of Manipulated Ontological Categories*. Levi understood "uncommon." Reading the rest, he had to agree.

Agree he needed drinks.

Nope nope nope.

None of these worked. Not even volume one of *The Cosmographic Bestiary of The Vale*, a massive tome embossed and painted with every creature he'd never encountered. He needed something on—

A small and thinning yellow volume tucked between two amber ones ensnared his eye. Canary in a coal mine. Paperback. Pressed as if by some old quilting club. *Bylaws of the Board for the Increase of Terran Ubiquitous Mechanical Expansion through the Northern Transept and Arcade of the Vale*.

He flipped it open, found within it bureaucratic words like quorum and continuance. A couple diagrams of rockets. This Board — from how they wrote and things they sketched like tea and bacon, playing cards — operated in a type of teashop. Or perhaps a small town diner? Cafe?

The book felt as if old ladies that once had served as legal clerks had written it. It contained, among much else, the rules of Bridge and Cribbage, some wild game called Spite and Malice, Euchre and Pinochle, and one card game with a curse word in the title Levi preferred to ignore. The book fretted more over what machines to smuggle onto the other planets than it did on expanding Overmorrow.

Perhaps that was the thing? Perhaps this...

Wait.

He flipped to the cover again and looked at the capital letters of the name of The Board's book. Did they make a word? He wrote them out tallways down a page:

Board for the
Increase of
Terran
Ubiquitous
Mechanical
Expansion through the
Northern
Transept and
Arcade of the
Vale

The letters spelled a word. Or seemed to do so.

B.I.T.U.M.E.N.T.A.V.

He pulled the dictionary off the shelf, the big blue one. Searched it for bitumentav. He couldn't find bitumentav, but he found bitumen:

A black viscous mixture of hydrocarbons obtained naturally or as a residue from petroleum distillation. It is used for road surfacing and roofing.

On a whim, he looked up tav. Tov showed up as the Hebrew for "good," as in mazel tov. But no such tav. Or maybe it was backwards? Vat? A big bitumen vat?

"Gross."

That or the good version of road tar. Good tar.

What was a good road through The Vale? Or a good roof?

He went to put back both books. When the dictionary's turn had come to be replaced, where its pages had leaned against the wall at the back of the shelf sat a goblet like the Angler King's. Barnacles upon its prow. Redder coral. Grey-green stone encrusting black-and-bronze figurines.

Something twinged in his mind again. Not everything needs drunk, not everything is edible, not everything needs swallowed down a gullet. Some things would leave you dry. Some couldn't even quench your thirst.

Maybe he didn't need to drink everything?

Maybe he only needed to drink one thing?

That was the right call.

Right?

He snatched it up in his hand, replacing the dictionary as he did so, and looked inside. Nothing but dust. He took it over to the sink and washed it out.

But when he washed the basin, it filled with seawine, same stuff as before.

He didn't want to sip it. He did. But didn't too.

Did won. He sipped it gone. "Ohhhh that's the stuff." He sipped again. "Ohhh yeah that's good."

But he got no further because the door was cracking. Dumping it out, he shoved the whole goblet inside of his pants pocket, which sagged further, slushing against the messy fart he still hadn't cleaned out of his drawers. He turned to greet the Author, Maker, and his sisters. That went over as well as if he'd extracted some farts from a zombie donkey and tried to sell them to the crowd at five pence a pound. He started gagging. Massive, slimy eels escaped his throat onto the floor.

"Eeeewwwwy eww," Annie said.

The Author squatted down and eyed him close. His big eye hit upon the bit of coffee grounds that Levi hadn't cleared, the dampened runner for the table. Seven beans had spilled upon the floor. Instead of saying anything, the Author eyed the boy in neither condemnation nor indifference. Waiting, gently. Curious and sad.

Levi swallowed, took a swing of water from his water cup, left there on the table. And then he said, "I think I have a lead." He slammed the bylaws book upon the table. Then he burped.

12

BOOKS HOLD UP THE ROSE

After flipping through The Board's book a minute, Ellie saw how deep it went. They kept tabs on all of Overmorrow and The Vale. They kept an eye on anyone who crossed a threshold— any major door or Tor gate or wormhole between any major world. She'd counted five that bore names.

That book revealed a SLEW of guilty parties. All connected to The Board, who thought of Overmorrow rains as if they made a threshold. Oblivion, according to the book, wanted to erase not only Overmorrow, but The Vale. Of course, the Angler King knew a good deal about Charlie and about waters.

So which should they go after first?

On whom should they set their hook?

MEANWHILE, LEVI WONDERED *WHY OH WHY* HE'D DRUNK THE Author's seawine right before the Author walked back inside. Shades of blue and grey had shimmered while he watched: The Author eyed Levi's eyes curiously, unjudging. Under that unjudgemental gaze, deep judgement squirmed within Levi's

129

soul. For he and he alone saw the standard he was failing to achieve. He knew he could give up the game, expose himself before his sisters. It seemed the Author knew what he had done. He could yield the goblet.

Or hide it. Bury it in books or deep in Brooklyn alleys. He felt the coarseness of it against the inside of his pocket liner, against his *leg*. It felt like a slimy old hull had formed around a spheroid. Star iron gone ovoid, an egg of Neptune. The coarseness called to him.

Or he could hide the Author's goblet book where he found it, then search around to try and find the Angler King as pretext for more seawine. Try to get away and drink it on his lonesome. All alone, an amber lamp in a darkness, cool and slick and oily sharpness down his throat. He knew that The Board — and the book of The Board — would abet the girls. He'd done his part, deserved indulgence.

And yet…

And yet he didn't want to.

ELLIE WAVERED BACKWARDS, FORWARDS: CHARLIE, WATERS, ANGLER King *or* Overmorrow, Board, Oblivion.

She focused on her brother. The living, present one.

Levi glanced back up, his hand still rooting in his pant pocket.

They started speaking over one another. Ellie gestured, raised her voice. She felt it straining at her throat. The vibration of it rattling down into her gut. They argued for a time on several subjects. The final two? The Board and Fish. Then Levi argued to revisit Angler King inside his haunt. But Ellie wanted all the folks who hurt her brothers bound and tamed and maybe dead. Levi clearly wanted liquid in his sloshy belly. In the end they visited the Angler King. The way the fish had treated Levi irritated Ellie.

But the distance seemed so close because, deep down, she wanted too to see this Biggest Bass.

And Levi had his own selfish reasons. Still he muttered, "That is great. I'll help."

BACK AT THE LAKE IN THE CENTER OF CENTRAL, THE SISTERS AND brother meandered around. They found no hint of the Angler King's pother, though she had her blue lined notebook at the ready. Something weighted down her brother's baggy pocket. That bothered her. But no Angler King in evidence. Not in the ruts where a fish may've bedded down. In the detritus of the shoreline rush, no fish scales remained from Levi's encounter. Even fewer fishermen along the shore than had been earlier that day.

Levi gurgled and mumbled on his failure getting sea wine. A single, solitary nightcrawler he belched, his very mouth a white noise foaming with its little waves. It gave Ellie the shivers. They ducked their heads under the water of the reservoir and found some oversized lures from eras of fishing gone by. Short of that no evidence remained of a once tall tale. Of The One That Got Away. And now he'd gotten far away from every fisherman.

The girls started wandering around to older folks who lined the shore in winter weather woolens, scarves. Any subject for an interview would do in a storm. Most folk had no interest. Most folk glazed their eyes the way that folks in Lutheran's trauma section did. They looked beyond the heads of everybody.

Ellie groaned. This wouldn't get them what they needed.

And yet.

One's eyes blinked as if waking from long and laborious dreams about turning his taxes in late. As if he'd been a child for longer than average, for all his life, however long his white old beard had grown, however shaggy his white hair stretched, however patched his green and tattered wizard's hat might sit.

They approached the man.

He had a Singaporean timbre, but sang a song of sixpence even there in Thai. "Ho there, Earthbound daughters."

"Hello, sir," said Ellie. "How are you this finest morning?"

He frowned and said somberly, "It seems like it's not going to rain."

Ellie flipped open a clean page in her notebook. "Overmorrow, do you mean?"

Levi kept fiddling with something in his pocket, fingertips hidden under the flap of the satchel.

She turned to him and asked him, "Will you stop? What is it?"

Levi blushed, removed his hand. "It's nothing."

"Well yes, Overmorrow," the fisher said, "What other kind of rain do you mean?"

"A sprinkle," Annie said.

"A splash." Levi gurgled.

"A drizzle, downpour, deluge," Ellie said, "but none of those make a magic rainbow rain."

"Ha! A magic rainbow rain," he said. "You can tell when someone doesn't spend many seasons in reality, talking after Overmorrow thus. You know what is magic? Thinking the physical's all that there is. That is magical thinking, yes, it is, you see? Tell me: if none of the Physical creates itself, and it don't, it surely do not do, and all you see and think is matter and mere stuff, how is that not magic? That physical's all that there is when it doesn't make sense of itself, *that* is playing pretend is it not?"

Ellie shook her head in disbelief, not disagreement.

"Course it is," he said. "That's the problem: blind folk all around forgetting what is real and what is the black veil of dead priests."

Ellie half folded her journal as her siblings stared into her eyes. Unfortunately this conversation was proving less than useful.

Levi's face went crooked, googly eyed, and water-logged. As if the seal in his goggles broke and water'd gotten into his irises somehow.

"What do you mean?" Annie inquired. "Blind folk?"

"Well that's the problem, in'it? If no one gets their eyes to see The Real, they might as well go blind. And no more Overmorrow would just be awful. That's happened before, in yesteryears, not to be confused with Yestereve." He cocked his head at them, his hat tip flopping on its side. "Say there, you look fresh. This is all new to you, in'it?"

Ellie nodded.

Annie nodded.

Levi shrugged — barely.

"Thought so. Just so's I know that you get it: what would it be like if no one got the chance to see what all you've seen?"

"Bad," Ellie said.

The other kids nodded, Levi a little too vigorously, as if selling something. Something in his pocket, something in his hand. What was it he had?

Ellie picked at her cuticles and kept an eye on Levi at her vision's edge. She thought about those whom she didn't know personally who might know of a thing or two. This man might be among them. "Were you there the day Overmorrow was restricted?"

"Round about here. That day I see the lights go out — or feel they is. Back in my first Overmorrow, I see miles and miles. Every building sparkles on that day. Tall prisms. Paperweights on some accounting god's own desk. The sky was flashing blue and green. Some who are not on the day before *now are*. Some who are around a moment prior now *are not*. Witches brewing, pipes of Angler King are churning—"

"The Angler King!" Ellie shouted.

Levi said, "Quit."

"He was here?" Ellie asked.

"Yes, of course, among the interviews and musing students. Some phoenix children start a war of flames with one another. So, yes, I remember. Why?"

"When'd you see the Angler King?!" Levi said much louder than the question justified.

The other three turned at the boy, the old man's head whipping fast enough his hair strands wafted. Willowswitches.

Levi blushed. "Was I too loud?"

The girls nodded.

So'd the man.

"Levi, you alright?" asked Annie.

Ellie looked at stillness out upon the waters. How it grew disturbed in whipping wilderwinds like large slop buckets of oil, good bitumen, its liquid switching speeds and heights and angles. She turned to her brother.

Levi seemed to feel a great weight of something in his baggy pocket. His hands weren't in it, but a churning grew in that pocket. Then it stopped, the fidgeting that didn't come from him. And he went still as well. Looked at her and she averted her eyes to what the man was saying.

"—check the A/C Union," said the man. "I never trust those dryad union boys."

"We will," said Ellie, glancing back at Levi's purple pocket, daring it to shake all by itself. "Tell me more about the way you saw the rains restricted. What has happened?"

The man shuffled his feet. "Well I don't know if I can say."

"Oh, you can say," Annie said. "You can trust us with whatever you need to tell us."

He raised a single eyebrow, then the other. He pointed to the reservoir. "That day was like what I always hear you Westerns talk about: the wind laid bedrock bare on the bottom of the sea, and all souls crossed over dryshod. It was pushed back. Pushed by the North Wind."

The children looked at each other. Ellie flipped back in her notebook to where the witches said Boreas the North Wind brought the rains. She wrote down *North Wind suspect?* That possibility muddied her mind, made her reconsider every law of thinking. It felt *slow*. It hurt, that suspect. And the hurting pounded her heart and shallowed her breath.

Levi stomped ahead of them and *finally* unsheathed something from his pocket, fiddled at the water's edge, brought it to his lips. Resheathed it in his pocket. He had found a small fishhook with a scale stuck to it there in the mud. He picked it up between his ring finger and thumb. He held the fishhook out to

Ellie. "I don't think I trust this silly little old man's account. None of it's real." Then he swaggered on off.

"Come now," Ellie said. She kneaded knuckles like dough. "The wind may be important. North Wind's one of the suspects."

Levi hollered at her over his shoulder, not seeing how his phrases landed. She squinted at him hard. He may as well have tossed a bucket full of dog saliva windward, unmindful of the folding of Ellie's nose's tip. Then he turned and said to her disgusted face, "You're talking about all the wind and the waves and then here waits our Annie pretending. Pretending she saw some magic. How do you arrest the wind? Or a bridge troll for that matter? Annie complained about people passing over her bridge and —"

"You did, too!" Annie said. "You saw it. You see it now. *You* saw it, didn't you, Ellie! You saw the—"

Ellie said, "I—"

Levi stopped and turned. "And anyways, if it true, I don't think—" murky water tumbled out his loosened with some shellfish carapace "—what's the point of going everywhere to figure out weather? Who talks about the weather anymore? Let alone of yesterday's?" He coughed, wetly. "Unless it's whether or not it'll get on your phone on the way to the train?" He couldn't help but ask, but tried in fact to whisper, "And have you guys seen any seawine around here? I cannot find the Angler King."

They both started at him.

Ellie looked to his pocket again. She suspected she knew what was sheathed inside it now, though she had no idea how he'd gotten one.

Annie screwed up her face in confusion.

Ellie could tell her sister hadn't figured it out.

Annie said, "Let's go ask the wind. That's next."

"Ask the wind?" Levi said, "This. Is. Not. Real. What about the bitumen Board?"

Annie started crying.

"Oh, Levi, will you listen to yourself?" Ellie asked. "Can't you tell how cruel you sound right now? What is in your pocket?"

He didn't answer, but fidgeted under the weight of direct questions.

"What is in your pocket, Levi? What did you drink?"

He said nothing.

Ellie hissed at him like feral wildcat. "I don't know where the Angler King has gone. You saw him first."

Levi said nothing.

Ellie nodded. "I would ask him questions till he cried. I'd give him a piece of my mind for whatever he did to you. Whatever he's still doing."

Levi cocked his head as if to say, without saying it, what an odd thing to accuse him of being: cruel. He'd cocked it the moment she asked him how cruel he sounded. He only cocked it further the longer she'd talked. At that angle, it looked like it hurt.

"Can't you see?" Ellie said, more at him than to him. "This is what's at stake, my brother. You could fail to think of Overmorrow. Hunger could blind."

"Thirst."

"AH! Forget it."

"Forget what?" Levi said.

Annie, in a burst of tears of joy and bits of anger, shouted, "That fairies, Ents, and dragons, unicorns and flying people, mermaids — it's all real, you see?"

"No." Levi sounded less sure of himself. His eyes wavered, irising, unirising. "No, it's fuzzy."

She harrumphed. "Levi. How can we hide this from people?"

"Doesn't seem like they want to know," he said, but he pawed the concrete with his foot. A half dozen acorns broke loose from a large fresh pile and fell into the waters. Floomp-flosh-swish-floomp-plooppity.

Annie said through the tears, though they'd slowed and dried a bit, "What if they're holding back from telling everyone of Overmorrow?"

Ellie's heart went out to her sister: Annie merely wanted to feel sincerely.

"They who?" Levi said. Seaweed fell from his sideburns — not beard sideburns, but the juvenile hair points that needed trimmed.

"We don't know!"

"A motive," Ellie said. "We found a motive, but the opportunity and means are more important. Who'd restrict it? Who was there? Who knows what we don't?"

"Everybody," Levi said. "Of everything. And no one. Silly questions."

"That's the point."

"Silliness?"

"No, everyone."

"We didn't see what we thought that we saw," Levi said. "Suppose our senses tricked us? Suppose there's no magical, mystical world behind it?" Something throbbed in his baggy pocket; he started shifting his thigh, twisting it.

Ellie wondered if money ever literally burned a hole in one's pocket. And if so, probably this goblet was like money in that way. "Well then... well then... well, if you faced all the evidence of magic and spirit in the world, but you didn't think it was possible to begin with, you could *still* lie to yourself and never accept the evidence."

The small man cleared his throat.

The children looked at him as one. They'd honestly forgotten he was there. He had waited awkwardly while they argued, spending the time reeling in and stringing up three different kinds of fish.

Levi's eyes bugged. What had he realized? Ellie wanted to ask him.

But the man was speaking. "Well, your sister's right, Young Levi. Whether magic *can* happen's a logical problem. Whether magic *did* happen on days in *specific* is an evidence mystery. Evidence is not the province of assumptions. Logic is."

Levi started walking as if on a circular balancing beam, arms out. Ellie noticed slime creeping at the seams of his mouth. "Of course magic can't happen. I can't have seen what my sisters think I saw. We're just playing some game together." He turned to his sister, twigs gritting underfoot. "And it's a stupid game, and I'm through playing it with them both."

Ellie was unmoved. She had her beat now. She wasn't turning loose of its rigging.

Annie moved, not so much away from her brother, but towards belief. Her younger sister turned completely from her younger brother and faced Ellie square on. "This is not you," she whispered over her shoulder towards Levi. A single salty tear fell from her eye's corner to her lip, where her other lip hid a prior tear in the shadow of its wing. She kept it from falling and twirled to Ellie. "How do we fix him?"

Ellie turned to Levi. "Forgive me."

Levi asked, "For wh—?"

The slap from Ellie's hand cut him short.

It took a moment, but Levi said, "Good Lord, how ya gonna do me that way for? What have I ever done to the two of you?"

"I said, forgive me," Ellie said. "But you should know that you are not yourself. You are a cynical, sarcastic jerk right now."

He laughed in her face. Slime and scales left his gullet, gone to ground, a morsel fleeing molars. "If not me, who am I?"

"Not-You," Ellie said.

"UnYou," Annie said.

He laughed. "Now I'm gonna go dissect some butterflies and pull the legs off beetles to learn of what they're made of. Maybe that'll offer *clues*." He walked from them toward the edge of the park and towards the subway. He was gone. It felt like gone for good.

Annie collapsed and grabbed her knee.

"What's wrong?" Ellie said.

"It feels… it feels as if I whacked my kneecap on a doorjamb and… like …" She gagged, dry heaved. Ellie thought of concussions and worried. "Like the funny bone in my knee got hit and the pain's gonna make me puke. He is so *rotten* right now"

Oh. Ellie helped her up. The grit ground between their grips.

"I don't know if we can find the Angler King without him. We failed again. I think I made him worse."

"I think we both did," Annie said.

"I've never had a problem fixing him. Even at his worst. When once he broke his leg…"

"He jumped off the house," Annie said. "Off the balcony to see if he could ninja roll down the hill onto the other side of the apartment complex."

Ellie laughed. "He couldn't. He just landed. Pieces of him broke. His leg, his—"

"I saw it from the top," said Annie. "Saw him try it. I wanted to throw the bedsheet down like Rapunzel. It didn't make a rope. The wind caught it, threw it like awful sails."

"I was on the ground. He snapped like groaning trees in storms." Ellie shivered. "I splinted it. You made the call." She whirled her mood ring on her pointer finger. Churning like a ring of marble, blue and white and orange. Moving, moving, painted ocean. She met eyes with Annie, misty. "This time broke him worse than that." She looked across the waters. "I broke it, didn't get a chance to set the break. If Charlie had been there to set the bone… If Charlie had been here…"

Both girls stilled. It went unsaid: they needed Charlie for many things. Or their parents for that matter.

A flock of stranger ducks flew overhead, a starling murmuration. A crowd of beetles charged the ground, all armored up in golden, greener plate.

Ellie broke the silence. "I suppose we could leave him alone. He'd grow into a Charlie."

"Maybe not."

"Or maybe we just help him. Bring some help along. Go up."

"Go up?"

"Go up the chain of command. Find another adult we can trust. Get help helping Levi." They'd walked down the potholed mud walk, one of the few in Central Park, where they'd interrogated fishermen and women. The mud splashing her boots and her knees, no matter where she turned. Trapped.

Annie said, "Leaving him alone is good. Maybe he can sort his thoughts."

Ellie said, "Yeah. I find when I refuse to sit in silence, lonely in a room, that's when most of my problems start. Maybe if he finds a quiet place, *then* he can come to us to help us find the way?"

"We need better help," said Annie. Looked she to her left, which — walking parallel — was Ellie's left as well.

The Author sat there on the ridge, upon the shoreline in his rocking chair.

How did he get there?

In a rocking chair?

Ellie met the eyes of Annie. She was sure the Author hadn't been outside before now. And certainly not in a rocking chair. Let alone fabric. The blue one from his Great-Grandma with tons of cushions fraying from the warspaniel's… claws's… influence. How had he gotten it all the way out here so fast without a car? Intermittently he read, looking up occasionally and pondering. How had they noticed everything but him? Ellie asked, "Have you been listening to me this whole entire time?"

"You weren't really whispering, now were you, girls? I think even the police horses on the other side of the park may have the whole story by now."

They said nothing.

He waited.

"Can you help us?"

"Ah, at last. When *asked*. I cannot give you anything beyond what you will need. And I also can't give you anything you don't ask for. I cannot make you do a thing or help you fill your greed. Or, rather, I could, but you would not be you. The goal's to help you do what only you would do, and do it best. If what you want is what you do not need, I cannot help. And if you're not yourself, I cannot help. And if you don't ask, you can't receive. I only help when True You truly wants what only True You truly needs. I cannot take your tasks away. That'd make me you, and you me." He stood. The rocking chair recoiled, then dissolved into the mist.

The girls had little time to react to that.

The fountain misted them again. They climbed the hillock, stood beside him there upon the waters.

"Come, let's hit the subway," said the Author. They walked and talked. "What do you think that you need?"

"Well," said Ellie. "Magic happened, right?"

"Is that what you want or that what you need?"

"Well, Levi said when he was raging, 'Magic cannot happen.' Is that true?"

"Whether magic did or didn't happen — and who did or didn't do it — is up to physical evidence. But whether magic can or cannot happen — and who can or cannot do it — is up to metaphysics."

"What?"

"Evidence for *whether* it happened verses thinking through whether it *can* happen or *ought* to happen. As far as I know, you're looking for evidence. Come." He walked them further south through swaying pine and bending oak and many, many grassy fields turned muddy.

"Are you saying Levi's wrong?" Ellie asked.

"I'm saying think a moment. Is there anything that you believe, rock solid?"

Both girls said, "Yes."

"Do you think thinking leads you to those things you believe?"

They nodded.

"How does Thinking happen in the butterfly your brother is currently dissecting unto death? In the wings or in antennae?"

Ellie said, "Thinking can't happen in wings."

"So you can't get Thinking from things that don't think?"

The girls nodded. A racket of rickshaws — a tatting of taxi bikes — passed them. Full of college girls, phones in their faces and lights where the grace goes, music louder than senses. The pink and purple rope lights in the back curtains of the rickshaws blinded Ellie.

The Author said, "If Levi—"

"UnLevi," Annie said.

"If UnLevi is right, then we account for everything you believe with 'nonThinking.' If there's nothing but nature, then every event has a natural cause. Including thinking. Each physical event has to have a merely physical cause. The antenna thinks for everything the antenna touches, including your brother who dissects it."

"Okay…"

The Author smiled, head up, shoulders back, almost strutting into the wind. "But you just said things like wings, chemicals, and rocks do not think."

The girls were at a loss. A squirrel of the black Central Park variety was fumbling an acorn.

"If your brother's right, then nothing you believe or he believes is born of thinking. Your brother's only right if his belief emerges from *good* thinking on *good* evidence. I see no cause to think whatever Levi thinks. If Levi's right in what he thinks, he never thought it in the first place. Why think what can't be thought?"

Ellie laughed. Her laugh caught up in the gut of Annie and the Author and bubbled over for the both of them. The three of them laughed for some time, passing a great purple and indigo bucket full of swill and pellets. Fifteen pigeons fled the bucket as a race-horse named *Front Loader* dove his total bit and bridle in the hole.

A billion influencers took pictures of themselves and ignored the runnels where the rain had gone. Ignored the gilded *Columbia Triumphant* riding a chariot pulled by hippocampi, towering above the monument to the U.S.S. Maine. Around the great circular stairwell down into the subway. Where they swiped their transit cards and passed the turnstile just ahead of several mages.

Annie said, "But what about the magic? Can it happen?"

The Author watched wearily as a very, very large hawkrhino barreled through the stairwell to catch a 1 Train chased by the screams of many. The Author focused back on Annie and Ellie, snorting. "Since all of nature, in your brother's view, can be explained without Thinking, then Thinking's got to come from something outside nature."

"If thinking came from non-thinking," Ellie said, "wouldn't it still be thinking?"

"Yes! So where does thinking come from?"

Annie said, "Outside non-thinking nature. Some source. From … thinking."

"Yes," The Author said. "Now, what's the word for above? Beyond?"

Ellie said, "Up? Ex? Super?"

"We tend to like super," said the Author, "Super to what?"

"Natural stuff," said Annie.

"All together now?"

Both girls whispered, "*Supernatural.*"

The train pulled up to the platform, and they crowded aboard. Ellie still gawked so much at what the Author had said that she had to close her mouth when the train full of folks in jumpsuits, rompers, ascots stared right back.

"If the boy can Think that Thinking is the most real, then deep down he knows the supernatural. Magic. He knows his faith that this universe comes from nowhere is really magic Thinking. And what we all do?" He pointed at himself with one hand and at a family of fauns on the train with another. "Is real. It's very, very real. Real in the imagination of the reader, here and now as I am speaking, deep enough to give the reader chills."

"But why would he say that he didn't believe in the supernatural?" asked Ellie.

"Why do you say you do?"

"Because I do. I see it. Right now."

"If you had said you didn't, why would you have disbelieved?"

"Cause I hadn't thought it through. Or witnessed something. Or, worse because… somebody hut me and I was unable to."

Ellie gripped the stainless steel, the pole clicking on her smoke stone rings. "I know where we could go for Thinking," Ellie said. "For stories written by the people seeing things. Records of bad guys intimidating people like us."

Annie said, "The New York Public Library!"

The Author said. "Perhaps it's better to let sleeping dogs lie? There's better—"

But the girls had ran with his first advice. "Who knows it best?" asked Ellie. "Where is the best library for the normal side *and* Overmorrow side. Surely there's a magical branch to the New York Public Library?"

"The oldest branch," he said. "The Rose Reading Room. Books hold up its very floor: it's just a bunch of catwalks. But I don't think—"

"Who knows the library best?" asked Ellie.

The Author didn't say a thing for long. "I won't convince you otherwise?"

Ellie shook her head.

"Then I cannot make you take the shorter way," the Author said. "It looks like you must go the long way around until you learn to want what you need. I know the library best, but you seem disinterested. Second best's a newsman. You won't get the help you need from him."

"The one from the lake?" asked Annie.

"The very soul," he said. "He has researched too much of man and not enough of magic. He reports on both as if they're math. The madman and the mathematician see the world as never-ending squares of chess: black and white in checks forever. No curve, no color, and no time for anything but summoning whatever's needed to control the rest."

"Where will we find the magic man?" Annie asked.

The Author sighed as if he'd suffered many whippings. "I don't know that I'd call him that. But forget that for now. For now you have the Overmorrow sight. You need to find the centaur who keeps the trollies. At the NYPL, the trollies will lead you down into the Archive's belly."

"Then that's just what we'll do." Annie said.

That's just what they did. Because of weird construction, the girls eventually had to take the D train to the 6 at Broadway Lafayette, and ride that up to Grand Central. But Levi, or rather UnLevi, had gone elsewhere.

THE GREEN LIGHT OF
MINATORY EYES

The case had grown worse in Levi's mind. For starters, his sisters had taken this magic stuff hook, line, and sinker. Swallowed it whole like a black marble at the fish end of the reel, rod, and line. They'd taken to putting the blame on The Angler, which made no sense to him.

He paced down the subway car, ducking, weaving as poles allowed.

How could any creature willing to introduce him to seawine treat him poorly? Perhaps the perp of Overmorrow lived away from the scene of the crime. Maybe in the hood where the Author lived, where Levi headed now. Maybe the perp wanted to blow things up. How bad was he?

There at the other end of the subway car a tiny figure in a shadowed hood caught his eye. Black hood, red seats.

He thought of the question he'd asked of the Author: story-weavers with their hoods, the ones who rescued the Wright children from the monster. Or, for all he knew, had murdered Charlie. Why had the Author winked at him whenever he'd asked, *why the hoods?* Levi scooted towards the end of the D train, wondering, stirring. Though the posters normally bedecked the walls of the station, the emergency repairs were so bad that posters bedecked its walls said significant delays had stopped it in recent days.

Delays from what?

They really needed to put money in these subways, these New Yorkers. It wasn't like some giant wolfdrake smashed the train to pieces. Like those great scales and freight feathers and fine fur that had smashed through their house and eaten Charlie. It wasn't like some great phoenix had torn the tunnels. Or that the trains themselves had turned into a giant mechanistic hydra to fight off giant statues in the Hudson.

He needed the train to get away. Faster.

He needed to get away so that he wouldn't be seen by the Author or others.

He needed to move unseen by them to drink his seawine on his own in peace.

The logic seemed inevitable.

As he moved towards the end of the car where the hooded person lurked against the a read seat, their starry hood lifted ever so slightly. The green light of minatory eyes pierced out. He froze. Deep muscle pain locked up, vibration sense stilled, two-point discrimination went all antiparallax, visceral indigestion hardened.

The hood rose. It stared at him — no one else. It breathed in, it breathed out.

Levi mirrored its breath and took a sip while it eyed him.

The doors opened. Those green eyes snapped towards the exit.

"Coney Island bound D train, 36th Street. Next stop 9th Avenue," the conductor said.

The Hooded One bolted out the door.

Levi thought for half a second, came up with no good reason something would stare at him so. Horrified it had watched him drinking — that he hadn't thought about his seawine in peace. *No one* exposed his shame. *No one* exposed his secret. "Scuse me!

Scuse me!" He shuffled past all of the shopping folks bending and standing and holding their overfull totes and bags all manner of angles. He ducked and dodged and knocked his knee into a bench, chasing the hood that hid the green light of those minatory eyes.

14

CRUX PLANET

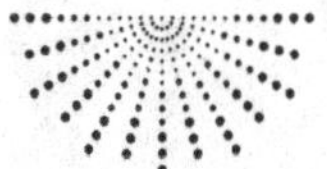

The hooded figure bolted up the yellow painted stair set, blasting forward off the stainless steel railing.

Levi followed suit, refusing to be spied upon, ducking left and ducking right around the people galloping towards his face. They hoped to make the train he'd fled. Static and screeching resounded from speakers. A conductor booth microphone too close to the conductor's face had the gain level turned up too high. "STAND CLEAR." *SCREEEEEEEEEE.*

Levi slid like a baseball runner over sopping cinders of ceramic tile flooring, under tripod turnstiles spinning in the air above his head like three silver jellyfish tentacles. He was up and gaining twenty feet of ground upon the hooded one, who exited at 36th. They entered the underground of Sunset Park, which hosted the Author's homesteads, his columbaria in the clouds of Brooklyn's climb.

But the hooded figure didn't hike the eastern hill towards the Jackie Gleason Depot. Nor did it turn west towards the gentrification experiment of Factory Shire and its hidden real estate development peers. Instead, the hooded figure soared southward across busy streets, hurtling car hoods down the otherwise crammed sidewalk of 4th Avenue.

Levi couldn't stomach letting someone flee who'd seen him drink his fill.

The hooded figure fled.

He followed it past saplings sprouting oak leaves someone had sown in cracks and crevices and rain holes of the concrete barriers. Levi careened around the alley one of the neighborhood's gas station. Up 42nd Street — the Brooklyn one — in the shadow of the tower of St. Michael's. Its bells rang over all the neighborhood, remembering their roots, an echo of the sister call of bells sounding from Our Lady of Perpetual Help. Levi chased up 42nd making it through the door of one apartment complex. Two stairs at a time. He'd was practically upon the perp in the hood.

Said person jangled a set of keys, swung the door, and slammed it.

But not before Levi crammed his foot in the crack. Fool's mistake. It nearly crushed his foot. "AAARGH," he hollered. But he pushed his way into a room that blew out fresh pan-fried dumpling steams.

A very short and very youthful Asian-looking girl stood before him, hood draped upon her shoulders. Her eyes were glowing green.

"I... Hello," he said. "So why you running off? And can I come inside?"

"The time to ask was *before* you shoved your foot in," she said.

He felt like smacking her face the way that Ellie'd smacked his face. But he knew this situation was extremely different. His ashamed eyes shifted to the floor. He stepped fully inside. The door closed. "May I ask a couple questions?"

"You already have."

His hands rubbed together while his eyes inspected the mishmash of plant life: bamboo, orange tree, redwood, and a pot of English Ivy. Kudzu? Some weird woody fernish shrub he'd never seen before. "I have a treat to share," he said.

"I'm running away from you," she said. "You weren't supposed to see me following you."

Levi stepped back. His butt hit the door. Cold seeped through the seat of his pants. "You were following me?"

She shrugged.

"Who has you following me?"

"You mentioned a treat?"

Perhaps he could hide all his seawine drinking in plain sight if he nonchalantly did it in the open? He felt the press of the ship-wrecked goblet on his thigh. Then walked up to the water tap to fill it.

She asked him, "What is that?"

"Water," Levi said.

She was looking in the belly of the goblet. "What's it now?"

Down inside it, water writhed. Shells and crawlies, sea mist and sea foam roiled among the seaweed. "Oh that? A better drink."

"Than water?"

"Than Adam's ale," he said. He poured from the goblet into two clear glasses from the cabinet. How had he not noticed before? The color of it? The stuff inside? Sure, the other goblet had been solid and opaque, but surely he may have noticed? The seawine took on turquoise hues with bits of ocean sediment, the way you might expect a dark red wine with bits of cork to do.

They drank.

The seawine took effect, blurring faculties and making them happydumb, filling their pores with the briniest sweat of deep sea work.

She smiled at Levi.

Levi smiled at her. Something twinged within him: he'd gotten more than he'd bargained for. Not only had she watched him, but had joined him. Deep in the back of his mind, another something twinged. Something felt... off.

As if, perhaps, he'd done a foolish thing. As if, perhaps, he'd mitigate his guilt by making her drink with him. Perhaps he'd get some information out of her while they were in their cups? Keep her from asking him the questions? Or... why not both? Why not keep her distracted and get information out of her?

"What do you want?"

"Why were you following me?" He tried to pluck the seaweed from his middle finger knuckle.

"I told you, I needed to keep out an eye just in case you acted like a fool."

He raised up his glass. Indolently seawine sloshed. "Like what?"

"I don't know." She sipped her glass. "But I's supposed to keep an eye."

He chuckled to himself and set his glass upon the bright red metal table. "What's your name?"

"Gossamer," she said. "Or Sammi if you need it short."

He pulled a little pen from out of his other pocket, the fountain pen he'd swiped from Ellie. Looked for something he might write on, settled for his hand. He hoped to keep track of as many notes as he could, given the limited resources. First he wrote *Sammi*. "So Sammi. No one here but you?"

"It's a safe house," she said. "Mom's back in Gergia."

He wrote a note. "Where's that? Djerzuh?"

"Gergia? Crux planet." She affected a longing gaze at him, which he saw when she looked at him in a floor mirror.

Levi said, "Is that where my mom is? A safe house in Djerzuh?"

Sammi said nothing.

Levi looked in the mirror on the floor to meet her eyes. Something almost eternal separated him in his longing for her then. "...Planet? Crux?"

"In The Vale. You've never been offworld?"

He wrote a few more notes. "I've never heard of offworld. Or even non-humans until very recently."

She shivered and the shivering creaked the parquet flooring. "Silent planets. Golly, you guys. They're all *humans*, some just look different from you."

Levi downed his glass and filled another for them both. His head went swimming. Both eyes bulged. "Know of anything about the Overmorrow case?"

"Someone's bounding rains," she said. "A wind's involved? Some sort of wind strike? Something?"

"Huh," he said. He wrote an indiscernible note on his hand in a dark black ink.

They drank awhile. A horn honked outside once. Twice. The third time the driver laid on the horn. Then other horns joined the chorus, a call and response trying to out-*you're-inconsiderate!* one another.

"Have any espresso coffee beans?" he asked.

"Aren't you young for coffee?"

"Pffft." He felt himself going back on the drip, dosing the real beans. The energy of the Emerald City tamper feeding his veins. Now he was addicted even worse to not one, but two substances. He gave off a flick of his wrist at her face like he'd shot her a free-throw.

She shrugged and started making coffee.

They drank more seawine while the other brewed. Then mutually started puking slugs. And he was smiling. She was smiling. Both their teeth went green.

The coffee burbled to an end.

He felt wonderful. If they kept this up, he'd learn gobs from her. Tidy bits about the world and Charlie, Overmorrow, this *Vale*. If he could keep distracting her with something foolish.

At his abnormal moment of discernment, every floor of every room went sideways. Not from drink. Literally. Physically sideways. A hole had opened in the northern wall and chunks of it were sliding down into a sinkhole far below in earth's salt and sod. A massive grave. A cave in the shape of a maw right in the middle of Sunset Park, Brooklyn.

People screamed on every floor. He heard them through the hole where wall had been a moment prior.

Levi could do nothing for it, but ride it out, hide inside, hope to not get caught.

That wasn't true. He *could* do a thing or two about it. If he wanted. If he decided to take responsibility for himself and exercise his freedom.

So.

Levi downed his coffee.

Perked up more than he really should have.

Devised a stupid, stupid plan. He'd take the rug that ran the length of the room and fashion a slide. "Help me lift this slide."

Sammi, out of wits, didn't argue. She held it up and rolled.

Some folks had already fallen past the hole in their wall, ceiling to floor and beyond. Levi went and unrolled the rug at the end of the floor. "Hold it!" He didn't have what it took to hold it on his lonesome, which made him feel so weak.

She would not hold it.

Levi growled and groaned as the rug flopped about and threatened to fall out of his little hands entirely.

But yet... she had some long, slender dried bamboo quill in her hand and was saying some nonsense while pointing at the rug. Even with the nonsense words, he heard her speech slur. The rug was *listening* to her. It curled into a giant slide, a wide mouth at the top. It *hardened*.

They held together now. Person after person rode it down over the rubble into the place where backyard enclosures met. Beyond the sinkhole. Scraped knees and bruises. Plenty of crying kids. But person after person landed free and still alive. Together Levi and Sammi made a few more rug and blanket slides. Everyone eventually found safety through their makeshift playground. Finally they were the last upon the makeshift chutes and ended on the other side.

And then the building collapsed behind them all in the sinkhole.

"Wow," Sammi said.

Levi felt a fool. Yeah, they'd helped those people. But he'd been out of his mind on seawine and coffee the whole time. It got worse. The cops showed. They praised him, but wanted an interview. The newscasters magically appeared. They praised Levi, but also wanted interviews. Then folks in starry robes hustled him and Sammi in a special black ambulance. Off they went to the hospital in a special escort. *They* did not praise him. *They* sought no interview. This is not at all what Levi had in mind when he went off to prove himself. Perhaps the opposite of what he had in mind. He did not want to spend the night in a trauma ward. His sisters might be wondering just where he'd gone.

Worse: he had been caught, he knew it. And the folks at the hospital would keep him from his seawine. Thanks a lot, Sammi. Thanks, stupid sinkhole.

WHAT HAPPENED WITH THE SISTERS A DAY LATER:
Ellie felt angry. Livid. Not with Levi. Him she felt some sympathy for, knowing he was… sick. At least inside the head. No, she felt a fury at the Author holding back the information on the library centaur. As if the Author wanted them to stall. Delays alone made her want to interrogate him again for his ideas on how to curb Overmorrow, steal Charlie. That or go forward with the plan? Detour to see him squirm?

Going forward with the plan had its problems, but so did spiting the Author. Of course, he was possibly innocent. She munched a macaron. Raspberry. They'd nothing better to do than to go to the library because otherwise they were having a sleep-over at the house of their ultimate enemy. He still could be. But she didn't *really* want to go there in her mind. Not yet. Good Lord, that would be awful if the bad guy you were chasing was the guy who wrote the book on the chase itself. All Ellie wanted was information from the secret end of the NYPL. Perhaps she couldn't get it. But she had to go forward with their plan anyway.

15

GRAND CENTRAL

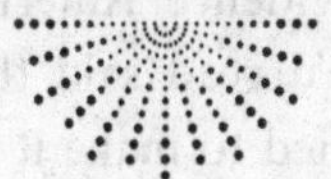

It was busy that morning in Midtown Manhattan, with morning commuters — a couple of leprechauns decked in three-piece suits. Sirens dressed like women of the night experiencing homelessness — fish netting, heels higher. Annie and Ellie traded places as they ducked and dove between shifting currents in the stair-climbing worker zombies. The newly renovated grey tile and sheetmetal undercavern of the subway — its ruthless, self-reflective efficiency — gave way to marble and gilded framing. In several steps, they crossed Americana's 1920's science fiction border into Roman Legionary fantasy. What if someone could write Roman legionary science fiction? A space opera?

"Wow," said Annie.

"I forget you haven't been here," Ellie said. "The oldest and bestest American train station.

Ellie laughed darker than her younger siblings could. "I guess American architecture takes gorgeous historical marble and columns. After thinking on a beauty honed over years of studious fine and manual art, Americans take it and—"

"Blow it up," Annie said. Her eyes glowed, remembering the

cauldron and the sassafras. "Lots and lots of dynamite. Big boom."

Ellie shrugged sadly and nodded. Mrs. Wright had once taken Ellie to Europe. Europe showed sculptures could save you. America's a country of gunpowder treasons and plots, whereas England celebrates the day Guy Fawkes *failed*. Could an architecture of peace even exist in the country of her birth?

In any case, by providence Americans had spared Grand Central. An article Ellie'd read said they'd lost the first Penn Station, though they'd tried to make it anew in the most recent construction project. The foremen behind said project went hostile to those experiencing homelessness, pregnant women, children, and anyone that didn't stand up in a suit with a briefcase full of money. Early on, they locked and chained the family restroom so that one pregnant woman peed her pants and her other baby screamed, "I'm poopy!"

Yet Americans hold enough "my grievous fault" they couldn't quite bring themselves to demolish TWO gorgeous marble train stations. The magic of the New World clung to cream bricks, train baron vault apartment or no. Gilded inlays ran around the room's patchwork slabs of marble, even around the giant mother of pearl clock worth twelve million dollars. Ellie wondered why in the heist movies, thieves never went after classic architectural features. Ellie and Annie passed under the low tunnels in a cloud of chocolate croissants, newspapers hot off presses, bourbon barrels, and coffee, coffee, coffee. The girls did not drink coffee or bourbon, but seeing it all helped them remember to refuse both to UnLevi.

Today, so many passengers passed through the ranks of tourists cloaked and hooded. The tunnel gave way to a great verdant vault above, its sunny stars and constellations — of gods and globes, the music of the spheres — a writhing sea of fantastic life stuck in deepest heavens. Gilded light cataracted into the room through sable-seamed windows holding up the catwalks. Ellie gasped. Between those windows, shadows of selves walked. A great foghorn offered its lone bellow.

A ghost train with wings came barreling into the hall, hovering twenty feet above them, dropping down the wraiths of escalators so fantastic folk could board. Another clarion shouted out its mouth, "NEXT STOP: NO'AD." Two sets of wings flanked every car. Ellie wondered if in earlier models, Pegasi had pulled that sleigh.

No common NYC folk, the Undernaehts, heeded the ghost train or its wings or the folk boarding. The commoners seemed caught in the drudgery, rocked to sleep by the vibrations of machines in tunnels beneath. Or they focused on the time boards showing what trains New Yorkers used to head up the Hudson or towards New Haven via nethersky tunnels.

Annie said, "Wow."

Hand-drawn map from the Author in hand, Ellie remembered the library. "Come on."

Annie had asked the Author before she followed Ellie why she couldn't use her phone's navigation.

The Author had laughed and asked her if her phone had ever led her towards anyone belonging to Overmorrow?

The more Ellie looked up and out to the world, the more she wondered at the folk bowed double over phones. Hunchbacked hags, black holes on legs navel-gazing themselves into Oblivion's clutches. She'd taken to shouting at the phone zombies, "Eyes up, brother! Eyes up, sister."

They followed the Author's map to the front of the old hewn, once polished, weathered cedar doors. The brass handles caught the elven candlelight from the great old chandeliers behind them. Down the road they went, more mindful of the crossing lights than the natives.

Waiting for the walking man sign, they watched natives walk whenever the risk/reward calculation tilted toward cream, as if any changing light initiated a game of Frogger. Traffic lights must not have wanted them to find the library.

They hung a right and the uniform sidewalk gave way to intermittent bronze-stamped placards quoting many a famous author, many a famous work, stamped with images of varied worlds their minds had made up, graven images of living cosmi-cloaks. The brass quotes formed the opposite of Hollywood's walk of stars: wisdom and wonder instead of fame and fortune.

Both girls lifted eyes. Before them reclined two great carved granite lions named Fortitude and Patience. The lions guarded a palace flanked by statues of Truth and Beauty. The common humans — Undernaehts — went in and went out, around and round revolving doors. But the Overmorrow folk used both the doors and the dirigible airship dock at the top of the building. This library and the Empire State Building seemed to be the most common docks for steampunk airships. Others dove headlong into the great fountains Truth and Beauty guarded. They passed as ghosts would through the angled stones.

Ellie hesitated before the many ways of entry. But Annie, oblivious, went through the normal brass revolving doors. Ellie followed since fewer barriers were there to prevent them from walking inside. A man sat guarding all the Y-shaped red ropes of velvet, checking the contents of totes. Ellie ran her fingers on the velvet ropes as she approached. He hassled a young man wearing felted headphones, long black locks licking out a green beanie. His pants were pulled tighter than either of the girls saw fit to wear. "Oh you brought soup but you didn't bring me soup?" he asked the young man. They haggled back and forth, loud enough to echo in the space with Mr. Astor's name on the wall. Ellie heard no more because the security man waved them on.

Annie audibly sighed, a Saturday morning cartoon sound.

Opposite the guard, a valkyrie, shimmering unseen by the Undernaehts, winnowed Overmorrow folken through with equal purpose. Had they stolen books? Did they bring in magic bombs? Ellie shuddered. Was that what Overmorrow folken could do?

They passed an open book upon a great East Indian rosewood table. A Dryden manuscript behind a glass read:

As those who unripe veins in Mines explore,
On the rich bed again the warm turf lay,
Till time digest the yet imperfect Ore,
And know it will be Gold another day.

Whoever restricted Overmorrow, were they trying to keep the world from being good and gilded, alive and well? Why not allow something to bring wonder to as many as possible?

The girls followed the directions to the Rose Reading Room. Climbing the large white marble stair sets yanked at Ellie's belly-button and the stitches in her sides, making her gasp. In front of them hung brass lions who spat out water for drinking fountains. Four paintings hung before them, floor to ceiling, of (1) minds recorded and reciting around a campfire, (2) minds recorded on tablets of stone, (3) minds as scrolls, as Gutenberg's press, and finally (4) minds upon the daily newspaper.

"At least there isn't a painting of commoners worshipping phone zombies," Ellie said.

"Amen," said Annie.

They walked through the Reading Room and remarked on how the skies outside had been perfectly painted on the ceilings above. The paint boiled, mirroring the weather as if painted according to Monet's ideals. All the wood was carved with tiniest swoops and leafing, inlayed with gold. The reading room sat full of folks alongside brass lamps, wooden armchairs, perfect books for the best stories and solutions. Multi-volume series. Exclusive commentaries on each.

"Whoa," Ellie said.

"Shhhhhh," said one of the guards.

At the quiet counter stood a greying centaur, his salt-and-pepper beard matching the horsehair on his body, blue roan and brindle. White hair fell about his shoulders. Green cloak tails spread out upon his back into a horse blanket. He was whispering, *"Pray for us centaurs, now and at the hour of our death."*

Ellie said, "Isn't it sinners?"

"You think any half man, half horse is perfect?"

Ellie hesitated.

"No?" he hussed.

Ellie shuffled. Hedged and hesitated.

Annie whispered, confidently: "Mr. Centaur Man—"

"Centaur Men are half breeds," he said. "I am a full centaur, half man, half horse. Mr. Centaur shall suffice, though that is not—"

Ellie, hands shaking, backed away some more.

Annie said, "Mr. Centaur—"

"Please," he said. "I am Boethius. How—"

"Boethius," Annie said. "We seek the magic library. An Author had us come to you."

Boethius turned for a moment. A little grey train like the one on Mr. Roger's Neighborhood came around the bend in the hardwood hauling mouldering old brown-leather volumes, pages cracking off of them.

Annie cleared her throat. "Mr. Boethius, sir—"

"One moment."

"But Mr. Boethius—"

"One moment, child, these are very rare."

"Because of what's inside?"

"Yes, but also because they're brown."

"Books are always brown."

"Not these."

"Why?"

Exasperated, the man-horse turned his full form to face the little child. The noise and inertia of his sheer size caused both girls to back off. "Be*cause*, child, it—" He seemed to see Ellie's sister's face anew. He started again. "Considering the source, it's hard for you to know their rarity, since they're brown books at what *seems* to be a normal New York Public library. I can see that, yes. However, on the planet where *these* books originated, the soil is purple. The *trees* are tinted purple. There is no *brown*, not naturally. Most of their brown comes from off world."

Annie's and Ellie's mouths and eyes were unabashedly gaping as they each in their own way imagined a world in which the color *brown* was rare. Only then did they reconsider the color of the books. They felt *regal*.

Each took a step back from the books and the centaur.

Boethius bound the books together in a small band with a label, wrote in a few numbers with a fountain pen. Those five numbers appeared on the large scroll sitting right beside the digital display controlled by a portly young librarian gal. Someone along the tables behind them rose. That person moved toward them while the centaur refilled the tiny train car with some other materials (old treasure maps, in this case, of sunken ships in the sea). He sent the little guy along his way again.

Ellie found her voice. It had been tingling alongside her jugular. "Are these trains used all over this library?"

Boethius smiled. "For miles and miles below us. Leagues."

Annie spoke. "We need to learn about the folk who live in Overmorrow. We have a case to solve. Overmorrow, The Board, seawine, Oblivion, Ch—"

"What'll happen if you *don't*? I'm really rather busy, poor banished children of Eve. I—"

"Overmorrow will be no more," Ellie said.

He laughed in her face. A horse whinny paired with a chuckle. "You can't end a world full of immortal fae folk. You might be able to end a world with *some* wandering immortals that will not taste death 'til kingdom come. *Canticle for Leibowitz* talks about that. Hendrick van der Decken. Others."

"No," Ellie said. "Not Overmorrow. The rain."

"You can't."

"But you won't be able to open any new eyes or hearts," Ellie said, blinking two colors. "The rain is ending. Its waters are drying up. Or getting bought up and the spigot turned or something."

He grew so still and quiet that Ellie thought he'd turned into one of those hyper-realistic sculptures she'd seen in Crystal Bridges back at home. The room sounded louder because he went so still. The other workers mirrored him. In that unique librarian silence, elder pages turned, softer keyboards clacked, wood and rubber on marble squeaked.

The eyes of the centaur moved around, looking at nothing particular in the air that the girls could see. He twitched, then moved quickly. "Come." He disappeared behind the wooden walls that held the service window and went through a door with a brass mesh window. Ellie remembered the confession booth at her neighbor's church back home.

Down they followed him to pulley-based lifts. An extremely gaunt, pale, and slimy creature hovered above the lift they chose. Her eyes were blindfolded and her skin sagged. The very ropes that manned the pulley system bound half her body and so she said, "I love ropes, children, do you like ropes?"

Annie, stoic, stood up straight and asked the creature. "Do you like your job?"

It snapped its attention onto her. Then on Ellie. Ellie felt its piercing blindfolded gaze *scraping* the inside of her iris, as if the world's smallest trowel made of sharpened lacewings were drilling on the lens of her pupil, as if the creature's mind was clawing on the doorway of her soul. Trying to get inside. *I am not afraid. I am not afraid.* It grinned a slime-toothed grin, nodding left and right and left and right, an Eastern gesture meaning *yes. Yesssss.*

"Do not taunt the Borda, child," Boethius said. "It likes its ropes a little much, you'll find. And though it has no water by the lift, these depths—" He pointed down as if the floor did not exist. The elevator shaft. "—would suffice for such a one when roused. For your sake and the sake of your children's children, leave it. And for his sake too and therefore the library's: we need him for the lift and it's the one thing that keeps him out of tremble."

"Trouble?" Ellie asked.

"That too. Out of trouble *and* out of the nightmares of children who tremble."

Down they went through the stacks and stacks that held up the floor of the Rose Reading Room. Books that held up both the floor and other books. "What if you want to read a book in one of the pillars holding up the floor?"

"To know the pillar is to know the books, for those books contain the true name of the pillars themselves."

"Long name," Annie said.

"A name tells all possible stories of a thing in and of itself. Noun means name. Nominative means name. Without having possession of the white stone holding the single name of any given thing — the white stone outside space and time — its full name's manifestation takes a very, very long time to say. Thus the books *are* the pillars, the pillars *are* its name."

"How long?" Annie asked.

"The length of its existence, if you're saying it in the same existential plane."

"The pillars *grow*?" Annie asked.

"All things grow."

"What about entropy?" Ellie asked.

"Even entropy will grow and change. It takes even *more* time to say a name if the Author cannot use two words when one will do."

"Doesn't he know his characters?"

"He does."

"Why doesn't that lead to shorter names? Nicknames?"

The centaur smiled. "What he knows he puts in his books from the perspective of those things. Books take ages to write, longer ages to revise, a reasonably long time to read through even the first time through, who knows how many rereads they can withstand, and then it will take generations to properly criticize and form a fandom or school of thought around them. *And that's only the books we pay attention to.* Books take eight or ten hours to read. Sometimes eight or ten years to write *the right way*, as Master Rothfuss and Master Martin and *certainly* Master Joyce and Master Tolkien know and knew good and well."

The lift slowed and they exited. The Borda licked its lipless jagged pock-pock-pocker and toothy tines, then said, "Fifteenth sub Archive."

Ellie's eyes went all wide. Before she exited, she asked, "What all is stored here?"

"If you go deep enough, it connects to the Akashic field and records."

Wide open prairies and her father's vinyls came to mind. Her father. Where'd *he* gone? *Had* he been taken too?

The centaur stared at her, confused at her confusion.

"I'm sorry, the what?" she asked.

"The Library of Babylon?"

The girls shook their heads.

"The Archive of the Redemptive Clockwork. ARC for short. It's the giant library with everything in it. One day you'll be old enough to delve it."

Annie's eyes went as huge as novas.

The centaur added, "A little. Delve *a little* of it."

"Everything of what?" Annie asked. "Everything of what's in this library?"

"The known. And the unknown. Though the unknowable parts of the library cannot be reached by any creature. But it has everything that's real or imagined or explorable by creatures with personal consciousness of self."

"It even stores lies?" Ellie asked.

"All counterfeits, properly marked."

"Isn't a lie an unknowable thing?" Ellie asked. "You can't know what's not true."

"A lie is a knowable unreal, not an unknowable unreal or an unknowable real."

"So fiction," he said.

"NO! Child, fiction is speculative philosophy, not a lie. The hypothesis stage of science and logic."

"I don't get it."

"It's the difference between the counterfeit twenty dollar bill in your hand and the idea of a counterfeit bill that never existed. Or the fiction and nonfiction section elsewhere in the library. They don't contain unwritten fiction and nonfiction books, do they?"

Ellie shook her head.

"You'd never dream of... I mean it's unthinkable where we store the undreamable dreams and unthinkable thoughts. One mind alone knows where they are."

Annie looked around and seemed to remember something. "This is that?"

Boethius nodded. "This is merely the Rose branch that

connects to a tiny province in an obscure corner of *that*." He stood as tall as a horse man can stand and no taller. He hoofed the floor and the horseshoes sparked bright fire against the steel walkway. "This way, poor banished children of Eve."

They followed him beyond the arches of brass and arches of bone and arches of horn and arches of stone. Each arch held a column of bookshelves heavy laden with tomes. They came to a catwalk. Annie had built momentum. She almost careened over the edge of the railing into the abyss that went down for forever.

The prehensile tail of the centaur worked in a braided horse-hair bullwhip and caught her in a coil. He pulled her back. "Take care, Annie."

But Annie's eyes focused on the writhing lava-bright thing at the bottom of the library's gravity well. She whispered, "That's why they call it The Rose."

Ellie followed her sister's eyes and peered down in there. At the very bottom of the cavernous hole, a great unflowering red rose swallowed the stairs and catwalk. Every shelf and stair and detail first faded towards the vanishing point. Petals of that great red blooming thing subsumed them. "It's so pretty," Ellie said.

"It'll drive you mad, unless you fall inside in your current state of mind, in which case it will kill you. Keep this way, child."

So books held up the Rose Reading Room, but the Rose held up the books? How'd that work? Down the shaft, a great sign hung: V.I.T.R.I.O.L. "Vitriol?"

"*Visita interiora terrae; rectificando invenies occultum lapidem,*" the centaur said.

The girls stared at him, baffled. They both looked back down at the great molten corolla, a mandala of meaning.

"Keep this way, child," he whispered. He slipped hooves into a set of centaur slippers made of raw cotton and dry leaves.

The children figured out why. The slow tink tonk of their sneakers on the cold-wrought iron catwalk echoed above and below the layered books that held up the floor of the Rose Reading Room at the main branch of the New York Public Library.

But the centaur's iron-shod hooves made no more sound on cold-wrought iron, thanks to the raw cotton barrier he'd slipped onto his feet. They also didn't spark, which Ellie thought was a good idea, considering all the old paper. He trod carefully, touching none of it. "Here," he said. "It's everything we have that's easily accessible about the Overmorrow rains. Hopefully it helps." He nickered and muttered. Then he said, "Take care. Fear not." He muffle-clip clopped down the metal walkway. As he did he bumped a stack of books waiting to be returned to the shelves. They thudded like many large splinters on the grate. "Come now, sister wisdoms." He neighed and clapped a sonic clap. Those books whisked up off the floor in a flock, dodged his wide-load horsehind, and reshelved themselves. As they did, little golden number ones flew off into the shaft and upwards.

"Whoa," Annie whispered. "What are all the golden ones for?"

"Magical librarians and otherwise are all the same. None of us want you to reshelve books."

"Why?"

"We keep an ever-moving record on what's used and what lies dormant. Undernaeht nonmagical folk will use their records of internal circulation to justify purging old, unused books. *Overmorrow* folk, however, tend to seek tomes used the *least* in recent years or decades. Modern society ignorance is reason enough to seek them. Other than the classics: there's a core canon of a few hundred or so books from which everything else stems — like the genus of flora and fauna. A canine is not always a dog: could be a wolf or a coyote or a jackal. But they're always a canine. The classics work like this." He turned to leave again.

"What makes those so special?" Annie said.

He stopped.

Ellie asked, "Aren't the classics biased?"

"Biased how, child?"

"Written by men?"

"No. Sappho. Hildegard of Bingen. Waellomi, of course. She is highest."

"What about white people?"

"Augustine was black, child. Gilgamesh was Arab. Sun Tzu was Asian. Diogenes was not a centaur like I, but a cynocephalus."

"A what?"

"He was half dog, child. Why do you think he barked so loud at Alexander the Great?"

"Diogenes barked?"

"I will not tell you everything right now, but the Dominicans — the hounds of God — know this. Plato once defined a man as a featherless biped. Diogenes responded by running into Plato's academy with a plucked chicken barking, 'Behold a man!'"

Ellie laughed.

"He was half dog. Canine. They're not biased in that way, for all kinds of men and women have always told stories and all kinds have always existed. So yes, classics first. The root first. But even then, so many versions exist that less-read versions and adaptations yield up true wonders of the world. Wasn't Dante writing Virgil fan fiction? Time's another kind of golden sieve." He whinnied and went his way.

The girls propped books in sections on The Board and seawine, Overmorrow, Charlie and Oblivion. They delved stacks and stacks to learn about the source of magic water. Overmorrow had such a varied history, so many forms.

It had its springs in Joplin and Eureka. Rivers in the land of Jordan. Mountain lakes in history and times when Nile and Mississippi rivers turned on back. Sometimes it hides even amid the dirty water of the Ganges where the poor bathe, clean swirls amid the filth. Dripping cyclic fountains in obscure Japanese villages under Tor gates. History of times when the Amazon ran but a trickle and the waters washed over a jaded Atlantian city.

Wells deeper and older as man in the deserts. Wars were fought for wells. Legendary wells in Florida wetlands now drowning under the sea level. Founts like octagons and fountains carved of marble hidden deep in stone stair sets in Perugia. Those sprayed forth from cherub kisses. Sprinkler systems in the Vatican. In Antisian hollows in some ocean. Overmorrow had a long and varied history, but they couldn't find a reason it would stop or get stolen, locally or otherwise. It moved, it was ignored, but to actually be suppressed? Forcefully restricted?

They found an old crusty book that gave them hope some Author or reporter would find an answer, but only because it was less about Overmorrow and more about the power of water in the worlds of the Vale. Something to do with a thing called weaving and storyweaving, but they couldn't make heads or tails of it. How could water catch fire? How could it persuade a mountain to move in waves? In any case, clearly water in this magical new world had properties normal water did not hold for them.

"Hello there, girls," a familiar voice said. "You doing okay here?"

They turned unto the newsman Sy, who looked so shriveled up and tired. A ghost-eyed, frail thing.

"Fine," Ellie said. "You?"

"I'm hanging in. Where's that energetic brother of yours, the one who acts all strung out on coffee?"

The girls shared a look.

"Don't mean to pry." He turned his head sideways to read over Ellie's shoulder. *Leaned* over, *leered* over. "You can tell me when you're ready. What are you researching?"

"Overmorrow," Annie said. "We want—"

"—to learn everything we can since we're new to the magical world," Ellie said quickly.

"I could teach you. I know my way around."

"That would help," said Ellie. "if you could get us to the magical folk at the site of the problems."

He looked across the railing into Rose abyss. It seemed to blind him. With every effort he pulled back and looked. "Oh sure. Sure, sure."

Annie said, "If you can get us to living magic folk so fast, can you bring us to the Angler King?"

The man cocked his head. "Of course. Again, not to pry, but why?"

"The Angler King's messing with our brother."

"Charlie?"

"Levi," Annie said. "The Angler King was there when Overmorrow dried. We think he's behind it."

The newsman nodded. "No time. Pack up."

Ellie folded up her book on the words *out of the darkness has come a great light* and thought of Undernaeght and Overmorrow. She started to reshelve the book, but Annie said, "Remember the golden ones." So Ellie left the book alone. It would shelve itself and be recorded. As they left, she felt a certain dread. After all, they'd failed their task. Their research had been interrupted. Would they ever make time to come back there and really read?

⤝⤞

WHAT HAPPENED WITH LEVI STARTING ON THE DAY BEFORE:

For some who only felt safe on stage, an injury that left Levi in a hospital bed could only be tolerated by turning his entire bed into a stage. He thought it his job to hearten all of those reduced to working dullest drudgeries in the hospital. He flirted with the nurses. He pranked the janitors and aides and techs.

On the other hand, for some who like to run about and play the hero, hospital beds are prisons.

Being tied down with wires, tubes, sheets, and gown straps didn't help Levi.

An athletic-at-all-costs type, Levi had to be restrained his first evening in the hospital. Feeling tied-down became officially literal for him. Folks in megacosm cloaks watched him as his "visitors" before "visiting hours" were over. He glanced at his belonging bag as would a shifty ferret, making sure no one had disturbed it. Mostly afraid one of them might find the goblet.

Levi felt a fool. He felt a hero. A heroic fool, perhaps. A foolish hero. Whatever this combination of courage, disgust, anger, and fear felt like. He also felt an absolute buffoon for having grown addicted to seawine. But most of all under padded restraints and rubber tubes, he felt imprisoned. He wasn't the type to show off in a hospital bed or flirt or prank the staff. He was the type who wanted to be up and out of that hospital, moving towards whatever he'd set before him as his goal. Was this hospital in Sunset Park? He thought they hadn't gone too far.

What could he do?

"Six deaths," one megacosm cloak said to him without turning. "Six dead in that collapse." The man in the cloak was named Jeremiah. He wore a golden yoke around his neck.

Levi stared at the man. Something about him felt hauntingly familiar. "Do I know you?"

16

AT WHAT COST?

The man wearing the golden yoke standing in the threshold of Levi's hospital room stared at him in unblinking silence. After a moment, "Six," he repeated, "six human souls have died, can you—"

A click sounded on their side of the door. The nurse came in with a heave-ho push on the giant lever doorknob. "Oh honey, shut ya jambalaya hole and see them papers. Not the funnies. Not the crosswords. Turn the front. There, ya see? Boy's a hero. Absolutely. Full stop hero." Looking at Levi, she added, "Stay up, honey. You a hero. Stay up."

Sure, Levi felt a hero. But he also felt a fool, fully addicted. Even as he raised his head a little higher, blush crept into his cheeks, hot yet hopeful to be hidden.

After the nurse spoke, a great crowd of women entered clacking eyeglass lanyards affixed to the ends of their bifocals. Their floral garb from some Midwest chic boutique blinded Levi. Their permanents in sundry shades of blue and grey alongside their perfumes as strong as a nuclear option overwhelmed his nose. These women snatched testimony right out of him, out of Sammi, out of anyone else amid the cosmicloaks and nursing staff that they could get to speak.

171

All of those in cosmicloaks eyed the women, curious and judging.

At this, the blush crept higher up Levi's cheeks and the inner wringing of his throat choked him further. The testimonies everyone had shared with these old women worked on him. Something deeper and better and full of happy longing (more than guilt or shame) stirred in his chest, warming him from within. He wanted to speak the unspoken truth: to lay bare his acts and those of others.

He didn't think he'd seen the women prior, but felt he knew about them from the way they'd eyed him over their clacking bifocals. A dozen different grandmas had come to keep him from thinking he'd done nothing wrong. More than a dozen: seventy or seventy-two of them.

Had he done nothing wrong?

Soon after, Overmorrow folk rushed into his hotel room with weavers. These fashioned giant tapestries with moving figures recounting his deeds in painful interior and exterior precision. More primitive folk used cameras, handheld recorders. They kept asking questions such as, "How's it feel to be a hero?"

All Levi could linger upon was the amount of seawine in their bellies. Man, he felt a fool.

After a while the crowd subsided — the two in the hoods who had guarded him pushed out the rest. When it quieted, the one named Jeremiah asked, "Odd position to find yourself in, huh?"

Levi didn't answer. Was he a hero? Or would he be found out? He looked closer at the man. That golden yoke on his neck. Where had he seen that before? "Do I know you?"

Jeremiah grimaced. "Not really."

"I have seen you once before. But where?"

Jeremiah said, "When He took your brother."

It came in a rush to Levi's mind. The capturing. The rescuers. The flight from Carthage, Missouri to NYC. The witness protection. Among them all had stood the man in the golden yoke. Fear came in Levi's chest, but also hope. "Are you here to steal me away?"

"I didn't then," Jeremiah said, "And will not now."

"Then what are you here for?" The ache in his soul wanted to know, so he whispered, "And do you know what happened to my brother?"

Jeremiah breathed in many breaths, slow, watching the boy. Other than the beeps and pumps of the IV tower and the whir of the A/C that Levi assumed the dwarves had installed, nothing much sounded but the slow and steady breathing of the story-weaver with the golden yoke. Jeremiah said, "I'm not certain. What little I know would help you less than what your sister knows. And what of my first question? Odd place to find your-self, eh?"

"A hospital?"

"A hero."

Levi looked at him and didn't answer. He knew he needed out of there, but didn't have a word for all the hero feeling stuff. So could he summon Angler King and all his friends? Where would he begin? Probably with standing water. His bag still hung beside his coat upon the rack. The cup weighed it down. Could he get out? Ought he? If The Angler King inched any closer it would ruin him. Yet he would end up with better seawine.

No, he didn't need to be a hero. He didn't *want* to be a hero. However much the questions bugged him, Levi didn't need to save his brother. Nor did he want to be a fool again. What if he run and hid? But heroes stayed. He could remain, learn from these people and better himself. Become a hero for real.

Though he'd never had the time for heroes.

Whether as the fool who wanted drink or the fool who hoped to hide himself, he wouldn't stay.

He'd wander.

That night, he waited till three in the night's death, then dressed and opened his anorak, zipping it up over his hospital gown. He grabbed his bag of garments and belongings — his little wallet warded within. When one of the men in a megacosm cloak perked up at his person, Levi muttered, "Bathroom." In the bath-room, he barred the door. He turned on the fan so that it washed over his little sounds with white noise. Plugging the sink with towels and pads, he turned on the faucet. It filled and he wondered. The last time he brushed his teeth with his brother, the sink had been clogged with the shaving gunk of their dad's beard. Charlie'd brushed it open for them both, letting water wash and flow.

No! Don't remember all that now, don't try. Forget. When the sink was almost full of cold water, Levi whispered, "What to do?" But he knew that he knew that *he knew.* Somehow. He dipped the goblet down into the gushing. Then with its stem submerged and soused, seawine ran into cotton runnels.

He felt a foolish child. But sometimes waters connect in this world. He whispered, "Angler King. Lutheran Hospital has me prisoner. Come pick me up. Get me out."

The water lay still and heavy laden with seawine.

It hadn't worked. Oh what had he expected? Fool.

But then the basin shook as something neared. A voice hissed out. "SSsssssssssokay little fisherpriest. The ice mouth cometh."

Lights flicker flashed and fluttered out in the room as if stirred by a cosmicloak's dream about paying utility bills much later than he'd planned.

Levi slipped the goblet back into his pocket and opened the door. Lights dazzled in the room — first off, then on all around. On and off and over again, faster and faster, freaking out.

"Stay here," Jeremiah and the Earthbound men in megacosm cloaks said, then took off down the hall.

The doorjamb hid most of the jowls and hair on Levi's face as he peeked. Lights flickered and flashed all along the massive hall. Nurses, orderlies, and techs went running and hollering, hoping to figure what they should do. Levi reeled into the room. Out the window that overlooked the Hudson Bay, the Statue of Liberty lit up like a lime in the limelight in the middle of the night. A clear night, no rain, Overmorrow or the usual variety.

He squinted. Something like a blackened spot arose way out upon the waters.

It grew. By reflected light a wild fountain climbed up the

waters, climbed up the waters's edge into the twilight, roughly at the altitude of Levi's room. It sped. A snake of water. Rope. A great cylinder of seawater.

Levi's chest went cold and fluttery. What on earth — or off earth — had he summoned? He backed up towards the door, then towards the corner of the room.

The water came closer and closer, faster and faster. It hit the window, which exploded inwards. Ocean chilled and filled the chambers of his hospital room. Something big passed him underwater. Then several even bigger masses. A splintering crunch sounded beneath the waves. Was that the room's door? A great clanking as the door gave way. Medical equipment flushed out the open hole. Levi barely held on in the corner.

The waters subsided. He walked out into the hall.

The Angler King filled up the hall on one end. His mermen had land legs, held strong harpooning guns that shot nets, and had shimmering scales made of emeralds. They looked like they'd lost and then won a thousand bar brawls: each one fishy. "We haven't the option to chat, little fisher. So come."

The workers and folks in cosmicloaks had found themselves swilled down the hall. These lay in a heap of googly eyes, waterlogged. He glanced at the vitals that hung from the wall of the room across from his chambers. His neighbor. A pill overdose.

"She's dealing with similar problems to me," said Levi. "We have to rescue her."

"I must do nothing you say."

"You *must*."

"No, fisherboy," the Angler King reminded, "I—"

Levi went into the room where stood a younger girl, frail. "What's your name?"

"Sammi," she said.

Yes, that's right. That was her. "Let's go, Sammi."

"Who are you?"

"Levi," How did she not remember him? "I am here to rescue you."

"Okay. But first, my purse." She found her things. "Pills for me. What sullied you?"

Levi looked upon the angry eyes of the Angler King, the evil whale, the good scarred fish who'd got away from so many fishermen. It one squinted back at Levi, then turned back to room and window smashing. Levi said, "Had to be admitted after a collapse." That still was true, correct?

"Go on and get," the Angler King said.

They hustled down the floor.

Levi trusted the Angler King would flop. Instead of flopping, he swam through the air, like luck dragons in myth books. A flying fish, a dryad. A living version of the whale suspended from the ceiling at the Natural History Museum.

The men in megacosm cloaks turned to them from down the soaked hospital hallway and pulled out various long and slender stylets. Levi had seen these in the book he'd found upon the Author's shelves. He didn't have time to consider their shapes cause the men were now netted to walls, thanks to the mermen's harpoon. They turned back towards Levi's room. A wandering patient passed them in the hall, his IV hanging from a caster wheel tower. Fourteen different bags all bouncing after every available hook.

This patient said, "You live through a building collapse and meet not one —" He nodded at the television showing images of the collapse and Levi's interview with Sammi. "—but two pretty girls." He nodded to Sammi, unaware she was the same as the girl on the screen. "You're alive, kid, don't whine. Control yourself."

Levi didn't like how relevant it felt. The goblet in his pocket threw his shallow questions to the wind and anchored there. Would the pocket hold or tear?

Then the men at the end of the hall shredded the nets from their limbs with these net-addicted flames. They turned twine to torched fuses that burned brightly.

The Angler King bellowed, "NOW!"

Water flushed them airborne. An extended column took them to the sky and stratosphere until it rained them down to land right on the front of the Author's four floor walkup. A darker sort of Overmorrow, an inverted Overmorrow: it came from the magic sky down to the mundane. Levi paused. Perhaps the Angler King *did* have a motive for stopping the rains? Maybe he had his own rain that would not *stop* a vision, but give a *worse* one. That made Levi very, very afraid. Dark Overmorrow. What would that kind of dark rite do?

But he had landed on the doorstep. That was good. Levi sprung his spare key, let himself in and looked behind.

The Angler King and lackeys were long gone. It made him more afraid, vanishing like that. "Let's get you inside, Sammi," he said.

In the apartment, he offered her a shower, a change into Ellie's pajamas, and while Sammi was settled, he looked through his father's old wallet fold up of pictures. The one in Levi's backup pants. A little album. Ellie, Annie. Even Charlie. All of them in the former life. All of them happy and safe.

"Where are you, dad?" he whispered in the cold and dark apartment, worried he'd been awfully, awfully wrong. Yes, he had gotten himself out the hospital bed that had felt like a prison. But at what gloomy cost?

THE MORNING AFTER ALL OF THAT WAS THE MORNING ELLIE, Annie, and Sy departed from the library. Ellie worried that they'd never get the time to come back and read. She dreaded it. She could, of course, ignore reporter man and stay. But that would likely split her from her sister. Hellbent, Annie was, on following this guy.

Of course Ellie *could* go, but the research would tarnish. And then they would start all over again. She didn't want to leave her Annie. But getting derailed from research bothered her. At long last she'd something significant to study, a lead to follow. It felt good.

Annie asked, "Where to?"

That made up Ellie's mind. She submitted, though she didn't like it. Took a single longing look at the granite lions named Patience and Fortitude. "I'll call for you again." The paw of Patience shifted, she was sure. She opened up her mouth. "To the reservoir," the lion said. "That lady in waiting shares its name." Traversing pathways, streets, and tunnels Ellie, Annie, and Sy retraced their path to Central Park. *Central* Park. Did the name of the place connect with that old *central* board? Ellie walked up the eastern side of the park. They passed an obelisk. A nearby bronze sign claimed it hid something deep inside and beneath its base — no one living knew exactly what it hid.

A slug crawled along its foundation. UnLevi. She needed to find an answer quickly for the sake of both brothers. Ellie didn't like to use any person, let alone Levi. Using this reporter for his skills felt off to her, yet she didn't feel *so* bad because she felt as if this reporter would have led her where she needed anyways, regardless as to whether or not she requested his help.

Though the journalist turned out to be a great guide, the traffic lights still restrained them. They moved beyond the lights, the street so soft and rickety Ellie half wondered if hundreds of years ago the street hadn't been made of oak parquet floor that some city manager later coated first in cobblestone, then in asphalt, mindful of where the stone and street had failed. Extended traffic barrels piped out steam clouds, which delayed them further. Nethersky belched visible heat down the wind tunnel's chill, smoky off gasses.

They dodged the cabs, which thwarted progress, dodged the buses threatening to run them over. Those left rainbow trails in their wake.

"How bad do you have to go?" Ellie asked Annie.

"I feel as full as seawine-bloated Levi."

"Ah."

They came to Columbus Circle, north and east into the mall. Ellie wished they had a normal compass. Past the alcoves of Authors, past fountain and path. Up to the reservoir that shared the jilted Lady's name. She and Annie (with this helpful man) would unearth the Angler King. Or unwave. They would—

A crowd had gathered round a CRIME SCENE DO NOT CROSS blockade. The words scrolled in midair as if by hidden lights and LEDs, which with the crowd made it difficult to shift around to see the Angler King.

But Sy said, "I am confident."

When Ellie and Annie wound their way to get up closer, they saw that fireflies were flying in formation to make the letters CRIME SCENE DO NOT CROSS. Those fireflies ducked around the barest edge of poplar tree, hydrangea, forming cleaner boundaries rubberneckers shouldn't — wouldn't — cross. A couple fireflies were a blue species from Tennessee. They offered counterpoints to neon green.

The newsman raised his badge, which parted crowds and let them through.

By the time that the sisters were standing upright they had gasped. The Angler King no longer held his magic sway above their brother. And the reason why The Angler King no longer had power over Levi was very, very obvious.

17

TRAVELS WITH MARTY
THROUGH TIME AND
THRESHOLDS

Someone had filleted the giant fish. Majestic bones lay white and blood red on concrete shores. Scales were scattered like so many iron cornflakes.

"Ahhhhh!" Annie shrieked. "Oh nooooo."

Ellie went dead silent.

The newsman whispered, "Oofy," evidently plagued by thoughts alike.

Who had murdered the Angler King? Magical detectives turned to them, each one robed with trenchcoats Dick Tracy might have donned. Had they all gone to the same cartoon detective school? A large Detective toad turned to face the newsman. "G'day chief, it's a bad thing righty here, y'see?"

"I do see. Have any idea who done it?"

The frog eyed him. One eye. Turned his head to use the other and eyed him with *that*. Then he turned back and eyed him with the first. With his tongue, the frog lifted his fedora, whipped it back into his mouth. It fell out as soon as he spoke. "Know who made him—" Here he croaked. "Ahumm?"

Ellie stiffened both shoulders.

The newsman said, "I think the girls witnessed the shrinkage of the rains. I think they have a clue."

The toad, his brows gone livid, turned to face the girls.

Both of them curdled and huddled backwards. Frigging Silas, throwing them both out in the open. Ellie grabbed her sister's hand.

But Annie stood up tall as if upon a stool. "We saw warlocks, heard The Angler King's involvement, the North Wind, something of an A/C Union." Annie rambled for a minute on exploding cauldrons, shivering brothers, the Author's house. Other than initial leads, she gave not much away.

Ellie dropped her sister's hand. Did honest answers help?

"Author, say ya?" Toad, P.I. asked. "What sort of Author?"

Annie told about their stay and how the Author rescued Levi at their home in Brooklyn. About pizza and a movie. About how their little brother'd come back late and smelling fishy. How she wasn't certain why he'd slept in late or why there'd been that unknown girl at the house.

Then the Toad grew very, very interested.

Ellie flinched. Now *that* was getting too close to home. But Annie would have to stick with his line of questioning. "There isn't reason for more yapping, Annie, come."

"She has to talk to us," the toad said.

"Not without a magic lawyer," Ellie said. "She can keep her silence. As can I." Ellie had no idea if their laws worked the same way in Overmorrow as they did in normal, non magical, Undernaeht New York. But she was willing to go out on a limb to find any way out of the conversation.

The Toad eyed her again, one eye then the other. Started scribbling furiously.

"Where are we going?" Annie asked.

Ellie looked at Sy.

Sy was eyeing greedily the bus-sized fish the crows had cleaned of meat. Once magical and terrible. Once upon a time he'd been the greatest catch for any fishing story. Now he'd passed on to the waterways beyond, a myth awaiting deconstruction. "Where should we go?" asked Sy, sadly.

Ellie, dreading standing by the dead fish any longer, thought *home.* First to check on Levi face to face. Or at least with the compass. Levi who'd slept in after drinking too much of his "good stuff."

But half the day'd be gone by then. Forty-five minutes to train back to Brooklyn, then forty-five minutes to get back to Midtown. If they'd utilize their time, they'd need to check on someone else they didn't know, but might know Charlie. If only they'd a threshold like what they'd seen the day that Charlie had been taken: that hole in the special rock. Home? Or onward?

"Let's check the air conditioning union," Ellie said, thinking of the book of bylaws.

"Follow me," said Sy.

THE AUTHOR'D LEFT TO GET SOME CURED MEATS AT A BODEGA ON 41st and 7th, Brooklyn, right at the corner of Sunset Park, the one by the coffee shop who sold ham cachitos. They brought the meats back home to Levi. He tried to eat. Long hair got in the way, hair long enough the Author called it "primed for tonsure." The boy could barely stomach any, what with the meatiness and lack of things like mermaid vegetation.

Sammi wolfed it down.

Levi craved his kelp and plankton. Krill. He complained when they proffered none. "Why won't you take me back to my sisters?"

Water and sewage, bits of toilet paper, fishing line with rusted hooks all fell out of his gagging mouth. Algae blooms followed. He hated that he'd let the Angler King aid him. Hated it, however much he loved the creature. Hated it, however much he knew the fish belonged among the pages of that copy of *The Cosmographic Bestiary of The Vale.* But he felt so alone in having to be the one to get out. He just looked at the toilet paper, fishing line, and algae blooms upon the floor. He'd rather have vomited.

"Good Lord," the Author said. "As Grandma Beth has said, let's fix you up."

THE PROCESS OF
INVESTIGATION

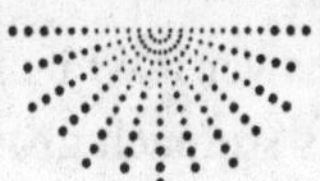

They took him to the kitchen sink, nursed his wounds. Such spare efforts helped him little. Slugs shot out, their chemtrails like rainbows. He wanted to return to folk with cloaks, his sickly bed, to learn to be a hero. To mean to be hero, not to stumble into heroism by accident. He'd paid enough for living, hadn't he? Considering the memory loss and the loss of what he might have done to have one more play session with Charlie in the future?

He'd lost Charlie's memory. He'd lost his sobriety. He'd returned a soiled hero. He had no right to wear the badge of *hero*. He wasn't an *imposter*, but still he knew he wasn't worthy. Why had he gotten thrust into this role? He was weak. He was frail.

His balance went off in a fit of this vertigo. Bathroom ceramic slammed cold on his cheek. Should he wait in the apartment until the girls came back? How long would they be? Ellie's list. Why not pick up where he left? Finish what he'd started before the seawine took him off his course again?

He stood. He didn't need help getting up.

Levi let them welcome Sammi. He was looking at the Author's books again, carefully pushing the bluish thesaurus in line with the others. He didn't want it sticking off the shelf the way he'd left it when he'd fled in haste, having swiped the Author's seawine goblet. He grabbed an old book called *The Process of Investigation*. It was not an answer, but a map for finding answers. He took notes on how to better study the subjects of crimes: keep in mind motives, opportunities, and means. To store them in his loci. It wasn't much, but helping *even a little* felt as if he were moving towards his sister Ellie. Sometimes those little steps matter more than—

A knocking at the door.

The Author went to answer it while holding forth a gyrocompass made of river silt, his stomach growling. Opened it a crack. A softer rumbling issued from the other side. "Yes, he is. And may I ask you who asked?"

More rumbling.

"Ah. You may ask him questions if he's willing. Levi?"

Levi perked up even more, hesitant to set his research down at any interruption, but also terrified to see whomever had arrived. He walked around a loom self-weaving tapestries of tower prisons. Past the bathroom's closed door which held in the still-singing, showering, preening, and titivating Sammi.

To the door.

On the front step stood three hair-slicked, clean-shorn dwarves in pinstripe suits. What they lacked in height, they made up for in raw intimidation: the brawn, the swagger, the power suits. One of them had bright red skin and a brighter green beard, at least a third of it made of moss and clover.

"Are you Lev the Maker?" clover-beard said.

Levi lifted up his chin.

The second, darker one with wavy hair unclogged his throat. "Levi Wright?"

He nodded, picked his cuticles. The skin, not the nail. He really wanted to get back to his research.

"We," said clover-beard, "obtained some evidence of seawater, seaweed, and micro organic organisms, seawine, slugs at the scene of the murder of King of the Anglers. Each has traces of human saliva."

Levi's eyes went wide. What had he forgotten?

So'd the Author's eyes.

"The Angler King is dead?" Levi asked.

The loom behind them stopped.

"The Angler King is dead?" Levi asked a second time, barely catching breath enough from the hitch in his throat. "Did you say the Angler King was…. he was murdered?"

The elder of the three inclined his brow.

"I did nothing wrong," said Levi. What was the point of research now?

"Then," clover-beard said, "you will have no problem completely cooperating with us."

"You don't need to talk to them," the Author said. "We should get you legal help. Have a great day, gentlemen." He went to shut the door.

A red arm blocked its closing. A grumble sounded out behind. "You cannot hide him for an age, Tobias."

"Neither can you keep your arm inside my door and, once it finally opens, get it back in one whole piece."

The arm was yanked away.

The Author latched the lock. It… glowed greenish.

Levi, horrified the arm had entered, felt a deeper shock before the Author's open threat. "You'd really take his arm?"

"Not exactly," said the Author. "Soon they'll dismember me in their world. That's about the only way I vest my life upon this multiplicity. So … it's coming due. What happened?"

"I went to talk to him myself and nothing happened. I'm hurt you think that something did."

The Author laughed. "You're unhurt, but you *are* scared."

Levi kept his peace and blushed.

Sammi left the bathroom wearing a woolen winter outfit she'd found in one of the Maker's storage bins. It didn't fit well. "Everything okay?"

"Fine," said Levi before the Author answered. "How are you?"

"Having landlord problems. Is it cool if I camp for a while?"

The Author shrugged. More than that he smiled at the girl

who needed a home. "Why don't we go for flour for sourdough, babe?" The Maker nodded, so the Author eyed the kids, then he nodded back. He warned them not to answer, left, and when he locked the door, it glowed green again.

The Angler King. Dead. The *Angler King*. Who could kill a flying Natural-History-Museum-sized whale? Such a massive monster? The thought, it bored a hole in Levi's courage. He'd been so stupid to be scared of it. Scared of what it could do to him, but a bigger fish had come along and caught the one who'd always got away.

What—

Sammi was grinning as the Author departed. As soon as their footsteps had silenced in stairwells, she wheeled upon Levi. "So now is when you need to give it here."

"Give what where?"

"The cup," said she. "The goblet. Even if The Angler King had never come to save us from the place—"

"You know The Angler King?"

"You've got it written on your eyeballs. Course I do. You stink of seaport, brine, and seaweed. Don't you see you smell like seawine? Give it here."

He eyed his newfound bestest friend.

"When the building collapsed you were drunk on the seaw-ine." It wasn't a question. "I saw it in your eyes at the hospital, the way you looked at the television news."

Levi hung his head and watched a cockroach skittle on the wall and out the window where its sisters hung in the musk of the restaurants below. "I was," he whispered. "That and coffee, a close second to seawine. Lots — and lots — of coffee. Had to get my stomach pumped."

She looked him up and down.

He shrugged. "I am a high-functioning coffeeholic. On the drip too long, dosing and grinding."

"Someone has to pay for those who departed whenever it fell."

"Don't worry."

"Why not? You are."

He nodded.

The news, streaming in the background from an open computer, mentioned both their names. They turned to watch. The wall was collapsing. Then he and then Sammi were subjects of interview. They showed that the funeral for someone began in mere minutes. The church of St. Michael's was hosting, the one with the spire icon of Sunset Park.

How large of a grave would they need for a creature like the Angler King? Would all the fishes of the sea pay respect to such a skull?

"You want to go?" she asked.

He sure as heck didn't want to stay there thinking on a dead fish king and seawine. He nodded again, wiped his runny nose with an acrylic sleeve. It itched, however smooth.

∞

THE FUNERAL HAD ANY NUMBER OF NEIGHBORHOOD GUESTS FILLING the pews. They watched faithfully as the priest talked of tragedy. Of living in the wake of something no one could foresee. Over in a corner, Sammi sat. Levi walked to her and whispered, "Hey…"

She nodded. "We should have saved more."

"Hey, listen. If anyone in the investigation asks if I had any seawine or coffee at the collapse, I need you to tell them I only had water."

"Who's going to investigate you?"

"I don't know," he said. "The men in megacosm cloaks. Police. The A/C Union. Angler King's cronies. Lawyers. The Board. My mom." Where was his mom? He was starting to worry about his parents: it was easily the longest they had gone without them and here in New York City. "There're a lot of people asking where I've been, what I've been doing."

"So you want me to lie. Lie even to my *order*."

He shrugged.

Angry tears bubbled up in her eyes. He watched them rise and wondered if he'd see some steam emerge. Her hands gripped and wrung the worn out wooden edge of the pew before her. Even the fabric on the kneelers beneath their knees looked putrefied. But she said, "I'll do it. But know I hate it. There weren't that many deaths, you know, but one was a cloak like me."

Levi raised his eyebrow.

"A cloak like me." She pointed to the whirling world upon her megacosm cloak.

Levi sucked in air past his canines. "Yeah… Sorry about that."

"You know you have a problem. You're gonna be the death of you or me. And maybe both." She shuffled teeter totter on her knees upon the kneeler and looked forward.

"Huh," he said. "I thank you, Sammi." Yeah, he got what he wanted. Sammi would lie. But then again: at what cost?

Did he really want her to lie for him?

Had he already lost his brand new bestest friend?

19

AN AIR CONDITIONING
SUBSIDIARY

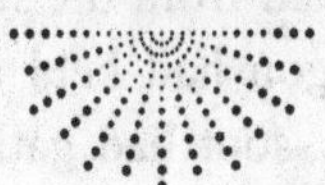

By way of special water fairy, Sy took both girls over the Hudson, down the estuary to Atlantic City towards a long abandoned casino. Ellie and Annie were not quite sure, but they followed. Years prior, some wannabe real estate mogul had plastered his name all over that building, then drove the whole thing into the ground. What a terrible, terrible curse, his name. How could you bankrupt a CASINO, whose very purpose for existing was rigging the odds of your own games in order to steal the money from the pensions your elders saved or from the food stamps of the poor?

Hard to imagine how someone could mismanage a cast-iron con. But this crook not only mismanaged it, he managed to force someone *else* to hold all his debt. The casino had been sold, pawned, foreclosed, traded for pink slips, lost in poker, lost in Grand High Tarock, lost yet again in other games (like Phi), lumped into auctions, sold again.

Then a great firm of dwarves from the second-Tor planet of No'ad had gobbled it up. The planet functioned like a large corporation of companies, merging and acquiring other little firms and planets till that globe had STUNTAZ INC emblazoned over every living thing. And dead thing. And inanimate. Now the

189

bankrupt casino had turned into a tall subsidiary of STUNTAZ INC. An air conditioning subsidiary.

This was where Ellie had demanded Sy take them.

THE DOORS CARRIED NEAR-APOCALYPTIC LEVELS OF GRIM AND grime. The windows only allowed a glimpse of light through their muddied glass rescued from the silt wreck of a hurricane's storm surge. As if a dragon had held the tower sideways over cauldron fires until thick soot had gathered on them all. Once they crossed the threshold, it did not improve.

A once crimson carpet was now mildewed green and black, except where the sun had bleached spots dry and orange. Bits had folded up as the glue'd come loose. Other bits had succumbed to the blackest of black molds.

A semi-circle of dwarves in ill-fitting pinstripe suits blockaded Ellie and Annie and Sy the newspaperman. Ill-fitting not because a respectable dwarf had no source for procuring tailored fashion. Ill-fitting because these particular dwarves had no respect for fashion. No eye. They were, in the end, not truly dwarves — the kind who liked their birth height and birth shape, the kind who appreciated other dwarves.

They were not *Earthen* dwarves.

No, these were different. They were giants whose stature reversed through years and years of avarice. Dwarfhood didn't fit their disposition, personhood, or place. It didn't suit them.

In fact, if you looked close, it looked like someone had squeezed some thirty yards of height into their figures. As if a giant had been forcible compressed into a mould and gravity had done its work to harden them and make them dense. Distant children of fallen angels, daughters of men. Once-giants whose bad habits had dwarfed their bodies from the fading of their souls.

No, not the same thing as human dwarfism at all.

"Welcome to STUNTAZ, Jersey branch on the Tor of Leukgalos." This came from a well-dressed, well-armed (at least by medieval knight standards) dwarf behind the counter. His armor was dented and squeaky-jointed. He looked ridiculous amid his peers in pinstripes. He lifted his visor by gauntlet in semi-salute and asked them, "Which division?"

Sy stepped forward. The carpet puffed dust.

Ellie coughed.

Sy said, "Air Conditioning Union. Which floor?"

The one behind the counter took a bite out of his faux-bacon egg and cheese and gave him the slightest glance. "Which was that?"

"The A/C Union."

The man behind the counter looked around at the others in the room and then reluctantly said, "Fifteenth." He slammed his visor down.

Several snakelike things, wisps with teeth, bowed their heads in threat. Ellie, more from fear than anything, hissed at them through her flared teeth.

They hissed back.

But Annie, Ellie, and Sy passed beyond unstricken and unharmed.

Up the elevator and out without incident, though Ellie tripped over the egress.

They emerged into a large hall with wood panels, linoleum flooring, and the occasional head nod toward vast wealth hoarded elsewhere. A leather couch made of the skin of some creature Annie, for all of her cryptozoology, never identified. A chandelier made of some red precious gem. A drinking horn cut clean off of a gryphon.

The compressed giant workers there perked up at the very unexpected, very unusual appearance of this motley troupe. Until they noticed Sy. Then some shrank away to offices, others to water coolers, others to orifices – break rooms and bathrooms. Obviously he'd dug up something awful on this company before.

Ellie sucked her teeth. They would make for harder interview subjects.

Sy covered cubical after cubical, and the girls followed. A/C repair men moved in and out in jumpsuits decked in blue and gray and black. Others wheeled greater dollies that outstripped their own height, the overflowing contents barely secured by orange straps.

The two girls and the elder man moved on further, dodging swooping bats with wires and soldering guns in tow. It seemed the building's very veins and nerves were fraying. The three went into the backroom, met up with a former giant compressed and fractured and crammed into the suit of a two-year-old child.

"Whatdya want?" he asked. "Especially you two. Names?"

"I'm here on assignment with these two job shadows. I'll be taking notes." Sy pulled his notepad out, flipped it, and started scribbling into the silence and the hum of the nearby window unit A/C. It still had the plastic streamers to remind the girls that yes, oh yes, it still blew *air*.

"So," Ellie said, worried that Sy's aggression with the notebook would clam them up, but was interrupted by Annie shouting:

"WHERE WERE YOU ON THE NIGHT OF TONIGHT?"

"Uh..." the pinstripe dwarf started.

"WHAT RELATIONS HAVE YOU HAD WITH MRS. JOHNSON?"

Ellie whistled low.

"Who?"

"Annie ... " Ellie laughed. "Annie please. Please, Annie."

"What? That's how people on our binge watches did it."

"There's no Mrs. Johnson on this case."

"I don't know," Annie said. "Seemed we might encounter someone named The Johnsons."

"What gave you that idea?" Ellie asked. She'd turned completely from the dwarven office desk to her sister's presence.

Annie shrugged. "Saw it before me in gold and in rainbow. Overmorrow vision." She squinted. "Maybe a trailer park? Maybe a commercial?"

Ellie winced. Doodled six-point stars upon her journal. "Uh, Annie? There's no trailer park in New York City."

"Actually there are," the dwarf said. "You're not too quick upon your feet."

A younger, slightly larger dwarf assistant poked his head inside and said, "That's just the name. The Trailer Park's a fashion store in SoHo. Kind of offensive, when you—"

"Well, I—"

"Quit it," Ellie said to both, and turning back to Annie said, "Don't be so desperate to detect that you make up crimes to solve. If you accuse folks of doing things they didn't do in order to have work, then you're just as bad as spies who groom assets."

"Oh." Annie thought in the silence. Nothing but the whir of A/C streamers kept accompaniment. "Yeah, I guess that could be bad."

"Or downright evil," Ellie said. "And rude to this old gentleman."

The gentleman in question jammed a five-tine fork into a bowlful of chicken hearts while his admin retired into the anteroom. "Don't call me gentle. I'm harsh deep down. And don't call me a man. I am a giant."

"Are you now?" Ellie asked.

"A giant in this business."

Ellie sighed and furrowed her brow.

Sy scribbled. His pen ran out of ink as fast as Levi ran. He shook it down to get it yielding ink as he might shake thermometers. To no avail. He threw it at the window unit, where it made a hollow thunk on the plastic and rattled within. He pulled out another, doffed the cap with teeth. The pen he'd thrown rattled in the vent, stuck. It got to where the constant stream of new air made it rickety and noisy.

The sound reminded Annie of something climbing the stairs, something furry, full of scales. Her palms slicked with sweat.

"Awwww come on," the dwarf said. With a quick palm heel strike he dislodged his pen, never looking back to see if he'd succeeded.

Ellie thought this through. She tweaked her neck behind, before. She said, "I guess you *are* a giant in the business. Does your union know about the weather restrictions of late?"

He stopped up short. And short. "What do you mean?"

"The changes in the sky, in the forecast," Ellie said, "and the way that affected everyone?"

Sy scribbled, even though no information was forthcoming. Not any that immediately presented itself to the girls, anyways.

Annie picked her cuticles. She wasn't a nail biter. She judged nail biters. So she picked the skin around her nails until they bled instead. She thought it more sophisticated than nail biting. She had no idea that her brother had the selfsame habit alongside nail biting. She had thought Levi simply bit his nails and they bled.

The dwarf watched them for a minute or so. "It… it… it… It's true," he said to them. "We did try to manage the outer weather. We do it inside, why not do it outside?"

"Why?" Annie asked, voice found.

"Why when you're good at something, do it well! Do it often! Do it everywhere! Make other people do it! Get paid to—"

"Give it a rest," Ellie said. "Rest is a thing."

"What do you mean?"

"To a hammer, everything's a nail. To an Air Conditioning Union, every puff of air needs changing. You don't really care HOW you're changing it so much as THAT you're changing it. You ever think some mountain climbers like hot air if they're climbing in Phoenix? That some Vikings move north to be in the cold? Not everyone wants cool indoors and warm outdoors. Some people like it very cold and others very hot." She glanced at the buzzing A/C unit. "And A/C gives these folk a headache."

He chuckled. "Nah, people love changing air. Every deal needs a middleman."

"Does every partnership need a deal?" Ellie asked.

He stared blankly at her. "Oh, you want my answer?"

Ellie waited.

"Oh, well then, of course. Of course it does. There's no partnership point otherwise. What are you fishing for?"

Ellie gaped at him. "I don't think so. What of marriage?"

"Prenuptial agreement."

"Divorce prep?"

"You sound like one who thinks that Yondertryst exists."

"Marriage?"

"Vows," he said. "The men who built the Brooklyn Bridge believed vows exist. Vows from their employer. But that didn't stop the shakes or what it was they got emerging from those pressure chambers."

She said, "I'll make an appointment with my future self right here, right now: someday, I'll marry a man and be faithful unto him until the day I die."

The dwarves gasped, the one in the room and the one outside.

Sy raised a very, very frightened eyebrow. An eyebrow that trembled to rise, trembled to stay afloat.

Then the earth itself *shook*.

She had... Done... *Something*. But what on earth was it? Whatever it was, it thrilled her more than stage fright. Into the silence, frantically searching their eyes she asked the dwarf, "Did you alter Overmorrow?"

"What?" His face betrayed something other than surprise. Something like fear. "Did I *what*?"

"The Overmorrow." Perhaps they would heed her, answer questions.

"The rains that give the sight — why would I do that? We need more ranks to fill the unions, to give us customers among the Overmorrow folken. There's a hundred reasons to expand the rain, but restrict it? Why? Is it smaller somehow? It had been behaving oddly, but not around the pond. We feared our tampering had something to do with it. But how can you even magically shrink a magical rain that opens your mind to wonder and magic in the first place?"

Sy cleared his throat looking pointedly at Ellie.

She felt nudged to offer a rebuttal, but she didn't. "Did you change the temperature of the reservoir in any drastic way?" Ellie asked.

He waited longer, brown eyes scanning as if trying to remember something he forgot. "I can't think of why, but I don't run every department, so I can't answer definitively, young girl. Did something happen?"

"WHERE WERE YOU ON THE NIGHT OF TONIGHT?" Annie demanded.

"You did that one already," he said.

"Oh. In that case, how do you know that the rains could grow?"

Sy and Ellie looked at Annie. Sy puckered his lip and nodded twice.

Ellie shrugged. There were worse questions she herself could have asked.

"Quick whip, that one," the dwarf said. "We have experimented with the moisture increase out of doors through hydrates we have pulled indoors. In certain urban densities, we've found a way to make a little rain *kaboom*."

"A bomb?"

"Of rain. It's useful pranking smaller groups of friends who wanted a meal on the town. Other than that, it's useless. Tends to flood out agricultural planes and small towns like Salem and Bellhammer, Illinois. You could use it maliciously and wreak havoc on a film set, but then why would you want to?"

"Did you think it can grow Overmorrow?" Annie asked.

He eyed the youngest of the three. Those eyes narrowed and flared a little green flash. "We hoped."

"For more... customers? And..."

"For pulling us away from humans. They're so bad at demythologizing, corporatizing, optimizing social benefits, production, story deconstruction. In a world mostly speaking narrative, you'd have thought they'd figure how to misquote, misread, misunderstand, and utterly misguide the readers, characters. Or more.

"But they do not do this. They miss the point. So it would be nice to present them the sight or to wake up enough of the bestiary here to gentrify humanity away from this planet. Or this universe, even. Exile them to uninhabited rocks. Then we dwarves could take the reins of deconstruction. Yes, in shorter term, it would be nice to grow the Overmorrow. We need more able-bodied workers." He thumbed at an organization chart on the wall, then a delivery schedule on the wall opposite, as if he'd rather hitch a ride from both.

"You're certain your efforts reduced nothing?" Ellie asked.

He looked away. Stared for a while at crumbling plaster on the wall. Looked back. "I cannot think of anything, Child, no. Would that I could. I honestly don't think our effort to expand it succeeded either. I don't think we changed it one way or another. I think the only thing we figured out was how to soak a party of five with rainwater at the local outdoor pasta joint, much good that did us. Or them."

"Did you have some partners?" Annie asked.

"Excuse me?"

"Partners. Other people in the —what'd you call it? — deal?"

"Hrmph," he said.

Sy said, "Answer the question."

"Huh-uh."

"Uh-huh."

He looked to the north. The A/C blew. He looked to Sy, stared at the man for a good, long while.

"The North Wind?" Sy asked.

The dwarf shot him a look of astonishment. "How… would?" Then looked back at the rattling air conditioning unit and at a bill pinned to the wall.

Sy appeared to follow the gaze of the dwarf to it, swallowed, and said. "Seemed to fit… uh… the bill."

Ellie said, "Oh yes. You'd need a great personified Boreas to help you on the way. To blow the clouds down. Haven't you read the poets? Langston Hughes? Ovid?"

He harrumphed. "Langston Hughes, bah! Well it's certainly true that it could help. I won't deny that riding wind could help." He looked to Sy, to the girls, then back to Sy and narrowed his eyes further.

In some way, this dwarf reminded Ellie of the bad parts of her father: all work, no play. "Where would we find him?"

"Wherever North Wind blows the strongest. Wherever you can stand at her back."

"He's a she?"

"Just cause it's cold and strong don't make the North Wind male."

Ellie said, "I like her already. But where would we have both such a strong northern wind and a shelter away from her?"

Sy said, "It's November."

Ellie said to the dwarf, "You really don't have anything for us, do you? Not a bit of information?"

The dwarf looked to Sy first, then to Annie and Ellie. "Afraid not. Sorry."

20

ST(I)LLBORN

Levi returned to the house shortly after the funeral. The cloud in his head swelled big enough he worried it might rain despair upon the place. The shame within — that he'd lost his new friend for — a lie. For a lie, of all things! He fished for books that might help, but his fingers trembled. He looked out the window: there in the awning, a mud dauber nest buzzed along with stinging things. Various elements of the case — its Pb and Au; its O2 and H2O — of the dead Angler King and Board who had interrogated him. Something was off that he couldn't place. As if they weren't looking correctly.

How could he do it without a friend? And more than that: hadn't he wanted enjoyment himself? Perhaps his self was not what he should have enjoyed. Perhaps his self should have enjoyed some object: a sunset or a run. Why'd he even need to look?

"You need some time away from the case?" The Author asked his back.

Levi could feel the weariness of the addiction and the case both under swollen eyes. He wanted to let Swevenfall ensnare him, sweep him off to Somnolory, spend some time *in somno*, realm of dreams. Of course, if resting, Levi couldn't work to finish up the … thing. He felt the Author *feeling him feel it* underneath those swollen eyes of his, all eyes on him and his exhaustion. So he sat down at the table with Sammi and let the Author bring out his copy of Time Stories.

Fine. He'd decide in a second.

Time Stories was a French boardgame where you play time traveling detectives. Levi wished he himself could go back in time and undo some of his mistakes on their case. Tell himself things like, "Refuse the cup the giant bully bass tries to give ya."

They played the game, but the scenario of its story had an undercurrent of addiction matching his own.

Unless that wasn't the case. Had that happened?

Perhaps it was the seawine. Mixing up the memories.

He looked at the board, the colors of the characters. Each of them trading little baggies of things, who knew what was inside? He could give the addiction up and be stone sober and hopefully finish the case or he could keep it, stay tired, flee Somnolory. Of course that meant remaining if not happy, then satisfied by the drug. Satisfied, yes. At least if he kept it, he wouldn't have to feel as crappy as he did withdrawing from it in the hospital. Though giving it up did appeal. He tried to remember what his life had felt like prior to seawine.

And then, in character, Sammi — from across the table — started saying things that also had meaning out of her boardgame character. Things that had specific meanings to him in real life, like, "When will you admit you have a problem Lev?" and "When will you just quit?" And "Yeah, you maybe could have solved it if you had your faculties."

It offended him, every word. He felt the dentals of her words in his own teeth, the labials in his tongue, which he bit. Shame on *her* for so publicly trying to shame him like that. Especially cause it *worked*. The shame welled up in him like a blossom of bad coffee and turned into something else. Not dignity. No, not. It wasn't awkward enough for that. It frothed inside him into a raging pride. Why would he ever even listen to such a fool as Sammi?

And so finally Levi said, "No."

The Author perked up.

"No what?" Sammi asked.

Levi shifted on soles. "No, I don't think I'll give it up."

Sammi spat. "You have to. I did."

"I don't have to do anything." He pointed to the board, but he wasn't talking about the game anymore than she. "I like my life the way it is."

"You're... You're just gonna rescue me and then do nothing about yourself?"

He didn't answer. He wouldn't answer.

The other players looked between them both awkwardly.

She threw her cards in everyone's faces. The tantrum had an impotent effect, wind resistance being what it is. The cards fell, so many helpless autumn leaves of black and white and red. They flipped their blue backs towards them as a break in their fluttering alchemy. She scattered the board's pieces, made an animal cry, and rushed the door. She shoved the outer door open. Behind it lay all of their coats and shoes, so the bottom of the door on the inside smushed against then snowdrift of wet fabric and rubber and leather slowly and awkwardly. In response, she snatched her coat, threw it on, slammed the door shut

Or tried to.

The coat had gotten between the door and the jam. So she shoved her coat out, tried to slam it again. The door bounced off a pencil in the doorframe. She screamed, "WHATEVER! ARGH!" She stomped down all the stairs with the door undramatically closed behind her.

"I'll get the door," the Author said. Locked it again to the green glow.

Levi in what he perceived as loneliness had already gone to the goblet. Had already filled it with seawine. Had already started his chugging. Finished. Started puking snails and catfish.

The Author watched him still. "You had that stuff in you when the building fell?"

Levi shook his head no.

"That's my goblet, Levi."

Levi shook his head no.

The Author led him around to the bookshelf. Pulled out the dictionary. "Then where's my goblet that hasn't moved in eons?"

Levi glanced, just for a moment, down at the goblet. He looked back up at the Author. "But why do you have it?"

"Research, for one. But it's not the seawine, it's how you use it. Few people know how to use it well. Very, very few of us use it responsibly. With temperance. The stakes of temperance get higher the harsher the substance. And seawine is mighty harsh, son."

Levi looked down at his puke-stained hands and, for the first time in his most childish voice, said, "I am too little for this."

"Yes. You're gonna need a lawyer. I'll call up old Rudy. I can't call the one my grandad hired cause Grandad represented himself, member? Of course you don't remember, silly me. But the man who represents himself in court has a fool for a lawyer. Grandad Remmy wasn't a fool. Most of the time," the Author said. "I'll call Rudy."

RUDY CHARLEMAGNE WAS A WONDERFUL YOUNG LAWYER FROM Boston who attended a liberal arts college up in New Hampshire. Along with some activists in NYC, he had helped end the policy whereby people in power who hired police to stop and frisk anyone that looked black or brown, and then sent them before a judge who wielded a squeaky hammer.

The mayor got his stormtroopers to stop people, pat down all of their private parts in search of guns and knives that didn't exist. Most people of color who went through the subway station or any public building got roughed up and patted down by the cops during those years. Rudy had helped put an end to that evil law with a hunger strike and a series of protests.

The lawyer showed up at the Author's apartment in a Hugo Boss suit, a strawberry pocky stick hitching a ride twixt his lips.

"Kid," he said, "let's see whatcha did wrong. Take a walk with me."

The city, even still, remained eminently walkable: a hill, a grocer, a pharmacy, a beer. Rudy took Levi to the scene of the collapse less than three full city blocks from where the Author lived (and took notes for stories on giant post-its). Rudy had already obtained access to the building to inspect it. He pulled out his phone, showing Levi some pictures.

"Looks like, from what I can tell, they have evidence of you drinking another draft. Whether you got that one from the Author's house or not, whether from a fridge in a house the size of a room or a wet bar the size of a house, I neither know, nor care. But you were one of the last to see the Angler King and now he's dead. He's dead, Levi, dead and you were last to see him. Or at least you're the last to use the Angler King as a means by which to see.

"That's gonna look bad for you. You realize The Board could send you to jail for a really, really long time? We're going to take you before the board tomorrow and you're going to need to stay away from that cup. No seawine. No coffee. No slathering fish mud on a pair of glasses so you see through a glass darkly. Nothing. Got it?"

Levi nodded. He blushed. Tears came to his eyes. "Wait… are you magic?"

Rudy laughed at him and said, "No."

"And you know about Overmorrow?"

"And Bellwether, Yestereve, Wayfare, Averrue, Yondertryst, Almshouse. Way more magics than those."

"How?" Levi asked.

"St(i)llborn," Rudy said. "It's that thing Dr. Giltner talked about in his poem."

"Who is Dr. Giltner?"

"Another storyweaver. We are legion. Being st(i)llborn happens to a lot of us."

He had said the "I" weird enough that even without audible pronunciation, Levi caught something *off* about it. "Style-born?

St... aisle... born? Is that like that the accidental virgin birth insurance policy the Author talked about?"

"Stillborn with an I."

"What's the difference?"

"I'm a person now," he said. "Just haven't really moved beyond that. Anyways, yes. I'm a st(i)llborn."

"Styleborn?" Levi asked. "Like being born with style?"

"I suppose I have a certain style too." Rudy looked down at the three-piece suit he wore down to the law mines every day. "And, come to think of it, I was born stylet-aware, but without one in hand. I can't do magic even though I *can* see it."

Levi thought of his sisters. Would they cast him out? His magical family? He really hadn't wanted to give up the seawine. He really had. Both. It helped, in the end, to have the decision made for him. But he accepted it. Grabbed hold of Rudy's hand. Now to tell the truth and rid himself of this addiction.

21

RIDABLE WINDS

Ellie sulked as the girls took the ferry back north to Pier 78 at Hudson River Park. She didn't want to have failed with the Air Conditioning Union. Here she was: a failed detective who had no leads to follow. She cried a little as the cold air off the waters hit her face. That wasn't true, maybe she was spiraling: she'd learned about the North Wind. The East Wind taunted her: faceless, mindless, formless. Unknown to them unlike the North Wind. She followed along aimlessly, listless every step, unsure what options lay before her. Ellie needed leads.

Sy escorted both girls along the streets, beyond Madison Square Garden, past herds of humans and halfmans. Pizza dealers tossed their pies and ridable quintapeds carried red bolts of eerie cloth, none of them nervous about what bothered Ellie.

The orange reflector plastic chimneys — construction barrel tubes towering an entire story high — spewed sewage fog as ethereal as Ellie felt inside. Past these, they made their way to doors with art deco in the metal: all right angles as if molded and designed by Tolkien's dwarves (not real world dwarves nor Overmorrow giants dwarfing their statures).

Interesting choice, the building rising up before them. If that's where they met the North Wind… maybe North Wind really was wise? The North Wind, even innocent, could have ideas about the case. Ellie could question her about the case. Or about herself. Her… Self… perhaps that was the way to go?

"Empire State Building," Ellie said.

"You're close. Wrong building," Sy said.

"I love Sleepless in Seattle," Annie said.

"Whatsit?" the newsman asked.

Ellie smiled for the first time in a while. It hurt, to smile like that.

"A *classic* film. Two fall in love and live at the top of the build-ing," Annie said.

"*Met* at the top of the building, Annie," Ellie corrected.

"Ah," Annie said. "Sure. Lived. Loved. Same thing."

Sy said, "Better to have the former and the latter than never to have had the latter at all."

Both girls squinted in the matching way sisters only can and said, "What?"

Sy said, "We're not going to Empire State, but right idea."

As Ellie debated which way to go in her mind, they followed Sy up the avenue for several blocks — past people chowing down on cookies and far, far too many young men in slim-fitting blue suits. All of these young men got in the way and the girls had to duck and dive around them all. They came to the Rockefeller Center instead. They went inside, took the stairs into the base-ment, and walked into the Top of the Rock tour.

They bought their tickets, rode the elevator to the top and waited for the lunch crowd to thin out.

"Why here?" Ellie asked.

Sy pointed to the north. Almost nothing stood in their way as they looked past Central Park into the north, all the way up to Yonkers. Bonkers, Yonkers. An open, higher north face in the city, closer to the cold, up in the teeth of winds.

Ellie focused on Central Park.

Great boulders. Tiny people played on them. The rowboats in

the lake where all of this started. Structures to the west included a rooftop with a new funnel. Various museums to the east: the giant layer cake of the Guggenheim, the sprawling labyrinth of the Met. The wind was bitter iced and blinding. Made of light that brushed the lenses of your eyes with irritating vitriol. Enough to make you cry. Enough to chase those tears away again. Enough you had to cry all over again just to catch its blinding blast. Wet and dry and wet and then red. Nothing — not the curvature of earth — stood in the way of that glacial blast coming down from the Northern Poles.

"Come," Sy said, and led them around to the sheltered southern exposure.

Annie and Ellie heard nothing but the wind, right near the eastern corner of the wall, blowing past.

Herself? Or her case?

What would she ask about? She searched within and as she did she noticed Sy searching.

Sy looked around before her. Most of the tourists had gone. He looked down towards a door to nowhere with a hinge on it. The door sat folded upon the side of the building there. The tiniest hole — a pinhole camera puncture — was in it. He nodded towards that pinhole.

Ellie grabbed hold of the doorknob and looked at Sy. Who nodded. Ellie flung wide the door, which moved easily enough, but it opened in such a way as to cover the entire walkway on that corner of the roof of the TOP OF THE ROCK. She heard a voice again, close to her ear. She felt about with her hand. Her fingers brushed the little pinhole.

Against that hole she laid her ear and heard a whispering voice as clear and soft and high as a tiny bell hammer. "What do you intend — my little banished child of Eden — closing up my wind tunnel?"

"What wind tunnel?" asked Ellie.

"You opened a door in the path of my tunnel and now there's naught but a little hole for me as egress and ingress. You see this tiny hole?"

"This little hole?" Ellie asked. "It isn't a tunnel, it's just a tiny pinhole in a big old door atop a big old building."

"I did not call it *a* wind tunnel. I called it *mine*."

"Can't be a wind tunnel," Annie said to the whispering voice. "Not a big underground run for wind to blow through."

"That's why I made this sky tunnel."

Ellie said, "You can't have a tunnel in the sky. They're underground." She needed to keep this door open as a shield for when the North Wind came. This whisper was starting to annoy her. And anyways, which question would she ask?

"I am under my grounds," the whisper replied. "And I want a tunnel to pass through."

Ellie sighed. They could be stuck all day debating with this whisper. Only in Overmorrow. "But you've made a tunnel into a large tourist destination where tons of people are. A tunnel through a very important landmark."

"Well, your mayor put three tunnels into my den, and you yourself with your siblings dug three tunnels into my bolt hole back in Joplin."

"But … my father said, when mother wanted him to make a tunnel for her blackberry bushes, that it was against the law, for it would get into the Electrician's tunnels. I heard something about tunnels through the blackberry bushes themselves, but mayhap that's a different thing."

The voice laughed. "That law would have trouble catching me. And The Law who brings that law."

Annie tsked. "Are you above the law?"

Ellie cut the question off saying, "If it isn't right, you shouldn't do it."

The voice chuckled. "I am so tall I am above THAT law. But not Law, no no. Of course not."

"Sounds like you have a tall house," said Annie.

"Clouds are in it, not the top."

Ellie started, spine ramrod. This whispering creature had given her an idea: she needed to know her role in all of this, just like the whisper. So questions about herself long before questions about the case might yield more fruit. She slowly said, "You can hardly expect all of us to keep a tunnel in our tower for you. Why don't you make a tunnel into Madison Square Garden?"

"Nobody fashions a window over a dog fighting ring or a cesspool. I like to end up in nice places on the other side of my tunnels. Just look behind you."

The girls did. There sprawled the better part of midtown, the older buildings in the midst of Manhattan, the great towers of Wall Street beyond, and the great sea beyond that, a canopy of bright glass and bright steel. All things bright and beautiful.

"Madison Square Garden is a nice enough view," Annie said.

"It's not the view I care about, but what's within. Viewing's only there to see something. Open the door."

"If I did," Annie said, "You see… the North Wind will blow right in our faces."

"I am the North Wind."

Both girls cooed. Ellie said, "I knew it."

The North Wind asked, "Did you?"

"No."

"Then why did you say you did?"

"I was ashamed to say I didn't know something."

"But child," the North Wind said, "there is no shame in ignorance. The only shame lies in saying a thing arrogantly when you do not know whether it's true or false. You neither know, nor think you know, and that is wonder. Say that."

"You're right. I neither know nor think that I know," Ellie said.

"Good. Now open the door."

Ellie blushed. At least she was still technically seeking her goal of learning something about herself.

"Do you promise not to blow in our faces?" Annie asked.

"I cannot promise that for I am made to blow in your faces. For what purpose are you two meant?"

Ellie didn't like that question, however much she sought its answer. She put her tongue upon her tooth and thought up some distraction. "You'll give us toothaches."

Sy nodded vigorously and scribbled notes. "Sinus infections."

"Whatever, whiny," Ellie said.

"You'll make my ears hurt," Annie said.

"What would I be without a tunnel?" asked the North Wind.

"I don't know," Ellie said. "But I think it'll be worse for us little girls than for someone so big as you."

"No. You shall not be the worse, I promise. You'll be the better for it. Just believe what I say and do as I tell you."

"But what if she did it?" Sy whispered to the girls. "What if The North Wind committed the Overmorrow restrictions and killed off the Angler King? She'll blow us clean off this wall!"

Ellie ignored him and thought more about herself and the North Wind's self. "Well, we CAN cinch up our scarves and hoods." They did, grabbed hold of the edge of the great door, and slammed it against the tension. It took some effort until the North Wind took over. The door slammed the rest of the way. KABLOONG. OONG. OOONG. A great whistling, whirling, growling warhammer of cold struck their chests.

They scrambled and tumbled to cover themselves and turn their backs to it, worried it would blow them over the edge into thin air and a quick plunge to their deaths. No door stood between them and the voice. They feared not. But they felt… odd. What a weird person to live "Out of Doors" and still think getting outside was really getting inside.

The voice started up again. Gentler, but six times as large and loud as before. A bit like their mother. "What are your names, little girls?"

"Ellie?" asked Ellie.

"You're unsure?" The North Wind asked.

Ellie didn't want to say *yes*, but she realized she was indeed unsure. Why?

"Annie," said Annie.

"Sy," said Sy.

"What funny names. Are you a little girl, Sy?"

He blushed. "Well, no."

The girls giggled.

"Why are you not sure of your name, child?" The North Wind asked.

Ellie said, "I… don't know."

"Funny names," The North Wind said. "Funny indeed."

"They're very nice names," Annie said and stamped.

"I don't know," the North Wind said.

Annie reared up a little. "I do."

"Do you know to whom you speak?" The North Wind asked.

"No," Annie said, and she didn't. To know a person's name is not to know the person's self.

"I mustn't be angry with you both, but you had better take a look before you continue to act a fool's act on Broadway. We have plenty of those, few enough make a decent living."

"Well then teach us, Mr. North Wind," Annie said.

Sy slapped his own face, then buried it in both gloved hands.

"I'm not Mr. North Wind," said the voice.

"You told us you were the North Wind," the girls said.

"I did not say MISTER North Wind."

"Well, then, I do," Annie said. "Mom tells me to be polite, mister."

"Then let me tell you I don't think it at all polite to say MISTER to me. Take your heads out of those hoods and look at what you've just called MISTER."

"No!" Ellie was half frightened, now.

As soon as Ellie had shouted, a horrid blast of hoary wind crashed into the three of them — alone there on the tower — and swept all of their outer clothes off them so that they stood there merely in pajama shorts and t-shirts while their coats blew off down below.

"Hey, that had my sieve!" Annie said.

Sy's pajamas had tiddlywinks and penguins on them.

They three looked up.

Ellie gasped from the cold and the shock of the realization: she had not known either herself or the North Wind at all, however much she had wanted to interrogate those who knew Charlie but whom she had not met.

Leaning over them was the large, beautiful, pale face of a woman. Then Ellie remembered what the dwarf had said. The North Wind's dark eyes looked a splidget angry. But a trembling in that soft upper lip made her seem as if she were on the verge of tears. Away from her head, as if underwater, streamed out her black hair in every direction, so that the shadows of the towers around her looked almost... made of her hair. Her mighty beauty entranced them all. They swayed together with her hair. Her hair flailed, spun, withered, recoiled, waved, floated, then gathered itself out of the shadows and fell down about her as a veil. Her face looked out of the veil as a moon peeks through cloud. Light came from her eyes to illumine her face in that darkness.

The wind ceased.

"Will you ride with me now, Annie and Ellie?"

"On what subway?" Annie asked.

The North Wind laughed.

"Or what police horse can carry us?" Ellie asked. "I have never called the cavalry, but I suppose Levi would like to."

Both girls cast their faces down at that. Levi wasn't here – wasn't anywhere, really, except as UnLevi — and they worried about him. Especially if they had mostly killed him and not fixed him. Annie worried for Levi's physical health, Ellie about the state of his mind.

The North Wind got to giggling the sort of laughter that shook the very foundations of the Rockefeller Center. Oblivious patrons at the other end of the tower's roof grasped desperately for a handhold or a foothold along the ledges there. Laughter that shakes the earth. Laughter that shakes even the earth's graves.

"Come with me now, girls? I am truly sorry I had to be so rough."

"I will," Annie said.

"Yes," Ellie said. "Though I'm unsure of my standing."

"You never know," said the North Wind. "But you can be sure of my presence, and that's enough to stand upon."

"But," Annie asked, "how can we get our coats back?" She

looked over the edge. It was a long, long way down. "And my sieve?"

"Never mind that."

"Won't we freeze?"

"No one's cold with the North Wind."

"I thought everyone was?" Ellie asked.

"Common mistake," the North Wind said and smirked. "Most people are cold not because they are with the North Wind, but without it or against it. When I batter those who are stubbornly set against me, then they grow cold. Come."

"We will come, ma'am," said Ellie. "Can you teach me a bit more about us? About me? About why we can see like this?"

The North Wind scoffed in Ellie's face. "Don't call me ma'am like that. Call me my name, respectfully, child: North Wind."

"You're so beautiful, North Wind," Annie said. "I was ready to follow you anywhere, and that's why I would like to call you ma'am. Respectfully."

"Don't go along with everything that seems beautiful the first chance you get, sweet Annie."

"But what's beautiful can't be bad. You're not bad, are you North Wind?"

Ellie dogpiled her question on Annie's and asked, "Aren't we beautiful?" For this was a part of herself she'd been unsure about.

"It depends. It is true that The Good and Beauty and Truth and Being are all synonyms for one another. But a beautiful thing can sometimes grow bad if it does enough bad, and in that case, if it started out beautiful, sometimes it takes a good long while for inner badness to infect the outer beauty. Sometimes it takes a long time for the rot on the inside of a willow to reach the bark and beautiful boughs. That doesn't mean the seemingly beautiful tree won't crash before it's truly dead. Little girls may make big mistakes if they go after something merely because it *appears* pretty. The pretty is not the same as the beautiful. And little boys *often* make this mistake. Imagine climbing such a rotten tree! Especially if the beautiful rotten thing is a young man or young woman."

Ellie said, "We'll go with you because you're good and beautiful too."

"Ah, but again, what if I look ugly without being bad? Look ugly because I'm too busy making ugly things beautiful? What then, Ellie? What if I feel the fairer but look the fouler?"

The girls had no answer.

The wind blasted the three of them.

Sy winced.

"I will tell you then," the North Wind said. "If you see me with my face all black, don't afright. If you see me flapping wings like a bat's, big as the sky, fear not. If you hear me raging ten times worse than your brother when he's foaming at the mouth cause of—"

"Our brother is foaming at the mouth," Ellie said. "How did you know?"

"Ah. Is he rabid?"

"He was given something by the Angler King."

"I see," the North Wind said. She paused a great long time. Then she said, "Yes, even if I am worse than this. Even if you see me looking in people's windows—" she gestured to the towers of New York "—while most New Yorkers use telescopes for such activities, even then, you must believe that I am doing my work. If I become a python or a lynx, a Kodiak bear or a great old lion — mane shaved or mane intact — never let me go. Luck dragon or phoenix. If you hang on, you'll know me even if I look nothing like Boreas."

"Boreas?"

"One of my truer names. Yes?"

"Yes," the girls said.

Sy nodded. Timidly.

"Can you teach me about me?" Ellie asked.

"Come then." She turned into a great whale with wings the length of ten whales. They were going to ride over New York atop a flying whale? Were they crazy? They hopped on, Sy most reluctant, and took off.

"Do you know about Overmorrow?" Ellie asked, soon as she

was aboard the flying whale that was The North Wind. "What it did to me?"

The North Wind chuckled. "Of course. Anyone in my world is IN my world because of Overmorrow."

"Even babies? We experienced it — well all of us but Annie, more or less — without knowing what we were getting into."

"Did you?" North Wind asked.

"Well, we decided to anyways. Does that still count?"

"And can you name, child, a single decision in life you fully understand, even now? Or their orders? And what of the decisions made before you could decide, but are very much a part of you?"

Both girls could not answer right then, though, as they rose up in the air, tucked into the streaming white hair and feather-down on the back of the whale. The earth rushed past like a river or a roiling ocean. Stock and stone and stream fled beneath, and a din of something like a zoo stood up in the silence. Either the Central Park Zoo or the Bronx Zoo, Annie couldn't tell.

Breach and branch and towers and Brooklyn passed behind and hushed away in a great torrent. A roar rose up as the wind forced the Hudson down south to meet the rushing rising tide, a Boreal bore tide.

Yet there at the back of the North Wind, the girls and Sy felt nothing. No stirring. No bitter cold. No whipping of well-manicured hairdos.

Perfect calm met them, sounds of the chaos behind. They looked over the edge of the North Wind's body: apartments rushed up and fell away, houses stacked on top of apartment complexes, and the winding twist of special architecture met them there.

In the midst of this madness, the North Wind said, "Well?"

"I'm sorry?" Ellie asked.

"I asked which of your decisions do you truly understand?"

"I guess… I guess none of them, North Wind," Ellie said.

"And who are the wisest people in your life?"

"An old man — my elder — named Chris. Another named Pier

Giorgio. Both of them take really, really good care of their neighbors."

"And when did they decide to start acting so wise?"

Ellie stirred over the slime of the whale skin. She picked up her hands and opened and closed them, noting the slimy glueyness, the spittle strings stretching betwixt her fingers. "About the age they started being able to think. And choose."

"But weren't they thinking and choosing their whole lives?"

"Well yes," Ellie said. "They were, but they didn't understand all of the choices."

"And have they arrived?"

"No," Annie said. "They can grow up more. Everyone can always grow up more, as long as they aren't obsessed with being a grownup. I guess I mean everyone can be more childlike."

"So you're telling me they haven't fully understood their decision?"

"Um … yes," Annie guessed. Ellie knew she was guessing.

"So then why would it matter if babies couldn't understand Overmorrow's nudge toward the real? Don't uncorrupted churches dedicate babies? Don't Jews circumcise?" The girls had no answer. "Don't Park Slope mothers who've said they hate babies get pregnant? And when pregnant, do these same self-declared antibreeders give their babies classical music while inside the womb and hand-mashed organic fruits from their food co-op? Don't they take prenatal vitamins?"The girls had no answer. "And if those babies, born in your world, were truly made for ours, wouldn't you want their parents — in faithfulness and wisdom and by swift and sure action — to raise their children as children of our world?"

The girls nodded. Especially Ellie. She thought and thought about that. About being not merely children of the Wrights, her parents, but also children of another world. About their parents leaving them. Or, rather, being forced to leave them for security reasons. About whether that could be faithful. Or wise. It was certainly swift and sure for their parents.

Were they being raised for another world?

She felt the slick back of the flying whale once more, the wind in her hair as she soared above New York. What else was she being raised for?

Perhaps… perhaps her parents hadn't left her with some crazy babysitter. Perhaps they had intended all of this. Perhaps they, trusting in the care of the Author, knew that Ellie would forever become a certain kind of person in the care of the Overmorrow waters.

Perhaps her parents had given her a sort of Fuseparents: parents of her pouring, of her oblation, of her washing, of her goodwater. Gothparents. God parents. Mom and Dad had said they trusted the couple. Could she actually trust the Author and the Maker?

"Overmorrow is awakening for the first time," the North Wind said. "Greater than that first cry when you come out of the birth canal and breathe your first breath as an infant: your being from one world — the world of your womb — enters another world of wind and breath — the womb of all worlds."

Their hair and smallclothes stirred slightly in a chill breeze. Ellie felt something stir even deeper in her soul, an echo of what possessed her on the boat lake in Central Park. As if, after a long run, she'd gotten a second wind.

"And if you could come from the world of wind and breath and awaken in a world of spirit and vision and dreams-made-real, wouldn't you want to get your first gasp of real air over with as quickly as possible so you could go on learning, go on growing up?"

Ellie said, "Suppose so."

"Then it seems there are two kinds. Those who have merely grown old in Overmorrow," the North Wind said. Sy grumbled. "And on the other hand, those who continue to grow up in Overmorrow."

They rode for some time.

"North Wind?" Annie asked. "Has Overmorrow shrunk?"

"No, child."

That startled the girls.

22

A THOUSAND SPLINTERS

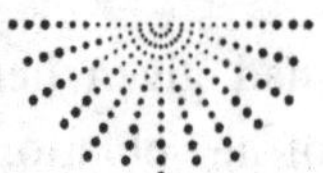

Ellie felt shaken, still wanting to ask questions about herself, but Annie continued, ignorant of Ellie's feelings. "You haven't noticed the clouds over the Central Park Lake growing smaller?"

The North Wind laughed. "Well of course, child. But conflate not one season's rain with Overmorrow."

"One season?" Sy asked. "One season! This has been happening for the last ten years! Worse and worse, shrinking and shrinking, but to shrink so much, so fast: surely this is the work of someone nefarious. Someone terribly clever and nefarious."

"I have no doubt of nefarious interference in the rains," the North Wind said. "But again, child—" this time she was speaking to elder Sy as if to a toddler "—conflate not one season's rain with Overmorrow."

The elder newspaper man scoffed. "A season? Spring only lasts a blink, not a decade. This is careful planning, this."

"A decade, too, lasts only a blink, not a millennium, child."

Sy hesitated. Blinked. Opened his mouth. Closed it. Opened it again. But he had nothing to say.

"Overmorrow rains come and go." The North Wind's voice

now boomed while intimate, boomed within them and without them all at once. "Overmorrow dews, Overmorrow living waters, Overmorrow cisterns (though one will return in the future at the Montauk lighthouse), Overmorrow fountains and geysers and single source aquifers. They come, they go. The waters of the golden bough run throughout the golden water's cycle, not some petty rain cycle. They move as moves a spirit. Or a wind like me."

Sy gaped like a hooked fish.

The North Wind didn't stop. "So, no, I do not conflate the shrinking of local clouds with any reduction of the efficacy or longevity of Overmorrow. Either universally. Or throughout time. Or even here and now. Overmorrow has existed, exists, and will exist with or without you, for those who have the eyes to see and ears to hear and nose to catch its scent. Those with a head on their shoulders to feel all the tremoring coming on strong. And those who know Overmorrow will pass the Overmorrow sight down to one another, time after time after time."

"Like with me?" Annie said. "My name and soul and body?"

The North Wind nodded her whale head.

"Like the Author did for Levi?" Ellie asked. The land whisked away below their flight upon the great blue whale in the great blue rain. Towers passed beneath like so many tiny twigs.

"You have met the Author?" the North Wind asked.

"Yes."

"What an honor!"

"...I... guess?" Annie asked. "He's a nerd."

Ellie said, "Goes off in his own little world a lot."

"Of course he does! What else would you expect from a Starling?"

"A what?" Ellie asked.

"A Storyweaver."

"A what?" Annie asked this time.

"Worldmaker. What a gift for one like you to meet one like him in the flesh, in his auctophany."

The girls stared at the creature. Why did it care so much?

"What did the Author do for your Levi?" the North Wind asked.

"Our brother," Ellie said.

"Ah."

"When the rains didn't take for us, The Author poured tap water through a golden sieve. He dunked Levi in a tub full of Overmorrow," Ellie said. "Then me."

"Why not Annie?"

Ellie looked at her sister. "I don't know. Maybe because she was soaked through? Or younger?"

"Wow," the North Wind said, "I had not heard it existed still. I had thought it lost to time."

"What?"

"The golden sieve. There are many golden instruments. But this one was lost."

"He made it," Ellie said. "From scratch, I think? Or summoned it?"

"Very curious," the North Wind said. "Hrm."

"What's so important about gold?" Ellie asked. "Is he greedy?"

"It's more about what it means than what it's made of. Most things — most people — are."

Annie pointed ahead and frowned in despair. "It was in my pocket until you blew it away, the sieve."

The North Wind grunted and flew them hard towards where their coats had fallen. Down and fast into the wind tunnel, the great blue winged whale barreled them towards the pedestrians. They clung to her. The North Wind paid this no mind, but said, "Yes, I suppose you have as pure an Overmorrow experience as anyone, Ellie. What happened to your brother is a way to pass it down without the rains."

Sy growled and shouted over the rush of air. "But clouds have shrunk all the same! People don't so easily discover Overmorrow on their own, don't you think? They don't just randomly run into it these days. Some malign genius is at work here!"

"Of course," the North Wind said. "To be expected every now

and again. Illumination comes and goes with the generations. Some want to darken the illuminated. Anti-limners. Wait a hundred and fifty years, it will shift again. If not then, in five hundred after three prime cycles conclude."

Ellie pounded her fist into the blubber of the whale and felt ashamed she had, but even worse that her punching did no damage. *I am solving this crime*, she insisted vainly as she punched. The heat went out of her. With how the North Wind passively received the hit, she had half a mind to ignore the whole mystery and ride the wind, let her take her where she may. But then what about her witness? "You haven't seen anything?" Ellie asked. "Now, I mean? Within the last few years?"

"Hrmm," the North Wind said. "Dwarves tried to barter with me to govern the Air Conditioning Union, something about getting air to go in the right direction in the right building and in the right speed and place. But I am no household fanblade nor windward scythe." The North Wind's growl disturbed a manhole far down below. A yellow taxi fell inside like a sun whose shadow didn't fit.

They rode on.

She punched into the wind again, but it was as fruitless as punching the whale blubber. This whole thing felt as awkward as the AC Union. The dwarves had refused to answer poor Mr. Sy's questions. "What did all of the air control have to do with the clouds?"

"Clouds are the children of winds and seas, winds and lakes. They grow up, and when they come of age, they weep as human children weep. They wither into cirrus things, and their bodies return to the winds and seas, as do human children."

Annie asked, "That's the only way a cloud has a life cycle?"

The North Wind rumbled. It sounded like cold thunder in a blizzard. Folks below ran for cover. "This question is wiser than you know child, but to give you the right words in the right order: a cloud's life cycle decides how its mass flux turns to cloud cover, thereby setting Earth's albedo."

"Its what?" Annie asked.

"Its whiteness that reflects sun. A shallow cumulus cloud, for instance, is it a bubble or a plume? Is it active or forced? These are a wind's questions. Clouds, you see, switch between active and forced, but act more like bubbles than plumes. Lab-made clouds are more active and plumelike."

"What's a plume?" Annie asked.

"One liquid moving through another. Have you seen videos of colored liquid in white liquid?"

Annie hadn't.

Ellie had.

Sy looked searched the horizon for something else entirely. For what?

Annie said, "A bubble is water with air that floats."

"Yes."

"Why do bubbles float?" she asked.

"No one knows," The North Wind said.

"Even scientists?"

"Especially scientists. Scientists vary wildly. In your time and place, they're shooting lasers at bubbles and have hit the fifth dimension, but no answers. Eventually they'll think they'll find answers, but no real ones. So yes, clouds tend to wither and return to the winds and seas. Whether it's from popping the bubble or disturbing the plume. They return as human kids return."

"Overmorrow too?" Ellie asked and, thinking of her own mortality. "And will I?"

"Overmorrow rains return in a way dissimilar, and you too, child. But not all Overmorrow waters—"

"Are Overmorrow rains," Annie said. "You're sure didn't do it?"

"Shrink Overmorrow? Child, you cannot—"

"Shrink these rains," Annie said. "Did you shrink *this storm*?"

"Oh. Well, no. Why would I?"

"Did the dwarves?" Ellie asked and then a darker question formed about herself. It felt… disgusting. Shameful.

Sy scribbled. Furiously. His journal was jerking left and right.

"It seemed to me the dwarves wanted to grow the rains," the North Wind said, still darting towards the south, where the coats had tumbled and tumbled still.

Ellie let that darker question bloom in her soul and, horrified at the shame she felt of the evil in herself, decided to ask it: "Did… did we?"

"What?"

"Did my presence shrink them?"

The North Wind laughed. "A small, sweet, pitiful thing like you, child? You couldn't possibly."

If a child could become wind, Ellie would have then, what for all the relief she breathed out. A couple of clothes danced on the wind ahead, ghosts of themselves. "Could the dwarves have failed terribly and done the opposite of their intent?"

The North Wind made a sound like BAROOM, clearing her boreal throat. "I suppose… I suppose that is possible. But those dwarves are crafty."

"Like Tolkien dwarves?" Ellie asked.

The North Wind chuckled. "No, no, child, Aulë exists not in this megacosm other than as a memory. That creature Aulë belongs to another storyweaver's robe and auctophany. You can only get to there, as anywhere outside the megacosm, from Gergia, with counsel approval, and access to that wing of the Archive. Ideally escorted by our Starling's auctophany himself. Or you could learn the old, slow way."

"What's that?"

"Reading Tolkien's books. Not even I have that much access beyond those books except in key parts of Tolkien's imagination which, frankly, disapprove of me and my kin in certain ways."

"Who is Aulë?"

"The maker of Tolkien's dwarves. He did not make Overmorrow dwarves. Ours are corrupted from their height."

Ellie listened instead of answering. She had nothing to offer other than sadness. She wanted to cry for a creature bent lower than its purpose. And though relieved, she felt frustrated that she and Annie had gotten no further. She looked at Sy and felt the man was useless. This annoyance saddened her further, for she wanted — needed — good help.

The North Wind said, "If our dwarves made an error, it was pursuing this with such tenacity they ruined it for everyone: to grow the rains as *rains*, not as Overmorrow. Their dreams for what it could be — not what it is — go poorly when it's wonder, restricted."

"I wonder," Annie said.

Sy shuffled his feet.

Ellie laughed a short, curt laugh and asked, "So nothing went wrong?"

"I did not say that," the North Wind said. The howling around the air bubble of their aerodynamic ride grew louder, shriller, as they picked up speed. "If something *they* did went wrong, it made rains bigger, not smaller."

"Why would someone want to shrink such a wonderful thing as Overmorrow?" Annie asked.

"They shrank not Overmorrow," The North Wind repeated yet again. "Are you—?"

Annie said, "Why would someone shrink *these* rains?"

The North Wind howled low and somber like. A Boreal whistle? Then she went still. "Perhaps one who does not want wonder to grow in the world. Perhaps one who wants to hoard all potential wonder. Perhaps one who wants wonder to grow in a very specific way. Perhaps one precious with memories." She waited a beat. "Perhaps the East Wind grew bored."

"Bored?" Annie asked.

"East Wind?" Ellie asked.

"Yes, bored," the North Wind said. "Have you never done anything impulsive due to boredom, sweet Annie?"

Ellie raged inside, "Well of course. Once she—"

Annie slugged her sister in the arm.

Ellie angrily added, "Then once I—"

Annie slugged her again.

"She-once-shoved-Levi-into-the-lake!"

"LEVI!" Annie said. "Take us to Brooklyn RIGHT NOW."

"The North Wind shall not be commanded by a child."

"AHHHHH… I'm sorry. Please?"

"Let us go." They hung on for dear life. Ellie, less deterred and less afeared, looked at the list she had safety-pinned inside her vest. She opened that vest wider, uncapped her sharpie with her teeth, went to kiss the cap onto the end of the sharpie. It slipped, fell to the earth.

"N—"

The North Wind caught it and blew it back up alongside them, up in the air in a great spiral and slammed it — laser fast — into the end of the sharpie with a miniature spear cyclone. Ellie read and crossed off items as she read:

⋙⋘

1. ~~INTERVIEW ANGLER KING, PREFERABLY WITH LEVI PRESENT.~~

   2. ~~Interview Boreas, as the witches suggested.~~

   3. ~~Interview private water CEO.~~

   4. ~~Interview A/C union.~~

   5. Check cauldron for residue and test with someone who knows potions.

Yes, Overmorrow couldn't be stopped. But the local rains were still being stolen somehow, restricted *locally*. She still needed to test it.

   6. Where were our parents?

She really stared at number six. She didn't know what to do with it, but it welled up like a great, slow bubble in a vat of oil or maybe even molasses in her chest. Something viscous and black and putrefied. Had it been months? She looked out over the leaves. Were they changing? Still no sign of mom and dad. *They had promised.* They probably should have told them *precisely* how long they'd be gone. Precisely. Ellie didn't feel abandoned, she just felt like this was the most she had ever been expected to trust them both. What a huge trust.

Sure, the kids were managing. Coping. It was just odd and

there was nothing for it, nothing for seeing their parents. Would she slip up still more without them? The best way was to move forward. She needed more leads for that to happen. Lucky for her, her own list said:

7. Ask newspaper man for more leads.

8. See if centralized board knows something of Oblivion's movements.

9. Separate warlocks from witches.

10. Buy Author some more toilet paper. He's out again.

11. Learn Akkadian. Use to decipher runes.

She laughed at that. The simple statement implied *years* of work. A doctoral program. And why not?

12. Tell backpack it is leaking again and we expect more from backpacks.

"North Wind?" she asked softly. "May we please stop by a bodega and go back to Central Park?"

Annie asked, almost at a shriek: "What are you doing?"

"Of course, dear," North Wind said to Ellie.

"What? What, what?" Annie asked.

Ellie needed time to process what The North Wind had said, needed time to be able to move forwards. She'd tried to ask about the case and got nothing much at all, and that honestly devastated her, knowing she couldn't really move much further. "Easy, Annie. I'm sure Levi will be fine. He's with the Author. Let's go get what we need first."

"No, no, no," Annie said.

"Trust me, sister. You're feeling the memory of shoving him into the lake, I think he'll be okay."

Annie looked at her. The look told of how much trust she had left, how much trust it had taken to go this long without her parents, this long with these new godparents. How much she was trusting them and how much she didn't want to have to trust Ellie for something huge.

Ellie looked at the slimy whale back of the North Wind. "And The North Wind's also right: you don't have your boon, Annie." What did Ellie need? To find her place in this case. It felt like the whole interview route went cold. Perhaps more evidence? Back to the scene of the crime.

The North Wind giggled and dove them towards the street level and a great number of cardboard signs, plastic orange barriers, and flocks of pigeons.

She looked at her list again: check cauldron for residue. Buy Author toilet paper. Learn Akkadian. Those were non-interview options she saw. Akkadian would take forever. Why even write *that* down instead of *find an interpreter*? Did she have what she needed for the cauldron? She wasn't sure. Toilet paper would be easiest, but useless to the case. But she could do toilet paper first, then talk Annie into the other. Find a new backpack. It wouldn't help a whit. Might give her more time to think, though.

Folks passed on the street in various winter clothes. Hordes of black woolen trench coats and puffer coats. Some had wrapped in stylish horse blankets. Others dressed scantily in sequins, keeping warm only God knows how.

The North Wind flew them down toward the outside of a large bodega hiding under the hunter green painted plywood of a great scaffolding at the base of a great tower. Always something to fix in New York, particularly perfectly good classic architecture. If it ain't broke, New York fixes it until it is like the last eleven presidents.

As the three started to land, the people below (fleeing from the front of Lady Wind), got caught in the great wind tunnel and found themselves blown every single way. The rumble of the turbulence rattled their rears like a colossal horse. WWI-style softback backpacks were blown open, scattering storyboards to the wind. Hardbacked briefcases spilled out fifteen kinds of sampler lipstick from a pyramid scheme display. Folks immediately tripped on the lipsticks.

Right in front of them, all of their coats and outer clothes fluttered down.

"Thy boon," a still, small voice whispered.

"Oh wow, thanks!" Annie robed herself once more and checked her pocket. The sieve was still there. "Wow."

"Never lose a boon. Particularly one lost so long. You always need a boon in a story, story girl."

The girls and Sy disembarked from the back of the North Wind and headed into the store for toilet paper.

"I don't *understand*," Annie said. "Why aren't we going to Levi?"

Ellie said, "Now I think whatever happened to Levi is the same sort of thing that killed the Angler King. Or they're connected somehow."

"I thought the Angler King hurt Levi?"

"He did," she said. "But I think it's all connected to the same rot Oblivion keeps spreading. In fact, I think Uncle Corey's in on it, much as he drinks. He probably even made Levi sick with his addiction. Uncle Corey's the king of sickness. But there's no way to know for sure unless we get a sample of the stuff in the cauldron. We need a solid bottle made of something containing the least amount of Overmorrow possible. And maybe toilet paper. Or a sponge." Yes, toilet paper could do double duty.

Annie touched her eyebrows, which had started to grow back in all prickly. "The cauldron I exploded?"

"The cauldron you exploded."

"Sweet beans and juicy juicy. I love explosions."

"Your eyebrows don't." Ellie found a package of T.P., paper towels. She searched and searched for a bottle and Q-tips.

"What about this?" Annie tried to lift a great plastic water cooler, but the thing outweighed her by a great deal. It was an old brown Coleman, hard white plastic ridges on the bottom, with a plastic handle and a spigot. It wasn't an orange monstrosity football players dump on coaches, but close for young girls.

"That's too big for you," Ellie said.

"But not us," Annie said.

Ellie sighed and stepped towards her sister to touch the brown, ridged plastic. "What, you just want to dump water out? Out in the street where folks faced with homelessness can watch us waste water?"

"I ... guess not?"

Ellie thought about it. Yes, it might actually work and attract attention the way the rains themselves had. "I have an idea that won't waste it at all." Ellie pointed to Annie's pocket, whose hands brushed the wicker of golden threads that made up the golden sieve. Ellie looked around for Sy. Sy was nowhere to be found. Wait. Where had he gone?

Moments later, Ellie and Annie rode the North Wind above the crowds on 5th and 6th Avenues. They had hauled the great water cooler up onto the back of the North Wind together. Had hung onto it together, had now affixed the sieve together, and tilting it, giggled along with the North Wind. From that great blue spigot poured a golden spray out onto the crowds whose dreary disposition braced against that great wind, pushing against the cold and hoarfrost, gave way to joy. They as one and at once noticed faelings gathered at the Rockefeller Center, winged and horned and hoofed and scaled creatures of divine intellect and reason who liked a good concert as much as the next pre-magical, Undernaeght guy or gal. Or ghoul.

The girls woke the world to wonder. They garnered a glow from within each city dweller, an inside to every outside that was, at heart, as infinite as the furthest without. Every individual thing became, deep within, the center of the universe and also its outer rim. Those girls glugged and glugged the great gilded rain out onto the crowds until their little store of waters ran dry.

When they finished, Ellie clung tight to the barreled bottle, beaming. "We could hold the sample in here now."

Annie nodded.

"See there?" the North Wind asked. "Overmorrow finds a way. In this case you two of It found it for It: Is and Thinkart and Bliss for all. How happy they look."

"But still," Ellie said. "It took a great amount of work for two little humans to make up for what is lacking in the rains, when the great rains themselves forget."

"Well it wouldn't be forgetting if it hadn't, would it?"

"I suppose not," Ellie said.

They descended back to the park.

Annie said, "Look there!"

They glimpsed a form slinking away from the edge of the pond, one with rags and an evening suit, unkempt hair, a drunken stagger.

"Uncle Corey returning to the scene of the crime," Ellie said. "We'll nail him."

The man moved further and further away from the water's edge, moving south *fast*.

The North Wind, however, laughed and laughed as she took the girls to the western edge, where that permanent cauldron installation sat. New York's one of the places in the world where any given art installation could be an actual artifact from an ancient world. And any ancient artifact in New York could be an old art installation. Hard to tell. Hard to distinguish between performing magicians and magic performers here.

So a great old cast iron cauldron on the edge of Central Park gets no attention. You *might* get some attention as an occasional sidewalk chalker (rains wash off colored ash and bone) or ambitious graffiti artist (spray paint and wheat paste seldom stay up), or opportunistic drug dealer (though unsuspecting dealers had found themselves — surprise — as the key ingredient in a brutal potion).

Though a clear day, it was still a cold day, and in the middle of the week. The coldness had driven off others with their big old thermoses full of mulled cider.

That left the girls alone, dropped off near the cauldron by the North Wind (who had other business to attend to in Niagara). They stood beside the cauldron they planned to sponge with toilet paper. Ellie immediately looked inside while Annie stood guard. There in the bottom, little else than scraps of sassafras remained but barest resin and residue pooling around the lip of the bottommost circle.

Ellie daubed it with a full roll of paper towels. She couldn't reach it without the full length of the cylinder. With a gloved hand (only fools touch unknown substances with bare hands and even the very wise won't touch unknown substance even with the bare hands of their pet grizzly bear's bear hands), Ellie squeezed the daubing into the lip of the water cooler. She grabbed the last of the sassafras and dropped it into the cooler. Capped it.

The tree above her exploded into a thousand splinters.

Annie screamed.

THE MECH

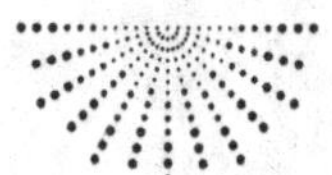

Ellie fell down from the concussion blast, immediately afraid and also oddly happy. Then ashamed she was happy to be afraid. Ashamed she was happy, happy she was afraid because that fearsome explosion meant *progress*. All at once she felt these three while she lay there, reeling. Her coat flew off, the gilded sieve shot off the end of the cooler. The cooler rolled. Its sponged contents and leafy bits spiraled. Stuff sloshed in the center.

When she got her bearings, she rolled out from underneath her armpit. Gunmetal grey, an enormous hulking MECH towered over her, cocking back to swing again. Great gouts of steam hissed from its joints where cogs, pneumatic pistons, steel cable, wires, magnets, and bolts met in a mess of movement.

It roared.

Ellie scrambled back and cartwheeled away as the machine rose and plowed its fist of earth tillers and oily pneumatic joints into the rocky earth below. Scythe blades met flint and bedrock, sending up a shower of sparks.

Annie threw a rock at its knee. The rock bounced.

The mech turned on her.

Annie screamed again and moved to run away. It bounded

after her — boom doom doom boom — over rock and stock and the green of the vale. Annie slid away from it down a slicked wet rock and onto the platform of a gazebo there on the waterfront. It smashed its fist into the gazebo roof. It opened the roof as a can opener cuts tops of tin cans. She screamed for a third time. A small flock of pigeons flapped overhead, distracting the mech a moment.

Feather.

Fluid.

Splinter.

Steel.

Stock and stone and water wheel.

Ellie stood on the shore with her coat, scaring pigeons from the rocks. "Shoo! Shoo!" The wings flapped off in multiple directions, but mostly with the west wind towards the mech's face, bombarding it with white pigeon poop, so looked like a spotted cowboy.

The mech clapped.

Six pigeons exploded out from between its fingers in a featherdown rain.

But Annie had dived into the frigid water. The splashing and swimming grabbed its attention. It started ripping the rest of the cedars and planks of gazebo before it was jumping — cannonball — in waters.

After *her*.

The wake gave Annie a great boost on the shore. As the mech swam furiously towards both girls, Annie found herself sprawled out on muddy tufts of unmowed prairie grass. How long before the mowers came? Stuck in the mud. Caught in the cattails. Did reapers mow down cattails with scythes?

"Quick, Annie, think! Think like you thought with the sassafras!" Ellie was searching, searching around for something to grab and whack it with, something to use, anything. She didn't know any spells, had no wand or stylet. There was nothing in the cauldron.

The mech's form emerged, dripping. Its metal had oxidized,

blacked and moist. Remembering the witches and mindful of the magic in the world, Ellie's witchy side had an urge to take an ounce of calx on the metal and store it in a cold place where she could later make some potion to fight it. What an odd urge: of course she had no time to fight it that way. She didn't even *know* any magic.

The mech leaned back with a great force and swung that scythe bladed fist towards Annie's face.

But Annie had grabbed the golden sieve and stretched it as wide as its gaps would go, stretched the grey cast net crocheted of golden threads. The fist of the mech met the golden sieve and melted into ten thousand drops of molten lava. The mech screeched and bellowed and immediately powered down as the fire spread up and up and up its fraying cords and pneumatics.

But the firewater had lashed out and landed on Annie's fire red hair. It burned it and her remaining eyebrows off, and she ran screaming into the lake to put it out.

Ellie was crying, both relieved and horrified for her sister. Relieved the machine was dead, horrified her sister might be too. Perhaps guilty it hadn't been her, crying about all of it. Angry she had to deal with the mech without Charlie or Mom or Dad or… where the heck was Levi? She swam down to meet Annie, and by the time she got there, her sister emerged from the water with blisters all over her bald head. Ellie wondered if it would ever grow flame red hair ever again. Doubtful: it seemed the mech had burned her true flame away.

"What happened?" asked a familiar voice.

They turned.

Sy stood next to Uncle Corey. Uncle Corey's arm was bleeding profoundly, and he was holding it, trying to catch up to Sy, who had arrived first, dragging Corey by the collar.

Ellie opened her mouth to explain, but a great rushing wind met the four of them and blew back the waters so that the very ground of the lake was laid bare, showing all manner of fake gold watches and petrified mounds of candied almonds and dozens and dozens of red-eared slider turtles and various New Year's

Eve glasses that boaters bygone had thrown exuberantly into the lake. A bobcat pirate lay exposed on the lake floor, hoarding some of those watches. He looked up at them awkwardly.

They looked at him. "Uh," said Ellie.

The bobcat said, "Uh. Hey?" Then bounded away, taking the watches with him.

"ENOUGH," the North Wind said. It wasn't a roar. It was a whisper turned up to eleven. It put a hissing pressure on their ears that made them all cry from the intensity, though Annie was already crying as the scars began to form. The North Wind passed a salve to Ellie and said to Annie, "This will not save your hair, child, but it may yet save your mind and skin and bone." Ellie applied the salve to her sister.

"All four of you youngsters, on my back this instant."

They obeyed without question, even Sy and Corey. They hopped on board and headed south.

"What happened to your arm, Uncle Corey?" Ellie asked him as she applied the salve to a whimpering Annie's skull.

Uncle Corey looked at Sy.

Sy seethed and looked forward to the horizon.

The North Wind, in Snow White luck dragon form, flew quickly to 26 Broadway. The Standard Oil Building.

"Built by Rockefeller himself," Sy said.

Annie whimpered and winced as she asked, "All by himself? One man?"

Sy blushed. "He had help, I suppose."

The North Wind said, "All managers do. They just take public credit from their betters."

"What's that?" Ellie pointed to the top of the building.

"A cauldron," The North Wind said.

"We don't need another cauldron!"

The cauldron on the tower burst into flame, turning the entire tower into a great, ominous torch.

"What powers it?" Ellie asked.

Uncle Corey mumbled, "Kerosene. Coal Oil. Bloody Williamson and Texarco's ladling off the Bellhammer find."

Sy hissed at him, hand still on his collar.

Ellie and Annie both grew very, very somber having learned that an honest-to-goodness skyscraper had been built by what seemed to be something like a comic book villain. And for nothing more than petrol.

The flame on the tower roared with dark red fire.

24

DARK FLAME BURNING

At the base of the Standard Oil Building, Ellie felt dwarfed in body and spirit. "Man, oh man. What is it with executive boards and big scary buildings?"

Sy said, "Well, the word executor has a sort of finality for both lawyers and killers."

A chill washed over her. She looked up at the thing, meditated long on the great kerosene cauldron at the top. She'd failed to get evidence from the witches's cauldron. Perhaps she should go back? But would she be able to go back easily, what with the North Wind practically forcing her and Annie to come here? Why here?

Maybe she could get evidence from this cauldron? After all, an oil baron might have motive to limit the amount of wonder in the world. She felt that chill. It reminded her of the ice bath. She looked at the bodegas below, their blinking lights on the walk-way, half expecting a more naive version of herself to emerge with a bag of ice.

"Sorry," Sy said, watching her shake.

Uncle Corey, dressed shabbily, drank. "Well, this is just where I get off, sunnies."

"We're your nieces," Annie said.

He squinted. "Sunny folk. Same difference."

"No," Annie said, "No it's not." She comforted herself by pulling out the golden sieve, the one the Author had pulled forth from the black, star-bedecked ether, and ran her finger along its flexible mesh.

Uncle Corey put a little bit of whisky in his open palm, splashed some in his beard, then splashed some on his armpits.

"You want to smell *more* like booze?" Sy asked.

"What's the difference between that and Pinaud?"

"Pinaud?" Sy asked.

"Cheap French aftershave that burns like the Dickens. Guy on the label even *looks* like he's from a Dickens novel."

"Oh that super strong smelling stuff that has al—"

"—cohol in ith," Uncle Corey slurred. He splashed away. He splashed in rude places most people don't put smelly good stuff, on outerwear.

The building they stood before climbed up like a series of old Renaissance revival towers, stacked up as a child might stack blocks into a pyramid shape. And there on top sat that great kerosene cauldron, lit by furious flame. Yes, she could get evidence from this cauldron. Or give up on getting evidence. Why was this cauldron any better than the one that singed her sister, other than being bigger?

"Hasn't been lit in eighty four years," The North Wind said. "Why now?"

"Why eighty four years?" Ellie said.

"I don't know for sure," The North Wind said, "but that's the year that marked the first time the Author tried to wombrove into our world. Maybe it has something to do with that and oil?"

Ellie looked at the great foreboding tower, and it warmed her to look up at the fire, but not in the way she wanted to be warmed. A sinister flame. Yeah, it would hide just as much evidence about this world as the other cauldron. Perhaps more. It was a dark flame burning the sky for some nefarious purposes.

And the North Wind had brought her here. She didn't want to quit, no. Not on Charlie, at least, which also meant she didn't want to quit on Levi, which meant she also wanted to stay the course in finding Overmorrow. Or at least the person who had culled the specific storm. Besides she couldn't easily get back to the other cauldron.

Witches used cauldrons. So did warlocks.

Here stood the tower of someone who knew something about magic, about where Charlie was, and yet whom she didn't know.

Yes, she'd get evidence from this cauldron about the other cauldron.

The great concrete and marble bricks of the place — the strategic cracks in the grey — made it imminently—

"Climbable," said Annie.

Ellie cooed to herself, proud of her sister. "Yes, and look at the clock."

A massive marble ball atop the entryway arch looked as if a giant had dipped it in the world's largest chocolate fondue fountain. Only instead of chocolate, the fountain poured molten time. A clock had been moulded to the face of the great sphere so that time itself conformed to the planet's shape. Great iron and pewter and brass Roman numerals and... were those zodiac signs? Only all wrong. Perhaps the ball had smashed a timebound compass, like what the Author had carried? That thought gave her as many chills in the base of her skull as did the idea of all of those symbols.

And the planets didn't look familiar. "What are those planets?"

Uncle Corey, almost stone-sober, said, "The Tors, Mounds, and Lamps of The Vale Megacosm."

"The what?"

"I'll tell you when you're grown up." He belched a disgustingly loud belch. You could smell the booze.

They passed under the arch engraved with 26 BROADWAY and found themselves in a large marble hall with way, way, way too many guards bearing naked, curved blades. You never really come across naked steel in NYC, whether blades or guns. When it happens, it scares you sober. Or would have if it weren't Uncle Corey we were talking about. Inside the hall stood a lawyer in a suit and their brother Levi, who looked half dead.

25

NO SOULS HOUR

Quick note: prior to showing up in that lobby where the girls met them, the lawyer Rudy Charlemagne had emptied and hid every goblet he could find in a four-block radius of Levi — including the Author's goblet. Rudy made Levi swear he wouldn't go seeking out a goblet again.

Then Rudy booked a hotel room down in the financial district near the Standard Oil cauldron. He locked Levi inside.

Levi had checked the fridge. The downstairs hallway. Every cabinet and drawer and nightstand he could for a drop of seawine. None of them hid a goblet. He double checked the spit cups, sink, a divot in the floor, even the bowl of fake fruit. None held that saccharine-umami-bitter sludge of snails and seaweed he craved. Not something so simple as a large Tupperware, tucked under his bed, had any. He hated it. He shouted at Rudy, "I WILL NOT GIVE UP SEAWINE!"

Rudy, bored, said, "Uh huh."

Someone — Rudy denied having done so — had gone behind the television and hacked apart the power cord that connected it to the wall. The hack job looked as if it had required the use of a machete. Levi relaxed into the silence and the great comfy sheets, thrilled that, even though he would have to face The Board in the morning, he would – for once – not be facing them alone.

Perhaps he could get some seawine before then?

He drifted off to sleep, looked at the sliding door that led out to the beautiful balcony that overlooked the financial district. The door's lock loosened. He didn't think much of the crack in the door opening onto the world, the subtle breeze blowing inside. He smiled and fell soundly asleep, Swevenfall — the hour of dreamers — came upon him. He wandered the land of Somnolory — the land where dreamers go — even there in search of seawine.

He found none in the land of dreams throughout the night.

Until three o'clock in the morning. No souls hour.

At three in the morning, a clicking sound and a whipping like tulle on glass got under his cold skin and mind. He thought at first the sound had come from deep inside the dream where he had hammered a wooden mallet on a toy assembly line as one of Santa's elves, paid in what they *called* seawine, but was merely water. He seemed to be the only little elf who noticed. Plus his payment was being held for his first two pay periods. He had long since stopped dreamworld hammering and started looking around the room for the source of the noise.

Whereupon he woke in the dream inside an Archive.

Then woke *again* in the room, first checking to see if the A/C had been turned on. He felt cold. But the heat still roared in the vents. He searched the room again.

Fridge still empty.

Phone still unplugged.

TV still disconnected with extreme prejudice.

No seawine in the fridge, cups...

Nothing in the bathtub, sink, door peephole, or...

The sliding door to the balcony was open wide, letting in all manner of cold wind. A flag flapped in the dark night light, a black flag hanging from a scythe that had been driven clean into the concrete of the balcony. The flag was suspended by a crystal cord. And the crystal cord was attached to a goblet, weighing it at the end.

He didn't think to ponder how the goblet had gotten there. Dangling *from a scythe*. He didn't think about anything other than the taste of it. And he knew the consequences. But like a helpless brown Labrador retriever who knows his owner will beat him bloody if he eats the tray of brownies, Levi found any consequence a fair price for the draught that hung before him.

Within the bright reflection of the sliding glass door stood a self of his. Standing outside, looking into his room illuminated by the yellow glow of the bathroom light. That self looked half dead: a corpse. He turned and looked over the balcony, considering the fall. How it might solve some things and ruin some others. Dark and stormy thoughts for a child. But children do have honest, brutal, dark thoughts when things get bleak. It was books like this one found in childhood that helped this Author out of some very, very dark childhood moments and darker again when his cousin hurt herself. So yes, in all honesty, that's what happened: Levi looked over the edge.

As he did, the soft hairs on his hand brushed up against the goblet, and he felt the thing almost pulling him towards it by the nape of his neck, the angle of his crown and shoulder resisting the pull of his nape. Hooked. Pulling.

Sever his nape. Sever his nape. The goblet seemed to whisper as if summoning Sweeney Todd.

Not resisting enough. Not near enough. He needed to flee or to jump. Avoid the very occasion of what could have happened. But his left hand — from muscle memory and against every bit of willpower he had — disobeyed his choices and snatched up the ancient bit of sunken treasure. Habits rule in moments like these, but Levi had few good habits at this point and fewer good mentors.

He was in the bathroom, filling it up. He was spending the evening drinking glass after glass after glass of mind-numbing myopic poison, filling the tub and toilet with slugs and snails and coral vomit, driven out of his mind by inner slime. Take that, Rudy.

In the morning, Rudy Charlemagne walked in. Levi had passed out next to a tub full of creepy crawlies. "Oh, my God, what have you done? AND HOW?"

The room looked like a washed up cove of Turnagain Arm had the grossest part of Kinmundy pond dumped on it before slathering in the silt of great and terrible tides that rise fourteen feet in an hour. As if some personified sea creature had rutted in the filth of the Mississippi River Delta for eons and then dumped it all in a lone hotel room. It was the most disgusting presentation of silt in the history of large tidal realities.

"That's it," Rudy said. "I'm leaving you."

Was he freezing? Was he shivering? "You can't l-l-l-leave," Levi said. "I need to g-g-g-get out of this."

"I can't help you," Rudy said. "Sorry."

"Someone can." Levi pulled out the compass he'd saved. He called into the Archive for Sammi. He whispered it, blindly into the compass. "Sssssssammi."

Somehow, it worked.

In minutes, she showed up with a merman, who brewed an awful, terrible stimulant from the blackest, most vile coffee beans you have ever seen. The beans hipsters talked about in Brooklyn. Some civet cat on some foreign mountain had eaten a coffee plant and pooped out one bean. Another cat had pooped out another and so on. A little village child had picked up the poops, washed the beans, and given them to the farmer, who filtered it all. Eventually, a whole bag of beans equated to a whole bag of handpicked civet poop. An Oompa Loompa situation, that, but at least they weren't paid in conscription.

"Oh no no no way man," Rudy said at the sight of the black ichor stimulant. "There's no way I'm going to stand here while a kid does all of this right in front of me."

"Quiet, londchild," the merman said. "It'll be fine in the wash."

"Listen to you," Rudy said. "Your people got him into this mess."

"Silence about the King, peace be upon him. And don't call us *your* people." The coffee was ready. The merman started feeding it to Levi, who had upturned his longhaired head as would a little raven. Hair primed for a tonsure. Levi drank it down as the merman fed it to him. "It'll be fine, lawyer."

"I cannot know about this and represent him."

"Just take him anyway," Sammi said. "Go through with it, and he can say the girls did it or something. I need to form a whole group of girls just to take care of this boy."

Levi looked unsure, but he was busy pouring the black dredge of doctored coffee into his slime-filled gullet, feeling it take the edge off the seawine. He had failed. Again. (He felt himself going back on the drip, dosing the real beans). He didn't need a pill, a prison, or a declaration from the powers that be. He needed a community, a village, to help him out of his habits and into new ones. But that would take admitting the failure. And he couldn't admit failure.

He guzzled instead.

"I have *got* to get into another career," Rudy said. "That or you have to come clean. I can't do this anymore."

26

THE BOARD

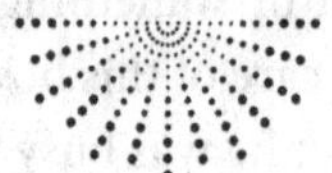

That's what happened to Levi before Ellie and Annie passed under the arch engraved with 26 BROADWAY. Yes, the girls found themselves in a large marble hall with way, way, way too many guards bearing naked, curved blades. Inside stood a lawyer in a suit. And their brother Levi. Who looked half dead.

"LEVI!" Annie hollered and ran up to him and threw her arms around his neck. They stood there awkwardly.

Ellie came up to hug her brother as well, slower, more cautiously, awkward from sincerity. When she embraced him, she gasped: how light his hug back had grown. How thin his middle section where her own arms reached. How weak his body and embrace.

How frail.

This wasn't the tough brother she remembered, running for miles at a time and growing into a latter day Charlie. Life had frayed this brother of hers. He'd been worn thin by the burden of carrying the role of two brothers and an addiction. She hugged him tighter. "What are you doing here?"

Levi said, "What happened to Annie's head?"

"Later. You first."

Levi looked at Rudy the lawyer, who shook his head. Seeing that filled Levi with pale, hollow dread: he had failed. *Again*, again. Failed to give up seawine and now failed to give up the super-stimulant coffee. On a normal week, he'd probably have to get his stomach pumped for the amount of coffee in his little body. Maybe he'd already had his stomach pumped and he didn't remember. Dosing, grinding, on the drip again.

The guard on the left, decorated with all manner of embroidered awards, said, "The Board awaits.

The lawyer raised his eyebrow at the guard, smiling.

The guard looked their frail forms up and down, scoffed, and continued walking. He lead them into a cast-iron crosshatched, square-brass-plate-paneled elevator. Ellie harrumphed. Levi saw crosshatches. Thought of how they might hide failures. The guard cranked a great lever (of the sort you might use to power up or power down the engines on a great steamer ship), and the elevator lurched the six of them forward into the library, deep into the doom that would be deemed.

The girls screeched.

Annie covered her face, its salve and bandages, as they rocketed towards the western wall.

Ellie had no evidence, but she would get evidence from this cauldron tower, so she watched the walls carefully, lights and pipes buzzing past.

Levi seemed oddly at peace. Two choices lay before him, now that he had a moment to think: either show people he had failed to quit seawine and the stimulant or hide the fact that he hadn't quit yet and try to win the case.

They all — folks and elevator — melted through the wall. A winding course took them through the belly of the building. It made a dizzying array Ellie couldn't track. Then it looped them back into the walls of various towers leading up to the cauldron. A human-sized version of hamster cage tunnels. The car stopped. But for the guard and The North Wind (who had been dancing in the form of a tiny girl on Ellie's shoulder since they left the

Author's house), all the others lurched forward and piled up against the other door.

Which opened.

They fell out atop one another in a white-linoleum-floored, wood-paneled hall. About two dozen large women over the age of seventy-two sat around tables. Some had hair like tight puffy chinchillas — white, midcentury secretary afros with fibers tight enough to stop bullets.

They wore costume jewelry that clacked and clattered, sequin laden white shirts that smacked of DIY crafting (more flea market DIY than Brooklyn Flea DIY), and a war of perfumes named after some fashionista's abstract concept of abstract concepts.

"Wait a minute," Levi said. "Some of these ladies were at my hospital."

"You went to the hospital?" Ellie asked. "When?"

Wings fluttered, paper hit thwack, thwack on wooden tables. Chicken fried steak, fried eggs, bacon, and the peppering of ketchup and the splashing of red pepper sauce all floated towards them in a Midwest fog.

Ellie coughed hard enough her eyes watered. It took a moment to gain control.

As one, about a fourth of these nice old white ladies — the ones sitting on the left sides of every table of four — said, "Trump is spades? Or diamonds? I forget."

The lawyer muttered, "Certainly not *our* hearts."

These old nice white ladies slapped down their bids from their hands and turned along with the rest to face the girls. The oldest, fattest, shrivelederest flabskiniest greyscalp of all sat up tall (which was still half the height of the rest) and strong (which was both an inner Rocky thing and somehow the frailest of the bunch). She smoked a cheap cigarette from the end of a long black cigarette holder whose paint was peeling to reveal a sickly green below. This one said, "Welcome, Wright matricies. Welcome, Wright scion."

The children had been scrutinizing the room. Watching the

room look back at them, they all reacted differently. Ellie curt-sied, scanning for evidence — cards, clattering costume jewelry. Levi bowed, hesitantly, yet low.

Annie sort of nodded and shrugged. "What is this?"

"The Board," the old woman said.

"Of..."

"Overmorrow's presence in New York. And Overmorrow's presence in Amerigon, but specifically we watch and attend to the consequences of those here who... get out of line."

Ellie felt heat in her face and hands. Charlie would have dodged Levi's and Annie's attempts at making torches. She and Charlie's juniors would find a way to wrap a stick in shredded t-shirt and dip it in kerosene anyways. Hrmm. "Why do you meet in a giant building made by an oil company that's topped with an evil kerosene cauldron?"

The old baroness smacked her gums, and her dentures came loose in her mouth. "Because, oil is simply old dinosaur goo—"

"Old ferns and big bugs, actually," Ellie said.

The baroness smacked her gums with such a violent POP that everything in the room went still as if glued. "WHICH entered this world through Overmorrow. Or rather, the world awoke to find giant ferns and giant bugs and dinosaurs were real, then pulverized them into viscous liquidity."

Ellie realized half the room was smacking gums in unison. "Burning oil isn't against Overmorrow?"

The old women cackled as one with almost tidal shakiness. Their collective laughs-then-gasps washed over the girls.

"Never heard of oilweavers? Not all oil dealers pump oceans full of plastic, atmospheres full of carbon, child."

The girls shook their heads. Annie less so, due to the fresh scarring.

Moreso Levi shook his head, hoping he would be ignored. Hiding seemed the better option.

"Never mind for now," the woman said. "I seek your brother fore I turn my focus on you two."

Levi tensed. He might not get to hide his addiction. He might have to give it up. He really wanted to fake as if he'd quit or never—

"Thanks for saving New Yorkers whose building collapsed."

Levi nodded. Hide it after all! If she gave him that big of a window, he'd crawl through it and hide, yes.

"Had you and Sammi—" a nod toward the black-robed girl "—been elsewhere it seems many, many more may have died."

Levi smiled. The smile rubbed against his other hidden feelings hard enough to hurt.

Sammi shifted in her seat. Levi knew *she* knew what she'd given him, what he'd consumed, what he'd hidden. Would they ask him directly?

"There's only one outstanding issue."

Crap. Here it would come. He swallowed against the desert spilling down his throat. The swallow did nothing.

"Found at the scene of the crime was a goblet of seawine and a leftover pot of oilspill coffee. Would you know anything about that, Levi whose name means little priest?"

Here it was. Everything from which he'd hid. Levi looked to his sisters, to Sammi. He knew, deep down, all he needed to do was say Ellie and Annie did it or Sammi did it to get it done with. He could hide it, yes. He could hide it spectacularly. So he opened his mouth to do so

And closed it again. Opened and closed.

"Are you blowing bubbles?" The old woman asked. "I demand an answer. Spit it out boy."

He could hide it. He would. He wanted to be done with this, right? Wanted to out them all as guilty parties and get off free as a phoenix, free to live, free to die, free to live again. Yet something stirred in him. Some wondrous irony said, deep down: Grow up.

He looked over at Rudy who nodded at him, defiantly. His sisters who looked worried for him, no expression of defiance there. Sammi who looked hurt, worried, defiant, but mostly ready for the other shoe to fall. Here it was. He could hide it, the lying didn't matter. Something weighed at his hip. He didn't feel hot enough. He didn't feel cold enough. He felt lukewarm. He looked at his hip. There hung the flask the Author had given him so long ago. When? But he knew what hid inside the flask. Overmorrow waters. Overmorrow waters not merely from the rain, but from the Author and his sieve and the tub. Overmorrow waters to remember his choice *to drown in the old world and wake in the new*. He unsqueaked the cap. It looked like liquid rainbow. He tasted it. Cold and sweet and savory at once. He opened his mouth to blame everyone in there for his addiction. He drank again. Opened his mouth to say something clever to get off *Scott free*. He drank a third time and then a heat rose in him, something deeper than the shame of it all. Something truer like a great boil needing lanced for once, needing healed. Instead of lukewarm, he felt frozen on his skin and as if his bones were on fire, burning and freezing at once. After that, he didn't open his lips. He looked around — truly looked — and it was as if the water that had once enacted drowning so that his old self had died, now it washed the inner man as well. He looked and a fresh wind and a fresh fire filled his lungs and bones. A hope and a wonder: each of these women, once so powerful, seemed so blessedly small. His sisters couldn't yet comprehend the whole of it. Sy seemed so dry. The North Wind so… so *thick*, so *sharp*, so *opaque* while the rest of them seemed a bit too translucent and thin. Good Lord, he felt awake for real, for true.

Full of that inner fire, he bellowed into that eerie noisy silence, "I am addicted to seawine."

Then it went silent for true.

The women stopped puttering about and trailing superfluous noise. All clattering stopped. All shuffling. Each machine and knife and whisk in the back kitchen went utterly still. Salt shaking, coffee stirring, elastic band adjusting, even the air conditioner's whirr stopped. It was as if this very diner were a sort of shadow that hadn't, until that moment, betrayed the reality leaning in towards Levi. And now it loomed over him, huge and dark — the diner and its every patron.

All seventy or so turned to look and asked him, "Did you drink it?"

It was almost deafening, the silence returning to him like that, but Levi said, "I did." He was failing pretty hard at this whole hiding thing. Gosh, could he climb out of this? Admit it was a false confession under duress and torture? Would his cheeks melt if they grew any hotter? His chest?

"The day of the collapse?"

"Yes."

"How did you function?"

"Coffee."

"How often do you drink it?"

"Maybe every day. I'm full of it right now."

"Is that it?" she pointed at the flask.

"That's Overmorrow water. Courage to confess."

"But you're full of the seawine?"

"And the oil spill coffee, both. Though it's subsiding. This coffee came from wild cat poop."

The women gasped at that; they had never expected him to be in such a compromised state.

"Civet cat poop, technically," said Sammi.

Both of his sisters were weeping. He looked closer. No, they weren't hurt, but… what was that look on their faces? Relief? Their faces red and puffy and wet *with relief?* For what? That someone else knew? They seemed relieved the burden was no longer theirs and theirs alone. He'd never considered how hard it might have been on them too, how they too ended up, in a way, with a shadow dependency upon the seawine.

"We will consider your sentence," the old woman said to Levi and then turning to the girls asked, "Why are *you* here?"

Ellie stammered to find a way to draw evidence out of this woman. Looking to Levi, she finally decided to try for directness. "What are you Board over?" She asked. "What do you govern?

"You came to me," the queen bee of pinochle proclaimed.

Ellie took in a breath. She could get evidence out of this woman, were she careful. "I did. I wrote down a list of folk to contact after recent… issues. I was told a board oversees the A/C union's movements and any contact between Earth and Overmorrow. Now you tell me you are over Overmorrow's presence and the consequences of those who get out of line." Ellie took in a deep breath, then asked the accusing question: "Do you watch Oblivion's movements?"

Levi looked over at her from across the Formica table, shocked at her direct approach.

The loud old women judges stilled again. Every sip of teacups. Every clatter of every raspberry spreader. Every shuffle and rattle of beads on bifocal chains and lanyards. Every stifled belch behind "polite" old lips, "Excuse me" prayers. All of it stopped. Worse than before. Silence ate sound, obliviated sound. Whereas with Levi's confession everything had simply left off making noise, in this instance, it seemed that something was swallowing even the potential of sound. The only sound came from Annie's fork, which fell upon the floor. Even that fell muffled.

Ellie waited. Good Lord, she was so bad at waiting. This whole entire time she'd pushed and prodded, searched for information, tried to do everything she could to get to the bottom of this. But something told her that no matter what she tried now, waiting and waiting alone would get the answers out of them. It hurt, truly, to be patient. She felt like a patient in the hospital, undergoing the longest surgery in the waiting. But wait she did.

Annie grew remarkably still for Annie.

Queen bee said, "Well, yes, of course we watch Oblivion. We know where he is right now."

NARRATIVE DEVIATION

Her heart put pressure on every vein in her neck and it was all Ellie could do to keep from screaming. "Wait. Do you know what happened to my brother Charlie?"

"Yes."

Levi gasped and stood from his chair. Then upon his armchair. Dizzy, he sat back down, but more upright, knees bent, feet on seat.

"What happened?" Ellie asked the board, shaking her head. Never again would she trust them. "Tell me this instant."

"No."

"No what?"

"No, I won't tell you."

"Why?"

"Because discretion is my job, my dear." She played a card.

The room resumed its playing cards, its slurping tea, its shifting chairs beneath its obese bottoms. The sound *roared* at them, the busybodiness of it all.

"You have to tell me," Ellie said and then her voice, small as a whisper, said, "He is my brother."

"And was he loyal to you?"

"Loyalty in family doesn't matter," Ellie said. "Higher loyalties matter more. And I am loyal to the Overmorrow waters, all of which have told me ask about my brother Charlie for the sake of all he has touched or will ever touch. For the sake of any mind connected to the archive."

Again the careless mentions of *deal* or *shuffle dear* or *will you pass the corn syrup?* When they all resumed their play, they grew again their individuality, at once. The raw uniformity of all had, if not shattered, smudged. Perhaps they only moved as one when it would matter most?

"Oh please," said Annie

Still, no answer. Ellie asked, "Then why do you watch Oblivion?"

Again the silence came crashing down, a whiplash of the sound, the room awaiting answer. Maybe the room itself was answer.

Woman, squat, remarked, "We don't wish to fail to call to mind, my dear. He does. We care, you see, for keeping track." She almost coughed the last.

Many others coughed while others sipped their cigarettes as if to wash their coughs on down with smoke. Still others took their coffee. Thwacking cards and tallying.

"Did he have anything to do with this?" inquired Ellie. "Taking Overmorrow?"

From there upon her shoulder perch, the North Wind prodded Ellie.

Nuance. "Overmorrow rains?"

"Certainly," the woman said, her clip-on earrings clattering.

"Well, was he here?"

"He's not."

"Was the A/C union all involved?"

"They were, but accidentally."

"And what of Angler King?"

She blushed. The ancient crone was *blushing.* Ellie was shocked, gasped at it. It took a while to settle down those ancient cheeks, but then the old woman said finally, "How is that elder flirt?"

The children balked at this. Especially Levi beside her. Ellie said, "He's dead, I fear."

The sudden news assaulted Levi: frigid ice filled his chest. He gasped, shocked.

The cards the room around cascaded out of slackened hands onto the tables and floors as muzzles dropped and drooped enough that one full set of dentures fell. The false teeth landed in a glass of cherry juice. It splashed blood red all over whitened tablecloths.

The speaker for The Board whispered, "Dead, you said?"

"I did."

Annie huffed, low and long. Blew out slow and steady, *hoooooooo.*

The woman shed a single tear that carved a path betwixt mascara, rouge, and eyeliner. Carved a line along her makeup fortress's foundation, leaving paths of liver-spotted whiteness in its wake. "Where? When?"

"Did you all know him well?" asked Annie.

"I did. We did."

"I'm sorry for your loss. We found him... cleaned..."

"As in sanitized?"

"Filleted."

They gasped.

"Ashore the lake," said Ellie. "I'm surprised Authorities haven't told you. Didn't you say that you followed larger happenings in Overmorrow?"

"Yes," she said and turned to look at Sy, along with every eye in every head of every woman connected to the hive. "This surely would have graced the morning papers by today?"

Sy shuffled both his feet. "We've b... b... been a little busy with the brother case."

Levi wondered who'd have killed the fish who started all his troubles, the fish who had first seemed so kind.

"Didn't you say, ma'am," said Ellie, "that you followed the pressure of *this* world upon The Vale and *not* The Vale upon our world?"

The woman's every wrinkle spoke her shock before she nodded.

"Wouldn't that include a murder?"

Looking slapped, the old lady sat back into her armchair and twiddled both her little thumbs. Again it all grew still.

Ellie pressed. "For murder — surely — didn't start in your perfect Vale? Didn't start in our world?"

"I suppose it didn't, no. See murder did in fact invade the rest of the Vale through Earth. But murder did not invade Earth first through The Vale, but from another world entire. Worse things entered deeper Heaven and other Tors in the Vale, but murder first was here."

"Again with due respect," said Ellie, "wouldn't you be blinded by your goals to murder in your yard?"

"Authorities—"

"Do you share phones with New York Police Department?"

"Cordial terms."

"So yes?" Ellie asked.

"No."

"They opened up the case, it seemed to me," said Ellie.

The woman acted shocked. "Well child, you somehow stumbled upon more info than you might have otherwise. One like you doesn't show up so often." She smiled the smile of very large and very hungry predators. "Tell me other questions."

"Do the witches — do the warlocks — often make their potions in a cauldron?"

All the women laughed in unison. Uncle Corey chuckle-belched. Even Silas laughed.

Young Levi looked around. "Did Ellie mention something funny?"

The women ceased their laughing. "Quiet you. We haven't sentenced you."

Levi went as still as a bone.

The elder woman said, "A witch or warlock makes their potions in cauldrons."

"Always?" Ellie asked.

"Unless they're terrible. It's in the job description. Sorry, but you'll need to get specific if you want to draw a helpful answer out of me."

"Could potions interrupt the weather?" Ellie asked.

"Or chem trails?" Levi asked.

"BE QUIET!"

Levi stiller went.

The old woman said, "A potion could, depending what they want to do. There's atmospheric charge that one can spread upon the ground to summon lightning to your feet. There's ways to make a fertilizer that reverses all photosynthesis in plants that drink it, getting plants to draw up energy from earth and shoot it out as light. What exactly do you think they cooked up?"

"Are there potions that could cull an Overmorrow storm?"

She stilled. A harp, of all things, plucked its melody from deep inside another room.

"There was a tincture long ago," she muttered slowly, "let a man rename a gilded rainbow rain. I guess it may be possible. By the docks they set this up?"

"They did," said Ellie. "Now, tell us all of Charlie."

The woman shook her head.

So Ellie put her foot down. Stomped. That sparest fork which fell before? Her foot stomped tips of tines. It flipped up in some twists, it flew, and speared into the ceiling tiles. Wavered there so sure until it stilled.

"Fine," said Ellie before it fully ceased its shaking. "We can find our parents. Then we'll bring them back to here, along with Mr. Author, to discover what you've hidden from us." She turned to leave.

The woman growled like Spaniels who've grown old with fat deposits. "You'll find that harder, dearie, than you ever would expect."

Ellie turned upon her heel.

Yet Annie stared with both hands down, unbandaging her head so scars appeared. Judging by the sound of gasps, her mangle horrified the weaker stomachs the room. Annie asked, "How so?"

Ellie smiled on her younger sister.

The women took a minute, gawking at the victim of the burns.

"How could it possibly be any harder than this?" Annie asked.

The Queen Be of the Board took a moment, then said to Annie, "Both your parents left this planet, sweet."

Levi gaped and gasped as if to speak, thinking about what Sammi said, staring at his sister, but remembering the threats. He stayed upon his seat and silent. None of that came easy to him, judging by his squirming.

Ellie went bug-eyed. "Where did they go?"

"I hope," the woman said, "they went to search the megacosm for your elder brother."

Ellie said, "We have to leave to find my parents. They can't leave us all alone."

"And did they leave you so?" The room grew still again, awaiting how they'd answer.

Said Ellie, softly, "Well… I guess they didn't…"

"Are they dead?"

"I think not. But they can't be safe."

"Depends on if they've travelled often off the planet and what sort of training they've received." The woman ripped an aluminum cover away from the top of a plastic packet of raspberry jam, all a-smile.

"How often?"

Every woman smiled creepy smiles as one, yet each of them different, discrete little horrors.

Ellie swallowed and said, "Well we can find them, surely."

"I am sure."

"But you just said … ?"

"It takes some time. Finding them wouldn't get you any closer to your fix for Overmorrow rains, assuming a fix is needed."

Ellie's eyes went wide and wild. She stamped her boot in vain. "Did you restrict it?"

The woman laughed. "Almost none of us leave this diner. When we do, it isn't long and almost only for interrogations. Your petty dogfights we ignore. Anyone who knows us knows that's true because the Queen demands her subjects come to her. Besides, we all were here when this restriction happened — anyone on trial that day could testify, and neither have we cause nor means to ever do this thing. It would be… unproductive."

"You want it to grow?"

"The more the rains will grow, the more Earth infects The Vale. The more the Earth infects The Vale, the more we settle lawsuits." Lit a cigarette. "Job security."

Though Ellie thought that sounded, in the final count, more evil than the crime she was currently investigating, it didn't, in the end, line up with whom she had in mind as culprit. "Anyone who will confirm you all were here?"

"Any record in the Rose Room on our meeting minutes," she said, "or ask your Author friend. He knows: *I* never leave."

Ellie slumped her shoulders: nothing. She looked to where she thought the Author might have stood if he'd been standing beside them. A ghost of him appeared to only her. The ghost didn't shake his head. He simply kept his eyes both level on the Elder Toad.

The old woman turned to Levi. "Do you see that if this were a drunk driving or drunk flying incident and someone died, you would go to jail for a long, long time via the NYPD?"

Levi nodded.

"Did you realize that, if you had seawine in your system and tried to navigate a windbreaker through a threshold in the seas of Gergia, if you sailed under the influence, you would be held for a decade in Ingenutvag for splicefraying your passengers?"

Levi shook his head *no*. He didn't know.

"Do you now?"

He nodded slowly, accepting this to be their boundary, their rule, a natural consequence of crime he never meant to commit in a world he barely knew. Even though he had no idea what splicefraying was or how it happened. But when did anyone intend to commit a crime? Truly? With full knowledge? A sinner in every sense of the word? No one, deep down, wanted to miss the mark so badly. Everyone, once they understand the absolute, qualitative, full implications of their actions with empathy for everyone involved chooses the good instead. Most folks would rather argue about where the mark was than look in the mirror and realize they were way, way off course from what they were trying to hit. Everyone thinks they're more right than they really are and this keeps them from being playful, creative, childlike.

"I find your escapade endearing, and you did save lives. And if your sisters carry on, I think giving you to them is a worse punishment than close quarters." She took a puff and hacked a raspy laugh. "Did you — of your own volition — chug this seawine and oil spill coffee?"

Levi said loud and clear, "I did. The fault was mine."

"Your own most grievous fault and no one else's?"

Levi nodded slow, his long hair flipping back and forth.

The North Wind whispered one single word in Ellie's ear that faded into something unintelligible, "Aver…"

Ellie turned to The North Wind and whispered, "Aver-what?"

The old woman blew out smoke. "I absolve you of your narrative deviation. Go do something else with your time."

Annie ran up and hugged her brother.

Rudy left, shaking his head, scattering his legal pads to the wind (not The Wind). He'd done everything he could, none of his advice had been heeded, and he'd succeeded anyway. "That's the way it goes sometimes."

Ellie looked up from her whispers with the North Wind. She looked from her brother to the women, and after realizing the sentencing was over, said, "How do I get my parents back? I don't know how and I want to help find Charlie."

The old woman nodded toward Uncle Corey.

Ellie's face darkened. There was nothing more here for them. The North Wind said no more, but nodded towards the shaft. "Elevator. Now."

They headed that way, the five of them.

"Thanks for coming to Sharon's Cafe," the clerk said.

"Sharon's Cafe?"

"Here in Little Egypt. Bellhammer, Illinois. You've never been to Sharon's Cafe for pinochle day? What about buckkeeper day?"

The girls looked at each other. "I thought we were in Wall Street."

"You are," she said. "26 Broadway under the Coal Oil Cauldron. But Broadway in Manhattan is entangled with Broadway in Bellhammer, Illinois at certain points, of course. Most Broadways and Main Streets are, you know, entangled at some point. It's a matter for algebraic topology."

"Of course," Ellie said, jotting down the word *algebraic topology* and reminding herself to look it up later. They exited the doors, and the elevator whisked them off.

"Where to, child?" The North Wind asked.

She turned to Uncle Corey, livid.

THE JOHNSONS

She didn't know where to start as they rattled back through the weird winding of the magic elevator. Uncle Corey had evidence? He probably hid all the evidence. May have done it himself. He'd probably swapped that slick king's robe for The Grim Reaper's own black shirt. She had half a mind to accuse him right then and there in the elevator. She wished she had handcuffs for the man, but couldn't prove anything yet. More evidence. She'd get it out of him. "You tell us," she said, finally.

He growled. "Tell you what?" He pulled from the pocket in his vest a thread of white and then a needle. An odder leather thimble. This he cinched around his middle finger's knuckle before he stitched a brighter thread throughout a navy patch in very subtle patterns. He fixed that combo to the hole inside his coat.

The North Wind pouted. "Now I cannot tickle you so often."

"Stay out of my personal space."

The North Wind snorted an airy snort.

"Stop," Levi said to Uncle Corey, sharply. "Where are my parents? Where's Charlie? What did you do with Overmorrow?"

Uncle Corey shrugged a soft shrug, the sort you might see in a schoolchild who couldn't care less if you discovered where he'd hidden your Halloween candy.

"Where are they, Uncle?"

The elevator continued its tumble through all manner of ways and means — and Ways and Means — underbellies and sidebellies of commercial and civic buildings. These filled their vision with pipes and conduits and whatnot. End over end. Barrel rolls.

"I don't know, El," Uncle Corey whispered. "I don't know Lev or Ann." He did not look up from his stitching. Then softer: "I don't really know, guys, I guess." The last word was inaudible, mouthed. Almost spoken to himself.

"What?"

He mumbled again, softer still. *Was* there actually something softer than inaudible sweet nothings?

Levi, now curious, though still reeling from his failure to hide, said, "I'm sorry, Uncle C—"

The man found his courage again. And his voice. "Someone does. I'm sure of it. Someone knows."

Ellie looked down at her list, wondering… wondering… still not believing him. Parents? Overmorrow? Charlie? She followed the others, almost without blinking, through the elevator doors and the entrance and back out onto the street. All while staring at her list. There was one on the list she hadn't interviewed. "Where do the Warlocks go on a night like tonight?"

"The Johnsons," Sy said without hesitation. "They're your target, that dangerous cauldron."

Annie looked at Ellie wide-eyed, almost shocked at her own delight. "See? Mrs. Johnson was part of this after all."

Ellie looked back at her and shrugged. So her sister had been right about that part, however crazed her question. She looked to her brother.

Levi looked curious, even still. He'd come out with it all, fessed up, and *they didn't hate him.* In fact, he'd emerged somehow stronger in the wake of it. That strength steeled the resolve he'd had before he met the Angler King, the resolve he'd had back when he'd started his last run.

Sure, Levi could fade into the background. But he could also choose to help his sisters all the more. To become a main character, a true one, in his sister's *mystery*. In the mystery they all were solving. That was the beauty: he just wanted a small part in the passion play. A small part was enough. He smiled his first real smile in a long time, no hint of sadness or sarcasm or fakery inside it.

"The Johnsons is where we'll find the perps?" Annie asked.

"And with that revelation," Sy said, "I bid you all a very fine evening, I am afraid I have other articles to attend to and a large bit of housework waiting on me. I do so seldom take out the trash on interview days." He looked long at Uncle Corey, who glared back and narrowed his eyes, and then took off down the street away from them all.

"Will you leave me too, Uncle?"

"What do you need?" Uncle Corey seemed concerned for once. His breath still reeked of booze and not just a little. Had he bathed in it?

"Who are The Johnsons?"

"It's not a couple."

"Dang," said Annie.

Uncle Corey said, "It's the name of one of these old ironic hipster bars."

Levi perked up.

"A very, very terrible bar." Uncle Corey belched. "One made terrible on purpose so that old men and young men alike who want to reexperience the memory of their first taste of booze can come and get their fill straight from the tap. Lower East Side. Ask round."

Ellie eyed him, blue and green.

He eyed her back, dramatically, the way a middle school girl might. He made a buffoon out of himself, merely reflecting her emotions and actions that way: smiling when she smiled, frowning when she frowned, glaring when she glared. But she also noticed behind all of the mockery of her facial expressions, he was also looking deeply in her eyes, back and forth: blue to green, green to blue. Searching deeply amid the buffoonery for something Ellie didn't know.

It was another lead. It meant *something*. But here she was with the perpetrator before her and no way to... to bring him in. Was he sending her on a wild goose chase? Probably. Somewhere in the middle distance, heavy metal sounded out in the New York night. Distortion. She was seeing through the distortion. But without some sort of cause... obviously *The Board* wouldn't do a thing about Uncle Corey. And The Author wouldn't help her much unless she solved it.

That left the magical police they'd brushed up against now and again, and if those functioned anything like unmagical police, she'd need probable cause. She'd need more than that: she'd need to trust they actually cared about justice instead of clinging to their jobs and doing the minimum necessary paperwork.

She had no probable cause yet, no trust. That meant she'd need to follow this one lead to The Johnsons. So they started walking, the girls.

Uncle Corey gave a very meaningful look, then took off down the alley at a sprint.

Ellie shouted, "Dang!"

The North Wind watched him go, then dissipated herself.

The kids were alone again, but at least together and halfway whole. The girls asked around: those experiencing homelessness, those in suits, those selling black-and-white cookies. Levi seemed ennobled, helping with routine interviews to find The Johnsons. They walked north and east towards the East Village.

New York at night is as of a hallucinogenic lightbulb, of a carnie-folk panoply as any given fly-by-night circus. You have to be very careful listening to only headphones in the city. Headphones can trick you into thinking you and you alone hear the soundtrack to a movie starring yourself, especially when you pass so many classic movie sets. Especially at night. You can't hear anyone sneaking up on you to beg you to buy into their electronic traded funds or large language model or cryptocurrency businesses. They might sneak up you to ask you to vote for a corrupt politician. Or to buy an umbrella or tee shirt or stolen watch or faked handbag. Or, yes, sometimes some drug. Levi could attest to that.

They passed coons big as cougars carrying eggs in both hands and sprinting on two legs while chefs shouted out the back doors of pasta shops, "Bring that back!" Another man shouted down from a kid-sized cage placed around the fifth-story window. New York has hundreds of these little boxes for kids to play in and be "outside" without being turned loose for their legs to dangle outside from several stories up. Outside dangling from a cage in the air like Houdini. The North Wind would have loved it.

The man had dressed up in about a thousand sequined scarves tied around his arms and legs and neck. Flailing in the wind like some sort of mist-born zeitgeist. He had rigged up a giant trash chute system from old plastic takeout soup containers, all with a hole in the bottom and no lid, so that he could "bomb" candy on passing tourists and children and shout "HAPPY HALLOWEEN!"

It wasn't Halloween. Not yet, anyways. Right? But it felt to Ellie as if it had come early. As if the entire week had taken them from Eastertide to Halloween without any real break between. Had it? How much time had passed?

Another costumed person — a little girl — had dressed herself up as a plush, fleece-white snowman, completely fuzzy and padded with memory foam. Days ago. Maybe weeks. Her street-wandering life had torn at the fleece to expose the foam, had sullied the fleece from white to cream to brown streaked with bits of greasy black. It stank.

When you added that to the minotaur dragging an all-electric cybertruck turned over on its passenger door down the street by the power cord, the crowd of Sasquatches who had shaved down their bodies punk rock style and styled their entire head and back fur into pink mohawks (was it still a mohawk when it touches the lower back?), and the pixies turning tricks on the corners of tiny dioramas…

It made for quite the walk for two young girls and a Levi.

Thirteen miles of NYC night can cow the fittest platoon of Midwestern national guardsmen, let alone a whiff of tweens.

But they made it to The Johnsons for what Ellie hoped would be the keystone bit of evidence. Uncle Corey had been right about one thing: some hipster had taken the hollowed out shell of a storefront, then replaced everything with junk and spare decor from the inside of some Midwestern trailer park. The walls had cheap plastic ships painted like brass, pictures of someone's tacky distant cousins, and the worst possible neon lights you could scrounge up from dumpsters behind the worst possible pubs.

Tasteless enough to be tasteful. As if they'd bought everything from some old man's estate sale in Joplin or Worthington just to make it chic.

Ellie looked at Annie again and Annie shrugged: trailer park, Johnsons. Close enough. The Johnsons felt like the sort of place where Uncle Corey may have started drinking back in Carthage, Missouri, where he'd been crowned king of the drinking sickness. Or maybe he'd come here and started? Perhaps that's what he was trying to tell them?

The place poured only two beers, a crappy dark and a crappy light, neither brewed on spot like at McSorley's, neither — they found out from one warlock — tasted anything like McSorley's. Their mirror behind and above the bar had faux gold cracks and a cheap smoking effect.

Their fridge was the lamest, shortest fridge covered in band stickers.

Their couches had been bought from the store cheaply: pre-collapsed, pre-shredded, the couch version of buying holey jeans. Using a pocketknife, someone had purposefully cut up their tables into grade-school-level heavy metal symbols. Their Super Mario embedded game table had been scratched to no end as if some stockboy had used its surface as a pallet beneath every other piece of furniture. Scratched to hell. The floor was fly-trap sticky, like *hard to pull your foot up to make a single step* sticky.

All three Wright children strode inside. Slowly, stickily, their wake sounding out *smack smack smacks*. They passed two couples aggressively kissing on the couch. Ellie gagged. Levi turned and blushed. Annie merely cocked her head and said, "They look like toddlers who can't make up their minds or control their hands."

Ellie and Levi looked at one another, back at the couples. After staring for a while Levi said, "Yeah," and Ellie said, "I get it now."

Both couples stopped and stared at the three children, scoffing, then resumed their positions.

The Wright children walked further past a series of identically clad men with the sides of their heads shaved short (similar to Sasquatches they'd passed, but no pink) and the tops of their heads cut long. They looked like a bunch of northern rich kids trying to dress as hobos from Appalachia. You know the type: the kind of rich WASP who thinks he knows what it's like to grow up poor in land settled by kindly white trash folk he hates. Like the English young brats who moved to Ireland after the potato famine genocide.

On second thought, maybe exactly that kind of brat, in the long tail of history.

Past them, the Wright children walked around a wooden-poled waist-high wall. Some folks shouted over a European boardgame — something or other about trading sheep and goats and copper ore — while others shouted over an arm-wrestling match between a freshman sorority girl and an ironman weightlifter. The girl was winning until the ironman snapped her wrist in half. She passed out, face white as a porcelain mask.

There at the blackened back, gathered around a broken down sectional couch, sat six warlocks. Two they recognized from the lakeside as well as four others.

Annie whispered, "I don't like that count."

Ellie shushed her.

"Better than thirteen," Levi said.

That nearly stopped Ellie's heart. Then jump started it again. "We don't need a coven."

But the man in the middle, the tall one, said, "I know what you mean. Seven would be better. Ten would be many. Twelve would be my people. We won't talk about a baker's dozen, but twenty-one would be a proper council, unless we called a Sanhedrin."

"Which would take seventy," the one beside him said. He was adorned in a robe that looked like a supernova had exploded on it. Ellie couldn't tell whether it was moving through some intergalactic orbit or if the robe was simply blowing in the wind.

Levi immediately recognized the patternless pattern: a specific mind wearing its own specific megacosm in a way that reflected the microcosm within him and the macrocosm beyond him. Levi compared this one with another, who had a white cloak. The white cloak bore nested bone planets orbiting ivory planets.

Annie thought both looked cute. "Aww."

"Or seventy-two," a third said. He wore a white robe speckled with black holes and black, visible superstrings.

"In any case," the first said. "I think this is the part where I say the titular line: Welcome to The Johnsons."

The one in white beside him said, "That ain't the story."

"It's the bar's story," he said. "We're in that bar. Why hold back its story?"

"Yeah, but titular lines are for the stories *they're in*."

"Well stories can be nested. I'd call this chapter The Johnsons, this section The Warlocks, this act The Drunk Perpetrator, but what's the name of the bigger story and therefore the titular line?"

"Overmorrow," Ellie said. "We're here to talk about Overmorrow."

The titular line warlock sighed. "There's been plenty of lines about that, though, *I* wanted to be the one to say the titular line. It's *my* titular line."

Ellie said, "I think you've had enough."

He sipped his beer and said, "Not of this."

Levi cleared his throat awkwardly.

Three of the warlocks leaned back towards the cushions, the head of one banging slightly on the wall. Another two leaned forwards. One tamped his egregiously long cigarette and the other rubbed his temples and looked at the floor. But the main warlock looked on.

"Did you brew a potion at the start of the week?" Annie asked, rubbing her scarred scalp. Ellie saw no bitterness upon her sister's brow and found it remarkable, all things considered.

"Yes," he said.

"Did it restrict Overmorrow?" Levi asked.

"No. What of her?"

Ellie squinted at the word *her*. She shifted her weight to her non-main foot. "Did you know that the rains were restricted?" Ellie asked.

"Yes, of course, I talked to the guy who came to play Phi with me."

"What's Phi?" Annie asked.

"Game invented by the dwarves. Infinite undos."

"Undos?" Levi asked.

"Takebacksies," sat the fat one in brown burlap.

"Past branches in the road to move forward along a different causal chain," said the one in the tarnished white.

"You're saying you can go back a move? Like your last move?"

"As many as you want," said the tall one in the middle.

"You don't do laid is played?" Levi asked.

"What is this, chess? It ain't about tricking your way to a win. You go back as far as you need to play your *best* game. It's *your* best potential game versus your *opponent's* best potential game. And it's all about the beauty of spirals intersecting forever and ever. Fractals."

"Fractals?" Ellie asked.

He grew super excited and started talking *very* fast and *very* nerdy. "A curve or geometric figure, each part of which has the same statistical character as the whole. Fractals are useful in modeling structures (such as eroded coastlines or snowflakes) in which similar patterns recur at progressively smaller scales, or larger scales, and in describing partly random or chaotic phenomena such as crystal growth, fluid turbulence, and galaxy formation. Same patterns nested in same patterns, no matter how large or small. The word *fractal* from the French for broken: but broken in a specific way. No matter how good of a game you play in Phi, there's always another game nested in the game. So it's a game of winning the set of all games. And whether or not *this* set is *that* set and—" he noticed her eyes glazing. He cleared his guzzler. "Anyways."

"You talked to a *guy* who came to play Phi with you?" Ellie asked.

"Yes."

"The North Wind?" Annie asked.

"No. North Wind's a *she*."

Annie raised her eyebrow and swayed, off balance.

"Dwarf?" Ellie asked.

"No."

"Giant…" Levi asked slower, "…fish?"

"No. Angler King's dead, I hear."

Levi spat. He didn't want seawine, but danggit… he did honestly like that old fish. The one that got away, who now had gotten away from every fisherman, forever.

Ellie scribbled a note in her book that she knew she didn't need. She looked up.

Annie said, "And not a woman who played with you?"

"No," he said. "Definitely a guy. Unless it was a very elaborate disguise, but I can see through most glamours. More enchantment. If a woman hid in that disguise, I would have known."

"What did this man want?" Ellie asked.

"Oh, he was just asking if there was a way to restrict rain."

Annie and Levi gasped.

"I told him we were trying to conjure up more rain for the dwarves, but he wanted to know if there was a way to restrict it. I told him he'd need to be pretty familiar with destroying thresholds like wardrobes and lampposts, portals and rabbit holes, ghostly brick walls and thinnies, fairy bridges and doors of stone, secret passages and wormholes and hyperspace booths — preferably with redundancies — and whatnot."

"You what?!"

"Oh yeah and he showed me his house where he'd done *just that* over the years. Kind of wild. Where he'd taken off the heads of all kinds of magical thresholds and objects, sure thing. Guy liked to drink, so I drank a lot with him."

The girls looked at each other, shocked.

"Where is this house?" Annie asked.

"Oh easy," he said. "Just down the road from where we were brewing all the potions for making the rain come harder. Just down that same street — 77th or something? Where it touches Central Park? The street by the same entrance to the park across from the cauldron. Make sure to bring whiskey, guy drinks it all the time."

The girls gasped, Ellie mouthed *Uncle Corey, No! How could you?* and took off.

"Aren't you gonna settle up?" The warlocks cackled after her.

The man at the bar said, "Easy, kiddos."

The aggressive couples stopped kissing again, in earnest, and their eyes went from consumed in their duality to shocked that someone — anyone — could be having more fun than the both of them were currently having. Enough for everyone else to stop and watch *someone else*. Almost *disappointed* they weren't the ones making a scene, the ones on exhibition. Their shoulders slumped. Levi wondered if the kissing was even the point: it seemed to him like most older folks he'd met in the world used romance as a way, not a goal. A fact, not a value.

Through the door Ellie shouted, "TAXI!"

"They don't call like that anymore," said a man outside in a green WWI jacket, complete with medals, a sign next to him saying *homeless vet, pancreatic cancer, hoping for a miracle*. "It's not a summoning spell."

Levi looked closer. Stars and moons on his robe. A homeless, veteran *wizard*. He gave him a fast food gift card he'd gotten the previous Christmas and had brought in order to spend on his first, best, New York trip. "Stay sober, brother," he said. "I get it."

The man smiled, though baffled at the little boy.

A taxi pulled over to them.

"Woah," the homeless wizard said. "It's magic! I didn't think they let people like me see magic anymore."

Ellie's eyes went sad while Annie's went curious — different wrinkles would form on those faces: one married, one chastened. Ellie told the cabbie the name of the street. The cab took off towards the house the warlocks had told her about. Ellie felt even sadder that the Overmorrow rains hadn't hit the man experiencing homelessness, sadder still that she'd gotten this last piece of evidence:

They knew now where Uncle Corey lived in town. He *wasn't* homeless. And he'd be there with all manner of evidence for all manner of crimes. She knew she should call the magical police. She probably wouldn't, since she could solve it herself. Yeah, she'd gotten what she wanted. But she hadn't expected it really and truly to incriminate her only uncle, however besotted a life he had lived.

THE RAIN FUNNEL

On the west side of Central Park, many rich folk live sometimes. And work sometimes. And sometimes play. Other times — most of the time — they live, work, and play in the South of France, Upstate, L.A., the Hamptons, Florida, London, Tokyo, Beijing, or any number of other manufactured playgrounds for the rich that *aren't* Central Park West. These types own five houses. They give their kids funds that generate endless amounts abstracted from the resources and companies and locals who built them like *Gold and Lead Mining INC*. This all creates a low occupancy rate in the houses and forces the neighborhood into a kind of tourism and crime churn.

The children exited at 77th and Central Park West on the park side where the warlock had told them to go. Ellie glanced back to the gate. The Author had said there was a gate for every kind of person. She looked at the name: *The Naturalist's Gate*. Naturalist.

Like a lover of nature?

Or like someone who believes nature is all there is?

She looked forward as they walked down the street between the New York Historical Society and the Museum of Natural History. Then they were at the house and saw the horror of flickering light.

Someone had taken a pipe cutter to cut the heads off lamp-posts by the hundreds, leaving them to flicker in their final dying light. The headless lamps twitched light in the front garden, fulgurating along all the walls. Lampposts you might find your first day in a magical foreign land. Ellie thought of the old street-lamp beneath their house in Missouri. It had had a gilded tip like a minaret, and black vine-like swirls with gold leafing and a gilded fairy crown above the black lampshade.

How horrible to think of someone cutting off its *head*.

Had it been their first encounter with Overmorrow, it may have given them a childish shock and awe. The lights of a thousand eldritch lamps in varied states of dying with no obvious source of fuel. The Gaslamp district headless, gasless, but flickering. A graveyard where fairy lights and will-o-wisps had gone to die.

Another corner held shards of wardrobes. Another shimmered from flickers of stargates and portals blinking in and out of being. A thousand other broken thresholds lay scattered, so much blackened lead held in such sacred light. Something possessed the children then, a kind of cadence, a spirit of song, a sort of call-and-response.

"We were meant to see another world," Annie said.

Ellie said, "One prevented that. Not a threshold guardian, a—"

"Threshold *distractor*," Levi suggested.

"Too soft," Ellie said.

"Threshold *assassin*," Levi said. "Threshold *breaker*. Threshclast. Threshold *forgetter*. Threshold demon."

"An image breaker not an image maker," Annie said.

Ellie nodded. "Threshold assassin. Overmorrow is the sight, but Overmorrow ain't the world."

Annie shook her head. "We've heard of bunches of them."

"The Vale," Levi said, "barely touches here. We stand on the furthest edge, the darkest corner of the universe." He pointed towards the sky. "And it's all up and into the megacosm from here on out my sisters." The bile and brine of seawine? Gone. His head had completely cleared for the first time in days, other than the withdrawal headache. He no longer wanted it. Especially looking around at the shattered remains of these portals. "Further up and in from here."

"From Earth," Annie said.

"Earth. Tara in Irish," Ellie said. "The grounding Tor. Satyrnalia."

"Lond," Levi echoed. "Lands. Terra as in Terra Firma."

"Lands. Lance in French," Ellie said. "Lance or Tara."

"Both," said Annie. "Both."

The lamplights flickered. Some went green, begging the children to find their abuser and bring them to justice. This particular house would have towered over many homes in Brooklyn. Astride spires it was dwarved like a giant that had corrupted itself and shrunk its own stature. As if the house had once been used for good, but now was only ill. A brownstone on its edifice that wasn't "Brownstone," so to speak.

It had all sorts of intricate moulding, handcarved by freemasons who'd led the Gothic revival. Not true Gothic, after all, since its bones weren't stones, but steel. Steel hid under that dark stone. It was a prophecy in building form that awaited true Gothic revival, what neoclassical folk might call barbaric. For good reason: the Goths invaded Rome. If Southern Gothic stories focus on mansions, if British Gothic stories focus on old decrepit Gothic ruins that creeped out younger children growing up in 18th, 19th centuries, then it seems a New York Gothic should focus on the haunted decrepit or even revived brownstones. The brownstone era thought it could wed nature to the steam engine: to simply slather brown and crumbling stone to the face of a building bricked by machines. It was Edith Wharton who called brownstones, "hidebound in their deadly deformity of mean ugliness."

They don't last, however cute for those rich folks flocking to them.

Let that sort of thing decay and draw in some ghosts. They built them with stoops to dodge the river of animal crap that flowed down average 18th century streets in New York

City — horses, pigs, the rest. This one, lit lamps or dark, leaned into the steam shovel side of creativity, leaned away from nature's proper wedding with the urban environ.

Somehow, all these remnants of broken thresholds to other worlds had been strewn about the front yard, arranged to resemble something worse than junk. Worse than a run-down hippy place. It looked like an elegant art installation. There were the remnants of fairy bridges of stone and fairy tunnels made of many trees that, through inosculation, had grown together into the single organism: the treetunnel. At least it had before it had been smashed. Garden gates, wardrobes, trap doors, door saddles, odd reflective pools that weren't reflecting the brownstone above but rather some other tower of dark light, glowing toilet bowls, and odd tent flaps. The types of thresholds filled the yard, all smashed.

Yes it looked like an elegant art installation.

A ghastly one.

Ellie reached out for the black wrought-iron gate, plated with green copper. It bore the symbol शनि and a sign with three seemingly contradictory messages upon it.

The first read:

Through me men go into that blissful place
Of hearts made whole and cures for deadly wounds
Through me men go unto the well of grace
There green and lusty May forever endures
This is the way to every good adventure.
Be glad, ye reader, caste thy sorrow off
For I am open: pass — be swift, be soft.

The second read:

Through me men go into the place of fear
Unto the mortal strokes of the sphere
Of which Disdain and Danger is the guide
From whom no man shall hide
There never trees shall fruit nor leaves bear.
This stream will lead you to the sorrowful where
There as fish in prison is all dried

The anguish of death pervades the neverdied.
The third said:
Through me lies the way into the everlasting city
Through me lies the way to every pain and bliss
Through me lies the way that passes through the lost
And past the losses, quest unto the found.
For Justice, Love are One who forged my hinges
Fire sinks us, even as it singes,
And makes the metal sound.
No things were made before my ditty
Except those things who bear eternal cost
Abandon every hope, ye shades who enter in.
Abandon all despair, ye real of dames and men.
Abandon not thyself, ye soots of steel.

Ellie had read it aloud to Annie since her pace was a bit slower than the other two. Then she stared at the lines. *That blissful place.*

Yeah, she'd gotten the evidence, but so what? Where did that leave Uncle Corey?

The anguish of death might await him. *Through me lies the way.*

The way to what? The solution? Charlie? Overmorrow? To getting her family back together for once? If she lost Uncle Corey for good and forever in exposing him to kidnapping Charlie... To shrinking Overmorrow... Would it be worth it? She didn't want to go inside. What if she found Uncle Corey in there for real? But she must. She grew quiet. Then to distract her own thoughts, she asked, "Which is telling the door's truth, Annie?"

Annie squinted to try to comprehend some of the words. "Read it again?"

Levi tried. He looked back up and read all three poems slower than his sister, without performative cadence and with determined effort. He focused in on the curve of *f* and *y* on the wrought metal, running his fingers on the green copper.

Ellie waited patiently, though inside she was downright intolerant of her brother's slowness in other arenas by this point. She *wanted* to be irritated with him, but for completely different reasons.

Annie sucked her canines with her tongue. "I think it's all three. I think it's the same message."

"But they contradict?" Levi asked.

"At first. But then, only as two sides of the same green penny contradict."

"Heads or tails?" Levi asked.

"Both," Ellie said. "But tails first for us, it seems, till wiser heads prevail."

"Huh," said Annie. "Burn us till we wisdom bleed." She patted her crown's scars and winked.

With that, Ellie made her call. She pushed open the gate to a shrill, high-pitched sound as if the steam whistle on an ancient train had been pressurized enough to power a ship, then whittled down to form a tiny whistle. It hurt their ears worse than a dog's.

Overhead, the sun went black as a hole. Immediate eclipse. The haunting stars at midday shone in wonder, for those who hadn't seen, and terror, for those who feared the night at noonday.

All went dark.

They covered their ears, ducked and covered as if in a World War I trench, and tried to press forwards beyond it. The doors slammed shut behind them. The cavernous low echo of the slam filled their ears with the last faint memory of sound. On the other side of the great cedar palace doors sat a cavernous hall.

"It's missing stairs," Annie said.

"What?" Ellie asked.

"Stairs. A foyer like this always has stairs."

The creepiest little old crusty housekeeper draped in shadow glanced at them, then skittered away. Ellie jumped.

The other two looked at her.

"Hello?" Ellie squeaked, her eyes so wide that zero blue or green remained.

Levi struggled to resume conversation, haltering in his breath.

"Some big old stairwell that a princess walks down? Some spiral stair up through the middle? This hall don't even have art."

"Doesn't," Ellie said.

"Don't works."

"Not in polite society," Ellie said.

"Manners are polished turds," Levi said.

"Sometimes manners are simple graces for someone else. Depends on what your manners mean. Dirt floors are just polished turds. Why not marble countertops?"

Levi said, "Huh."

Annie belched and nodded. "Everyone does *that*, one way or another."

Ellie rolled her eyes at her sister. "The room isn't empty, though."

Annie looked down from those cold, vacant heights and beheld the eyes of frozen creatures: creatures stuck in ice, creatures in stone, creatures captured in the hardened amber that had once been the sap of sacred maple and cypress and uncorrupted acacia trees. Annie gasped.

Ellie followed Annie's gaze, gasped too when she saw.

Levi went silent and still, which was quite something for him.

Mandibles and horns marred by hoarfrost. Feathers and scales squeezed by crystalline. Those of bone turned those of stone, even more skeletal types like the dead-but-flying reindeer. A slight tear formed at the corner of Ellie's vision, blurring it all to a muddy blue, muddy white. "Left or right," she choked out over the edge of the horror that so many Overmorrow folk had been petrified.

Most people turn right as soon as they go into a place. That's why you go into a grocery store and they get all those aisles to turn right on you as soon as you enter. A great sloping entrance to a maze of carrots and kiwi. But Annie wasn't most people. Stubbornly Ellie's sister turned left *first* instead.

From the lefthand room they heard grinding and smashing of bricks. Ellie knew she was going to stumble upon her Uncle Corey just throwing bricks at the wall. Annie turned the corner,

Ellie close enough to kick at her heels. The grinding, crunching grew so loud, it felt like it might turn their very teeth to pulp.

The ceiling had been changed into a great silver funnel — the same funnel they'd seen from the roof of the Rockefeller and from Central Park, the same funnel they'd seen from the rocks at the boat pond the day the waters had shrunk. It had all manner of rainbow rain and golden waters falling through it into a great bladder that swelled and swelled, then squeezed the waters it held into something below. A great prison for Overmorrow waters.

Heaven's drain.

There in the middle, a great wall of bricks quivered. They wriggled and holes in the fabric of reality appeared and disappeared. These grew wider and wider and smaller and smaller a sideways broken archway that was being smashed over and over again with this massive warhammer.

The person who was wielding it was *not* the Angler King, obviously, nor some zombie version of the Angler King. But the person who was wielding it was *also not* one of the three witches, one of the warlocks, The North Wind, one of the dwarves, one of the cosmicloaks, one of the random magical creatures they'd met like the centaurs or fauns, one of the old women from The Board, Sammi, Oblivion, their parents, The Author, or even Uncle Corey.

Ellie gasped.

30

MORE MECH THAN MAN

The person in front of Ellie who smashed thresholds with a warhammer was Sy. Sy, the reporter, smashed over and over with this massive warhammer. A giant, monstrous plant filled with cameras like chimeric eyes hovered around him, getting as many angles on his destruction as possible, cataloging all of it as a naturalist with notebook and colored pencil.

When Sy's warhammer struck the bricks, great tendrils of lightning flashed out from the hammer and great golden coins — tarnished and broken in twain, a foreign currency to the girls and even to most on Earth, cloak or no — flew out of the bricks. Coin bits and coin bobs. Some plumbum. Beside Sy sat a small vial of silver will-o'-the-wisps, or a similar something. Quicksilver in cloud form.

"Sy?" Ellie asked. "What are you doing here? We're looking for our Uncle Corey."

"Corey. Corey?! Oh sure, right. Fits the bill, him." He smashed away at his walls.

"What are you breaking?"

"A threshold. This one leads to a pretty famous shopping district of a world of wizards. Sort of place that sells cauldrons, brooms, wands, and wheezes. You get to it through an arch that forms from this wall of bricks."

"Why?"

"Because," he stopped swinging the warhammer, leaning on the handle of it and looking at the girls. "It's time we forget all of this magical nonsense and move on. Go back to being an *industrial* society, one of great *progress* and *factories*. American manufacturing!"

"But what about Overmorrow?"

"What about it? I'm tired of this world, kids. So tired. Magic world. Fantasy. Comics. Aren't you tired of it?"

"I'm just getting started," Levi said.

Sy scoffed. "Do you have any idea what it's like growing up off-planet?"

"We're third culture kids," Levi said. "We were born up off-country."

"It's not the same."

"Sure it is," Levi said. "We grew up a world away from our home. We only recently moved to Missouri."

"Have you any idea at all what it's like to spend your entire childhood on Gergia and only ever *hearing* of Earth? As if you weren't even *human*?"

Annie asked, "Aren't there humans on other planets?"

"Well sure," he said. "But we came from *here*, didn't we?"

"I don't know," Ellie said. "Did we?"

Sy scoffed. "What do you know?"

"Nothing," Ellie said. "Nor do I think I know."

He scoffed, stopped leaning, picked up and swung his warhammer and smashed more of the archway that had once led to the magical alleyway. "What do you even know? Why wouldn't we be from here?"

Annie said, "Well... Maybe because we're from a magical *elsewhere*?"

He swung harder and then pointed the hammerhead at them both. An odd hourglass shape aimed at her eyes. He opened his mouth, then closed it again. "It's time we get everyone back here, back to Earth, and hit the reset button."

"Cut us off from Overmorrow?" Ellie asked.

"Cut us off from *The Vale*," he said. "Gergia's connected to all of the other universes of all *their* creators. Why can't we severe our connection from them all?" He smashed more bricks. "Why can't we just go back to being a *silent* planet, hiding in our dark little corner of the megacosm? Don't you *want* to forget this cosmic madness?"

More smashed garden gates, hedge mazes, wardrobes, and crystal cave entrances. He swung and he swung and he swung. So many thresholds rendered unstable, unusable, so many of them torn asunder from their worlds. And now their own threshold to The Vale — their Overmorrow — was getting sucked through a massive funnel into God only knows where.

Ellie said, "It can't be you. You weren't there."

"At the scene of the shrinkage? What? Sure I was. I was interviewing everyone as soon as it happened. I interviewed *you*, silly girl."

Ellie thought. She *had* remembered the funnel looking thing over in the sky on this side of the park. And he'd been with them all along the way. Guiding questions. Guiding answers. Hadn't The Author straight-up *warned* her not to go to the library with Sy?

Annie whispered at the broken thresholds more than at Sy: "Why would you take away the magic way to open our eyes? Why would you make Levis out of everyone on Earth?"

Levi looked at her and said, "Hey!"

Annie shrugged. "Sorry, not *Levis*, but UnLevis."

Levi nodded as he swayed on either foot. "Yeah, no one should be so full of seawine."

Sy stopped up cold. He looked compassionate for a moment. "What happened to your brother?"

"I'm standing right here," Levi said.

"So?" Sy asked. "What happened?"

"The Angler King."

"Is dead," Sy said. "So?"

"He fed me some seawine that made me forget who I was, temporarily forget Overmorrow, and all sorts of other things."

"Yes, I'd planned on that," Sy said.

Levi pawed the old flooring with his toe. "Had to do oilspill coffee just to get lucid enough to function."

"Ah, yes. An antiwayfare. It'll sever you from any of those silly ideas that you live in a magic world or that something like an Author exists." He swung his hammer. "Haven't you ever read Philip Pullman or H.G. Wells or Heinlein?" He smashed the bricks of the alleyway. Bits flew off.

Ellie said, "Some. Seems to me none of them did what they set out to do. Kind of impossible."

Annie thought she could hear the faintest cry of despair from the brickwork, the sound of the *idea* of magical masonry *dying*. This was a place where even *ideas* came to die. Where maybe even the concept of concepts came to die. All of them, personified. "But Levi is sick."

"Was," Levi said.

"Sickness is a way of life," Sy said. "It's just part of humanity, toughen up and get over it. What doesn't kill you makes you stronger."

"It *could* have killed me," Levi said.

"You sure?" Sy asked.

Annie said, "I'm sure of it."

"Enough of this, you brats. Get over here and *help me*." He nodded to some similar hammers. They weren't bell hammers. They were meant to crack the resonant frequency of anything, not ring it out loud and proud. They were meant to make things say *what I do is never me for that I wouldn't ever come to be*.

"No," Ellie said. "We're turning you in."

He stopped mid-swing. He turned to the girls. Death glare and pointed the hammer at them. "No. You are not."

The doors slammed shut behind them.

But something else in the hollow of the room sounded like them. An older them. A boy. Perhaps an older brother. Ellie ran towards the great bladder and the spinning and swirling mess beneath it and her alike. "Charlie?" she asked into the hole down which she couldn't see the bottom.

Faint — fainter than the sort of adult conversations her parents had often shared that Ellie had often heard through a wall — so faint came a voice lost to time and memory. "Ellie?"

Ellie started pushing at the bladder, trying to find a way to move the billows and get down into there, but the more she pushed it, the more it ebbed and flowed and seemed to suck in *even more* Overmorrow rains above. A great slurshing. It funneled even more down and down in speed and intensity, the eldritch magic machine like a demon-possessed dehumidifier. One covered in black mold and putrefaction. She looked for something to smash with. Ellie eyed the warhammer, which now lay a ways away from Sy's hand. She ran towards it.

"You won't take the Overmorrow rites from my master's memory palace!" Sy shouted. "You won't steal his waremind storage!" He sprinted at Ellie, fist raised with a dagger made of lead. The dagger had already started turning his entire hand to charred ash, to charcoal, to prima materia. Burning him down to the raw stuff of creation. It would certainly kill them all.

Levi shouted, "Over here, ya nincompoop!"

"You said poop," said Annie and giggled.

Which slowed Sy for the briefest second. Silly thing to say, the both of them, but it was enough to give Ellie a head start. Sy cleared the room to his left.

Ellie scrambled to lift the warhammer to her right.

Annie fumbled in her pocket. Fumbling. Stick of gum. Fumble. Free comedy show tickets. Sample of coconut water. Half eaten bag of kettle chips. Uncashed lotto tickets found in some trash can. A sieve. A golden sieve? *I'll be: a golden sieve*, she thought. Wielding it, she ran to intercept the line Sy'd cut towards Ellie. Annie lifted the sieve.

Ellie lifted the warhammer with ease: how had it been made so light?

Sy lifted his leaden dagger to kill the eldest girl Wright.

Annie put the golden sieve between the dagger and her sister Ellie. The dagger hit the sieve and turned to a golden knife on the other end. But when Sy's fist, wrist, forearm, then arm hit it, the reporter's limb exploded in a burst of light and Overmorrow rain.

"WHAT HAVE YOU DONE, YOU DYSFUNCTIONAL MECHANISM OF SOCIETY'S DECAY TOWARDS THE PRIMITIVE!" He went to swing at Annie with his other arm.

Levi ran to help. "Odd cry."

Ellie swung at the bladder with the thunder warhammer. It didn't explode. It didn't even puncture. Rather it contracted, as you might deflate a balloon and the Overmorrow rains stuck within reversed their passage through the rain-collector funnel. Instead of draining, they sprayed out all into the stratosphere.

It rained gold. Outside in the eclipsed night-by-day, it rained gold everywhere like throwing sunlit snow in Death's shadowy face.

Meanwhile, Sy was screaming about burns. Howling and cussing.

The golden sieve had expanded from Annie's hands to the size of a cast net. Levi grabbed one end, she grabbed the other. They extended it. Then pulled it all the way down the length of the man and he screamed and hollered and turned into all sorts of flashing, flaring bits of watery light — even more of those quicksilver wisps like in the jar came out of his ears and nose and eyes as the two children pulled it down.

Levi half expected it to kill him, for there to be more blood or something, some sort of blood filter even, spleen-like, but it didn't. There wasn't blood.

Instead, at the bottom of the full filtered length of what had moments prior been a man, when all of that dissolved light once more coagulated and condensed there lay a tiny little newborn babe. The baby shared the same birthmark Sy had under his left eye. A birthmark in the shape of a little bullseye. The baby cooed and giggled.

Annie said, "I guess he was more mech than man?"

Ellie couldn't focus on baby Sy right now; she was possessed of the sound of her brother Charlie's voice. Rather, she found herself searching around the edge of the now-empty bladder (the side of which had hidden a manual override switch she'd pulled) and was muttering, "In here, Annie. Charlie's buried in here."

Annie ran over to help, but it didn't really seem that they could get to him from there. They moved the bladder around the edge of the drain hole, loosened it and found a little gap in the platform. It gave enough to reveal a little porthole leading to black.

The Wright children looked at one another.

Hesitated.

Give them that much grace at least, they thought: to jump or not to jump.

Then they pushed to stretch the hole and leapt down into the black abyss below.

31

MY BROTHER'S KEEPER

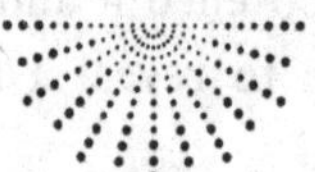

Beneath the Overmorrow collector and bladder billows, a great drain stretched above them, a circle like the circle leading to the water fountain column in the center of the Ben Gurion airport. Only the water had dried. Now only drips of Overmorrow flicked down into that blackened space. Those splashed their golden rainbows all upon the lifted platform. A faint calling again, though less faint than before. Stronger and closer.

The way the platform refracted the light of the water splashing summoned Ellie. She cocked her head and climbed upon it. The platform gave out beneath her. What if it gave out completely? That's when she noticed her feet were upon a massive pane of glass. It was dark in the room she occupied and dark below.

And yet, the reflection *gave* concave. It wasn't perfectly reflected. Another room, a different room shone from the pane below.

There in that room beneath that pane sat an older boy. He had burnished green eyes that illumined the very dark. His hair reminded Ellie of Annie's mop. Or the mop Annie had *had* prior to blackening and singeing it off in the first of the fires of the sieve in their fight with the mech. The more she thought about it, why on earth did they keep on carrying that sieve? Speaking of carrying: his hands had the lithe dexterity that Levi's slender fingers had. Somewhere Ellie's mind adjusted Levi's and Annie's ages. She saw again the elder boy and asked herself a solitary question: "Charlie?"

He was silent. He was bound. Bound hand and foot, face and back.

She pounded on the glass — a pound; a pound. Something was off. She wasn't really looking at the boy, but at a room, an ideal room. Too filled with tiny details like a cast-off centaur helmet or a floating hammock bed.

Odd things. Odd things oughtn't be there. They didn't fit her notion of the props you find in rooms like that. Or even with the sorts of things she'd seen since Overmorrow had woken her, things that didn't fit.

A silhouette creeped up behind the boy. An enormous silhouette, perhaps feathered, perhaps furry, perhaps scaled. The face of it peeked into the barest of lightbeams. It was the face of an ambitious young man. Or a snake. Or maybe a wolf. A wolf man, snake man, wolfsnake thing. She couldn't tell, really. She knew the name of the creature before she could say it. She didn't need to say it as the cowboy had so long ago and so far away from there. It was already summoned, already approaching, already clutching her chest from the inside like a hidden claw come to snatch her very heart and eat it, tooth and claw. All the fear of her mother's drifting memory and of the absence of her parents congealed in her lungs, all of her worries over Charlie caught in her throat so she couldn't speak, her anger over Levi's addiction and bafflement over the filleting of the monstrous old sea fish both leaked into her sweaty palms. Her sadness at the distance between her and the Author grew, her desperation to find the centaur's help or the witches or the warlocks. Where was the North Wind blowing? Why would she not help them in their flailing? Why had the dwarves and the whole wild world abandoned her as this eldritch horror rose up before her, old dread of Alzheimer's and Amnesia incarnate.

The monster opened its maw. "Well hello, Ellie. Charlie and I have been dreaming of you, you see. All three of you. You stirred up lots of dust in Somnolory."

"Oblivion?" She asked.

"They've called me worse," he said. "I see you all destroyed our Overmorrow hoarder?"

Annie spat and said, "Yeah and we will break the rest."

He bared his teeth. They looked crystalline and terrible-like wolf teeth made of diamond merged with the fangs of snakes. Almost like a fang-mouth eel. Shard mouth. As if it had eaten a mirror the size of God.

Levi growled back at him. Barked.

Ellie looked across the glass-covered wishing well and mouthed to Annie *rest of what?*

Annie shrugged and pointed at him.

The monster sputtered. Somehow, large flecks of spit and bile showered its room. Levi laughed at it. It asked, "How do you know about the others, Annie?"

Annie blew a raspberry.

Ellie said, "Let Charlie go."

"Oh child, even if I were to let him go, you couldn't find him. He'd get lost out in the void of space, you know. Quite an inconvenience, space. Even to one like me. And now I think I'll take my leave of you. We have so many things to remember, so many ideas to collect, me and Charlie." He pulled a five-gallon bucket of paint out, a roller brush, and started painting over his side of the glass mirror Ellie stood upon. Painting the convex window sable.

Ellie pounded on the glass.

Levi ran to the edge of the glass and drew the multitool he'd nicked from the Author's house. He fiddled with the seam of glass to see if he could pry it loose. Screwing with the screws he found, however tiny. Using tiny scythes to rip it as you'd rip the seam of jeans.

The creature painted on the dark, in the dark. The window of the glass, it slowly turned to blackened glass.

Ellie pounded.

Annie whispered, "Ellie."

Levi fiddled. Squeaks resounded, shrill, metallic, while he worked his blade.

Ellie hollered, "CHARLIE!"

Annie whispered, "Ellie."

The monster shrouded in shadow painted on. Painted the wall before him, the floor beneath their feet. She never stopped to think how gravity had shifted for the monster and the brother.

Ellie grabbed hold of the last tendrils unraveled beneath the empty bladder and funnel after the hammerfall. She power-climbed up the makeshift rope as she had done in. P.E. classes until she reached the edge of the drain.

"Ellie…"

Levi started ramming the blade into the seam. The tip snapped clean off. He opened up the saw.

Ellie emerged astride the great old hole in the ground with the flapping leathern bladder opening and closing the space between it and the wall of the perfectly circular hole. She hustled to where she had dropped that glowing, pink translucent warhammer. She picked up the warhammer without effort. Threw it at the mirror hole.

Annie had to dive away to keep from getting hit. The warhammer fell to the floor.

The hammer didn't clatter, but it stopped where it hit ground.

Sliding back down the torn strap of the bladder as a ninja might slide down a ripcord, Ellie sprang from the rope and scooped up the hammer of lighter light —

"Ellie," Annie whispered once again—

Levi snapped the saw and then pulled out the can opener—

—Ellie gripped it in those white-knuckled bony little well-tempered-clavier-playing hands of hers and swung for all she was worth. Right at the glass pane on the floor beneath her.

The hammer bounced.

The glass wouldn't shatter.

Oblivion painted on, tittering.

"ARRGH," said Levi and reversed to the handle just to pound on seam and screw.

Unlike when she faced the maw of the monster who took her brother, she did not freeze. Something then boiled in Ellie's bones to a heat she'd never felt in her life and she said without warrant or warning or plan: "I AM A CHILD OF OVERMORROW, MAKER OF GOLD AND RENOWN. THE ELDEST DAUGHTER OF MINE OWN LINE! I SHALL WIELD THIS THONTHORSTROKE HAMMER WELL AND TRUE AND BEAUTIFULLY!"

Annie said, "Please, El—"

She swung again. She swung for all her might and bigness. Glass beneath their feet exploded, Ellie was gasping, "Yes!"

But all three fell.

32

AM I MY BROTHER'S KEEPER?

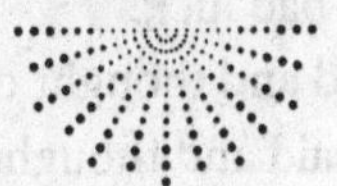

She gasped.

Down in the depth of the short little well of stones long erected to make a basin. There beneath the circle drain, above where the bladder for the Overmorrow rain had gone. The room had vanished along with the mirror.

Annie spoke first. "Ellie, I know it's not fair..."

Levi looked at his hands. Glass crunched beneath his boots.

Her elder sister stared at boney little hands. The hammer on the floor cast aside. Not her. Not her.

Annie started again. "We'll find him. I just didn't think it real, the mirror."

"It was real," Ellie said.

Levi said, "We just don't know enough to travel that way. Through a mirror."

"Mirror, mirror on the wall," Ellie whispered from some other story.

Annie said, "Next time, don't destroy the threshold we must use."

"Should have learned from Sy."

Annie perked up. "Oh no the poor baby!" She climbed the cobble wall of the well and went back to the trailing thread of the bladder and started climbing up it as her sister had, one hand after other. Much, much slower than Annie.

Ellie waited in the basin, boots were grinding glassy shards to powder. "Annie?"

Annie called down without eye contact, "Yeah, El?"

"I just shattered a massive mirror."

"Yeah?" Levi asked.

"It's seven volumes of bad luck."

"Seven *years*." Levi said and thought of all he'd drunk.

"Seven years." Annie said and thought of the hair she'd lost.

"No," Ellie said, thinking of the Author. "No, I think I spoke true."

Annie said, "Weird way of saying seven years."

Ellie said, "I'm starting to get the feeling that we're stuck inside a tragedy. I can't remember why."

Annie laughed. "Everyone is, sister." She climbed up to the top and heaved over. She grunted, "Until they aren't anymore."

Ellie said, "Why do I feel like I've heard you say that once before?"

Annie shrugged. "It's just something I say."

"I don't think so." Ellie followed Annie up the wellwall and the bladder shreds.

After staring long at both of his hands, Levi came.

They picked up the child, took a look around at the decimated thresholds. Annie said, "We need to tell."

Levi said, "It'll be really hard to get to other parts of The Vale without these thresholds."

Ellie looked around, "Or other parts of other worlds."

"You think these come from worlds beyond The Vale?" Levi asked.

Ellie said, "I think this crux planet everyone keeps mentioning connects to more than planets in our world. Maybe it even connects more than planets."

"Other kinds of places you can live?" Levi asked.

"I think so."

Baby Sy squalled. They shushed him, found a tapestry with a

unicorn upon it. It had floated down to them in the storm from the Cloisters. They wrapped him in that, in swaddling clothes, and took him to DCFS where they laid him in the hands of the manager. How could they explain it to Authorities? They still had keys to Sy's place. Annie looked at him and said, "Never mind, I'm taking him. He's my brother."

Ellie said, "But Annie…"

"Am I my brother's keeper? If we can't get our eldest," she said, "we'll have to settle for our youngest. Little Silas singing for us in this prison yard."

"Ma'am," the agent said. "Are you saying you tried to give your brother away?"

"Silly prank," Annie said.

"This is a serious joke and serious business ma'am. Do you—" The conversation took an hour but Ellie talked them down. Eventually they left and took the northern route, entering the park not through the Naturalists's Gate, but through the Hunter's Gate. Seek and find.

All over the park, folks were waking up. Artisans splashed in the Artisans's Gate. Artists painted and sculpted in the Artists's Gate. Boys and Women, Children and Engineers, Farmers and Girls, Mariners and Miners, Pioneers and Scholars, Strangers and Warriors and Woodmen all celebrated in the Central Park gates of their namesakes. And so many others in motley woke up in The Gate of All Saints.

Instead of training back from the Merchant's Gate to Brooklyn, they exited out the Artists's Gate and walked all the way to 34th street. All along the way, people dressed in costumes tossed them candy for Halloween. *How much time has passed?* Ellie wondered. How long had they been searching? How long had her parents been gone? Overmorrow indeed: time and space had gotten weird ever since the rain. She worried it would get weirder still before the end. Yes, the world was normal now, but there were real centaurs in the street dressed up like fake human bankers and real human bankers dressed up like fake centaurs. Everything was all jumbled.

They took the ferry back. As it rained and rained and rained, they watched as the frown lines and the crow's feet melted away on the faces of those they passed in the city. Those with downcast faces lifted up their heads to be washed, some even focused on the wonder of the rain that carried the light inside, each drop a little rainbow. Each drop a bit of liquid gold and a forever kind of life. They started to see the mystical nature of so many creatures who had hidden in their midst. Some of the citizens and tourists even realized that they, themselves, were mythic creatures and people of magic.

From the street, Ellie and Annie and Levi walked into the Author's apartment.

The Author promptly hung poor Levi upside down from the ceiling by his toenails.

33
REMEMBER HOW TO REMEMBER
THE RITES

Their brother Levi smelled of brine. His face looked ashen, but the kind of ash whose volatile spirit was loosened and captured. Not his breath, his body smelled of brine. He smelled like he'd been soaking in The Dead Sea for a solid month before he'd hung from rafters upside down. The blood was rushing to his face, begging to be free. "STOP," Ellie said to the Author. "What are you doing?"

"We're draining him dry," the Author said and then, "Oh Lordy, Annie, what has happened to your head and face? And who's this baby?"

The Maker said, "Oh my goodness," and went and grabbed some salve from the kitchen. When she returned, she tried to apply it to Annie's head.

Annie refused, "Already had some," and held baby Silas.

The Author turned from their suspended little brother. "Where on earth have you three been?"

Ellie said, "Solving some mysteries."

"Well you've wanted that since you arrived," the Author said. "Did what you find make you happy?"

Ellie started crying.

"No," Annie said. "No." She started on the story of their journey.

The Author whispered, "I tried to spare you."

Ellie carried on until she mentioned hammer throws that shattered glass.

The Author's eyes went wide and then he said, "So Charlie *is* alive. You solved the Overmorrow problem. Now we have a host of other issues to consider."

Ellie mentioned what The Board had said.

"Disturbing. Tormenting, that."

Levi asked him, "Have you heard from Mom and Dad?"

The Author looked to the Maker, who nodded, and then looked back to the kids. "I have. They have contacted me through an onyx compass gifted to him by one of the Negloa emissaries. A man of onyx. Actually, of scilian."

"What's scilian?"

"Precious metal. They used to turn it into ancient weapons. But onyx or obsidian is the closest stone that comes to mind. If both were made of metal. It's as if the man of darkened stone has given Mr. Wright a compass made of his flesh and his bone."

Annie's eyes went wide with horror.

Levi's went wide with excitement.

Ellie nervously looked between them both. Shifting in the doorframe.

"They received word during *their* escape that Charlie may be living, so they went to look for him."

"Where?"

The Author pointed up.

"Space?" said Annie.

"Womb of worlds, *The Vale*," he said. He looked to his wall where a map of planets hung. "To Gergia first. Then to other stars."

"They think they're gonna go without us?" Annie asked. "Solve a mystery without us?"

Levi, upside down, said softly, "What kind of parents leave?" Tears formed in his eyes.

Annie said, "Just leave two little girls and a boy—"

"Excuse me," Levi said, "I am a pirate, *grown*. I've had my freshman mutiny, I will remind you all."

The girls snorted. Ellie's snort was snotty.

Annie said, "He's not," and pointed down to Sy. "But leave us with, well no offense, but—"

"We are strangers, yes," the Author said. "But we are closer to your parents than even all of you have ever been."

The Maker brought them scones and cookies she had finished baking. Also some sourdough biscuits and jam from the currants, the black ones they'd picked, so the jam was more currants than jam. Ellie looked down at her nails: they had grown back out. The Maker had brought her over the softest pink down blanket. The one from her room in Missouri. Ellie gasped, "Where did you get this?"

"Here and there," the maker said.

Ellie snuggled it. It smelled and felt like home. How was *home* possible in such a strange place and world?

"We can beat them," Annie said. "Beat our parents to the punch."

"It's not a competition," Ellie said.

"OH YEAH IT IS NOW." Annie stamped her foot. "A race to find our Charlie. And we'll be first and that'll show them not to leave us here alone like this."

Levi said, "They didn't leave us."

Every eye on him.

"Not really," Levi said. "They're finding *one* of us. You guys would leave me all alone tomorrow if you found where Charlie's hiding fore I got myself together."

The girls nodded.

Ellie said, "Yeah, but we'd also leave one another to pull you up off the depths of the seabed."

Levi cried. And tried to mutter, "You left off the Overmorrow problem long enough." He smiled through the tears. His face was worn — worn thin by the seawine and thin by the coffee and thin by the hanging inverted, but happy. Happy for once. "I think I'd leave the hundred and forty-nine folks that I know to find my Charlie. So yeah, it's a race. We find the lost brother *before mom and dad.*"

"We'll win," said Ellie.

"If we find him," Levi said. "With Overmorrow on our side. What's next in the rites? We need to prepare."

The Maker said, "Bellwether."

"Whatsit?" Annie asked.

"A vow. One of two: Bellwether or Yondertryst are the two, you have to pick. Bellwether's the fast initiation into Story-weavers. Yondertryst the slow."

"Storyweavers?" Levi asked.

"An ancient order of makers preserving the things that they've made," the Author said. "A group of folk who believe in their Author and whose characters believe in them. You've already met so many."

Ellie answered, "That cowboy."

"Black Jack," the Author said.

"And that wolf thing and the girl. The ones who saved us from Oblivion."

The Author nodded.

Ellie left unsaid *and didn't save my Charlie.* Her expression darkened.

The Author nodded again at the thought, it seemed, more somber.

Ellie narrowed her eyelashes at him.

"Where are they?" Annie asked.

Levi coughed inverted.

The Author threw a dart. Where he got it, no one asked, but it struck on the hanging map of The Vale, the megacosm of the planets. Hit the bullseye, the planetary crossroads, Gergia.

"Pack your snacks and golden sieves," the Author said. "We leave in the morning."

Levi added in specific notes on glass and thresholds. "May I now get down?"

"Sorry," the Author said, "meant it more in jest and not to terrorize." He let down Levi, who had dried out. "Did it hurt?"

"Not at all."

"Good."

"Mr. Author?" Levi asked.

"Yes, Levi?"

"Why'd a man like Sy do what he did? I mean, I get the dwarves wanting to expand it for greed. I get the rains serve the Board for the moment. I get the North Wind's lack of empathy for our small little experience of it. I even—" He choked down tears. "I don't like what he did to me, but never wanted the Angler King to *die*. I wouldn't wish a death on... anybody."

Annie rubbed her older brother's back.

It only encouraged more tears. "I just don't get why someone'd want to hold back *wonder* like that. Why not just let people see?"

The Maker spoke softly. "Sometimes," she said, "there are threshold guardians and sometimes threshold assassins. Oblivion wants us to forget how to remember, forget how to wonder, forget your brother was taken. He wants to hoard the ways of memory. And Sy had made a deal with the memory hoarder. But we will remember and we will feel the wonder of creation, won't we?"

The girls nodded.

"Won't we, Levi?"

Levi took in a breath. He reached inside his pocket, pulled a leaden cockle shell he'd saved from coughing fits. The shell had turned to white lead. He said, "I never knew how grey my vision and hearing and feeling could get. But now that I know, I'm awake and alive, I never want to go back." He nodded. "So where do we begin?"

The Author started peeling an orange and, once he had a single slice in sticky fingers, shoved it in his mouth and said through the mouthful, "That's the thing about Overmorrow: having passed through the waters, we've *already* begun."

"Bellwether's next on the Overmorrow rites?" Levi said. "Good. Uh. What's a bellwether?"

"Lead sheep with the bell hammer round its neck. That's you, little priest." When *he* said the nickname to Levi, as opposed to all of the others, it made it feel as if all were right in the world. As if something rang out in Levi's soul. As if that ringing hit the girls and they were concussed with it — like a holy little bomb, like the tolling of a thing you never knew could chime. No matter how blind, deaf, dumb, and numb to wonder their perfectly normal new neighbors had grown, wonder had returned. Wonder: the beginning of wisdom for all three Wrights.

"I contain multitudes."
— Walt Whitman in 1885 writing to
— Bob Dylan in 2020 performing for
— Lancelot Schaubert in 2023 transcribing for
— You, right now reading.

"The world will never starve for want of wonders, but only for want of wonder."
— Chesterton, *Tremendous Trifles*

"Mother was comfort. Mother was home. A girl who lost her mother was suddenly a tiny boat on an angry ocean. Some boats eventually floated ashore. And some boats, like me, seemed to float farther and farther from land."
— Ruta Sepetys, Salt to the Sea

"Right now I'm having amnesia and déjà vu at the same time. I think I've forgotten this before."
— Steven Wright

ACKNOWLEDGMENTS

One early reviewer called it the mark of a rank amateur for me to express my gratitude to everyone who helped with this book, but as Brandon Sanderson and Stephen King do it, perhaps the term doesn't *quite* apply. I see this as an opportunity to cite my sources, praise who helped me, and (God willing) if I ever have another archivist in the family, they can keep track of the social connections of my time and station who helped. It's a useful thing, I think, just not intended for every reader. So I was, at least, convinced to put it at the end. And after this is a letter on the book for the children of my siblings: as that's an even more specific audience, and longer than Lewis's to his Lucy, it should follow the acknowledgements. You need not read either

If nothing else, I've found that my community and my hired help both appreciate when I give them credit. Many editors, for instance, cannot prove they worked on a book without an acknowledgment section. And to give honor to whom honor is due:

First, to that early reviewer who criticized this: thank you for reading my book and for making me weigh whether or not I wanted an acknowledgement section.

To Dr. Mark Scott, who when he was academic dean of my alma mater, allowed me to create a one-on-one masters level class on mythology that he took the time out of his busy schedule to oversee personally. Though not the last fruit, though not even connected directly to that project, this is some of the first fruit of that exercise. I always try to give my first fruits back to my fathers.

Thanks to Dave King who joined me in the tilling and pruning field as editor. And, when I still failed to make the book good according to early reviewers, to authors LJ Cohen and Emily Munro who gave insight early and often to improve upon the bones, and finally, to Cat Rambo for showing me — clearly and precisely — what all of those early reviews had identified. Thanks too for those reviewers for being so beautifully and in some cases brutally honest about the book.

To the Starling writers who heard not much of this, but who are always improving my craft: Angus MacIntyre, Emily Munro, Alexander Sirkman, Aaron Sirkman, Emory, Erin, Sarah, Steve Warner, Joe Geni, JP, Brice, and all of the rest over the years.

For Clayton Cormany, who has often personally preordered so many copies of one of my books, he single handedly funded that book's cover. That was the case for Tap and Die. That's a reader, you know? A true patron. He'll order a case and distribute them to all of the Little Free Libraries in Ohio.

For all of the other patrons who consistently make this possible in small and big ways, on the site, the nonprofit, newsletter subscriptions, elsewhere. There's almost 300 paid and 10,000 unpaid of you now. Thank you.

For Dr. John Granger who — via Dr. Doug Welch — got me into symbolism.

For all of the Dominican monks — past, present, and future — at the church and region where Dorothy Day got her start: for how you care for the artists and the poor of New York who make an appearance in this book.

For Maddie and Josh Huckabay as well as Autumn Neuenschwander and FC Shultz, who read early copies. Beta readers bear a unique cross that makes better books possible, even and perhaps especially when they don't finish: it lets us authors know where books went very, very wrong. I hope, if not the best possible book you could hav read, this final version is better. The same goes for the Starlings writers group in NYC, Erik Peters, TaniaRina Perry, Emma Thomas, Anja Peerdeman, Dan Rees,

Karl Mitchell, and so many others — I remain grateful for you if I neglected your name somehow. Sometimes the email search function fails me in finding the threads.

Thanks to the innovative team at Damonza for the cover design and for choosing Overmorrow as one of the top ten covers for the year in a list of thousands — I'm thrilled you thought it was as good as I did and doubly thrilled to see it on your backdrop for the AWP conference next to Dean Koontz.

The quotes from the gate to Sy's house come from Chaucer, Milton, a bit of Dante, and then my own combination of their poems to sort of make it an all-purpose gate into the eternal. There are other quotes from Tennyson, MacDonald, Chesterton and the like sprinkled throughout.

I would add, though, to one specific nibling (a nephew) and their parents: "The Johnsons" was an actual bar in Lower Manhattan and, as the disclaimer says at the beginning, didn't intend you. If I intended to describe the bar, it's only the aesthetic of the place, not the patrons. I went there once and remember zero people. Even the warlocks are different than the warlocks I know.

For the real family of five who really visited my home, though this book's characters are nothing like the real kids or parents: this one's for you. Come back any time. As for the names of the three children, though I received permission from the real Ellie, Levi, and Annie to use their names, they are absolutely nothing like those children and no comparisons should be drawn, whatsoever. If anything, the actual children I know are much better behaved, much kinder, wiser, and (in Levi's case) fun to be around and not addicted to seawine. They also look very, very different and should therefore be left alone. This is, if nothing else, a reminder that authors very, very seldom have someone specific in mind when they write a book or a song or a poem, even when they use the exact same names. This is why the song "You're so vain" exists: I simply liked their names and had a wonderful moment with them in the rain on a rowboat in

Central Park. That moment gave me the idea for the book, nothing more.

In the instance where Authors do use real names, they always ask specific permission. I can confidently say 99.99% authors absolutely are not writing about you. Unless it's a biography, of course, which I don't really do.

A LETTER TO THE CHILDREN OF OUR SIBLINGS — OUR NIECES AND NEPHEWS

Dear Niblings—

My orderly L., my clever C., my valiant S., my courageous M., my cuddly C., my dainty queen É., my bountifully joyful E., my pacifying C., my wide-eyed C., my giggly E, the unborn children who died unnamed, and my many other unnamed nieces and nephews to come (by water and by blood) —

There's a weird thought in our world that if a gift is given broadly, that breadth makes it less a gift. Only American selfishness and greed could come up with such silliness.

No one deserves a gift, custom-made or otherwise. Yet a gift need not be rare in order to be generous. A gift given to *everyone* is still a gift. A gift that is precious need not be rare in order to be an act of highest generosity. The saving of an entire city from an explosion is a generous gift to everyone who lived in the entire city. One gift given in millions of specific ways to millions of specific people with millions of specific stories of survival.

The Miracle on the Hudson was experienced by all New Yorkers. The defusing of a bomb similarly. 9/11 in tragic and heroic ways, both. To be one of the eight million spared from a wreck makes it no less a gift to be personally spared — you have a unique story of *how* and *why* and *whence* and *whither* you were spared.

In fact, a gift becomes no more precious — it actually grows less precious — if what *makes* it valuable in the first place is the giver's stinginess, restriction, and exclusivity. Privacy can help you be yourself, of course. Bears hibernate in caves, eggs develop, caterpillars have metamorphosis inside cocoons. But hoarding a gift doesn't help it grow. It's a lie you'll be told later in life of supply and demand: scarcity is manufactured so economies can exist. But true scarcity doesn't exist. We have enough food in the world to feed the hungry, we just don't share it properly. If hoarding makes the gift a gift, it's not a gift. It's the kind of behavior that creates dragons.

The world isn't against *you*.

And cutting out the world or new friends or old friends won't help you, however scary. You'll have to deal with them eventually and many times, they're more than willing to reconcile or at least achieve a kind of ceasefire.

Because we exist. That we even exist at all is an indescribable gift we don't deserve.

All of us.

That we move from Being to the majesty of birth is an experience not all humans get, yet it amplifies the gift of existing.

That we can move from that basic truth of existence and birth *unto wonder* is an even greater gift: the bliss of *knowing* we live and knowing why we live. To know what ends and purpose we strive. Wow. *Wow at the wonder of it all.* And not just wonder at everything once. Wonder at it all *forever*.

Wonder — the joy of seeing what we could become — makes us more and more like that vision of who we *really could become*. It will culminate in what we first glimpsed of the day when there will be no more tears.

Because you're *you*, each one of you, the exact same gift given to say each of you becomes a different gift entirely. I could give the same $100 to each of you and you'd spend it on or save it for wildly different things. You each would actually get a different gift because you would all receive the same thing in a unique way, spend it in a unique way. One would prefer chocolate, the other strawberry. One would prefer to save the money, the other to spend it. One would accept the award graciously, the other with boisterous pride. That's what makes you You.

It makes you you-i-er.

And Overmorrow's kind of like that, in the really real The End.

It's the same gift.

Given to everyone.

And yet…

And yet it makes us Us. Today you are You, that is truer than true. There is no one alive who is Youer than You. That kind of purpose makes the son of a tailor into the joyful beggar king who befriends all animals. Even as a young boy, it prompts the son of carpenter to sand his crossbeams.

Along the way, perhaps an uncle will want to write a book from out of that bountiful bliss and wonder. Perhaps he hopes to help each of you to forever throw away cynicism, criticism, nihilism, iconoclasm, Manichaeism. Perhaps he wants you to have the dignity of internal motivation and no more shame. Perhaps he wants you discover the path to who you really are, why you exist, why you live. That he offers this book to the rest of the world makes it no less personal, no less a labored love letter for each one of you for very, very different reasons.

When you grow old enough, you will each receive it differently, I am sure. Many of you may well be bored by it, I have no control over that. Living in NYC away from you is quite hard on me at present. I have no words other than that it's the way of things for now. I look forward to the day when each of you are grown adults and can come see me and Aunt Tara as you please.

And please do. I have a hunch we will enjoy one another even more once you're adults than we do now, mainly because of proximity and other factors beyond my control.

I may not be able to see you as often as I like, but I hope you can now carry a part of my mind with you in your bookbags, indeed a part of my very self, a very carefully written love letter to all of you, to each of you, my niblings.

With luck, your heart's bucket won't be able to hold all of the great unconditional love and respect and confidence I have for you and so it will overflow into the lives of other children just like you. Remember: that doesn't diminish the effort I made for you, doesn't diminish the gift I gave you. It isn't a scarce love — scarcity doesn't *truly* exist, only the particularity of any given thing, this rose compared to that rose. In fact, the overflow onto others makes this gift all the more bountiful: each one of *those* children and adults will have completely different thoughts and feelings that grow out of these books. Everyone will react differently: even *I* react differently every time I read this or any of my books. Sometimes they bore me, sometimes excite me. That's because no one is like me, even *future* me, no one is like you, no one is like any one of us.

May one day you wake up and find yourself in Overmorrow. Oh what stories we will tell then, eh? Stories for everyone that grow out of our love and respect for one another.

Until then, hang onto these books. For I will become an old uncle, particularly for how late in life circumstances required Aunt Tara and I to start having children (assuming we _can_ start having children). Perhaps we were never able to at all. Therefore I'll be worn out like an old oak bending wonderful ways for teenagers inside a 50-year-old body, 60-year-old body, 120-year-old-body, scribbling these old inkwells dry and typing the letters off my keyboard.

Assuming we still type things in the future.

Then you can give these book-length letters back to me by reading them as *my* bedtime stories in the ICU or the nursing home or live-in-care the way Tara and I did for our grandpas. They won't be my letters to you anymore. They will be your letters *back* to me so that I *remember, once more,* how to have wonder. So that I remember how to remember the rites.

Remembering is tricky, you see. The memories are all there, but accessing them is another story.

I'll need the Overmorrow waters to wake me up again, even then. We all need a quick splash, from time to time, to remember that first washing. We all need help remembering how to investigate, explore, be curious, be aware, to play in our work, to listen for the sake of *understanding* and not merely for the other person to "feel heard," to remember that the cynical and sarcastic person who says "I was only joking" is a madman shooting fiery arrows into the air unknowing where they will land, to let the spirit of life turn my attention to what's important. And just because each one of you gives *me* the same exact words I gave *you,* will that make them any less?

Will that ruin the first gift I gave you?

Oh no no no, it won't make them any less of a gift to 65-year-old or 75-year-old or 125-year-old man named Lance. That will make them suddenly *more,* even still, even then. For you will all read them differently to me than I ever could write them to you. I may have even forgotten that I wrote them. Perhaps, if the stories are decent enough and worthy, you'll read them even to your own children and best friend's children. And then we will know that the idea of the gift, the effort of the gift, and the power of the gift doesn't come from me.

Or from you.

The gift comes from beyond us all and we merely participate in Wonder.

❦

I remain your servant: your untamed, yet good—
Uncle Lance

November, 2020
Mid pandemic
Sunset Park
Brooklyn, NY
Where it's currently always winter and never Christmas

ALSO BY LANCELOT

- Substack essays and short fiction
- Of Gods and Globes I
- Of Gods and Globes II
- Of Gods and Globes III
- Bell Hammers: The True Folk Tale of Little Egypt — *historical humor novel*
- Tap & Die — *a "Die Bard" fantasy novella*
- 15 Vale Short Stories — *short stories from the universe where all of his fiction and nonfiction and poetry and photonovels connect*
- The Greenwood Poet — *poetry written during the pandemic in Greenwood cemetery, 500 acres of the oldest rural cemetery in America*
- Inconveniences Rightly Considered — *poems from his twenties*
- Harry Rides the Danger — *children's picture book on courage*
- The Elevator Out — *children's picture book on wonder*
- *H.A.L.T.S. — 90's alt-rock folk album*
- *All Who Wander — indie folk, experimental album*
- *Open — short film written for WRKR productions*
- *Cold Brewed — photo novel (graphic novel with still photographs) in a world where the prohibition made third wave coffee illegal*

Over at http://lanceschaubert.org you can find the archive of 400 academics, artists, and authors published in The Showbear Family Circus, resources for your own creative work, as well as ongoing serialized work by Lancelot.

Thanks for buying, reading, and sharing the work of living authors.